New Yor... ...Feehan has
thrilled le... ...sual 'Dark'
Carpathian tales. She has received numerous honours
throughout her career including being a nominee for the
Romance Writers of America RITA, and receiving a Career
Achievement Award from *Romantic Times*.

For more information about Christine Feehan visit her website: www.christinefeehan.com.

Also by Christine Feehan

Dark Melody

Christine Feehan

PIATKUS

⠿ *Visit the Piatkus website!*

Piatkus publishes a wide range of best-selling fiction and non-fiction, including books on health, mind, body & spirit, sex, self-help, cookery, biography and the paranormal.

If you want to:

- read descriptions of our popular titles
- buy our books over the Internet
- take advantage of our special offers
- enter our monthly competition
- learn more about your favourite Piatkus authors

VISIT OUR WEBSITE AT: www.piatkus.co.uk

Copyright © 2003 by Christine Feehan

First published in Great Britain in 2007 by
Piatkus Books Ltd.,
5 Windmill Street, London W1T 2JA
email: info@piatkus.co.uk

This edition published 2007

First published in the United States in 2003 by
Dorchester Publishing Co., Inc.

The moral right of the author has been asserted

A catalogue record for this book is available from the British Library

ISBN 978 0 7499 3851 2

Data manipulation by Phoenix Photosetting, Chatham, Kent
www.phoenixphotosetting.co.uk

Printed and bound in Great Britain by
Clays Ltd, Bungay, Suffolk

For my daughter Denise Feehan and for Cody Tucker,
two people who share a great love of music
among many other things.

Chapter One

Need crawled through his body and pounded out a rhythm in his mind. Music seethed and roared, filling the large bar, an edgy, compelling melody as dark and driven as he was. The notes were ripped from deep within his soul, moved through his fingers to the guitar cradled in his arms as he might cradle a woman. The music was one of the few things that reminded him he was alive and not one of the undead.

He could feel the stares, although he never looked up. He could hear the breathing of the crowd, the air moving through lungs like the rush of a freight train. He heard blood ebbing, flowing in veins, beckoning, a sweet seductress, teasing his senses until his craving was an obsession as dark and relentless as the shadow across his soul.

They whispered. Hundreds of conversations. Secrets. Pickup lines. The things whispered in bars under the cover of music. He heard every word clearly as he sat on the stage with the young, enthusiastic band he was jamming with. He heard the whispers of women as they

1

Christine Feehan

discussed him. Dayan. Lead guitarist for the Dark Troubadours. They wanted to bed him for all the wrong reasons, and he wanted them for reasons that would have terrified them.

The song ended, the crowd roared, stomping and clapping and yelling approval. Dayan glanced at the man waiting at the bar. Cullen Tucker raised a glass of water toward him, one eyebrow up. *What are we doing here?* Dayan read the expression clearly, read the man's mind. What were they doing there? What had compelled him to go into the bar, pick up his guitar and play for the crowd? His performance would only draw unwarranted attention to them. It wasn't safe. They were hunted, yet Dayan had no choice. He *needed* to be in this bar. He was waiting for something . . . for someone.

Dayan's fingers were already picking up another rhythm. Dark. Moody. The melody took hold of him, demanding to be released. His voice stilled the crowd, beckoned, seduced, tempted. He called to her. Commanded her. His lover. His lifemate. His other half. He called to her to complete him. To give him the emotions that had faded from his soul, leaving him an empty shell of growing darkness. A creature living in the shadows, vulnerable to the crouching beast. *Save me. Come to me.* The words took the breath from the listening crowd, brought tears to the eyes of the women.

They pushed closer to the stage, unaware that they did so. Unaware of the power of his voice, his eyes. He mesmerized them. Seduced them. Compelled them. He cast his spell, a dangerous predator among easy prey. *Save me. Please save me.* His voice washed over them, seeped into pores, soaked into brains so that they stared up at him completely enthralled. Hunger rose, a response to his heightening senses. He kept his eyes closed, blocking out the sight of the crowd, losing him-

2

self in his song to her. His lifemate. The one woman who could save him. Where was she?

The door opened, allowing the night breeze to rush into the room, dispelling the odor of too many bodies crushed together in too small a space. It was the sound of a heartbeat that made him lift his head. The heart was weak and irregular, beating too fast, laboring too hard. Dayan looked up and literally lost his ability to breathe. There she was. Just like that. His lungs burned for air and his fingers lost their age-old rhythm. His heart began to match the strange rhythm of hers.

Dayan forced a breath into his body. First one, then a second. The band was staring at him uncertainly. His fingers began a melody he had never played before, one that was always there, locked in his heart. Dimly he was aware the band had taken its cue from him, following his lead, but he paid no attention to the others. He couldn't look away from her, watching as she paused while her light-haired companion spoke with several acquaintances.

What was wrong with her heart?

His black eyes moved over her possessively, marking her, claiming her. She was small, curvy, with lush dark hair and enormous eyes. He watched the way she moved, watched the sway of her hips. To Dayan, she was incredibly beautiful. And she was human. He knew it was possible for one of his kind, a Carpathian, to have a human lifemate, but he had never imagined his other half would be one.

She paused for a moment to stare up at him in shock, her wide gaze colliding with his for the briefest instant. Her perfect mouth formed a round O as she recognized him. She swung her head toward the tall blonde who accompanied her. The other woman laughed and hugged her, led the way through the crowd to a booth in a dark corner of the club. He heard the soft murmur of her voice, and at once his world changed. Where before the club had been visible to him only in shades of gray, it was now brilliantly alive with vivid, dazzling color.

Emotions were crowding in on him fast and hard, so many he couldn't sort them out. He could only sit very still with his fingers flashing over his beloved guitar. He *felt* that. His guitar. It amazed him so much, he was aware of tears burning behind his eyes. Dayan was almost paralyzed by the different stimuli bombarding him. The music. Hunger. Colors. Lust. It was a volcano, molten hot, adding to his edgy feeling. And there was jealousy. Dark. Dangerous. He realized he didn't like to see the men crowding around her booth, leaning over to talk to her.

At once that thought triggered the rising of the beast in him and he had to crush it down. He was very dangerous in this state. The music poured out of him, through him; wild emotion almost choked him; he was blinded by a myriad of colors. He took a deep, calming breath, fought for control and won. *What was wrong with her heart?*

He kept his head bent over his guitar, but his empty black eyes were fixed on his prey, the only woman who mattered to him. He played to her, poured his heart out to her, allowed the beauty of his music to speak to her. He wanted her to see the poet in him, not the predator. Not the darkness. All the while he played, he listened to the conversation she was having, listened for the sound of her voice.

"I can't believe it's really him, Lisa. That's Dayan, of the Dark Troubadours. He's practically a god among musicians. I've never heard anyone play like him. What in the world is he doing with this band?" That was her voice, soft and feminine. She spoke in a reverent tone.

Her fingers were tapping out a rhythm on the table, following his guitar riff.

Lisa leaned across the booth to be heard over the noise in the bar. "I heard he was vacationing nearby. I guess he's just jamming here tonight, Corinne. I know how much you love music, and I wanted to give you a surprise."

That was her name. *Corinne.* Even her name fit the music in Dayan's mind. He unashamedly eavesdropped to learn what he could. She was listening to his music, her body responding naturally, but she wasn't staring at him in rapt adoration the way the other women in the bar were staring. The way he would have liked.

"But how did you know? He's not just anyone, Lisa. He's a genius when he's playing. How did you know he'd be here tonight?"

"Bruce—you remember Bruce, Corinne—he works for my photographer. Bruce knows you're a huge music fan. He stopped in for a drink and called to tell me a member of the Dark Troubadours was jamming here tonight. Bruce said that man at the bar is supposedly a friend of the lead guitarist's and that he travels with the Dark Troubadours." Lisa indicated Cullen. "Everyone's hoping it means the Troubadours are looking for new places to play."

"Well, they do prefer the smaller, more intimate clubs, but who would have ever thought they would play here?" Corinne said. Her gaze strayed to Dayan, their eyes met, and she hastily looked away.

The impact shook him. His fingers nearly lost their rhythm; his stomach gave a funny lurch and his very breath slammed out of his lungs.

"Is he really that famous?" Lisa asked, grinning at Corinne.

"He's absolutely famous, you heathen." Corinne's

5

laughter was affectionate, teasing. "His band doesn't have a contract with any label. Some people try to tape their music when they go to concerts. The tapes are worth a fortune."

"You have an old record and several tapes, don't you?" Lisa asked.

Color swept up Corinne's face. "Ssh! For heaven's sake, Lisa, those tapes are black-market. What if someone hears you?" Guilt was in her voice. "The band travels and plays mostly in small places, like old-fashioned troubadours. That's probably how they came up with the name."

Lisa leaned her chin on her hand. "He's looking this way. I swear, Rina, I really think he's noticed us."

"He's gorgeous. I had no idea." Corinne had never been one to fall for men in the spotlight, whether actor, musician or athlete. It wasn't her style; she was too down-to-earth. But Dayan resembled a sculpture of a Greek god. He was tall and sinewy, giving the impression of great strength and power without bulky muscles. His hair was very long, but well kept, shining like a raven's wing, pulled back at the nape of his neck and secured with a leather thong. But it was his face that caught and held Corinne's attention. It could have been chiseled from marble. His was the face of a man capable of great sensuality, or great cruelty. She couldn't get the impression of danger out of her mind when she looked at him.

His mouth was beautiful, as was the shape of his jaw with its faint blue-black beard shadow—she had always liked that on a man—but it was his eyes that ensnared her. She made the mistake of looking directly at him. His eyes were beautiful, shaped like a cat's eyes, dark and mysterious, empty, yet filled with a thousand secrets. She felt almost pulled into his gaze, captured for all time. She couldn't look away from him. Mesmerized.

The word came to her out of nowhere. She was definitely mesmerized by him. His head was bent toward his guitar, but his gaze seemed fixed on her face. Lisa, with her striking looks, garnished attention easily and was comfortable with it. Corinne could barely breathe with his gaze locked on her.

Her fingers curled into a tight fist, her long nails digging deeply into her palms. Her heart was doing a crazy somersault, and her breath seemed stolen right from her lungs. "I've never heard anyone play so beautifully." Her mouth was so dry she could barely get the words out.

"He can sit in my bedroom and play me to sleep every night," Lisa said.

Color crept up Corinne's neck to sweep into her face at the idea of this man in her bedroom. Playing his guitar was not what she had in mind. The image that did come to her was shocking. She had never thought of anyone like that. Not even John. Not only did it seem disloyal, but it was totally out of character for her. Suddenly she was very afraid. She wanted to run like a child and find a place to hide from his mesmerizing eyes and the strange effect he seemed to have on her. He frightened her, truly frightened her. Perhaps it was his music, so intense, so *hungry*, like his eyes.

"Corinne!" Lisa said her name sharply, breaking the spell. "Are you all right? Do you need your medication? You brought it, didn't you?" She had already grabbed Corinne's purse and was rummaging through it hastily. There was an edge of fear in her voice.

"I'm fine, Lisa," Corinne said. "I think my hero took my breath away for a minute there. He's potent. I wish he'd sing again." She forced herself to laugh.

"Oh, yeah," Lisa said dreamily, "he has a sexy voice."

"Be still, my heart," Corinne teased, clutching at her heart dramatically. It made Lisa laugh, wiping out the sudden fear in her eyes, just as Corinne knew it would.

With his superior hearing, Dayan could hear every word. He sorted through conversations easily, dismissing them from his mind, but not *hers*. *Corinne*. The other woman had called her Corinne. Although happy to know he had managed to steal her breath, he was busy assessing the situation. *Medication. What medication? What was wrong with her heart?* It was important to find out as soon as possible.

Dayan directed his attention toward Cullen. *Go to the far booth and strike up a conversation with the two women*. He pushed hard, making his words a command. He didn't like using Cullen—it wasn't in Dayan to use someone he was fond of—and now that he could once again experience emotions, he could feel the friendship he had with the human male. But he needed an emissary, someone to act quickly before Corinne bolted. He could read her fear easily enough, and he could not allow her to flee from him.

Cullen turned his head and spotted the beautiful blonde. To his astonishment he recognized her face. Lisa Wentworth. She was a model often seen on the cover of magazines. Ordinarily, he would never have the nerve to speak to her, but for some reason, he found himself covering the distance between them. He had been in love one time in his life and had lost his fiancée. Since then he had never really looked at another woman. He couldn't help noticing Lisa Wentworth. It wasn't just the fact that she was beautiful, it was something shining from deep within her.

"It would be an honor to get you two whatever you're drinking," he said as a greeting. "My name is Cullen Tucker." He wished he had a pickup line that would make him stand out from all the men staring at her, but he hadn't tried to attract a woman in years.

"Lisa Wentworth." Lisa stuck out her hand and

flashed a blazing smile while Corinne seemed to shrink back into the shadows, her face slightly averted, her hair spilling down like a silken shield. "This is Corinne. Corinne Wentworth."

Cullen raised an eyebrow in inquiry. They looked nothing alike, although he thought them both beautiful. "What would you like to drink?"

"We're both just drinking water," Lisa offered, a flirty smile curving her soft mouth. "I'll let you get it for us if you promise to sit with us."

"I'll be right back," Cullen commented, rather pleased that Lisa wasn't staring up at Dayan with that look he recognized in so many women. He had learned, in traveling with the band, that few of the groupies cared what the band members were like, only that they were famous and played in a band.

"What are you doing, Lisa?" Corinne hissed. "Are you crazy? You never pick up men. What are you thinking? Tell me you aren't using him to meet the guitar player."

"Of course I'm not. I don't know—there's just something about him. He's cute. He isn't looking at me as if I'm something to drape on his arm and show off. It gets tiring. Do you mind so much if he just talks to us? You can stare some more at Dayan while he plays." There was a hopeful note in Lisa's voice.

Corinne took a deep breath and let it out slowly. She wasn't being fair to Lisa. Lisa needed to have fun. She had been taking care of Corinne for months now. Carefully Corinne hid her trembling hand out of sight in her lap and forced herself to shrug casually. "I suppose I can do that. But I'm not looking at him anymore. Just hearing him play is overwhelming. He's almost *too* good."

Lisa's eyes were on the man at the bar, surveying him with interest. His shoulders were square and he stood very straight. She liked the way he looked her right in the eye. There was something else, something that touched her heart. She couldn't define or explain it to Corinne, but he looked like a man with the weight of the world on his shoulders and no one to ease his burden. The plain truth was, she liked the look of him.

"I'll take Cullen," Lisa said half seriously, "and you can go for the guitar player."

Corinne flashed a saucy smile. "He's too good to be true. Men like that break hearts everywhere they go. They have that element of danger because they really are bad boys. Women think they can change them, but the truth is, they're bad and there's nothing to be done about it. If you're a smart woman, which I am, you only stare at them and fantasize; you don't go near them or you get your fingers burned. I'll just listen to him play and be very happy."

Cullen made his way through the crowded club back to the booth where the two women were seated. He had no idea what he was going to say to them. The blonde was striking terror in his heart. He couldn't possibly become interested in a woman, not with a pack of murderers hounding his footsteps. Very carefully he set a bottle of water before each of them.

Lisa smiled up at him and scooted over, allowing Cullen to sit beside her. The room was crowded and it was very loud. She wanted to hear every word this man spoke. Corinne shifted slightly to give Lisa a little more privacy to work her magic. Lisa deserved to find a nice man. Someone. She would need someone very soon.

The music continued, but Corinne noticed the moment Dayan stopped playing. The beauty and clarity were gone from the music, leaving an okay group making up for their lack of genius with enthusiasm. She couldn't help it; she stole a quick look at him from under her long lashes. He was standing up, a casual, almost lazy move that reminded her of a large jungle cat stretching. He was careful with his guitar, setting it against the far wall out of reach of any light-fingered fans or rowdies. For a brief moment he surveyed the crowd, most of whom were staring up at him in rapt adoration. A flicker of what could have been impatience crossed his face.

He turned his head and looked directly at her. Instantly she felt the weight of his stare. Intent. Hungry. Corinne's heart seemed to stop beating. He was looking at her—not at his friend and not at Lisa, but straight at her. Their eyes met across the room, and immediately she could feel that mesmerizing pull. A spell of enchantment. Dayan leaned down and said something to the lead guitarist and then stepped off the stage. Over the crowd his black gaze held hers captive. Corinne couldn't look away.

Her heart was going crazy and her breath refused to enter her lungs. She could only stare helplessly at him, watching as he crossed the room to reach her side. Strangely, no one spoke to him, not a single woman in the crowd. Everyone moved quickly out of his way so that he approached her without interference. He stood at their booth, his black gaze seeing only her. Up close, he was even more intimidating than he'd been across the room. Power clung to him like a second skin. And he was more than sexy, he was darkly sensual. Terrifyingly so.

The band swung into a slow, dreamy song, and Dayan reached down and captured her small hand. "I need to dance with you." He said it like that, starkly, without embellishment, without worrying about his vulnerability. He *needed* to touch her, to hold her close in his arms. He *needed* to know she was real and not a figment of his imagination.

Corinne couldn't have resisted him for any reason. She let him take her over, pulling her with exquisite

11

gentleness to her feet, drawing her into his arms, close to his body. She held the palm of her hand over his strong heart. At once she could feel his heat, feel his solid, muscular frame. Her heart was beating overtime, and she felt strange. In another world. A dream world. Floating. He was taller than she was by quite a bit, yet she fit into him perfectly, as if she were made for him.

He bent his dark head to hers. "Breathe." He whispered the word against her skin, and her entire body came alive. Just like that. Every nerve ending. Every cell. His breath was warm and his arms were incredibly strong. He held her almost tenderly. It was a kind of magic, and she knew instinctively he was feeling it too.

For just one moment she closed her eyes and let herself be carried away. Their bodies moved together in perfect rhythm as if they had been dancing together for all their lives. As if they were making love. Corinne bit her lip. It was the most intimate thing she had ever done in her life, yet she had been married. He seemed to be everywhere, surrounding her, his body hard and his hands gentle. A curious thing was happening. Her heart, usually so erratic, was struggling to match the more even beat of his. She noticed it because every detail was so important. She wanted to carry this moment with her for the rest of her life.

The music moved through Dayan so that he became the music. The woman in his arms was already a part of him. He knew it with his deepest soul. She was the one, the only one. He could feel the struggle of her heart just as he felt her small, very feminine body imprinted against his masculine frame. But the situation was even more complex than he'd first realized. She was the only woman for him, yet there was a third heartbeat. He could clearly hear it racing as he held her to him. He could feel the life in her, the small mound beneath the loose clothing she wore.

He brought her palm under his chin and held her even closer as he examined that discovery. She was carrying a child. Another man's child. A human child. For a moment his mind was in chaos, a wild mix of jealousy, rage and fear, things he had never experienced. Breathing helped, and he focused on what was most important. If he gave her his blood, he could possibly fix her heart problem, but what would such an exchange do to an unborn infant? He could read her fear and her sadness. He moved with her, his body a hard, urgent ache, his mind a jumble of thoughts, his heart and soul truly at peace for the first time in his existence even while his brain worked on a solution to such a unique problem.

The song ended, and he reluctantly allowed her to slip out of his arms, retaining possession of her hand so she couldn't run. "My name is Dayan."

Corinne nodded her head, almost afraid to speak. He was leading her back to the safety of the booth. He moved easily through the crowd, keeping her safe beneath his broad shoulder. Dayan gave her the illusion of safety, taking great care that no one bumped her carelessly.

"Are you going to tell me your name?" He asked it softly, his voice a velvet seduction in itself.

Just the sound of his voice created a yearning to hear him sing again. "Corinne, Corinne Wentworth." She didn't look at him; it hurt, he was so good-looking. And sexy. That dark, dangerous sensuality she wanted no part of. They were close to the booth, to safety. She allowed herself to breathe again.

"When is your baby due, Corinne?" he asked, his voice a gentle thread of sound. She had never heard a voice quite like his. Hypnotic; mesmerizing. A bedroom voice. It whispered over her skin until she burned.

His words stopped her short, and she looked quickly,

13

guiltily at Lisa, afraid she might have somehow over-heard. For a moment she felt desperate. Lisa had her head close to Cullen Tucker's and was laughing at something he was telling her. Dayan leaned down, his larger body shielding hers protectively, effectively blocking her from the rowdy crowd. It occurred to her that he was a celebrity of sorts and the crowd should have been clamoring to meet him, pushing forward at least for his autograph, yet somehow no one went near him. Not even the women.

"Corinne." He did something to her name, made it sound exotic with his strange accent. "You are very pale. Would you like me to get your friend for you and take you outside into the night air? There are far too many people in this building."

"She doesn't know." She blurted out the truth and then was horrified that she had done so. What was it about him? She had danced with a perfect stranger, merged with him so that they seemed as intimate as lovers. Normally a private person, Corinne had a com-pelling urge to tell him the most personal details of her life.

Dayan changed direction immediately, gliding through the crowd once again toward the door, taking her along with effortless ease. *She wanted to go with him.* Corinne couldn't understand that irrational im-pulse. The cold air should have cleared her head, but he moved his body very close to hers, shattering what little composure she had left. She couldn't think straight with him so close to her.

Dayan took her into the shadows. Everything in him rose up to claim her for his own. He wanted her, he needed her, and his body was going up in flames. She stood there looking up at him with her enormous green eyes, and he was lost. Knew he would be lost for all time. "Good—your color is coming back. Your friend seems to care very much for you. I cannot imagine that she would not be happy about the baby."

Corinne lifted a hand to shove back the wild mass of her hair. "I shouldn't have given you the wrong impression. Lisa will be happy about the baby for a lot of reasons. It's just that I'm . . ." She trailed off, reluctant to reveal any details of her personal life to him. "It's complicated." Suddenly, inexplicably, she felt compelled to tell him everything about herself. He was looking down at her and his eyes were so—*hungry. Lonely.* She didn't know what it was, but those eyes were impossible to resist.

He made her feel as if she'd been cornered by a great jungle cat. His eyes didn't blink, they simply watched her. Completely focused on her. At times she could have sworn there was a red flicker of flame in the very depths. "You have to stop looking at me like that." The words left her throat before she could censor them, and she found herself laughing. She was a grown woman and ordinarily very logical. He was certainly getting a false impression of who she was.

His smile was slow and very sexy. It started her wayward heart pounding again. A slow burn was smoldering somewhere in the pit of her stomach. "Am I looking at you?" His voice brushed against her skin, heating, tantalizing.

Corinne tilted her head to one side and studied his perfect masculine features. "You know very well you are. You have that smug male look on your face. I can't think straight when you're looking at me like that."

"How am I looking at you?" He asked it softly, gently, a note of tenderness creeping in to turn her heart over.

Like a hungry leopard about to pounce. The thought came unbidden. The smile climbed to his eyes as if he could read her thoughts, making her blush. "Never mind. Just stop." She put out her hand as if she might hold him away from her.

"You were going to tell me about the baby." *And the baby's father. We do not want to leave him out of this conversation. You want to tell me.* Shamelessly he "pushed" her, needing to know. The man was dead. Dayan could feel that. He read it in the lingering sadness in her eyes. She had cared for another man enough to bring his child into the world. *Who was the man?*

He captured her outstretched hand, her left hand, found the circle of gold, the symbol of human marriage, the mark proclaiming she belonged to another man.

The thought triggered the dangerous aggression of his species, and Dayan fought down the rising beast. He would not chance frightening her. His thumb rubbed over the ring almost absently, back and forth, a gentle caress, persistent. Insistent. He brought her fingertips to his lips. All the while his black gaze focused completely on her, staring directly into her eyes.

His look was hypnotic. Strangely exhilarating. Corinne's breath caught in her throat as his teeth scraped along her finger, his mouth warm and moist. Butterfly wings brushed at her stomach. His teeth tugged gently at her gold wedding band. The sensation was so erotic, she shivered. She stared up at him for a long moment, completely fascinated, before remembering to pull her hand free.

"Tell me about your baby, honey," he commanded, his voice low, almost purring.

He touched her mind very gently, with great care. She was fighting the compulsion to tell him what he wanted to know, but she was human and he was an ancient, one in a long line of dominating males. He was far too strong for her to resist.

Corinne pressed her palm protectively over the baby.

The wind whipped down the street, gusted leaves and debris into whirling eddies. Unknowingly, she moved deeper into the shelter of his body. "I grew up with Lisa and her brother John." She stopped speaking abruptly, her throat closing on the name.

John. The name pierced him like a knife. The way she said it, the pain reflected in her eyes, told him how much the man had meant to her. *John.* Dayan had never liked that name. He didn't want to hear any more; he didn't want to hear the sound of her voice when she said that hated name.

Corinne twisted her wedding ring nervously. "The three of us had a difficult childhood, so I suppose we were closer than most. John and I were . . . different." She stole a quick look up at him from under her heavy dark lashes. She didn't want to explain to him what that word meant. She didn't know him, didn't know why she seemed to trust him when he was a virtual stranger to her. She didn't know why her body seemed to know him. *Crave him.* Corinne shoved her wayward thoughts away, concentrating entirely on how much she could tell him . . . or not tell him.

Dayan examined her mind, wanting an explanation of "different." He caught a hastily censored picture. Telekinesis. She could move objects with her mind. Of course, she was psychic. She would have to be psychic if she were his true lifemate. Dayan had no way of explaining to her exactly what a lifemate was. How could he reveal to her he was of another species? That he had been on earth a thousand years? That he needed blood to survive?

Dayan watched her fingers turn that small gold band. With every touch, every stroke, his stomach knotted tighter and tighter. He tried to force his gaze back to her face, but that small betraying movement fascinated him.

17

Corinne shrugged her shoulders. "To make a long story short, John and I were married and he was murdered a few months ago. I didn't even know I was pregnant. I haven't said anything to Lisa because . . . well . . ." She hesitated, searching for the right words.

That brought his dark gaze back to her face. She felt the impact of his focused stare all the way to her bones. His hands covered hers, stilling the nervous play of her fingers over her ring. Her heart leapt, a curious sensation that alarmed her.

His black eyes never left her face. Not once. And he still hadn't blinked. She felt almost as if she were falling forward into those strange, hypnotic eyes. What difference did it make if he thought she was a basket case? She hadn't asked for his sympathy, nor did she want it. She wasn't telling him the story for sympathy. Why *was* she telling him her story? Her chin lifted and she looked at him almost defiantly. "I have a heart condition." He could run like a rabbit and she'd be very happy. He was a complication, a fantasy, the worst sort of "bad boy," and she wanted no part of him.

Dayan touched her mind very gently. He caught an image of hospitals, machines, endless tests. Her asking about a waiting list for a heart. Doctor after doctor shaking their heads. She had severe allergies. She bled easily, too much. The specialists were amazed she had lived as long as she had. Dayan rubbed the bridge of his nose thoughtfully, his eyes intent on her face. "So the baby is a danger, then. Lisa would not like that."

Corinne let out her breath. It was almost a relief to tell someone. "No, Lisa won't like it all. She'll be so frightened." Corinne had waited until there was no possibility Lisa might try to talk her out of having the baby. She wanted a baby. Her little girl. Long after her death, after John's death, their daughter would live and breathe, run and play, and hopefully lead a perfectly normal life. Corinne had absolute faith that Lisa would cherish and love the baby. She pulled her hands away from his to place them protectively over the small mound where the baby rested.

"You are very small. How far along are you?" Even as the words left his mouth, he marveled that he could say them. In all his imaginings, he had never thought to be asking such a question. Heat blossomed and spread. A sense of belonging. Strangely, he felt as if he had a family already.

"The doctors are a little worried about that, but she looks good. She's growing fine. They've told me it's a girl. I'm six months along."

His breath hitched in concern. She was tiny. "Are the doctors concerned about your heart problem also? Do they view this pregnancy as risky? Perhaps very dangerous?" His voice was still as gentle as ever, yet it had an effect on her she couldn't seem to shake. He sounded almost as if he were reprimanding her in some way and assessing what he was going to do about the situation.

Corinne felt compelled to answer him, although it wasn't what she wanted. "My heart has enough trouble working for just me, let alone a child too," she conceded reluctantly. Her fingers once again found the circle of gold and began to twist, a nervous habit betraying her inner turmoil.

Dayan nodded his head even as his entire body knotted in protest against that small action. "And your husband—" He forced the words out despite the fact they wanted to stick in his throat. "Why was he murdered?" He couldn't help himself, he reached out and caught her hand, pulling her palm to his chest, right over his heart, effectively stopping her from touching the ring again.

Corinne's gaze flew to his. Electricity arced between

them. The air sizzled with the charge. She found it difficult to think with his black eyes mesmerizing her and his touch scattering her senses. Discussing the murder of her husband with him should have been impossible, yet she found the words tumbling out. "The police haven't come up with a motive. The killers didn't even take his wallet."

"But you have an idea." He made it a statement.

Corinne felt that same desire to confess every detail. Normally, she confided in Lisa and no one else, yet Corinne hadn't said a single word to Lisa about the baby or her own suspicions about John's death. *Why on earth was she telling a virtual stranger her every secret?* "John could do things that weren't considered normal. About a year ago, he went to a university and told someone there about his talent. From there, he was directed to a center where psychic ability was tested. The Morrison Center for Psychic Research. John believed he might be able to help people in some way, using his unique gift. Almost immediately after his appointment at the center, he told me he thought he was being followed." She withdrew her hand. "This is hardly something you would want to hear about."

"On the contrary. I'm extremely interested. Everything about you interests me."

Chapter Two

"Corinne!" Lisa burst from the club with Cullen one step behind her. She was obviously upset, her beautiful face betraying her anxiety. "Rina, are you ill? I'm so sorry, I should have been paying more attention." She clutched Corinne's purse protectively to her.

"I'm perfectly fine, Lisa," Corinne answered immediately. She stepped away from Dayan, but somehow he moved too in a ripple of power so that he was sheltering her body from the rising wind. Corinne looked up at his chiseled features and found her heart in her throat again. What was it about him? How could he so easily rob her of her breath and sanity with only a look? A movement?

"We were just talking away from the noise," Dayan drawled, smiling lazily, his teeth very white in the darkness. He raked his hand carelessly through his shining ebony hair, managing to tousle it more. Strands fell in disarray across his forehead, yet he looked more attractive than ever.

The two women exchanged a quick glance, rolling

their eyes in complete accord while Corinne stifled a groan. How could any man be real and look and act like he did? Corinne mouthed "bad boy" at Lisa, making her laugh.

Lisa leaned close to whisper, "Only you could look at a man too sexy to be on earth and reduce his incredible beauty to bad boy."

Corinne felt herself a fraud. Lisa didn't think Corinne was in the least susceptible to Dayan's dark sensuality. But she was more than susceptible. She was enthralled, under a spell of enchantment. She even briefly wondered if his songs, or his voice, might have somehow hypnotized her.

Dayan reached out and casually removed Corinne's purse from Lisa's hand, then gave it to Corinne. He would have been amused at her thoughts had her heart not been stuttering again, a laboring that bothered him immensely. How could he fix it without harming her child? His eyes moved possessively over Corinne's face as he watched her pull a small container from her purse and swallow a tiny pill. With the same easy strength he always exhibited, he shackled Corinne's bare wrist and brought it up for his inspection. "Why are you not wearing a medical bracelet? In an emergency it would alert strangers how to help you."

Lisa tossed her blond head. "At last! Someone with a little sense, unlike Rina. She never listens to anyone."

A small sensual smile tugged at the hard edge of Dayan's mouth. He leaned down close to Corinne so his warm breath stirred tendrils of hair at her temple. "You do not listen to others?"

"I'm perfectly capable of making my own decisions," Corinne informed him, her voice faintly haughty when all she really wanted to do was touch his mouth with her fingertips. Up close he robbed her of breath. Of good sense.

"Until now," Dayan corrected with infinite gentleness. His voice was very soft and, like velvet, it whispered sensuously over her skin, making her shiver. He brought her hand up to his perfectly molded mouth, rubbed the pads of her fingers over his lips.

Her heart stuttered; butterfly wings brushed at her stomach. For a moment she could only stare at him, lost in his magic. She dragged her gaze from his, withdrew her hand to curl her fingers into her palm, holding on to his warmth.

Cullen stared up at Dayan in total shock. He had camped with their leader for several weeks during the Dark Troubadours tour, yet Cullen had never seen Dayan exhibit the slightest interest in any woman. Now Dayan's body language shouted that he felt protective, even possessive, of Corinne. There was something else, something in Dayan's eyes that had never been there before. A flicker of something dangerous. Cullen had assured Lisa that her sister was perfectly safe with Dayan, but now he wasn't so certain.

"Perhaps we had better get the ladies out of the wind," Dayan drawled. "Cullen, let's escort them to their car, and then I'll pick up my guitar." His voice brushed over Corinne's skin again like fingers.

She shivered in reaction. At once he drew her into the shelter of his arms. "I should have realized it was too cold out here for you," he said softly, apologetically, his breath warm against her neck. His body was hot and hard against the satin softness of her cool skin. "I was being selfish, wanting you to myself."

He glanced at Lisa, and she unexpectedly found herself leading the men to her small sporty car, wondering why it was suddenly so important to her to get Corinne out of the wind. Dayan kept possession of Corinne, handing her carefully into the front seat. "Where can we meet you so we can talk in a quieter atmosphere?"

He asked it softly, his black eyes suddenly on Lisa's face.

Lisa blinked and blurted out her address, something she would never normally do. Corinne stared at her in horror. Lisa clapped a hand over her mouth guiltily and watched as Dayan reached casually across Corinne to buckle her seat belt.

Hard and defined with muscle, his body brushed Corinne's. He smelled of spice and woods. Totally masculine. He dwarfed the small car. His chin nuzzled Corinne's hair. "I am not a serial killer, although it is nice to know you have some instinct for self-preservation."

He closed the door on her shocked expression, his arrogant, bad-boy grin very much in evidence.

Lisa put her head down on the steering wheel. "Don't say it, Corinne. I don't know what I was thinking, giving him our address like that. He's just—I don't know, too much. I couldn't think straight for a minute there with his eyes staring at me as if he could see right through me. I'm sorry. You don't think he's some kind of crazy person, do you?"

"I think we're the crazy ones." It was a relief to be away from the potency of Dayan's company. He made Corinne feel out of control. Spinning madly. Wild. Sexy. Wanting. "And he did point out he wasn't a serial killer. That was comforting news, unless serial killers regularly make such statements to strange women."

Both women dissolved into laughter, dispelling most of the tension in the car. Corinne found she could breathe again, think again, as Lisa put the car in gear and, honking the horn, plunged bravely into traffic. "So, are you looking at Cullen? Because he's certainly looking at you." Corinne rubbed her palms up and down her arms over the exact spot Dayan's arms had held her. Oddly, she could still feel him close to her. She could smell his scent on her, and it was strangely comforting.

"I really think Cullen is great," Lisa admitted. "You know how I hate being the decorative doll on the big guy's arm. He didn't make me feel like that at all, not once. He's nice, Rina. Very nice. And when I realized you were gone, he was so sweet, reassuring me that Dayan wasn't a playboy preying on women. The truth is, I panicked. I don't feel comfortable when you're out of my sight anymore." She threw Corinne a quick, mischievous grin as she rolled through the next three stop signs and narrowly missed jumping a curb. "I sound like I'm two and afraid to leave my mommy. Cullen's cute, though not in a kiddy way." She tugged on Corinne's sleeve. "And what was *that*?"

"What was what?" Corinne tried to sound innocent, but a blush slowly crept up her neck into her face.

"You know exactly what I mean," Lisa accused, her eyes laughing. "That dance."

"Oh, that." Corinne pushed both hands through her mass of gleaming hair and lifted it off her neck, the gesture curiously sexy. "That was scorching."

Lisa let out a whistle. "Scorching? Not just hot?"

Corinne shook her head solemnly. "Absolutely, totally scorching. That man is lethal and shouldn't be allowed to live anywhere near the female population."

"I'm a believer. You've always been immune to men. If he can scorch you, he should definitely be locked up somewhere."

"Somewhere where we can still look at him," Corrine suggested with a little smile curving her soft mouth. An intriguing dimple appeared briefly, then melted away, leaving Lisa wondering where it had gone.

"You like him." Lisa made it a statement. She knew she was overprotective of Corinne. But Corinne was terribly vulnerable. A man like Dayan might easily sweep her off her feet. Anyone looking at him could see he was a dangerous man. A rock star, a musician. Half the female population was after him. But there was something about the way he looked at Corinne . . .

"*Like* him?" Corinne echoed the words thoughtfully. "I don't think he's a man who would inspire such an insipid word as *like*. I feel safe when I'm with him, and yet threatened at the same time. It makes no sense. I do and say things entirely out of character for me. What's really strange, Lisa, is I feel as if I've known him forever, that I'm supposed to be with him." She took a deep breath and made a hurried confession. "And I can't look at him without feeling like jumping into bed. At first I thought it was because I love his music. Ever since I ran across that old LP, I've worked at collecting everything of the Dark Troubadours I could. You know, the idol trap that women occasionally fall into when the musician happens to be a godlike creature. But I think he's rather like a flame and I'm a little moth flying way too close to him. It's called chemistry. Explosive, natural chemistry."

"Really?" There was definite interest in Lisa's voice. She lifted one eyebrow in inquiry. "Spill all, Corinne. Are we talking sex here?"

"You saw him. He oozes sex. I've never met anyone even remotely like him. I just thought I wasn't the sexy type. We talked about it, remember?"

Lisa nodded solemnly, hurtling around another corner, missing a parked car by half an inch. Corinne was so used to Lisa's driving, she didn't even wince. A horn blasted at them, and Lisa flashed a cheery smile and waved gaily as she cut off the driver to get to her turn. "I thought it was because it was your first time," Lisa answered carefully; "the beginner thing with John. You had a hard time of it." Corinne had always been honest with Lisa about her life with John. Everything had been

26

comfortable between them with the exception of the bedroom. Corinne blamed herself, believing she simply didn't have a strong sex drive.

"More likely it was the chemistry thing, because, believe me, this man and I have some kind of attraction. I'm not certain I would trust myself in a room alone with him," Corinne mused aloud, shocked at the blatant response of her body. "Maybe you've run across his type before in your crowd, Lisa, but for me, this is an absolutely new and very uncomfortable first experience. He could drop a woman at thirty paces." Corinne sighed and shook back her hair. "It makes me feel guilty over John." She made it a confession.

Lisa scowled darkly. "Don't be silly, Rina. John would hate your saying that. He loved you like crazy, but we both know you didn't love him the same way. You made him happy, you know you did, and for that I thank you from the bottom of my heart. You were always there for both of us."

"I did love John," Corinne said, "and I miss him terribly."

"I know you loved him. I didn't mean it like that. He isn't coming back, and he would want you to be happy. You know he would." Lisa pulled the car up to the driveway of their home. Her unusual, elegant, yet exotic looks had helped provide money for a beautiful home in an upscale neighborhood. The two women enjoyed just looking at their home sometimes. "Of course, I don't know if he'd approve of Mr. Sex Appeal. What were you talking about all that time? Alone. In the dark," Lisa teased.

"Babies." Corinne blurted it out, wanting to confess everything. How could she have told a perfect stranger before telling her beloved sister-in-law?

Something in Corinne's voice warned Lisa it wasn't a funny subject. Lisa went very still, her fingers freezing

27

around the car keys while her other hand tightened around the steering wheel. "I'm sorry, I thought you said babies. Why would you be discussing babies with him? I hope you told him babies were out of the question." There was an edge of challenge in Lisa's voice. At once her eyes were examining Corinne's figure, clad in jeans and loose-fitting top.

Corinne looked away from the accusation in her eyes. "I didn't know, Lisa, I swear I didn't. The morning John was killed we had made love. After he was murdered, everything was so terrible I didn't think about it for a couple months; then I noticed I was abnormally tired. Way more than usual. I spotted the entire time, so it just didn't occur to me I could be carrying a baby. But then when I was so ill, I went to the doctor. Remember I had to go to bed for a while?"

"You're pregnant? You're pregnant right now?" Lisa pushed Corinne's shirt away from her stomach to inspect her. "You'd have to be six months and you aren't showing." It was an accusation. It was a plea. But she saw the little mound where Corinne's flat stomach had been.

Corinne caught Lisa's hand in hers. "Come on, Lise, we can get through this together, just like we've always done."

Lisa was shaking her head in denial, tears swimming in her eyes. "You can't have a baby. The doctors said you couldn't. You were on birth control. I remember you were so upset when they said it would be a virtual death sentence for you to have a baby. John swore he would never allow you to chance it. He swore it to me. I made him swear it."

"I had to go off birth control some months ago. We were taking precautions and we were always careful." In the last few months before his death, John had begun to complain about using condoms. The pill made Corinne sick, and so did the shot. He hated everything else because it was "invasive." "It was just the one time. I knew better, but I wasn't thinking much about it at the time." John had gotten impatient with her inadequacies. Corinne hadn't blamed him. He had wanted her to feel for him the same things he felt for her. How could she explain how guilty she felt for not being sexually attracted to John in the way he needed her to be? She loved John—she knew she loved him. She loved him dearly, but she had never wanted the physical side of their relationship as he had. That morning she had tried hard for John.

"It was totally irresponsible of both of you," Lisa snapped. "I told John he should have an operation, but he didn't want to because . . ." She trailed off.

"Because he thought he might have children one day with someone else after I died," Corinne finished for her. "I wanted him to be happy."

Lisa's fingers tightened around Corinne's desperately. "What can we do? Can they take it early?"

"Take a deep breath, Lisa," Corinne advised gently. "This baby isn't an it. We're talking about a child. A part of John."

"I don't care who it's a part of. That baby is going to kill you."

"John and I have a daughter, Lisa. She's a living, breathing child, kicking and moving, a little girl." Very gently Corinne attempted to guide Lisa's hand over the small mound of her stomach.

Lisa snatched her hand back and shoved open the car door. She scooted out and slammed it very hard, a measure of her mood. Corinne sighed and slid from the vehicle, following her up to the house. As Lisa grabbed for the doorknob, Corinne stopped her with a gentle hand on her shoulder. "I know you're upset, Lisa. I should have told you right away, when the doctor confirmed it, but I wasn't certain I could carry the baby. After the horror of John's death, I didn't want you to suffer along with me. It was all such a nightmare, a terrible nightmare. What would be the point of making you worry even more? John was dead, I was already pregnant, and we both know the chances of my carrying successfully were slim. I didn't want to worry you."

Lisa spun around, her blue eyes reflecting a mixture of grief, fear and anger. "You didn't want me to tell you what you knew all along. You can't have this baby because you'll die if you do. You'll die, Corinne. That's the bottom line; it's always been the bottom line. I thought you had accepted the fact that you'd never have a baby. You're everything to me. My family, the only family I've got. We fought for the life we had, the three of us, but then when we finally made it, someone killed John and now you're planning on dying and leaving me all alone!"

Corinne wrapped her arms around Lisa and held her close until the stiffness melted away and Lisa was clinging to her. "I'm not planning to die, Lise, and if I did, you wouldn't be alone, you'd have a part of John and a part of me with you."

"I don't want a part of you, Corinne, I want *you*. I can't do this—I won't lose you too. I'm not like you. I'm not strong and brave and I don't want to be," Lisa said adamantly, then breathed a soft expletive under her breath as headlights caught them for a moment and the engine of a car died. "I can't possibly act normal now. I want everyone to go away so I can cry a river."

The moment Dayan stepped from the car and inhaled the night, he knew something was wrong. He was well aware of the dissension between the two women; he could easily read their thoughts. He wanted to comfort Corinne, knew she was fighting tears, but they were both in danger. Even as he read their minds for information, he scanned the area, his mind seeking the hidden threat. His heart in his throat, he glided toward the two women, putting on a burst of preternatural speed as they turned away from him to reach for the front door. His hand was there first, effectively blocking Lisa from entering. Even as Dayan jerked the door shut, Corinne gasped and pulled Lisa away from the house, across the lawn, back toward the car.

"It was open, Lisa. The door wasn't closed all the way." There was panic in Corinne's voice. She had been afraid someone was watching them ever since John's body had been found in the small park close to their home.

"You probably forgot to lock it," Lisa ventured, but her voice was shaking.

Corinne shook her head, her eyes meeting Dayan's over Lisa's head. "I locked it, I know I did. We have to call the police." She wanted him to believe her.

Dayan was already herding the two women toward Cullen. Dayan nodded his head as if in agreement, his hands very gentle on Corinne's arms, moving up and down over her skin, warming her, offering a measure of comfort. "Go with Cullen. I'll take care of things here." There were two human males waiting in concealment in the house. "Cullen, take them to the house where we're staying. I will come as soon as I am able."

The authority in his voice said he was a man used to being obeyed. Lisa immediately slid into the car, her face very pale. Corinne balked, just as he had known she would.

She lifted her chin at him, her green eyes flashing. "I don't think so! You're getting in the car too, Dayan. What are you thinking? My husband was murdered. Don't you think it's a bit of a coincidence that someone's in our house? You're coming with us!" Corinne caught his arm and tugged.

31

Dayan smiled down at her, his heart melting. "Thank you, Corinne." He framed her face with his hands, his black gaze holding her captive. "You will go with Cullen and wait for me, and you will not call the authorities." His mouth brushed the top of her head, the briefest contact; then he was smiling his reassurance as he put her gently in the car.

"Dayan, please, come with us. I have a bad feeling about this," she protested.

"It will be fine, Corinne. I am not easily killed." He leaned across the seat in the protective way he had and tightened her seat belt. "Your heart is beating too irregularly," he whispered against her ear, his mouth against her skin. "Listen to the rhythm of mine." He brought her hand to his heart.

For one moment she couldn't breathe, and then she could hear the sound of his heart. At once her heart seemed to work to follow his lead. It was impossible, but then, Corinne could move objects by simply willing them to move, so she believed in the impossible. With Dayan, everything seemed natural. She felt a jolt of electricity as his fingers brushed the silken top of her head before he closed the car door. Whips of lightning danced in her bloodstream. He did everything smoothly and efficiently, with no hurry, his confidence complete. It was impossible not to do as he said when he seemed in such complete control and utterly invincible. Corinne couldn't look away from him until the car pulled out from the curb.

The moment those black eyes were no longer on her, Corinne covered her face with her hands. "We shouldn't have left him like that. I don't know why I act so out of character around him. Cullen, we need to go back and help him. If someone is in our house, they could hurt him, or worse."

Cullen laughed softly. "Save your sympathy for anyone in the house. It won't be Dayan who goes down."

"I'm serious," Corinne said. "There could be several men with guns."

"Believe me, it won't matter. They won't hurt him." Cullen spoke with complete conviction.

"He's a musician, a gentle, sweet poet," Corinne protested, thinking of the beauty of his words, the tenderness in his smile.

Cullen laughed softly. "He's much more than that, Corinne. Don't worry about him. He really has an uncanny knack for taking care of himself."

Dayan watched the car until the taillights disappeared around a corner. Corinne feared for his safety. He read it easily in her eyes, in her mind. Heard her protest with his acute hearing. It warmed him as nothing else had ever done. Then he turned his head very slowly to look at the house. As he turned, his entire demeanor changed. There was nothing left of the elegant male. At once he looked like what he truly was. A dark, dangerous predator unsheathing his claws. Stalking his prey. He began to move in the darkness—his home, his world. He had the complete advantage. He could see easily on the darkest night, he could move with the silence of the wind, he could scent his prey as keenly as the wolf, and he could command the skies and the earth itself.

Dayan glided around the house, effortlessly vaulting the six-foot fence. As he did so he shifted shape, landing silently on four paws instead of two feet. The leopard padded softly on its large, cushioned paws, the grass barely moving as it circled the back of the house. Off the back porch a light shone beneath the door of a small room. In the shadow of the porch, the huge cat wavered and shimmered, its mottled fur almost iridescent for a brief moment, then it simply dissolved as if it had never been.

A stream of vapor poured through the crack of the door, flowing as quickly and silently as a lethal dose of carbon monoxide. Dayan gained the interior of the house and paused for a moment inside while the vapor wavered into transparency once more, only to re-form in the huge, well-muscled body of the cunning and silent predatory cat.

Dayan padded through the small, well-lit room into the darkened kitchen. He knew immediately where both hunters lay in wait. He could smell them, a pungent mixture of fear and excitement. They had been waiting for some time, pumped up and ready, sweat glands excreting their foul stench, but inevitably the wait had drained them and they had become restless and cramped in their positions. When the headlights of the car had signaled the arrival of the two women, the cycle had started all over again. Fear. Excitement. Adrenaline. And then the terrible letdown.

They were shifting their positions, uncertain what to do. Their orders were clear. Wait until the women arrived, grab them quickly and quietly. Dayan read their minds as clearly as he smelled the sweat from their bodies. Neither noticed the large leopard as it made its slow, patient approach in imperceptible silence.

The cat walked boldly out into the center of the spacious room, not even attempting to use the furniture for cover. This kind of cat-and-mouse game was as old as life itself to the predator. The leopard's eyes remained focused on its prey, a penetrating, piercing stare signaling that death was stalking. Those eyes held all the cunning and intelligence of a great hunter. They were not the yellow eyes of a leopard, but a fierce, calm black, empty of anything but lethal intent.

The leopard dropped low, belly to the ground, muscles incredibly controlled as it began to stalk the men. Inch by slow inch. In complete silence. There was not even the whisper of fur brushing the immaculate carpet as the cat gained on its prey. A man was leaning against the wall, sighing, moving restlessly, easing his cramped muscles. A gun was in his right hand and he continually checked it, caressing the trigger absently with his finger, wiping his forehead where beads of sweat were accumulating. Waiting was a difficult thing, and he didn't have the patience or stillness of the cat.

He never knew that he had gone from the hunter to the hunted. He felt the impact of the heavy body as it drove him into the wall. He felt the brush of fur and smelled the wild scent of death. Daggers pierced him where the heavy cat's crushing claws held him still while its long, sharp teeth punctured his throat. For one moment the man stared into the eyes of the cat, caught and held as his throat was crushed; the knowledge of his own death had come far too late to stop it. Those eyes held savage intelligence and were mesmerizing, compelling. As he died, he recalled the events leading up to this moment. He had been one of the men who'd stalked and murdered John Wentworth. One of the men who did security work at the Morrison Center for Psychic Research.

Dayan lowered his prey to the ground, breathing deeply, forcing the beast under control. In the body of the leopard, his own hunger was doubly difficult to restrain. He moved quickly from the temptation, padding softly around the corner of the room into the hall on his cushioned paws. Corinne had been correct: The kidnappers were after them because John had gone to the center. Whatever her husband had told them, it had aroused interest in Corinne and Lisa as well.

Once again in complete control of the beast raging inside him, Dayan began to stalk the other kidnapper.

He was on the other side of the room, oblivious to his partner's fate. Twice he lifted a small corner of the curtain and looked out into the dark night. The leopard could smell him, hear his sighs, his movements giving away his position as he constantly shifted his weight back and forth in an attempt to ease sore muscles and keep himself alert. This man was stroking his gun, too, fantasizing about what he would do to the two women when he had them in his hands.

The leopard padded forward until it was within several feet of its prey before it froze in position, sinking to the carpet in a low crouch. The cat remained perfectly motionless, its eyes fixed unblinkingly on its prey. The man turned and looked directly at the leopard without seeing it, without any awareness whatsoever. Dayan waited with all the patience of a thousand years of hunting. For him, the life cycle was endless and there was all the time in the world. He watched dispassionately as the intruder turned back to his post without seeing the body of his partner or the danger to himself.

The leopard inched forward once again without even a whisper of movement to betray him. He had stalked prey countless times and defeated his enemies time and again. The merciless black eyes never once left their target. When he was within striking distance, he gathered himself for the attack, watching, waiting for the perfect opportunity. He struck hard, going for the throat, the quick kill, and this time he shifted shape as he did so, bending his head to drink as he took the man unaware.

At once the rush of adrenaline-laced blood hit him hard, a fireball moving through his system. *The forbidden.* Addicting as any drug. He was hungry and he drank deeply, the beast rising, fighting for supremacy. Dayan calmly held the man's weight in his enormously strong hands and deliberately thought of Corinne. She anchored him, kept him safe. She was there to ensure he did not cross over to become the very thing this man was hunting. The vampire. The undead. Dayan was a Carpathian male, as old as time, one of the ancients walking the land in search of his lifemate. Without her he would eventually be forced to seek the dawn or choose to lose his soul and become the vampire.

The blood was moving through his system, reviving cells and muscles and tissue, soaking into his body and giving him a false high. Everything in him demanded more, demanded he feed while the life force faded from the body. *Corinne.* He called her name in his mind for strength to resist the wildness. A cool breeze seemed to find its way to his hot skin. *Corinne.* He could see her face—he had memorized every inch of it. Her soft skin begging for his touch. Her moss-green eyes, the color as rare as she was. The light inside her, shining out of her. *Corinne.* He felt her with him and it was enough. He closed the wound with his healing saliva, allowing the man to die at his own pace. The beast inside him raged for a moment, fighting him, wanting more, wanting to gorge itself, but Dayan ignored the terrible whispers of power and concentrated on Corinne.

Her mouth. The intriguing dimple that came and went. The way her lips curved into a smile. She was extremely kissable. He looked around the spacious house. Corinne's house. He inhaled her scent as he moved through the rooms. The house had high, vaulted ceilings, lots of wood and was very clean. Instinctively he knew that Corinne was the one who did the house-keeping. Lisa's bedroom had clothes on the floor and draped over chairs. Lipsticks and cosmetics were scattered over a vanity. A large gilded mirror was on the wall above the small vanity. The room held Lisa's scent and two pictures. One was of Corinne. The other was of a young male. Tall. Laughing. Blond like Lisa. It had to be John.

Dayan stared a long time at the man. He could see Lisa in him. The eyes were intelligent, the smile real. He wanted to find something not to like about the man, some hidden demon, but he seemed genuine. Dayan moved out of the room and wandered through the house getting a feel for those who lived there. A large room off the main living area held a gleaming piano and a drum set. He paused for a moment, inhaling Corinne's scent. This was a part of her domain; he knew she was often at the piano. It was only after he had inspected the area carefully that he allowed himself to enter Corinne's room. Various antique instruments hung on the wall.

The bedroom was decorated in soft colors, very neat and tidy, the bed with a multitude of throw pillows. Her clothes were neatly folded in the drawers and hung in the closet. Books were everywhere. Books of every kind. There was an entire section devoted to wild cats. Dayan found himself smiling as he picked up a particularly thick one on leopards. The pictures were excellent. His finger touched the snarling face on the cover. Books on weather and the ocean were in a pile on the left side of the bed. Thick volumes dedicated to the history of music were scattered on the floor beside a case holding a state-of-the-art music system.

On the walls were rare signed posters of various artists. A keyboard was set up in a corner of the room. There was an electric guitar leaning up against the wall and a beautifully crafted acoustic instrument lying in a padded case with the lid opened. A CD holder was packed with every type of music imaginable. Tapes were neatly fit into another case and records were in a third. Browsing through the tapes, he was shocked to find several cassettes marked "Dark Troubadours."

Looking further, he found rare and bootleg recordings of various artists.

On the bed lay a notebook filled with lyrics written in a small, neat script. Her handwriting. He looked at the signature and his eyes widened. A slow smile softened the line of his mouth. C. J. Wentworth. The name was respected in music circles. He'd had no idea C. J. Wentworth was a young woman. His young woman. Corinne. He leafed through the notebook. Her words were beautiful and touched his heart.

All at once Dayan couldn't wait any longer to get back to her. Her presence was everywhere in this room, her scent enfolding him in its embrace. He inhaled deeply, taking her fragrance deep into his lungs. Dayan caught up a photograph of Lisa and Corinne laughing together, Corinne looking up at Lisa as a spray of water showered down over the two of them. The pad of his thumb caressed her laughing face. The sun had bathed her in a ray of light, a surrounding halo. She was so beautiful she robbed him of the ability to breathe. It hurt to look at her. There were moments when a giant hand seemed to be squeezing his heart. He wondered whether it was because her heart labored so terribly, or because she was so beautiful it hurt to look at her.

His emotions were difficult to sort through. He wanted to be everything to her, the very air she breathed. He was concerned with the logistics of protecting her. If he bound her to him in the ritual manner, as every fiber of his being was demanding he do, they would be locked together for all time. She would not be able to endure separation from him during the daylight hours, and if he remained aboveground he would eventually be drained of the great strength needed for her protection. During the day, if he was not safe underground he would be helpless and vulnerable to his enemies.

Dayan sat on the edge of her bed, his palm absently running over the quilt in an uncharacteristic show of tenderness. He sent out a call, seeking information. He was far from his own kind, but Darius was strong and their connection had been powerful almost since the beginning of their time together. Theirs was a blood bond, unbreakable by time or distance. Darius was family and he would answer on their own private path, mind to mind. *'Darius. I have need of you.'*

Dayan had learned patience hundreds of years earlier, the patience of the leopard on the hunt, the patience of the ocean wearing away the rocks. He sat quietly, his mind replaying the events of the day so Darius could read his problem clearly. He could feel the connection between them, Darius's power filling his mind. Unexpectedly, he felt a rising emotion for this one man who had been so much a part of his life. Dayan had had only the memories of their closeness to sustain him for hundreds of years; he had lost his ability to feel early on, yet he had the music that poured out of his soul, reminding him he still lived. He had been fortunate that he had retained that priceless gift when so many others lost everything.

'We are happy for your find, Dayan.' The voice alone comforted and gave Dayan a sense of well-being, a sense of family. Darius had led their small group unerringly through terrible years of war and vampire hunts. He had kept them together, given them purpose, protected them and taught them how to survive in those early years. *'Desari and Tempest cannot wait to meet their new sister.'*

'I must consult with a healer. The need is great and the situation complicated. She is with child.'

'I will find the best our people have to offer and bring them to you as quickly as possible. We will start out immediately to come to you.'

'We have enemies here. Perhaps the society has found my lifemate, or perhaps we have a new enemy. Someone from the Morrison Center, a psychic research organization, was sent to acquire her. They were using guns and had violence in their minds. Come carefully, Darius, and caution the others to do so also.'

'I have already put out the word to the others. It will take us a few days, Dayan.'

'I thank you for your concern, Darius. I do not yet know if our enemy is her enemy, but I will find a way to keep Corinne safe. Should something happen to me . . .'

'She will always be under my protection and the protection of your family. You will keep her alive until the healer arrives.' It was a command. 'We will not lose either of you, Dayan.' The voice spoke with utmost confidence.

With a small sigh Dayan turned his attention to the problem at hand. He had to remove the bodies of the intruders from Corinne's home. The leopard had crushed the throats of the two men, strangling them rather than ripping and tearing. There was very little blood where the puncture wounds were. He had been careful to keep the carpets clean. He wanted no signs that the two men had ever been in the house.

Dayan lifted the bodies easily, slung them over his shoulder and stepped out into the backyard. The night was waning, and he had much to do. He launched himself into the air, shape-shifting as he did so, taking the men with him as he winged through the sky, gathering dark clouds together to shield himself from any observers. He was moving fast, a dark shape streaking across the heavens with his burden.

Dayan, like all his kind, was enormously strong, and the dead weight of the two bodies meant nothing to him. He was enjoying the night, the sounds, the songs, the sheer beauty of it all. It surrounded him, enfolded him in its music. The stars glittered like diamonds, a brilliant display, and below him trees dipped and swayed in the wind. In the darkness the leaves appeared a gleaming silver. He flew over a small lake and the surface glistened like glass. The world had never appeared so beautiful to him. Living so long without colors, Dayan found their return overwhelming. He wanted to take it all in, turning his head this way and that so he could see everything.

Far from the city he found what he was looking for, a deep forest. Dayan settled to earth, his wings dissolving as he took his own shape. With a wave of his hand he opened the earth and floated the bodies into the deep chasm, tossing the crushed guns on top of the remains. Overhead, he built a storm, gathering in dark clouds and roiling the air above him so that lightning arced, veins of white-hot energy leaping from cloud to cloud. The dancing whips were directed into the hole so that both bodies were incinerated quickly. No one would find this grave. With a wave of his hand, the earth settled back over the ashes. The wind scattered leaves and twigs across the grave so that it looked as if it had been undisturbed for years.

Dayan dispersed the storm and, in the shape of an owl, flew quickly back to the safe house where Cullen waited with Corinne and Lisa. He was eager to get back to her, to be in her company, to see that she was real and not a figment of his imagination.

Chapter Three

Corinne sat curled up in a deep-cushioned chair, her feet drawn under her and her head resting on her arm. Her hair cascaded in a silken curtain around her face. She sat in the dark waiting, her heart tapping out an uneven rhythm. She was trembling inside, feeling very shaky.

Lisa and Cullen had talked quietly for some time in the small bedroom off the hall before Lisa had finally fallen asleep. Cullen eventually sprawled close to Lisa, nodding off himself, his arm flung protectively around Lisa's waist.

Corinne waited up, fear beating in her like the pounding of a drum, as irregular as her heartbeat. She had no idea how she had come to be so wrapped up in a virtual stranger. Every cell in her body needed to know that nothing had harmed him. She could remember every detail of his face, every fleeting expression. She felt alone and frightened without him, and that was totally out of character for her. Corinne was unsure what to do. She was the one who had always seen to the details of everyday life. She juggled appointments and paid bills, made certain Lisa was where she was supposed to be and that John's business ran smoothly. She didn't fall for tall, handsome strangers in bars, certainly not one who was famous. She wrote songs for many famous musicians, but it had never occurred to her to be impressed with any of them.

She heard nothing but her own heartbeat, yet when she looked up, Dayan was looming over her, tall and strong and alive. Air rushed into her lungs and she could breathe again. Corinne had an unexpected and entirely unacceptable desire to trace the angles and planes of his face with her fingertips. She needed to touch him, to assure herself he was unharmed. A small smile found its way to her soft mouth. "I was worried."

Dayan reached down to lay his hand against her satin cheek. Her stomach did a funny little flip, his touch bringing a strange craving for more. "There was no need, Corinne, but I thank you for your concern." He said her name like a caress.

She shook her head, astonished at her reaction to him. He was truly lethal. No one had ever looked at her as he did. His eyes were intense, fathomless, dark and dangerous and mysterious, moving over her possessively. So *hungry*. Could anyone ever refuse such longing? Such intense need? "I should have called the police," she confessed in a little rush. "I don't know why I listened to Cullen. I *never* listen to anyone when they aren't being logical, but he was so adamant."

"It is just as well you did not," Dayan said softly.

She looked up at him from under long lashes. "You aren't a criminal of some sort, are you? It seemed the only explanation for Cullen to carry on so."

Again he smiled, a slow, sexy curve accenting the sensual line of his mouth. He hunkered down beside her chair so that his head was level with hers. "Do I

44

look like a criminal?" His voice held that strange black magic, whispering over her skin so that she shivered, but deep inside her a flame began to burn hotly and spread liquid heat like molten lava throughout her body.

"Even if you're not, you should be totally outlawed," she blurted out before she could censor her words.

Those black, black eyes glittered with male humor. "I will take that as a compliment. You did not say if you liked my playing."

She lifted her head, tossing her abundance of hair over her shoulder, the gesture purely feminine, entirely sexy. "You know very well you're phenomenal, I don't have to tell you. Everyone says so."

"But then, not everyone's opinion counts to me. Only yours." He was perfectly serious, as if she were the only one in his world. His deep black eyes did not leave her face. Did not even blink.

Corinne wanted to look away, afraid he was capable of mesmerizing her, but instead she felt herself falling into the depths of his eyes. They were so beautiful, unlike any eyes she had ever seen. He was compelling her to answer him. She *had* to answer him because it was necessary to him. He made her feel that way. "You play absolutely beautifully. I've never heard anything like it. I want to hear you sing again."

"You are C. J. Wentworth. You did not whisper a word about the famous C. J. who can make someone's career with one of her songs."

Color crept into her face again, and for a moment it was all he could do not to lean down and fasten his mouth to hers. She looked shy, yet so enticing he wanted to gather her to him and shelter her against his heart.

Corinne shrugged modestly. "I've had luck with my songs, but they're nothing like the ones you and Desari compose. Your music and lyrics linger in the mind."

"You have tapes of our gigs," he accused, a faint grin stealing into his eyes.

She flashed a saucy little smirk at him. "They didn't come cheap, either. I had to pay a fortune. The strange thing is, a few years ago I came across an old record. The band is called the Dark Troubadours, but the recording was made in the 1920s." She studied his face, feature by feature. It was a handsome mask, giving nothing of his thoughts away. "Most of the dealers know I love rare recordings and that I'm willing to pay for them. When one of them sold me that record, I became obsessed with the music. Its different, incredibly beautiful, almost haunting. You should hear it, Dayan. When I first heard the name of your band, I thought there might be some connection and I had to hear your music. It took a long time and a great deal of money to acquire the black-market tapes. I know you aren't the same band, but I swear, the similarities are amazing. The music is different, of course, of a different era, but the style, the way of playing is so like yours. I've listened to that record over and over, and I'd swear the musicians are the same. You know how you can listen and know who is playing just by the sound?" The words tumbled out of her in her excitement. She was speaking musician to musician.

He raked his hand through the dark silk of his hair, his intrigued gaze on her face, drinking her in. Devouring her with his eyes. That recording had been their one mistake. It had not occurred to them that technology would one day be able to identify individuals by voice. Fortunately, few of the records had been produced. They had quietly set about tracking down and destroying every copy. Obviously, they hadn't succeeded.

"Well, have you heard of them? Did you use their

name deliberately?" Corinne demanded, the mystery uppermost in her mind. "You have to hear this recording, Dayan. I've studied music all my life and I have a great ear. I'd swear it was you playing lead guitar."

"That's because it is me," he answered truthfully, allowing a mischievous smile to light the dark depths of his eyes.

Corinne blinked up at him. "So that would make you at least a hundred years old. You're so very well preserved, Dayan."

"Thank you." He bowed slightly from the waist with a curiously Old World elegance that suited him.

"You're welcome, although if you're thinking of a relationship, I'm afraid it's out of the question. I can't possibly go out with a man who's a hundred years old."

His smile widened until his white teeth gleamed at her, taking her breath away. He reached out to brush a stray tendril of hair behind her ear, his fingertips lingering against her skin in a light caress. "When I look at you I can barely breathe," he admitted starkly, melting her heart. "You are so beautiful."

Corinne took a deep breath, trying hard not to allow the wild color to creep up her neck into her face. Someone had to be sensible. She tried not to look at him so she could think more clearly. "Dayan, I'm very pregnant."

"You should be bigger." He spoke gently, but it was clearly a reprimand. "Now I will have to add that to my growing list of things to worry about where you are concerned." He reached out with lazy ease and caught a lock of her hair, rubbing it between his thumb and forefinger as if he couldn't help himself.

"The baby is perfectly healthy," she said defensively, trying desperately not to be affected by the intimacy of his touch.

He tugged at her hair. "What has the doctor said about your health?"

Corinne tried to duck her head, but Dayan's hand caught her chin, his black eyes capturing her gaze, refusing to relinquish his control. "Answer me, honey."

It was odd, but she could feel his voice brushing at the walls of her mind, compelling her to answer him. She *wanted* to tell him despite her natural inclination to keep certain parts of her life private. She shrugged. "Well, you know. Doctors have a way of making everything seem like a worst-case scenario. I'd rather talk about what you found at our house."

Dayan moved, a menacing ripple of muscles that had her heart pounding in her throat again, but he was just standing, stretching like a large jungle cat before reaching for her. He picked her up easily, as if her weight were that of a small child, and glided through the hall to a bedroom.

Corinne closed her eyes tightly for a moment, her hand creeping around his neck. "What are you doing?"

"If we are to talk, honey, I thought it best you be somewhere comfortable. I will not deny it is in my mind to make love to you all night, but I am fully aware of your pregnancy and the difficulties it presents, so I promise to behave myself." There was a slightly humorous drawl to his voice, as if he knew that just saying the words, admitting his desire for her, would send heat coursing through her body. As if he knew his desire was contagious.

Dayan placed her in the middle of the large double bed and bent over her, his black eyes moving over her face intently. Her palm pushed against his broad chest in alarm, an effort to restrain him. Her eyes were enormous in her face, apprehensive. The ritual words beat in Dayan's head; his very body strained with the need to bind her to him. She was his lifemate, she belonged with him, and he needed her desperately. He had been alone for so long, so many centuries. She was here. In the same room with him. *Corinne.*

She lay very still, like a small wild thing caught in a predator's stare, afraid to move. She couldn't look away from those black eyes, the intensity, the terrible naked need. She wanted to hold him, to banish that stark, lonely look for all time. Her palm, the tiny barrier between them, trembled as she stared up at him, mesmerized by his vulnerability when he seemed so invincible. "Dayan." She whispered his name—a soft sigh really, or was it an invitation? She didn't know, so how could he?

Dayan captured her hand, brought her fingers to the warmth of his mouth. "You have nothing to fear, Corinne. I would never do anything that might harm you or the child. I cannot help wanting you, but until it is safe, I think we will both have to suffer."

She found herself smiling as she moved over to allow him to stretch out beside her. Why she trusted him so much, so quickly, she couldn't fathom, but it didn't matter. She liked being beside him, felt comforted by his very presence. He was solid and warm, his arms strong as he pulled her to him, fit her into the curve of his body. She shivered, more from his close proximity than the cool night air, but she liked the way he instantly drew a comforter over them even though she knew he wasn't cold.

"Are you going to tell me what you found at our home?"

"Are you going to believe me?" He asked the question quietly, but she could feel him waiting in the darkness for her answer.

"You forget, my husband was murdered. I know someone was in the house," she answered firmly. "I felt it."

49

He winced inwardly at the word husband. John. Her husband, John. Dayan had to get over that sick feeling whenever she mentioned him. John had been a part of her life for many years, first as a childhood friend, then later as a husband. A part of her loved him, would always love him. His hand bunched in her hair and he brought the silken strands to his face, inhaling the fragrance that was so unique to her. "There were two men in the house. They had guns and orders to kidnap both of you."

Her large eyes moved over his face. "Why?"

"A few months ago our band received word that we were on a hit list. That was how I first met Cullen. He risked his life to warn us. There is a society, a group of fanatics who believe in vampires."

Corinne lifted her head off the pillow to stare at him in shock. "You've got to be kidding me. Vampires? In this day and age? And what does that have to do with me? Or with you, for that matter?"

"You said you were different, that John had gone to talk to someone about his differences. That is the kind of thing these people target. The moment he set foot in the Morrison Center, you were noticed. How are you different, Corinne?"

His voice was like magic in the darkness, soft velvet brushing over her skin and in her mind. She loved the sound of his voice, his interesting accent, which she could not identify. The way he twisted certain words and sounded such a mixture of Old World and modern.

"I can move objects without touching them." Somehow it was easier to make the confession in this dark room with his body lying close to hers, with her palm resting over the steady beat of his heart. She waited for his reaction, his derision, his shock. She waited for him to get up and quietly move away from her. Corinne didn't realize it, but her heart had gone crazy, beating irregularly again as she waited for Dayan to respond.

Dayan captured the hand over his heart, brought her knuckles to his mouth so that his breath moved over her skin, warm and reassuring. "What an amazing gift you have. I too can do such a thing."

Corinne turned her head to look at him. "You can? I've never met anyone else who could. It's so cool. Lisa doesn't like me to do it, but I can't help myself. John knew things. Like the telephone was going to ring and who would be calling. I've never met anyone else who could move objects."

"I can do other things too," he told her softly, his white teeth scraping along her fingers, back and forth in a soothing rhythm so that her heart settled down into the steady pattern of his.

Tears of relief were burning behind Corinne's eyes. Somebody who could understand. Even Lisa, who loved her, didn't really understand. She wanted Corinne to hide her differences from the world, and from her. Lisa pretended that Corinne was like everyone else. They had enough trauma in their lives without adding any more burdens.

"Can you read minds?"

Dayan nodded solemnly. "Yes. I do not have to touch the person to read his thoughts. I was very relieved to know you found me attractive when you saw me, because you took my breath away."

A slow smile curved Corinne's soft mouth. "That is so cheating. You honestly can read my mind?"

"Right now you are attempting to keep your mind totally blank and you are wondering if there is any way you can censor your more, ah . . . how shall I put this delicately . . . ?"

Corinne burst out laughing, the sound soft and inviting in the privacy of the bedroom. Dayan closed his eyes in an attempt to control himself. His body was burning with need, a hard, urgent ache. Little jackhammers seemed to be ripping at his skull. Her body was soft and tempting against his, her curves fitting into the hard angles and planes of his body. Fitting just right. He ached with need and loneliness. Inside him the beast was fighting to break free, raging against the restrictions Dayan was placing on himself. He reminded himself over and over that first and always came her health and well-being. He allowed the scent and sound of her to wash over him, into him, through him, so that he felt centered and balanced.

They weren't joined yet, but she was beside him, giving him the precious gift of color and emotion. She was there, alive and real, a truth he could barely grasp. *Corinne.* Her name was a light in the terrible darkness of his soul. Shining for him alone. Leading him away from a path down which so many of his kind had disappeared for all eternity. *Corinne.* He breathed her name and calmed his raging body with the knowledge that she was beside him.

"Let's not go there," Corinne said softly, laughter in her voice. "How did these people know about your gifts? And why would they think you were a vampire?" It was much safer to keep the conversation away from the almost bewitched way she felt in his company.

"I think there are many reasons. Our lifestyle, traveling from country to country, seems odd to many. The name of our band may even have contributed to the society's suspicions. We hand-raised two leopards and they travel with us. We sleep during the day and perform at night. Somehow it all added up to our being vampires. They tried to kill us by spraying the stage where we were performing with bullets." In the darkness he shrugged. "Cullen used to belong to the society."

"Cullen?" She echoed the name in alarm, astonished

that Dayan could say it so casually. Lisa was alone in the other room with Cullen, asleep and very vulnerable.

Dayan touched her gently, his hand moving over her face. "Be calm, honey. Cullen risked his life to warn us. Those killers want him more than they want us. I've stayed with him to help protect him. My family owes him a great debt. Thanks to you, I can feel friendship again, even affection, where before I felt only a debt of honor. You have already given me more than you will ever know."

"I don't understand the vampire thing. Why haven't the police found these men?" Corinne was deliberately ignoring his strange references to her. She didn't understand her attachment to him, the way she needed to be with him when she had never been a needy person in her life. She felt safe with Dayan, yet at the same time threatened in some elemental and very exciting way.

"This group operates the same way terrorist organizations work. Hit and run, meet in secret. Only those at the top know who belongs. No one trusts anyone else. Some of those on the bottom have no real idea that killing goes on. I know it sounds bizarre, but unfortunately the society is very real. We have to protect ourselves at all times. If these people have targeted you and Lisa, you need protection too. They will not stop hunting you. Somehow we have to find a way to convince Lisa she really is in danger. She is resisting the truth because she does not want anything else in her life to change."

"Lisa had it much harder than John or me. When we were very young, their father began to date my mother. It was mainly a drinking relationship. We didn't know it then, but their father when he drank was extremely violent. To make a long story short, their father murdered my mother. Lisa walked in when he was bludgeoning her with a tire iron, and he knocked Lisa down, put a bag over her head, threw her in the trunk of a car with my mother's body and doused them with gasoline. John knew—he always knew things, and between the two of us, we managed to free Lisa without her father knowing." Corinne had unlocked the trunk of the car using her unique gift. "Lisa, John and I stayed together. We lived mainly on the streets, sort of fending for ourselves." She said it hurriedly, in a little rush, not wanting to dwell on the painful details of her childhood. She never talked about that time, never revealed the details of her early life to anyone, yet she couldn't stop herself from giving Dayan whatever he asked for.

Dayan threaded his fingers through Corinne's, all too aware of the sorrow beating at her, the horror of those memories. "After the murder, Lisa was so battle-scarred she didn't talk for days on end. I sat with her for hours and rocked her back and forth, and she would hold me when I broke down and cried. John was our rock; he stole food for us and kept us safe as we grew up. Eventually we all landed jobs in a café. Lisa was discovered there by a huge modeling agency. After that we didn't have to worry about a roof over our heads. I was already making money writing songs, so I pursued music in college. John became very successful at landscaping. We lived together as a family."

He touched her mind very gently, not wanting to be intrusive when she was reliving painful memories, but he wanted to "see" the details. Her life had been difficult, and he could clearly see her loyalty and love for John and Lisa. They had formed a family together and kept one another safe in a world gone insane. They had virtually raised themselves in a harsh environment and managed to remain loving and sensitive despite the odds against them.

"Lisa is not different in the way you are." He made it

a statement, his hand tangling in her heavy mass of hair.

"We were terrified of Lisa's father. God only knows what he would do if he ever saw my gift, or found out about John. Lisa still is frightened and prefers not to talk about our differences." Without thinking, Corinne burrowed closer to his warmth. "Why would these people target Lisa? It isn't as if she does anything strange. No one could possibly think she's evil."

"It does not matter what their reasoning is, we will have to protect her. I have searched long for you, Corinne. I know you have accepted your death as inevitable because the human doctors have convinced you there is no hope, but it is not going to be that way. You are going to get well and spend your life with me." His thumb was rubbing the inside of her wrist, a caress that she felt all the way to her bones.

"You said human doctors. Is there any other kind?" She was trying to tease him because he sounded so intense.

"I want to try something. I am not a real healer, but I can help you, at least for a short time if you will allow me to do so," Dayan said tentatively. He was in new territory, feeling his way carefully. But her health was so fragile, he wanted to help in any way he could.

"What do you mean? Like faith healing?" She tried not to sound skeptical, but they were talking about vampires and religious fanatics and other highly impossible things. Still, Corinne didn't mind the strange conversation; she enjoyed lying in the darkness beside him, whispering softly.

"Do this for me." There was a magical quality to his voice that always made her want to do anything for him. How could anyone resist him? Ever?

"Tell me what to do."

"Just stay still and allow me to attempt this. I have to leave my body and enter yours. Usually a healer does this, not someone like me. I have sent for our best, but until the healer arrives, I am sure I can help you."

Corinne believed him. She didn't know why she believed he could do what he claimed—it was absurd—but she could see his confidence and she believed. It was odd to think he could read her thoughts, but it didn't bother her much, certainly not as it would if anyone else claimed such a thing. She lay perfectly still, waiting, without protest, to see what he did.

Beside her, Dayan became motionless, not a single muscle moving. Even his breath seemed to cease. She felt a warmth inside her, growing, moving, spreading. She heard a faraway chant. The words were in another language, quite beautiful and soothing, so she relaxed completely. The voice was male, definitely Dayan's, but it was in her mind, not spoken aloud. And he had a beautiful voice.

Dayan examined her enlarged heart carefully, then moved on to the baby. A tiny infant, a female. She was beautiful, fully formed and aware of his intrusion. He reassured the baby immediately, sending waves of serenity to surround her. She had the same abilities as her mother; perhaps they were even stronger. Although extremely small, the baby was perfectly formed, needing only to mature to thrive in the outside world. He left the child with encouragement and returned to his primary mission. Corinne's heart was definitely laboring.

He was not a healer and he didn't have the necessary skills to repair her heart. He could give her his blood to help strengthen her, but he had no idea what it would do to the child. He had touched the infant's mind, knew her as a person; he knew that Corinne already loved her. He couldn't chance harming the baby, not unless Corinne's time ran out. Still softly chanting the ancient healing ritual, Dayan did what he could to shore up her weak, laboring heart.

Corinne knew the exact moment he pulled out of her body. The warmth was gone, and she felt the loss of his presence instantly. She turned her head to look at him, slightly bemused. Perhaps he was a black-magic sorcerer. She was totally bewitched by him, completely under his spell. When his black gaze met hers, she saw hunger there, a terrible aching need, a void only she could fill. Corinne felt it, although she realized the intensity of their emotions made no sense.

"I just met you," she offered softly, her moss-green eyes examining his face.

Dayan linked their hands again, brought hers over his heart. "I have searched the world over for you, through time and distances you cannot imagine. You are the one. My other half. My lifemate." His voice was gentle, whispering over her like velvet.

Corinne shivered, edged closer to the protection of his strong body without realizing she did so. "I like that word. Lifemate. It sounds magical. Like we were meant to be together." Her eyes widened. "I can breathe easier, Dayan, I really can. What did you do?" She was experiencing that strange phenomenon again: Her heart was beating in the exact same rhythm as Dayan's. "Do you hear that? Listen to our hearts."

"We were made to be together, two halves of the same whole," he informed her gently, knowing she wouldn't understand. He meant it literally when she thought he was talking figuratively. "You are the other half of my soul, the light to my darkness. I hold the other half of your heart. We belong, Corinne."

She loved the way he said her name, a lazy drawl, his strange accent curling the vowel sounds until they were intriguingly sexy. "How strange, when I've never believed in love at first sight. You're overpowering, I'll give you that much. I can't make up my mind whether it's your guitar playing or the sound of your voice that's making me lose what little sense I had. Which do you think it is?"

"Something made me go into that bar tonight," he answered softly, his teeth teasing the pad of her thumb. She could feel each gentle scrape all the way down to her toes. "I dreamed you up. You're my fantasy come true."

She laughed then, the sound like music in his ears, a melody even his guitar couldn't match. "Complete with baby on the way, a broken-down heart, and killers stalking me. I'd say you need to try dreaming again, Dayan, you didn't do a very good job." She wanted to be his dream come true, wished she were the one he needed.

"You are the *only* one I need."

He was so certain, so intense. There was no hint of a smile in his black eyes, rather that strange look that reminded Corinne of a predatory animal. He looked dangerous. She changed the subject abruptly. Their relationship couldn't really go anywhere, so what was the use in speculation? "How did you find out the two men were in our house without their seeing you?"

Dayan turned on his side, propping his elbow on the bed so he could rest his head in his palm and gaze down at her face. He could see her clearly in the darkness. He was a night creature and his eyes took in everything. Right now his gaze was focused on her face. She looked beautiful to him, lying there, unaware in her innocence of what he was, what he was capable of. "I needed the information," he replied gently, one fingertip tracing her lush mouth because he couldn't stop himself.

"That isn't an answer," she told him firmly. "Don't avoid the question."

"I do not want you to be afraid, Corinne. I am not always the gentlest of men. Those two were lying in wait to attack you and your friend. One of them had certainly participated in killing your husband. If it is the same organization that attempted to wipe out my entire family in one evening, they would have killed both you and Lisa. They are hunting Cullen, whose only sin was to warn us. I did not feel particularly kindly toward these individuals."

"You confronted them," she guessed. What was he not telling her? Surely he couldn't have faced two armed men alone and bested them. "Do you carry a gun?" She hated guns, those cold metallic instruments of death.

His broad shoulders shrugged casually. "I do not need a gun to kill," he said honestly. "I do not need a gun for any reason whatsoever."

She let her breath out slowly. "I'm glad to hear that."

He knew Corinne said it because she didn't have any idea what he was. A predator, dangerous and powerful. He had no need of a gun; he commanded the earth, the sky. He could shower the land with fire or buckle the ground beneath their feet. His voice alone could rob others of their will. He was a Carpathian male, a hunter of the vampire, his strength enormous, his ability to shape-shift only one of his many gifts. His was a dying species, a race of men doomed to wander the earth endlessly in search of the light that complemented their darkness, the one woman who was the other half of them. Without that woman they lost their ability to feel, lost the ability to see in color, so that they inhabited a dark, shadow world with only memories of honor to keep them from choosing the way of the vampire.

The insidious whisper of power was always with them, eating at them, calling to them, crouching in them, a dark beast filled with blood lust and the need to kill just to feel that momentary rush. As the centuries passed, the dark stain grew and spread, filling the males, until there was no hope, only the dark, dangerous hunger.

For the first few centuries, Dayan had suppressed the beast with his music and the poetry he had loved, but his struggle had increased in the last two hundred years. "Very recently there has been a change in our lives. You know all the band members, right?"

"Desari, of course, your singer. Barack and Syndil and you." Corinne rubbed his arm, sensing his unhappiness.

"And Darius, head of our family and bodyguard. The change was good for my brothers and sisters, not so good for me. First Julian arrived and claimed Desari as his lifemate. Then Darius found Tempest. Barack claimed Syndil, and I was left alone. I felt isolated, Corinne. I cannot explain how difficult it was. How alone I was." The sight of all of them so happy together had left him terribly alone. It had been a kind of hell without them all. They had been together during the centuries of their existence, yet he could no longer face them. The sight and sounds and smells of the mingling couples had made his loneliness even more intolerable.

He was different. He was a danger to them, to the women as well as the men. He saw the wary way Syndil always looked at him. She had been attacked by one of their own, Savon, after Savon had turned vampire. Darius had destroyed the vampire, but it had been a close thing.

Dayan knew the others worried about him, and it had disturbed him that he felt nothing at all. Just alone. Always and forever alone. He was not afraid of Darius and his power, as he should have been. He was Darius's second-in-command. Darius felt tremendous loyalty to him, and they had exchanged blood on more than one occasion when one or the other had been wounded. It enabled them to communicate privately; it also enabled them to track one another at will, no matter how great the distance.

"You aren't alone, Dayan; never think that," Corinne whispered, aching for him. She heard the loneliness in his voice and she wanted desperately to comfort him.

Dayan brought Corinne's fingers to his mouth once more, kissing them gently instead of crushing her to him as he wanted. She had changed his life for all time. He could return to his family now without worry, without the threat that he might turn vampire and have to be hunted and destroyed. He would never have to read in their minds their worry over him, sense their pity and sorrow, their fears. He could feel the love he held for them all, instead of just remembering it. Corinne had done that just by being in the world for him to find. All the long centuries had been worth the wait. All the loneliness, all the terrible emptiness.

Corinne filled him with hope again. No one would be completely safe until she was bound to him, until the ritual had been completed, but Dayan could breathe easier. He had found her at long last, his Corinne. She would save him, and with him, any that he might have endangered.

"I wish I could read minds," Corinne teased. "You go very quiet and you never exactly answer my questions. What happened to our conversation regarding those men in my house? It seemed very important to me."

"Was it?" His voice was that perfect whisper of sound. "I find you the most important thing in my life. It is difficult to keep my mind on anything else, but since it is of such importance to you, I will try."

He was staring down at her as if she were the most beautiful woman in the world. His black gaze drifted over her face, possessive, hungry, aching with need . . . with some inner torment she didn't understand. He was looking at her the way a man looks at a woman he wants to spend the entire night making love with.

"Eternity making love," he corrected, proving he really could read her mind.

Her eyes widened in astonishment. A blush worked its way up her neck to her face, putting color into her cheeks. She realized it could be embarrassing having Dayan read her mind. She thought about him way too much. Thought about every detail of his appearance—his long, thick hair as shiny as a raven's wing, his black eyes, so intense and needy, his sculpted mouth, perfectly chiseled, molded and shaped into a sensual masterpiece. Half laughing, embarrassed that she couldn't control her wayward thoughts, she put her hand over her eyes to block him out.

"Do not do that, honey," he reprimanded softly. "Do not ever do that. I would not be happy if you did not find me attractive."

"You're too attractive," she confessed. "Not real. I don't exactly have these kinds of feelings every day."

His perfect white teeth flashed at her. "That is a relief."

"Now you're laughing at me." She tried to stifle the yawn welling up. "It's almost morning and we haven't gotten anywhere with this. Did you call the police? Is it safe to go back into our house?"

Dayan shook his head. "Maybe to get a few things, but you cannot stay there. When those two men do not return to their people, others will be sent after you. The first place they will look is your home."

"You didn't call the police, did you?"

"Why would we want to do that? The police cannot do anything to these people; they cannot touch them."

"What did you do with the two in my home? Why aren't they going to return to their people?"

"They had orders to kill you, honey. You did not expect me to allow them to walk away." He made it a statement. "It was fair enough—they had guns."

She tangled her fingers in the silky mass of his hair because she had wanted to do that from the first moment she laid eyes on him. "You don't make sense, Dayan. You answer me, but not so I can understand anything. I'm tired." Her long lashes were continually fluttering down despite her efforts to stay awake. "I'm too tired to figure out your sentences with all the holes in them. But don't worry, I'm fairly good at things like that when I'm fully awake."

Dayan stroked the hair from her forehead, his fingertips lingering in a gentle caress. "You can go to sleep, Corinne. You will be safe here and we can finish this conversation when you are not so tired. The baby needs to sleep too. A little girl." There was the slightest of "pushes" in his voice, a hidden compulsion to give in to her desire to sleep.

She smiled up at him, at his strong, sensual features. "That's right, a girl. How did you know?" Corinne found herself suppressing a yawn.

"When I attempted to heal you, I checked to make sure she was in good health. She is beautiful, and very aware of you already." He lowered his head, his heated gaze moving over her face, dropping to her mouth. It moved even lower to brush the slender column of her neck, rested on the pulse beating there.

Embarrassed again by the molten heat spreading through her body, Corinne tried to look away. Dayan's hand spanned her throat. "I want you to want me. Just for this one moment in time." He bent his dark head toward hers, slowly, relentlessly, his black gaze mesmerizing her so she couldn't breathe. Her lashes fluttered in anticipation, her lips parting slightly.

He took his time, in no hurry to end the moment, inhaling her fragrance, gathering her close to him, his body slanting protectively, possessively over hers. He could feel her body, soft and pliant, every curve pressed snugly into the hardness of his own powerful frame, and he savored the differences between a man and a woman. He could feel his blood heat, and he allowed himself the luxury.

Corinne watched the expression in his eyes change from black, sensual possession to a strange, almost predatory stare. Red flames seemed to dance in the very depths of his gaze, and he looked fiercely hungry and all at once threatening. Before she could react, before she could think to protect herself, Dayan's mouth found hers and time simply stopped for both of them.

His mouth was gentle, even tender, a direct contrast to the strength of his arms and the powerful muscles of his body. An electrical jolt flashed through her, through him, and a thousand tiny tongues of flame began to lick along every square inch of her skin. There was so much sensation, she could only cling to him, her mouth taking on a life of its own, matching the hunger in him as he fed on her. The long, drugging kisses made her feel as if the bed was spinning out of control beneath her and her body was no longer her own. She was drenched in hot fire, filled with aching need. She made a small sound of protest, yet her hands sought his back to hold him to her.

Nothing in her life had prepared her for such a firestorm of need. She *had* to have him right at that moment. She wanted him to possess her for all time. Her body seemed empty without him, every cell crying out for him. If she hadn't been pregnant, if it hadn't been risky, she would have become his entirely.

He was everywhere around her, blocking out the room, the world, narrowing her vision until only Dayan existed with his perfect mouth taking hers, his hands moving over her in a gentle exploration. Corinne closed her eyes as he deepened the kiss, as his hand shaped her breast, pushing aside the neckline of her blouse to explore the vulnerable line of her throat.

His mouth drifted to the corner of hers, moved along the curve of her chin to her soft throat. He murmured something soothing as if to quiet her, as if she might struggle. On some level her brain was protesting her behavior, but she couldn't move, couldn't lift her lashes, and self-preservation didn't seem to be so very important in that moment. She felt his tongue sweep over the pulse beating in her neck; his strong hands gathered her closer still. Her body clenched and pulsed with need, with anticipation. His teeth scraped gently, teasingly over the throbbing spot, drenching her with hot answering liquid. She felt she might be drowning, yet she couldn't move, so mesmerized was she by his black-magic spell.

White-hot heat flashed through her, a pleasure so intense it bordered on pain. For a moment she couldn't tell the difference. Then she was drifting in a dream world as Dayan indulged his erotic hunger, his mouth moving over her pulse, feeding on her until she thought she might die of pleasure. Her arms crept up to cradle his head to her, to hold his mouth against her skin.

Dayan heard his own heartbeat pounding in his head, roaring like the beast inside him trying to break free. The ritual words beat in his brain like a drum, filled his mind and heart and soul as he drank. Her blood was sweet, intoxicating, the pleasure coursing through him like wildfire. Fiery hot. The roar increased until his body was going up in flames, urgent, demanding, painful with need. He whispered her name like the talisman it was, forced himself to breathe, to hang on to his sanity, to fight the raging beast and its demands. His tongue stroked across the two tiny wounds, closing them with the healing agent in his saliva, resting his forehead against hers while he fought for total control.

Corinne felt drowsy, and yet her body was on fire, filled with an aching hunger that reduced her mind to erotic images which flared up like dancing flames. She didn't want him to leave her like this, her body throbbing and crying out for his, yet she couldn't summon the energy to move her arms. They felt like lead, sliding from him to lie uselessly on the sheets beside her.

When she managed to pry her lashes open a tiny bit, she could only see his eyes, those haunting eyes watching her with a terrible longing, a terrible need. Her throat worked, and tears burned behind her lashes and clogged her throat. She wanted to remove that look from his face for all time. He looked so alone. So terribly alone with that bleakness etched into the lines of his face, that emptiness in his eyes.

Corinne made a supreme effort and lifted her hand so that her finger could caress the shape of his mouth. *'Don't look so sad, Dayan. I'm not going anywhere.'* She could only say the words in her head because she was far too tired to speak them. Her lashes were already drifting down.

Dayan caught her wrist and brought her knuckles to his lips, a flare of surprise moving through him. He had not given her his blood, yet the connection between them was so strong! *'I will never allow you to escape from me, Corinne, not even through death. Nor will I allow any harm to come to you.'*

She carried that last thought with her as she succumbed to the demand for sleep. Dayan watched her for a long time as the sun began to climb in the sky. He held her hand and simply breathed her in, memorizing the curve of her cheek and the sweep of her lashes to take with him to ground. He murmured a soft command to her and reluctantly left her as the sun stained the darkness and the sky turned a silvery gray.

Chapter Four

"Rina, wake up." Lisa was leaning over the bed and shaking Corinne repeatedly. Her large blue eyes held worry as she looked rather helplessly at Cullen. "I can't wake her up. I can't believe I went to sleep last night and slept most of the day away. I just left her to take care of everything when she's so fragile."

"Don't worry," Cullen soothed as he took Corinne's pulse. "Dayan came back last night and he probably worked at healing her. She just needs to sleep. Feel, Lisa; her pulse is strong."

"I want her to wake up." Lisa was close to tears.

Corinne, buried in layers of fog, recognized Lisa's voice and knew from long experience that Lisa was very upset. Out of habit Corinne answered the call, struggling to the surface when she really wanted to sleep. Corinne's heart began to pound in alarm. What in the world was wrong with her? Her body felt like lead, and she didn't *want* to wake up. Her mind turned that piece of information over and over in an attempt to make some sense of it. Corinne concentrated on her hand, her fingers, each separate muscle. It was strange that she felt so disconnected from her own body.

Lisa gasped and reached down, clutching Corinne's hand. "She moved her fingers, Cullen. I think she's waking up. Rina, come on, girl, wake up," she encouraged.

Corinne heard the voice much more clearly as another layer of fog seemed to lift between her and the world. She struggled to raise her lashes. She *would* open her eyes. She forced herself to concentrate harder, bringing every ounce of her strong will to bear. It was odd, but she was certain something was preventing her, *commanding* her to remain asleep. That made her all the more determined to wake up.

"That's it, Corinne, come on, you can do it. Are you feeling ill?" Lisa bent over her, shaking her shoulders gently. "Please wake up, you're scaring me."

Corinne made a supreme effort, her lashes fluttering for several moments before she managed to raise them. She found herself staring up at Lisa's anxious face. Corinne made herself smile when all she wanted to do was curl up in a ball and snuggle beneath the covers. "I was up all night, pumpkin. I'm just really sleepy."

"You never sleep like this. I couldn't wake you up. You didn't take any sleeping pills or anything like that, did you?"

"Of course not. I'm pregnant. I would never do that." Corinne's words were drowsy and difficult to understand. Several times her lashes drifted down, and she turned on her side, curling deeper into the pillows. "I'm just tired, Lisa."

"Rina!" Lisa commanded sharply. "Don't you dare go back to sleep, or I swear I'm taking you to a hospital." There was real alarm in Lisa's voice.

Corinne sighed softly. "I'm awake, I promise. I'm awake."

"Did you see Dayan last night?" With great determination Lisa perched on the edge of the bed, retaining possession of Corinne's hand. She wasn't certain she wanted Dayan anywhere around Corinne. Corinne looked fragile, pale, more vulnerable than Lisa had ever seen her, even after John had died. Lisa wanted to take Corinne and run home. She was suddenly very afraid of Dayan. He seemed to have some kind of mystical power over Corinne; how else could her behavior be explained? Corinne *never* was impressed by men, by fame or money or good looks. Corinne was always the rock, the logical voice of reason. Dayan was too good-looking and talented to be trusted, too wealthy, a for-eigner, too charming with women.

She had to admit that Dayan didn't have a reputation with women. Even the tabloids had been unable to ex-ploit his sexual prowess in any way. His public appear-ances were not scheduled or publicized, and most reporters who had attempted to get interviews and pic-tures had written articles on how frustrating it was to find facts on him. Corinne had read every article she could get her hands on, because she had been such a serious fan, and she had shared that information with Lisa. Now Lisa wanted to go back and change the fact that she had taken Corinne to the bar.

Lisa frowned. But there was Cullen. She really thought Cullen was an exceptional man, not at all dan-gerous or mysterious, not the type to steal a woman's heart and leave her cold.

"What's wrong, honey?" Corinne whispered. Her voice was slumberous, drowsy, very sexy.

Lisa had never noticed that about Corinne before. She didn't think of Corinne as being sexy. She looked down at Corinne's face, really looked at her. Corinne had her eyes closed and she looked serene, her long lashes two thick, dark crescents on her face. Her abun-dance of silky hair spilled around her like a halo. She looked innocent in her repose, yet Lisa thought her so beautiful, it was almost as if she were seeing Corinne for the first time. Seeing Corinne the way Dayan had seen her.

"I want to go home. You scared me, Rina, when I couldn't wake you up. I want to go with you to the doctor and hear his prognosis about the pregnancy," Lisa said as firmly as she could.

"I'm too tired," Corinne said softly. "Let me sleep for another couple of hours, and then we'll decide what to do." She pulled the covers up to her chin.

Lisa glanced up at Cullen. "She never sleeps during the day. Corinne must be sick, really, Cullen. Maybe we should take her to a hospital."

Corinne roused herself enough to lift her long lashes and peer at Lisa. "I'm not sick—in fact, I'm breathing easier than normal. I stayed up all night, that's all. What time is it?"

"It's nearly six-thirty."

Corinne groaned. "Why are you waking me up, then? No one but a lunatic gets up that early. I think I went to bed at six."

"It's six-thirty in the evening," Lisa emphasized. "You've been in bed all day." She didn't admit she had slept most of the day snuggled right beside Cullen in the other bedroom. Lisa just wanted to go home and shut her front door, closing out the entire world.

Corinne's eyelashes fluttered in surprise. She forced herself to sit up, blinking as she looked around the unfamiliar room. "I can't believe it's so late." Shoving a hand through her thick, dark hair, she glanced over at Cullen. "Lisa worries endlessly about me, but really, I'm perfectly fine. I don't know why I slept so long." She was still exhausted, her arms and legs, heavy. All she wanted to do was go back to sleep.

Cullen smiled at her. "Lisa was frightened when she

couldn't wake you up. Would you like something to eat or drink? I could make you tea or coffee," he offered.

"He makes great tea," Lisa confirmed. "Rina loves tea, don't you?"

"That would be wonderful," Corinne agreed. Lisa was looking at Cullen with her heart in her eyes, something Corinne had never seen before. It wouldn't hurt to drink a cup of his tea to please her. "Where's Dayan?" She tried to sound casual, but it must not have come off that way, because Lisa glared at her, and Corinne couldn't help blushing.

"Just what went on last night?" Lisa hissed when Cullen stepped out of the room. "Don't you think you're in enough trouble without getting mixed up with a rock star?"

"He doesn't exactly play rock," Corinne answered mischievously.

Lisa frowned in reprimand. "Don't joke about this, Corinne. It isn't funny. You know very well you've always had an aversion to being in the public eye. What do you think is going to happen if you start running around with that man? The tabloids love people like him. Forget about him."

Corinne reached out and gently took Lisa's hand. "This isn't about Dayan at all, is it? I'm not going to die, Lisa. I won't. I'm a fighter, you know that. This baby is going to be a part of us—both of us, our family. You aren't going to lose me."

Instant tears were swimming in Lisa's blue eyes. Her fingers closed convulsively around Corinne's as if her grip could somehow keep death at bay. "You always overestimate your strength, Rina, you do. Even John said so. I want the baby too, but not at your expense. I don't want to be all alone. I couldn't stand that. I've already lost John." She laid her head in Corinne's lap for comfort. For the first time, she could feel the baby there, lying between them. She moved her head and placed her hand over the small mound. "It's moving," Lisa said with a kind of wonder.

"She's kicking," Corinne confirmed, stroking Lisa's hair. "A little girl, Lisa. It'll be okay, you'll see. I know I can do this. I want the baby so much."

"I'm sorry, Rina, I didn't mean to sound so awful about the baby. I really do want it too. I want to be excited. She'll be the only thing I have left of John, but I love you. I can't stand the thought of anything happening to you. I'm sure Dayan's a really nice person. Cullen says he is. And he doesn't have the reputation of being a womanizer. I didn't mean to imply that. I don't know why I was saying all those crazy things." Lisa wailed the words, ashamed of herself.

"I know, Lisa," Corinne crooned soothingly, "you're afraid of losing me. But I'm really not going anywhere. You just have to believe we'll be all right. It's natural, after what happened to John, to be afraid of losing family, but it won't happen. I'm *very* strong. I feel better than I have in years."

Lisa sat up slowly, taking a deep breath and giving Corinne a tentative smile. "So was there really someone in our house last night? Cullen didn't say one way or the other." She glanced toward the door and lowered her voice. "I thought it a little strange he didn't want to call the police or go back to help his friend, didn't you?"

Corinne leaned against the headboard of the bed. She was beginning to wake up, the heavy, fuzzy feeling was fading away. "Dayan talked to me about it last night, Lisa. He thinks we're both in danger from the same people who murdered John."

Lisa was silent for a moment. "You know more about John's death than you let on, don't you?" She looked down at her hands. "You never told me, because I never ask questions. I'm like an ostrich."

"You're not an ostrich," Corinne denied gently, refraining from smiling. "You're a beautiful young woman who suffered far too much trauma as a child. John and I both got in the habit of trying to protect you."

"We're the same age," Lisa pointed out, "but you're the one who always took care of the details of our lives. You've had to battle the same trauma as I have, and you have a heart condition. John may have been my brother, but he was your husband. We both loved him. We both lost him. Why am I such a chicken about life? Why am I so afraid to hear anything that might upset me? That's why you didn't tell me what you knew about John, and it's why you didn't tell me about the baby. You were afraid I'd fall apart." She looked down at her hands. "I would have fallen apart."

"Lisa"—Corinne said her name softly—"you're being way too hard on yourself. You always worried about me and took on all the jobs you thought were too strenuous for me. We work as a team together, we always have. I didn't tell you my suspicion about John's murder because that's exactly what it is, just suspicion. John and I are"—she searched for the right word—"different."

Lisa ducked her head, shaking it, ashamed. "And I never wanted to hear about it. Not once. It was because . . ." She trailed off.

"It was scary," Corinne finished for her.

Lisa shook her head adamantly. "It made me feel left out. It created a bond between you and John that I wasn't a part of. We were always together. I wanted John to love you because I was afraid someone would come along and steal you away from us. I was the one who talked you into marrying John, remember? You told him no so many times, but I cried and fussed and acted so childish. I was afraid we wouldn't be together anymore. I was lost there for a while, feeling like I couldn't breathe. I feel that way now. Everything is so scattered. John is dead. I know your heart's been acting up lately; I've seen you fighting for air, and taking more medicine. Now you're going to have a baby, and for the first time *ever* you're really interested in someone." The last was almost an accusation.

Corinne could feel Lisa's pain. Their world was changing around them very fast, and it was frightening to think of all the dangers they were facing. She couldn't blame Lisa for being scared or for wanting things to be the way they were before. "I loved John very much, Lisa—don't think for one moment I didn't. Maybe it wasn't romantic and passionate, but I loved him deeply and I'll never regret what we had. I don't want you to think I was forced into marrying John. I'm excited about the baby, but I'm nervous too. And meeting Dayan is very unexpected. I don't know how I feel about him. I don't know why I respond to him the way I do." She took a deep breath and admitted, "It is frightening, Lisa. I'm afraid too."

Lisa swallowed hard and summoned up her courage. "Tell me what you *think* happened—why someone wanted to kill John."

"John went to the university to talk to a professor about his talent." Corinne looked straight into Lisa's eyes. "You know what I'm talking about—his ability to know certain things before they happened." She took Lisa's hand in hers. "It was how we managed to save you. John knew you were in danger, and I was able to open the trunk of the car." She closed her eyes, remembering finding her mother's battered body lying next to Lisa. Her heart gave a lurch, and she forced her mind away from the haunting memories. "The university sent him to the Morrison Center, which does psychic research. John felt strongly that we should be using our talents to help others."

74

"Because of me; because you saved my life," Lisa said softly.

"He thought maybe he could save others," Corinne confirmed gently. "A few weeks later, he told me he thought someone was following him. He became secretive. You saw the changes in him. He left that morning to meet someone. He was nervous, edgy, and he wouldn't say why. I don't know if he had started working with them and discovered they were doing something illegal. You know John—he would have wanted to go to the authorities. Dayan suspects that the people who murdered John are part of some organization who fanatically believe in the existence of vampires."

Lisa's lips parted in an O shape, and her blue eyes went wide with shock. "You can't believe that nonsense. That man is crazy. Vampires! Good God, Corinne, he must be mentally ill!"

"Dayan's right," Cullen said as he entered the room carrying two cups of steaming liquid. "I belonged to the organization at one time. They investigate anyone who appears the least bit different. Most of those on the bottom rung are kids who love anything gothic and like to pretend they believe in vampires. They think it's all fun and games, but the information they supply often determines who is under investigation. Those at the top are very serious about killing anyone they think is a vampire. They do it in a ritualistic way. A stake through the heart, garlic in the mouth, beheading—the whole bit. These people are fanatical, and they're killers."

Lisa was staring at him in horror. "You joined something so stupid? Why would you do that?"

"I believe vampires exist," Cullen admitted. "I saw one." He kept his gaze fixed on Lisa, waiting for shock, for condemnation. Waiting to lose his chance with her.

Corinne and Lisa exchanged one long look. They were suddenly very aware they were alone in a house

75

with someone they didn't know very well. And the man was probably very ill. Last night, when Dayan was talking to her, Corinne thought he'd made perfect sense, but now it all seemed totally insane.

Cullen handed each of them a cup of tea. "Don't look at me that way. I know what you're thinking, but I'm not crazy. There was a time I thought I was losing my mind. Several years ago, I was engaged and my fiancée and I had gone out to dinner. At that time there was a serial killer loose in the city. He targeted women, and their bodies were always drained of blood. My fiancée was murdered that night, and I witnessed it. I saw him bite her neck and drain the blood out of her. I saw it with my own eyes. He would have killed me too, but something interrupted him." He tapped his finger against the palm of his hand. "I *saw* him kill her. No one would believe me. I wasn't drinking. I don't use drugs, but the cops wanted to lock me up in a mental institution instead of listening to me. Those in the organization listened to me. Unfortunately, my anger and terror bought me a membership into the inner sanctum of the group." He tried not to sound bitter, but even after all this time he still felt the pain of that time. He looked directly at Lisa. "I swear to you, I'm not crazy. I saw a monster. I saw it."

There was a look on his face, totally vulnerable, very sad. Lisa wanted to cry. There was an actual pain in her chest. It was all she could do not to run to him and comfort him. She didn't know what he had witnessed that horrible night, but he certainly believed he'd seen a vampire. "I know you're not crazy, Cullen," she said softly.

Cullen stared at her a moment longer, then began to blink rapidly, fighting some strong emotion. When he looked away, Lisa caught the sheen of tears in his eyes, and a large lump in her throat threatened to choke her.

She was happy she hadn't blurted out a condemnation. Whatever he had seen that night had changed his life for all time. Lisa knew about murder and trauma.

She glanced apprehensively at Corinne and caught her watching her thoughtfully. For no reason at all, Lisa found herself blushing. "What?"

"Don't 'what' me." Corinne took a cautious sip of tea. "Mmm, perfect, Cullen, thank you. I think you've revived me. I swear I was so sleepy I didn't think I could ever get up." Her hand crept up to cover a spot on her neck, just over her pulse, where she felt a sudden warmth, as if Dayan's mouth had moved over her skin.

"Are you sure we shouldn't take you to the doctor just to be on the safe side?" Lisa asked anxiously.

"Believe it or not," Cullen said, "I sometimes wake up that way in the middle of the afternoon. I actually have to go back to sleep. I think when you hang out with musicians, you start staying up most of the night and then you start sleeping all day like a bat. I've seen Dayan stay up all night just playing his guitar. When he plays, I can't seem to walk away and just quit listening. I tell myself to go to bed, but then I don't do it. I've seen a packed house stay that way all night, even when no one is drinking anymore. They just don't go home until he stops playing."

"Last night," Corinne said, "not one person went near Dayan when he stepped off the stage and we were dancing. The crowd just opened up and let him through. No one asked for his autograph, no one tried to talk to him, none of the girls even went up to flirt with him. When we went outside, not one single person attempted to stop him. Explain that to me."

"I noticed that too," Lisa said. "I was certain they would crush him, but no one went near him."

Cullen shrugged. "He's like that. I can't explain it, but I've seen it often enough. They come in wanting to meet him, they talk about it at the bar and on the dance floor. I've heard them, the women. They flirt outrageously while he's on the stage, but when he puts down his guitar, when he's finished playing, he always does the same thing. He looks at the audience just once and then he steps off the stage. No one ever approaches him. I honestly think he has some kind of look that terrifies everyone. He can scare the hell out of me when he looks a certain way. I've also wondered if maybe he's a psychic and simply warns everyone to leave him alone." He looked at Lisa. "Did you want to meet him?" He seemed to be holding his breath, waiting for her answer. "Was that why you went to the bar last night?"

Lisa shook her head. "I wanted to surprise Corinne. She loves music, and she's always talking about the Dark Troubadours. A friend called to tell me Dayan was playing."

Cullen arched an eyebrow. "A friend?"

Lisa smiled. "Bruce, an associate I work with. I did joke about meeting Dayan, but once I was in the bar all I could think about was . . ." She trailed off, the color rising steadily in her cheeks.

Corinne nudged her teasingly. Lisa scowled fiercely over her teacup, signaling Corinne to silence. Corinne smirked at her. Cullen looked at them both, and a slow grin spread across his face.

Corinne opened her mouth to tease Lisa some more, but words faded from her mind. Everything faded but the knowledge of Dayan's presence. She could feel the burning weight of his stare. She turned her head slowly, knowing he was standing in the doorway. A moment before, the doorway had been empty, and in the next instant it was filled with his powerful frame. He was simply standing there in total silence, his hungry gaze fixed on her face.

At once her heart accelerated, slamming alarmingly

hard. She swept one hand through her tousled hair. He looked immaculate. Elegant. *Dangerous*. So sexy he robbed her of breath. She found herself staring helplessly at him. Just drinking him in. His black eyes never left her. Intense. Hungry. He was everything she remembered from the previous night. All of her resolve went flying out the window. How could anyone look like he did and not be a mythical Greek god?

A slow smile curved his sculpted mouth, enhancing his sensual black magic. *'I am reading your mind.'* His voice brushed at the walls of her mind, velvet soft and very intimate. Sheer temptation.

For one moment Corinne could only blink up at him helplessly, a shiver running through her body. The illusion of being alone with him, his strong arms wrapped around her, was so strong, she forgot for a moment that Cullen and Lisa were beside her. "Just stop." Her voice wasn't her own, but instead a blatant invitation.

Lisa stared at her, open-mouthed in disbelief, and Cullen gallantly cleared his throat, drawing Corinne's attention. Dayan's white teeth flashed at her. *'Got yourself in trouble.'* He was laughing at her, warmth leaping into his fathomless eyes.

"Showoff." Corinne said it very softly, teasingly.

Lisa shared a puzzled look with Cullen and shrugged her shoulders. Dayan hadn't said a single word, but Corinne and Dayan were definitely communicating in a very intimate way. Lisa tried not to feel left out, tried not to be hurt by the look in Corinne's eyes when she stared at Dayan. Tried not to be totally shocked. Corinne had never looked at anyone the way she was looking at the musician.

Dayan glided into the room. A ripple of muscle. Casual. Silent. Lethal. There was something frightening about him that none of them could define. He emanated danger. He was wild. Untamed. Yet he was elegant, courtly even. Corinne smiled up at him, a dimple appearing in the corner of her mouth. She watched him cross the room effortlessly, his body so perfectly coordinated it was sheer poetry.

Dayan reached down and took possession of her hand, bringing her knuckles to the warmth of his mouth. "Did you sleep?" His teeth nibbled, teased.

He knew she had slept deeply, Corinne realized instinctively. She studied his sculpted features. "You should know." It was half a guess, but she was becoming slightly alarmed. Could he somehow force her compliance? Her reaction to him? She had a strong talent. If she could do unusual things, why couldn't Dayan?

Amusement crept into the depths of his black eyes. *'Of course I can do those things. But I do not need or want to force your reaction to me. What good would that do? You are my true lifemate, the light to my darkness. It would be an abomination to force your compliance.'*

Her eyes flashed at him, a hint that she was not amused. *'Stop talking to me in my mind and talk aloud. It's very disconcerting.'* She tried thinking the words, picturing them in her mind and throwing them at him along the same mental path he was using.

'This method of communication is as natural to me as breathing, but I will speak aloud if you insist.' Dayan looked more amused than ever. "Good evening, Lisa. I trust you slept well. Corinne looks rested." His voice was soft and unbelievably gentle.

Lisa tried not to stare at him. He was claiming Corinne. He was letting all of them know his intentions. His possession was in the way he held Corinne's hand, the way he looked at her, even his protective body posture. Very male. Territorial. The word crept into her mind uninvited. There was something about him she didn't

quite trust. He was too *untamed*. She let out her breath
and glanced at Cullen for protection.

Cullen smiled encouragingly at her even as he spoke
to his friend. "This is early for you, Dayan. We just got
up a little while ago."

Corinne moved her wrist, a subtle motion designed
to get her hand back. Dayan simply leaned into her, his
powerful frame looming over her. "You are not drinking
your tea, honey, Cullen's tea is very good."

Cullen's eyebrow shot up. "Quite a compliment."

Lisa scooted closer to Cullen, sliding off the bed to
give Dayan a place to sit. "Rina told me you found two
men in our house last night. Are we really in danger?"

"I am afraid so, Lisa," Dayan answered quietly. "Do
not worry. Cullen and I are quite capable of protecting
you and Corinne." He looked around the small room.
"But I prefer to move you to a place easier to defend."

"What do you mean, defend?" Lisa asked suspiciously. She looked at Corinne. "My sister is pregnant.
She can't be traveling all over the country," she said,
hoping to shock him.

"I am well aware of Corinne's pregnancy," Dayan replied gently. "Do not worry, Lisa. On my word of honor,
I will always place Corinne's health and happiness
above my own. I would never allow anything to harm
her." His black eyes rested on Cullen. "I have family.
The band is scattered at the moment, but I've called
them and they are on their way to meet us. I contacted
Darius last night, and he is sending for one of our
greatest healers. I believe we should move toward
them." His gaze was steady on Cullen's, but there was
no "push" for approval of his plan. He was being cour-
teous for the moment.

Cullen caught Lisa's hand. "Darius and the others
would make it impossible for any harm to come to you

or Corinne. I agree with Dayan. I think we should leave."

Lisa withdrew her hand. "I work. Tomorrow I have a major photo shoot with one of the top photographers in the country. I signed a contract with a cosmetic company to do ads. It may not seem like a big deal to you, but I take my business very seriously. These people are counting on me. I can't very well run out on them. And Corinne needs to be close to her own doctors, who understand her case." She looked at Corinne. "I want to go to the police, Rina. We can't let someone else run our lives or scare us into leaving everything we've ever worked for. We didn't see anyone at our house. I'm not even sure someone was there. Are you?"

It was the first time Corinne had ever seen Lisa take a stand on anything. She obviously felt very strongly about what she'd said. Corinne believed someone had been in their home waiting to harm them. She believed those same people had killed John. She glanced at Dayan. His expression hadn't changed, but there was something about him that gave her pause. There was an impression of menace. Of ruthlessness. A merciless slash to his mouth, something in his eyes perhaps, but she couldn't put her finger on what it was. She shivered unexpectedly. It was that menace more than anything else that made her throw her support behind Lisa.

"In all honesty, Lisa, I think someone *was* in the house, and I'm certain we're in danger. But if you want to handle the situation by going to the police, then that's what we'll do." Corinne watched Dayan carefully as she gave her reply.

His black eyes swept her face, then rested there thoughtfully. Corinne lifted her chin in defiance. He was nothing to her. What could he do?

Amusement crept into the depths of his eyes as he read her thoughts. *'I am everything to you, honey. You will know that in time, and there is much I can do if it is needed.'* His words brushed at her mind, a sensual velvet caress, wrapped in warm humor. His strong teeth scraped gently, almost tenderly over her knuckles.

"That's exactly what I think we should do," Lisa said, glaring triumphantly at Dayan. If he thought for one minute she was going to let him walk in and take over Corinne's life because he was a good-looking musician, he was in for a surprise.

Dayan shrugged his broad shoulders, a lazy ripple of muscle. He had deliberately safeguarded Lisa from the mesmerizing effect he had on humans; now he thought he might have done too good a job of it. Prompted by her protective instincts and her fear of losing Corinne, Lisa was reacting with outright hostility toward him. Corinne loved Lisa and considered her family. Dayan couldn't have Lisa so antagonistic toward him.

"Lisa." He said her name very gently, very softly, commanding her attention. There was something hypnotic about his voice, something impossible to ignore.

"Dayan." Cullen made it a protest.

Lisa couldn't look away from those demanding black eyes. They were empty, fathomless; she found herself falling forward into them. Why was she afraid of him? Dayan had her best interests at heart. He would protect Corinne with his very life, protect Lisa. He was trustworthy, completely so. Why had she ever doubted him? Everything he said was the truth. They were in terrible danger and they needed to leave with him.

Suddenly furious, Corinne attempted to reach around Dayan to grab Lisa's shoulder. She had a feeling that his brooding black eyes were working black magic. He was a wicked sorcerer bent on having his way. Dayan restrained her easily, a casual move of his body that was almost no movement at all. He wrapped his arms around her slender shoulders and pulled her back against his chest. "And just what do you think you are going to do, honey, leap out of bed and run away? Your running days are over." His lips were against the nape of her neck, his warm breath stirring tendrils of hair and causing a minor earthquake somewhere deep inside her.

Corinne forced herself to lean forward and away from him. She knew he had used his psychic gifts to influence Lisa. It angered her that he would do so. She knew Cullen realized it too, yet he was simply standing there, watching her reaction. "Let go, Dayan. I want to get up." She resisted the desire to dump her tea on him. "I think we should call the police, Lisa. Absolutely. In any case, I don't want to stay here." And she wouldn't. Who was Dayan anyway? Nothing to her.

'Everything to you,' he repeated, his voice calm, tranquil even, as it brushed in her mind. His arms unlocked, releasing her, and at once she felt bereft. That annoyed her more than ever. Dayan casually helped her to her feet, his obsidian eyes laughing as she shoved his hands away from her.

"I'm not sure," Lisa said thoughtfully. "What do you think, Cullen? You know these people. Do you think we're really in danger? Can the police help us?" She looked up at him, her heart in her eyes.

Corinne nearly groaned aloud. She took a breath, determined to save Lisa from whatever black-magic spell Dayan had placed her under. The palm of his hand slipped gently over her mouth, and he pulled her back into the hard frame of his body. "Let them figure it out together. I want to talk with you." He breathed the words against the nape of her neck even as he walked her out of the room, his body hot and hard, so needy against hers.

The moment they were outside in the cool evening air, Corinne wrenched herself away from him, then turned to glare at him. "You had no right to do that to her. And don't even try to play innocent."

He didn't look at all remorseful as his possessive gaze drifted over every inch of her. "You are even more beautiful than I remember from last night. When I woke, I thought I might have dreamed you up. My night fantasy."

His voice was mesmerizing, so beautiful Corinne found herself wanting to hear him speak more. She wished he had his guitar in his hands so she could listen to him sing. No one had ever called her a night fantasy before. She was certain she wasn't beautiful, but he made her *feel* beautiful. For a moment she could only stand there, blinking up at him, caught in his spell.

Corinne bit her lower lip hard to wake herself up. "You must have been a poet in another life. Or a gigolo. Stay on track here, Dayan. I'm not letting you off the hook."

"I did not want your friend to be falsely attracted to me," he said quietly, without any embellishment, yet modestly, almost humbly. "Sometimes women think they want me just because I am performing on stage. I will admit to you, I influence them to turn away from me. Perhaps I did so a little too strongly in her case."

Corinne was astonished that he'd told her the truth. When he looked at her with those black eyes, his hair tumbling onto his forehead, all she could think about was kissing him. "Did you make her want to be with Cullen?" she asked suspiciously.

"I would not do such a thing." A mischievous grin softened the edges of his mouth. "I did send Cullen to your table. The moment you walked in, I knew you were the one who held the other half of my heart."

She tilted her chin at him. "Are you influencing me?"

"I hope so. I want you. I need you in my life. I am

not using mind control on you, but I am attempting to be *very* charming. Is it working?"

He could melt a woman's heart at sixty paces. "No." She said it very firmly, but inside she was doing a slow burn. "I don't want you influencing Lisa in any way. It makes me very uncomfortable."

"I know you love her, Corinne," he said softly. "Anyone who is family to you is my family. I would not do anything to harm her or belittle her worth. I will protect her as if she were my own sister."

Corinne took a deep breath and forced herself to look away from him. Staring into the gathering darkness, she tapped out a nervous rhythm with her bare foot. "You can't feel this way about me so fast, Dayan. The truth is, I'm not going to live very long. I'm not saying that to make you feel sorry for me; it's a fact. I've faced it, but Lisa hasn't. You need to be practical, Dayan. It's hard enough with Lisa pretending all the time— I feel like I have to protect her from the truth. I don't want you to be that way too." For no reason at all she felt tears burning behind her eyes. Not for herself—she had gone beyond dreaming—but for him, for that utter loneliness she occasionally glimpsed in the depths of his eyes.

Dayan caught her chin firmly in his fingers, forcing her to face his glittering black eyes burning with such intensity. "You will not die, honey. I will not allow such a thing. Make up your mind to live in this world, because you *will* share your life with me. I will allow nothing less."

"You don't understand, Dayan," she replied gently. "The doctors—"

"Are human," he interrupted. "And they are very much mistaken. I agree we will take precautions until such time as one of our healers can examine you, but you will *not* die. Is that perfectly clear? You do understand me in this, and you will obey."

She found herself laughing at his sheer arrogance despite the gravity of their conversation. "Dayan, you can't just command someone to live. I have a bad heart; I've had it for years. I'm carrying a child. My heart isn't going to last forever."

His black gaze bore straight into hers until she felt as if he were taking possession of her, forcing compliance in some way. "You will obey me in this." There was absolute authority in his voice.

The smile faded from Corinne's soft mouth so that her intriguing dimple simply melted away. "I promise to do my best, Dayan," she capitulated solemnly.

He bent his dark head to hers, his mouth brushing the top of her silky head. "It is always better to see things my way," he said with great satisfaction.

Chapter Five

Corinne pulled away from Dayan, a delicate retreat. The slightest contact with him sent a shiver of anticipation down her spine, turned her insides to mush. "You're a bit on the arrogant side, but I doubt I'm the first person to tell you that." She glanced over her shoulder at him, teasing, enticing, without realizing her heart was in her eyes.

He felt the breath slam right out of his lungs. He glided after her, a great jungle cat stalking his prey. Silent. Intense. His gaze fixed on her face as she backed away. Corinne forgot they were on a porch and stepped off the platform without looking. Somehow Dayan managed to catch her. She blinked, and that fast he was cradling her safely in his arms. "Fortunately for you, I can live up to my reputation. Look where you are going next time." Deliberately he flashed his immaculate white teeth at her, displaying masculine amusement at her predicament.

Corinne raised her eyebrow, managing to look haughty even while cradled in his arms. "How did you do that? How could you move fast enough to catch me?"

"I am a superhero," he confessed soberly. "I never told you because I feared you would not like men in capes. Mine is very traditional, but nice all the same."

She laughed so hard she had to clutch at his shoulder, afraid she might fall out of his arms. "You'd like me to believe you're a superhero. I want to see the all-important cape. You can't be a superhero without one." She liked being in his arms. She *loved* being in his arms. He was enormously strong, yet surprisingly gentle. He could say the most outrageous things with a straight face and innocent black eyes. She looked up at him from under her long lashes. "You need tights to be a superhero too. Bright blue tights," Corinne pointed out wickedly.

One black eyebrow shot up eloquently. "Tights?" He repeated the word as if it were not in his vocabulary. "Blue tights?"

She tried to look serious but she couldn't stop laughing and her heart was beginning to hurt. A hard, painful weight was pressing down on her, squeezing the air from her lungs so that she wanted not to gasp for air. Corinne looked away from him, not wanting him to see the struggle. It was amazing to her that she could be so happy, could forget everything so completely in his company. Her body had to remind her it was wearing out fast. Corinne blinked back sudden tears and buried her face against his shoulder.

Dayan remained silent, allowing his heart to find the scattered, irregular rhythm of hers and slowly guide it back to normal. He cleared his mind of desperation, finding a calm center and reached across time and space as his kind could do. *'Darius. My need for the healer increases. I do not think I have much time.'*

There was a moment of time, a heartbeat of silence.

Dayan never doubted, not even in his desperation. Darius's gentle voice flowed into his mind, flooded him with conviction. *'Two of our greatest healers are making their way to the Cascades. We will meet you there. We will not fail you, Dayan.'*

He took the directions straight from Darius's mind, learning the way to a safe house owned by one of the Carpathians' greatest healers, Gregori, and his wife, Savannah, daughter of their Prince. *'I thank you for moving so quickly. All is well with you?'*

'Yes. The women are anxious to see you and your lifemate.'

Dayan took comfort in Darius's voice and words. In his long lifetime, Dayan had never known Darius to fail at a task. If he gave his word about something, it was done. They were family. They had traveled together for nearly a thousand years. To know that his family was mobilizing swiftly, moving to help him save his lifemate, gave him added confidence it could be done. They would find a way to save her. If possible, the child also, but it was imperative they save Corinne. Without her, Dayan could not continue. He would not want to face the darkness and the emptiness. Wherever she traveled, he would choose to be at her side, to protect and guard her in the next life.

It was only after a few minutes of breathing normally that Corinne realized their hearts were beating with the same rhythm. Keeping her head pillowed on his shoulder, she looked up at him with her large green eyes. "Where are you? You've gone very solemn and serious on me."

"I was 'talking' with my brother."

"He's telepathic too?" Corinne lifted her head to look at him more closely. "Put me down, Dayan. I'm really capable of walking without breaking my neck. It must have been wonderful to grow up with someone who shared your talent."

Dayan shrugged his powerful shoulders, a lazy ripple of muscle. "I never thought about it. All of us are telepathic. The entire family." Reluctantly he lowered her feet to the ground.

"Do you think it's genetic, then?" Corinne pressed her hands protectively over her baby, suddenly afraid for her. Her own life had been at times very difficult because of her special gifts. She knew she wouldn't be around to protect and reassure her child when times were hard.

Dayan's hands framed her face. "I call the Troubadours my family because we've been together since we were small children, but only Darius and Desari are truly brother and sister. Syndil, Barack and I are related the way you and Lisa are related. The ties are stronger than blood."

"Of course, the members of your band. They all have interesting names."

Dayan laughed softly. "I forget what a serious little fan you are. You have inflated my ego for all time."

"A serious little fan," she echoed, her eyes beginning to smolder with hidden fire. She tossed her head, the copper highlights in her hair sizzling from the walkway light as it came on automatically. "I'll have you know that it isn't *you* I'm a fan of, but *music*. There is a difference, you know. Don't get me wrong—" She held up her hand to ward him off as he advanced rather purposefully on her. She found herself laughing again, watching his eyes glinting at her. "You've convinced me to be a fan. Really, you have. I'll stare adoringly at you next time you play." She batted her eyelashes and fanned herself. "I could act the perfect little groupie if your ego needs a boost."

"I'm flattered," he said, catching her small hand in

his. "So tell me what you know of our band."

She shrugged casually. "You play guitar, as does Barack. Syndil plays the drums and just about any other instrument. Desari is your lead singer, and she has an amazing voice. You sing only when the mood strikes you or if a particular song warrants it. My guess is, you both write the lyrics to your songs." She smiled up at him. "And your music is awesome, although there are a few others who are right up there with you." She looked down at her fingernails. "Legends."

His eyebrows shot up. "Who? Name a legend."

"In what category? I like rock and roll myself."

"Rock and roll?" There was a slight sneer in his voice. "Who would you consider a legend in rock and roll? Tread carefully, your reputation is on the line."

"What year are we talking here? In the fifties there was so much going on. If you're going to be all snobby about modern rock and roll, we can raise the stakes and talk blues or jazz. Surely you'll admit there are legends in blues and jazz."

"I'll concede that point to you, but you can't start looking in the fifties. The origins of rock and roll began long before the fifties. Have you listened to the tribal music and the original beats coming out of Africa?"

She grinned at him, one eyebrow shooting up. "Surely you aren't testing me, thinking I don't know my music history. That isn't the point. Do you honestly think there aren't legends from the fifties and sixties?"

"Maybe the Dark Troubadours," he mused, his black eyes laughing at her wickedly.

"Excuse me, Mr. Legend, what about Louis Armstrong? Do *not* make the mistake of turning up your nose at him. Muddy Waters, for heaven's sake, and BB King, he's awesome. He just has such presence. And Stevie Ray Vaughn. I could name several others."

"You are only supposed to think of *me* as a legend."

He meant to tease her, but as he bent his dark head toward her passionate little face, his gaze found her lips and his heart nearly stopped. He closed the small gap between them, fastening his mouth on hers, taking her breath and giving her air. The earth stopped moving for him. The world dissolved and there was only Corinne in his mind, in his arms. His eyes burned strangely, his body hardened like a rock, his stomach did a curious somersault, and his heart simply melted. There was everything in her kiss. Passion and fire. Exquisite tenderness. A promise. Dayan lifted his head before it was too late to pull back.

Corinne blinked up at him, clearly bemused. "How do you do that?"

"You and I are lifemates . . ."

"Lifemates?" Corinne echoed. The word was beautiful and implied something permanent and binding. She wondered if it was an interpretation of a term from his native language. She had heard him use the word several times before.

His black eyes moved over her face in a serious, intent study. His gaze was brooding. Incredibly sexy. "Lifemates," he affirmed. "Married, but more. Married as in an eternal commitment."

"That's a beautiful concept, Dayan, but don't most people think they'll be married for all time?" His eyes reminded her of a great jungle cat. There was a burning intensity about him when he looked at her. Deep inside her there was an answering need, calling out for him alone.

His hand capturing hers, he tugged gently until her small body was pressed up against his. "You are my lifemate, Corinne. I recognized you the moment I laid eyes on you. I know you are the light to my darkness, that your soul is the other half of my own. Each of the members of my family has found a lifemate. Barack and

Syndil were meant for one another. Desari's lifemate is Julian. Darius has Tempest, and I am amazed I found you. I had no hope that you existed."

Corinne ducked her head. Dayan believed every word he said. They barely knew one another, yet he was so certain. He almost made her believe they had a future together. She knew better; she knew her heart was deteriorating. Dayan had slowed the inevitable by whatever he had done the night before, but she knew her heart would never last beyond the birth of her child. She was already worn, her heart laboring and her lungs struggling. "I like all of your names," she said, determined to change the direction of their conversation. "Are they stage names or your actual names?"

Dayan smiled without humor. "We change many things about ourselves, but we have always kept the names we were given at birth."

Mysterious secrets were locked behind his extraordinary eyes. His eyes looked old, as if he had seen far too many things. There was a quiet strength in the sculpted features of his face. At times he could look quite young, and at others, older and more worn. His body could be so still, not even revealing he was breathing, yet when he chose to move, he was so fast that if she blinked she missed the actual movement. Dayan. He filled her mind as no one had ever done. He gave her dreams she dared not have.

Corinne touched his face with gentle fingers, sorrow for him welling up so that it overwhelmed her. She had thought to warn him, to allow him to make his own decision regarding their relationship, but he was breaking her heart. "Don't do this, Dayan. Don't build your dreams around me. I'm so afraid for you. You deserve to be happy. I want you happy. Don't be like Lisa. She wants a miracle." The pad of her index finger outlined his perfect lips. "I don't want to cause you pain. I really don't."

"I believe in miracles, Corinne. I found you. I have traveled the world for more years than you can possibly conceive, and never once did I hope for such a thing. Yet you are real. You walked right through the door of that bar. You came to me when I was certain my time was running out. I know there are miracles. Each one of our males who finds his lifemate knows there are such things as miracles. We have had this discussion before, but you refuse to listen. You are not going to die. I want you to believe that, Corinne. Start believing that."

Corinne sighed softly and looked away from the hungry intensity of his eyes. He could convince anyone with that compelling look. She wanted to be convinced, to think that she might have a chance at a future with her child and a man she felt passionate about. The thought came unbidden, and at once she slammed the door on it. She didn't really know Dayan at all. Would she still be feeling the same way in a month? Two months? Would Dayan even want her around after a month or two? She knew absolutely nothing about him except that he was a musician who drifted from town to town with his band.

'A brilliant musician. A legend of a musician.' Dayan corrected her thoughts, his black eyebrow slanting up as she tried to convince herself she didn't want him. "Get it right, Corinne. You know more of me than that. You know I do not chase women, that I am protective. You must know I am honest and trustworthy."

"The ultimate Boy Scout, who eavesdrops on other people's thoughts," she reprimanded even as she wondered why it didn't embarrass her that he knew what she was thinking. She arced one eyebrow at him in a small taunt. "Pregnant women often think sexual thoughts, so don't flatter yourself."

"I am only interested in the sexual thoughts of one pregnant woman. It is only natural that you would be sexually attracted to me, Corinne. If you were not, it would be a difficult merging for us. But you are my true lifemate, and I intend to claim you as my own for all time. I think sex should hold a place in our relationship." He grinned boyishly at her. "A very important place. That is how it is supposed to be."

She found herself reluctantly smiling. "You sound so certain, so matter-of-fact, as if none of the obstacles matter at all."

"Of course they do not matter. We *must* be together, we are meant to be. You feel it too, Corinne, I know you do. We do not have a choice. If you accept that we must be together, than we will find a way for it to be so."

She looked away from the intensity in his glittering eyes. "I think you really must be a poet, Dayan. You believe in romance. Real life does not necessarily mirror poetry. All of us die, some just go a little sooner than others. My body is wearing out faster than it should. I was born that way, and I've always known it would happen. According to the doctors, I shouldn't have lived beyond my fourteenth birthday. I'm luckier than others who were born like me. That is reality." He was giving her a headache by refusing to accept the seriousness of her illness.

He gave her a gentle little shake because he couldn't help himself. "I would like to tell you about the reality of my life, Corinne, what I have experienced without you, but you are not ready for such a confession. In the meantime I think we should talk to Lisa and Cullen and begin our journey tonight. We have a great distance to travel."

Corinne shook her head. "We can't just pick up and leave. We have a life we've worked very hard for, Dayan. Lisa's profession demands she be available when she's needed."

Dayan's black eyes moved over her face, brooding, moody, with a hint of menace she found disconcerting. There was something undefined about him that she couldn't quite name; it made her feel afraid.

'Not afraid. You should never fear me. I could never harm you, Corinne. I will do everything in my power to see to your protection. And my powers are considerable.' He had shifted into the much more intimate communication of lifemates almost automatically. Dayan's arm circled her slender shoulders, held her very close in the moonlight. She was fragile, delicate, her bones small. Unexpectedly, fear slammed into him along with a kind of helpless fury. He needed a healer fast; he needed to find a way to gently steer her in the direction he wanted her to go. If necessary, he would use his telepathic ability to persuade her, but it was against his code of honor to influence his own lifemate in such a way

"It's the way you look sometimes, Dayan," Corinne said with a small self-mocking laugh. "You can look very intimidating when you choose." She smiled up at him, her fingertips going up to smooth the hard edge from his sensually sculpted lips. "Like now, when you aren't getting your way."

His black eyes burned over her face. "I will always get my way, honey, when it comes to protecting you. I do not think there is a rational argument you can make about this. Lisa will not care much for her job if you are dead. You are capable of writing songs anywhere. I also know that you are far more frightened than you are letting on and you agree with me that we should protect Lisa despite her refusal to accept how grave your situation is."

"Is this what it's going to be like with you?" Corinne sent him a smoldering look of warning from under her long lashes. "I don't like you reading my mind."

"You will soon be reading mine," he answered without censoring his thoughts.

Corinne raised an eyebrow at him. "I'm just supposed to suddenly acquire the ability to be telepathic? Does it rub off on people when you're around them too much?"

Dayan shrugged again. "We will have to see, Corinne." His hand moved up and down her arms to warm her. "You are getting cold out here."

"It's beautiful, though. I hate to be indoors at night. The sky always looks so incredible." Corinne laughed softly. "Of course, I feel that way during the day too. I love to look at clouds. Lisa drives like a maniac, but she says I'm worse because I can't keep my eyes off the sky." She looked up at him. "I don't want to miss anything, you know? The world is such a beautiful place; I want to see as much of it as I can." She walked a little further along the pavement. "Where are you from originally? You have an accent, but I can't place it."

"I have traveled so much over the years I do not know if my way of speaking reflects any one place. I speak several languages. But I was born in the Carpathian Mountains in Europe. I spent most of my younger years in Africa."

"How interesting. What did your parents do?"

"I was a mere boy when they were killed. Darius raised us, the band members. We were all children, and we grew up a little wild." Dayan smiled at her, his teeth very white in the darkness. "I think we are still a little wild."

Corinne allowed him to lace his fingers through hers, though she wasn't altogether certain why. A part of her wanted to be realistic and strong, while the other, more treacherous side whispered of temptation, whispered she should enjoy his company while she could. "So Darius is much older than you are?"

"Darius is an extraordinary individual. He was six years old when our parents were killed. I was four. He kept us alive." He waved his hand, the movement graceful as he dismissed the past. "It was a long time ago."

Corinne reached up to rub his jaw with the palm of her hand. "You sound so sad, Dayan. It couldn't have been that long ago. Was your childhood difficult?"

"It was an adventure, Corinne, unlike yours. Remember, all of us are telepathic, and we are used to our differences. It was a wild, fun, very exciting time. Tell me about your childhood. I know bits and pieces through your memories, but you have locked most of it behind a heavy door I do not wish to open without permission."

They walked together unhurriedly along the pavement. Dayan seemed to glide beside her, making no noise. If she hadn't felt the security of his large frame brushing hers and his hand wrapped around her fingers, she would not have known he was beside her. In a way it was reassuring, yet it was also eerie to feel such raw power and stealth in him. "You aren't like everyone else." She said it quietly, intuitively.

There was a small silence, the space of several heartbeats. "I am from an ancient lineage," he admitted softly. "I have gifts, special gifts granted to me."

She smiled in the darkness. "I am very glad we met, Dayan. There is something wonderful and beautiful about you. When I'm with you I feel as if I could go on forever. The words to your songs and the beautiful music you play are exceptional. I love the sound of your voice, speaking or singing."

He curled her hand against his chest, so that she could feel his heart beating strongly beneath her skin, right through his shirt. She could feel the heat of his skin, the call of his masculine body as his muscles moved subtly. Above her head, Dayan smiled, his smile slightly wolfish. "You are deliberately trying to direct the conversation away from your childhood." He was secretly pleased by the sincerity he detected in her mind. He had placed no compulsion on Corinne, nothing to enhance her feelings for him. He was relying on the fact that she was his true lifemate, yet he had not bound her to him with the ritual words. He feared their forced parting during the daylight hours might be too difficult for her strained heart.

"Why would you want to hear a boring story on such a beautiful night?" Corinne kept her head down, not wanting to look into his eyes when they saw far too much.

"I want to know everything about you, Corinne," he said softly, his voice sheer black magic in the dark of the night.

How could anyone refuse the beauty of that voice? She took a breath, let it out. "The bad memories are of my mother drinking. I can't really recall much of her doing anything else. There were always men and awful little rooms we lived in, stuffy and hot. I spent all my time listening to music. I'd sneak out and find places where there was live music." She tossed him a quick grin. "It was an advantage being small—I could fit anywhere, and using telekinesis, I could remove locks and open heavy doors."

His hand moved over her hair in a small caress. He had to touch her. He could feel the contrasting emotions accompanying her memories.

"I lived for music. I dreamed it and heard it night and day in my head. It kept me sane when I was alone. It balanced my world, was something I escaped into. And then, of course, I met John and Lisa and their father."

There was such a wealth of sadness in her voice, Dayan gathered her into his arms, gently, protectively, his body sheltering hers in the dark of the night. He held her as if she were fragile porcelain, a precious treasure. "I'm grateful you had John and Lisa." And he meant it. John had saved Lisa's life and protected Corinne. He had done his best to create a family for them. Dayan was grateful someone had been there for her when he could not.

"Don't fall in love with me, Dayan," she murmured softly, pleading with him. She was fighting for him, wanting him to understand he couldn't feel so strongly about her. It was going to be bad enough with Lisa; she couldn't bear for Dayan to count on her and then lose her too.

His hand cupped her chin, tilting her head so that her eyes met his steady gaze. "I know you better than anyone has ever known you. How could I not love you when I see into your mind and heart? You are *everything* to me. I know you cannot understand, and to you it does not make sense, but to me—a wanderer with no one to love him, no one to chase away the demons—you are a miracle."

"Is that what I do for you?" She smiled in spite of herself, the thought beautiful to her. "Do I really chase away the demons?"

Without hurry, almost lazily, he bent his dark head and took possession of her mouth. He was gentle; there was nothing but gentleness in Dayan when he touched her, a gentleness so at odds with his enormous strength. But his mouth was pure magic, opening a door to a world she had never known existed before he had come into her life. His mouth was masculine and hot, dominating hers; the very earth shifted beneath her feet so that she clung to him for support. He swept her up against his hard frame, yet he held her with exquisite tenderness, infinite tenderness. His mouth was sheer magic.

He swept Corinne into another world, one of passion and exotic fantasies. One she had never dared to imagine. She might chase away demons for him, but he was something altogether different to her. Unreal. A mythical god. A man of legend. A hero. She smiled against his perfectly sculpted lips, velvet soft and hotly erotic. Every time she looked into his black eyes, so intense, so *hungry,* she melted inside.

'I am reading your thoughts.' The voice brushed intimately at the walls of her mind, a flutter of butterfly wings creating the same sensation in the pit of her stomach.

"Well, stop." Corinne pulled out of his arms, the only sane thing to do with her heart pounding and her body turning to molten fire. "We have to stop. You know we do." Her heart wasn't going to take much more; it was already working far too hard.

He rested his forehead against hers, breathing heavily, attempting to recover. "I'm sorry, honey. Think of something mundane for me."

She laughed softly, nibbling at the corner of his mouth. "Lisa and I need clothes. We'll have to go back to our house and get enough clothes to last a few days until these people lose interest in us."

Dayan's hand curled slowly around the nape of her neck. His fingerprints were like a brand on her skin. She could feel it all the way down to her toes. And she was melting again, coming apart inside, her heart somersaulting dangerously. He straightened slowly, his black eyes staring down into her beautiful gaze. "Those people will not lose their interest in you, honey. You cannot go back to the house. I will get the things you and Lisa need and bring them to you. Make me a list." His voice was low, a whisper of sound like velvet over skin.

Corinne closed her eyes to shut out the sight of him. He was overwhelming at such close quarters. Every breath she took, she inhaled his masculine scent. Clean. Wild. Male. "You can't go through our things, Dayan. It just wouldn't be right. One of us will have to go with you."

He shook his head slowly. He didn't blink. Everything he did, he did with a fluid power, a ripple of pure energy impossible to ignore. "To keep you safe, Corinne, I can do this small thing." He said it softly, patiently. "These people sprayed the stage with bullets where Desari was singing. She is a beautiful, vibrant woman, unique in this world, yet they were willing to murder her, to silence her voice for all time. They managed to wound Desari, Barack and me. We were lucky that Julian was there along with Darius to save us. I am not so willing to take a chance with your life. Or the life of your child."

"You said those men were gone. They aren't going to send someone around so quickly. We need our things, Dayan. Sooner or later we'll have to return. And Lisa is famous—anyone can find her." Corinne tapped her fingernail against her palm. "We could hire bodyguards."

His features remained expressionless, yet he went completely still, something deep within him roaring silently, raging immediate denial. For one moment Corinne thought she saw red flames flickering in the depths of his black eyes. Her breath caught in her throat. She took a step backward, but his hand was still wrapped around the nape of her neck, anchoring her to him. "What is it, Dayan?"

His smile was slow in coming, his teeth very white. "What is it you see that you could possibly fear in me, honey?"

"I don't know . . . sometimes you look like something more than you are. I know that doesn't make sense, but you can look very intimidating." She brushed back her hair, a small shiver running through her body. "Let's go back."

"I do not want you to be afraid of me, Corinne. I realize it is unexpected the way we met and came together. You were not looking for such a thing, but it has happened. We cannot pretend or go back." His thumb was moving over her skin, a small caress, feather light, but so erotic she was shivering beneath his touch.

"I was talking about going back to your house," Corinne clarified, attempting to move out from under his hand. Was he using his unique mental telepathy to "push" her in a direction he wanted her to go?

Dayan shook his head sadly. "I thought we had covered all of this, honey. I am a wanderer, a poet, a musician. I am a male who has roamed the earth in search of one woman. I know that woman to be you. If I influenced your decision in my favor by using telepathy, our relationship would not last. What I want with you, I want for eternity."

Corinne turned away from him, from his brooding good looks and the smoldering intensity of his black eyes. He needed someone to love him. He looked so alone, standing tall and confident, yet so *hungry* for someone to love him. God help her, she wanted to be that woman. For just one time in her life she wanted something to be real.

Dayan reached out and took her hand, needing to pull her smaller body close under the protection of his wide shoulder. He simply walked beside her in the night, enjoying the moment, thankful he could feel it, savor it. Thankful she was in his world.

"Every line of every song, every note I've ever played was written for you, played for you. The other half of my soul. My heart. In the hope that you were somewhere in my world and you would hear." In her frail condition, Dayan didn't dare reveal the truth of what he was to her. He knew the healer would find a way to save her life. There was no other possible outcome. He was very concerned that there might not be a way to save the baby. He was a shadow in her mind, connected to her. He knew she was willing to trade her life for her daughter's life. He was not. He was her lifemate. It was his sworn duty to see to her health.

Corinne blinked back tears at the utter sincerity in his voice. "You can't say things like that to me, Dayan." If he did, she would be lost and so would he. How could she resist him?

Dayan smiled down at her, tightened his fingers around hers. With every step he took beside her, he felt the heat rising between them, felt the way she was wrapping herself around his heart. It was the little things, like feeling her hand so small, entwined with his. Her breath. The scent of her. The way she smiled. He loved the way she smiled, the way she moved. The way she fought so desperately to protect him from possible loss.

Deep within his heart he was learning about true terror. The thought of losing her was beyond the scope of his imagination. He had never experienced fear in his adult life. Even during battles with vampires, he had experienced no ripple of feeling through the long centuries to give him the wisdom to handle such an intense emotion. Terror. He tasted the word. Could he face the loss of his lifemate without ever having lived with her, without ever having the time to love her and bind her to him? Dayan knew he would not want to. His life had been bleak and empty, so barren and cold he had been losing his ability to create songs, to feel the music inside of him. But now, with Corinne close to him, songs and words and notes were pouring out of his soul, begging to be heard.

She was the world. Colors and excitement and beautiful poetry. He would not lose her to mortal death. He knew now where his ability to play, to create, had come from. It was her half of his soul. He had been left with some small part of her light when they had been split, to find their way back to one another. He felt the songs in her, the music. It was in the way she walked, the way she flowed through a room, her small, slender figure so balanced. It was in the turn of her head and the way her smile lit up a room.

There was something about Corinne, something that had drawn his eye immediately. Lisa was beautiful, tall and blond and quite obviously a model. She belonged on the covers of magazines. Corinne's light shone from the inside out. Just watching her made Dayan smile. When he touched her mind to share her thoughts, he found she was thinking of others, how they felt, what they needed. She was happy despite the fact that she had recently lost someone she loved, and believed she herself was going to die soon. Corinne lived each moment as it was given to her, determined to see beauty around her, even while she grounded herself in reality.

Dayan found the way her mind worked interesting. She often used telekinesis without thinking about it. She would glance at an object across the room that she needed and she would start to draw it to her. He could feel the difference immediately in her brain, a warmth, the building of the image and the focus on it. The image was always sharp and crystal clear, and then she would remember she was not alone and would heave a small sigh.

"What?" She was smiling up at him, her intriguing dimple mesmerizing him, so that he had no other choice but to lean down and kiss it.

Butterfly wings fluttered in her stomach at the touch of his mouth against her skin. "You have to stop doing that," she told him softly, without much conviction.

"I thought I should practice as often as possible," he replied, rejecting her idea immediately. "I am without extensive experience, and I must make certain I do not lack in the area of a lover. After all, I wish to make you happy."

His voice was a whispered caress feathering over her skin. Corinne looked up at him, her large eyes dancing. "You know very well you don't need any practice at all. And you make me very happy." She reached up to touch his chin, a gentle brush of her fingers. "Tell me about your life."

"I am a wandering musician. That is the truth, honey—a poet who has found his missing heart. I have long been without it." It wasn't simply the words he said, it was the way he said them, with hunger in his eyes.

"Do you love playing?"

"It is who I am," he replied thoughtfully. "When I pick up my guitar, it is a part of me, like my arms. The notes and the words are somewhere deep inside me and they just flow out. I was born with this ability, a great gift bestowed on me."

His humility surprised her because he was usually very confident, so much so it bordered on arrogance. But not when it came to his extraordinary talent.

As much as she was enjoying walking with Dayan, she was already exhausted. She became aware of the way her heart seemed to struggle to find the exact rhythm of his. She smiled up at him as he bent down to swing her effortlessly into his arms. "You really can read my mind, can't you?" The sound of her own voice was more of an invitation than she would have liked.

'Of course."

"Do you have to be touching the person?"

"No. I was not always touching you when I was reading your mind. And I have never touched Lisa. It is easy to read the thoughts of mortals." He said it casually, so comfortable in her presence, he didn't think to censor his words. In the short time they had been together, he was already thinking of them as one, a partnership, life-mates rather than two separate entities.

Corinne's arms were clasped around his neck as he carried her through the night back toward the house where he and Cullen were staying. "Mortals? That implies all kinds of things, Dayan. Why would you use a word like *mortals?* Aren't you mortal?"

Chapter Six

There was a long silence while Dayan listened to the sounds of the night, the murmur of the wind as it whispered to him of secret things. "Sometimes, honey, it is better not to inquire too closely into things you might not want to know about. I used the word *mortal* when another might have been a better choice. Are we not all both mortal and immortal at the same time? If you were to die, you would leave a part of you behind here on this earth, yet you would continue in another life elsewhere."

"You believe that?"

"Absolutely," Dayan answered solemnly, knowing she needed reassurance. For a brief moment he stopped walking to bury his face in the warmth of her neck, inhaling her scent. "Wherever you are, Corinne, you will never be alone. I will always be with you."

At once the fragrance of her, the reality of her, rose up to overwhelm him, and just that fast he was battling the demon inside. It rose sharply, swift and furious, fangs exploding in his mouth, the male Carpathian demanding he complete the ritual and bind her to him. She was his savior. The keeper of his soul. Light. Colors. Without her, there was only an empty, barren existence he could never return to. Never endure. Her pulse beat beneath his mouth, her life force ebbing and flowing with a dark richness he craved, he *needed.* Red flames flickered and danced in the depths of his black eyes as he fought the demon.

Sensing danger, Corinne held herself very still, her arms cradling his head to her. She was aware of his great inner struggle, although she understood nothing of it. His body trembled for a moment, and she felt his mouth moving erotically, back and forth over her soft skin. Her fingers crushed his silky hair, rubbing at the strands in agitation. What was it he needed from her? Sex?

'No!' The word shimmered in her mind emphatically. His voice gentled. *'Not just sex, my love, I need to make love to you all night. I need to bind us together for all eternity. I do not know how to tell you these things so you can understand, but it is as necessary to me as breathing.'* There was such intimacy in the way he spoke to her, in the tenderness of his voice as much as in the way he could communicate, mind to mind. *'I need you so much, Corinne,'* he sighed against her pulse, his breath warm and intimate; *'so much.'* There was something very dangerous in him—she could feel it in his enormous strength, in the possessive way he held her—but his need was so great, she couldn't think straight, couldn't think to deny him, not even for her own self-preservation.

The answer was shimmering in her mind, in his mind. *'I want to be whatever you need.'* There were no words spoken aloud, yet he heard her acceptance of him, of his differences, of his wild, untamed nature. It echoed in her mind and in her heart. He murmured her name softly, his sacred talisman to guide him back from the precipice of danger, the whisperings of madness she could not hope to understand.

His mouth moved over the slender column of her neck, touched her ear briefly, while both of them seemed to drown in a rush of molten heat. He could feel her body molding itself to his, responsive, inviting, enticing. She moved restlessly in his arms, and his body reacted with a hot surging of blood, creating a painful ache that would not go away.

Dayan closed his eyes and gave himself up to the luxury of feeling. His mouth moved up her throat to her chin, nibbled lightly before settling over her mouth. At once there was that curious sensation of the earth shifting beneath his feet, of the ground rocking, falling away from him until there was only Corinne. He felt every sensation—the satin softness of her skin, the silk of her hair, the hot need of her mouth as he took possession. She clung to him as the storm of need and hunger washed over them, as his mind filled hers with his hungry desire, with dark, erotic images and the ever building fire in his blood.

Her mouth was a silken haven he was lost in, his blood roaring in his ears. Dayan held her tightly, possessively; she was his only refuge after a thousand years of utter loneliness. He lifted his head so that his mouth could drift in a dancing flame of heat and light over her skin back to her irresistible pulse. It beckoned him in an age-old call. She could hear his voice, a soft murmur, a whisper of sensuous command, and her blood quickened, heating in answer. His tongue caressed her skin, his teeth nipped gently, teasingly, erotically, and then she gasped as white-hot lightning arced through her, sizzling, streaking through her blood so that she was on fire. His mouth moved against her and he held her even tighter, fitting her to him almost as if they were making love.

It was like a dream, hazy and unreal, sensuous and erotic. It was unlike anything she had ever experienced. Corinne felt weak, unable to move, yet she didn't want to, cradling his head to her, her hands in his wealth of hair, giving herself up to his hot, seeking mouth. She closed her eyes, the illusion of being made love to so real she could almost feel him touching her intimately. His voice was in her head, and somehow she *felt* his desire, the hunger in him, his intense pleasure. She never wanted him to stop. Her fingers slipped from his hair and her hands fell limply to her sides.

At once Dayan lifted his head, breaking the connection between them. Curiously, she felt warm liquid running from her neck along the creamy swell of her breast. She didn't lift her heavy lashes to examine the cause, not wanting to break the magical spell of heat and desire. He lowered his mouth to pursue the liquid trail so that her entire body responded, clenching with pleasure. Corinne smiled that he could make her feel so much without any real effort.

"I left my mark on you." It was a black-velvet whisper that moved through her body with the same heat as her blood. "I could not help myself." He nibbled and teased the corner of her mouth until she obediently opened for him. There was a faint coppery taste as his tongue swept inside, claiming her for his own. Before she could give it any thought, he had taken possession of her soul, her body, so that she was no longer a thinking woman, but a living flame of need and hunger.

His hand came up to cup the weight of her breast, his thumb caressing her nipple through the thin material of her blouse. Flames raced through her bloodstream. His mouth left hers, his teeth nibbling her chin, down the side of her neck and along her vulnerable throat so that she arced closer to him. A soft moan escaped her as his mouth nudged the edge of her blouse.

"We have to stop," she said softly, not convincing either of them.

Her heart was laboring far too hard. That, more than anything else, caused Dayan to gain total control of the demon battling for supremacy. He wanted so much to claim her for his own, to bind her to him. He wanted to secure her life by exchanging blood, not simply tasting the essence of what would be his. He needed her, but more importantly, she needed him. "You are right, honey," he said with deep regret. "Follow my breathing pattern to allow your heart to rest."

She was relaxed in his arms, her eyes closed, her body on fire, yet she felt as if she couldn't move to save her life. She was inexplicably tired, drained. "I need to get things from my house. Medicine. Important things. If we really can't go back for a while, we'll need clothes."

"Make a list," he suggested again. He was moving through the night, his arms cradling her effortlessly, his strides long and easy. He was silent as he carried her toward the small house he shared with Cullen. Every now and then he bent his head to brush the top of her silky head with a kiss.

"I can't make a list, Dayan, you know that. Some things are private. Lisa might let me get her things, but she would never let you go through her personal drawers."

"Then I will buy clothes for you. And makeup, and whatever else you think is necessary." There was no impatience in his voice, rather a mild male amusement as if mundane things like clothes and makeup were of no consequence to him.

Corinne struggled to open her eyes to pin him with a smoldering gaze. "I do not need you to buy me

Christine Feehan

clothes. At least I'm willing to take you with me when I go back to the house. Think of it as a concession."

He paused for a moment, studying her delicate features. "You do not really want to return to the house." He made it a statement. His voice was a soft lure.

She made a supreme effort and caught at the nape of his neck. "You can stop with the voice, Dayan, because I *am* going. It's important. If you want to come with me, you may, but you aren't going to use your voice to persuade me otherwise. In any case, I know you'll protect me."

"You sound very stern," he commented with great admiration. "I am certain I am very impressed." He couldn't stop the warmth her words produced. She did trust him whether she knew it or not.

"Kissing you is enough to make a woman weak, Dayan," she said, exasperated with herself. "It's bad enough to lie here like a sixteenth-century heroine without you teasing me about how I sound."

He kissed her forehead again. "You do sound impressive. It was a compliment."

They had arrived at the house, and without conscious thought, Corinne waved her hand to open the door. He laughed softly in her ear. "Now that was very impressive. I do not think you do that in front of many people. You are becoming very comfortable in my presence."

"Well, don't flatter yourself. It isn't *you* at all. It's your voice. I like to hear you talk even if you spout a lot of nonsense and macho male rhetoric."

He bent his head and found her mouth with his, easily, unerringly, as if it were the most natural, necessary thing in the world. And he made time stop for that brief moment. "It *is* me," he said complacently as he carried her through the door. "And I *never* spout macho male rhetoric."

114

Lisa and Cullen sprang hastily apart as they entered. They glanced at one another with small, guilty grins, Lisa's beautiful face crimson. She looked alarmed to see Corinne lying so limply in Dayan's arms. "Is she all right?" she asked quickly.

"Absolutely," Dayan assured her. "I would never allow anything to harm her." He was looking directly into Lisa's eyes, and, as always, she subsided. "Corinne insists the two of you need clothes and makeup from your house."

Lisa nodded solemnly. "I was just telling Cullen I will need quite a few things. We should go there tonight before those men come back."

"I do not think it is safe, Lisa," Dayan replied gently, still holding her gaze captive. "I think you should stay here with Cullen while I go and retrieve whatever you need."

"With me," Corinne roused herself enough to say. "You can give the list to me, Lisa." She pushed at the wealth of hair tumbling around her face. "I'm going too, so whatever you need, I can get for you."

"Is it safe?" Cullen asked anxiously, looking at Dayan.

"Of course it is not safe," Dayan answered, his words a clear reprimand. "I am certain the house is being watched. Going there is a sure form of lunacy. And we should be on the road already. It is imperative we meet the healers as soon as possible. It is the only way to ensure that Corinne's heart becomes strong again."

"What healer?" Lisa asked, a note of fear in her voice. "I don't want Corinne anywhere near a quack. I mean it, Dayan. She's had enough crazy people in her life to last us both a lifetime."

Dayan's eyes remained steady on Lisa's face. "She did not bring those people into her life, Lisa," he said quietly.

115

At once Lisa's eyes filled with tears. "I didn't mean it like that."

Corinne shoved at Dayan's chest hard, furious all at once. "Of *course* you didn't mean anything, Lisa, no one thought you did. What do you want us to do, honey? Tell me and we'll do it."

Dayan was as gentle as ever, his expression never changing as he continued to look directly into Lisa's eyes. "I am sorry to cause you pain, Lisa. You love Corinne. I know that. I will be happy to get anything from the house that you need, and I guarantee that no quack ever touches Corinne. We are becoming friends, beginning to trust one another." His voice was utterly beautiful, a soft melody of words, the cadence pure and perfectly pitched so that they all strained to hear him.

Corinne framed Dayan's face between her small hands and turned him to face her. "You are doing something I don't like." She said each word distinctly. "Don't do it again."

"You can come with me back to your house," he said very gently, smiling at her, looking more handsome than she wanted to admit. He could rob her of her ability to breathe. It astonished her just how much he could affect her.

"Put me down."

"Can you stand up without my help?" he asked softly, teasingly, whispering the words against her ear.

"Of course," she lied. "And just to set the record straight, Lisa, *I'm* allowing him to come to the house with me."

Lisa and Cullen burst out laughing. "It looks like it," Lisa said.

The house was dark and forbidding, giving off a strange vibration of evil to Corinne. As she looked uncertainly at her home, she began to shake. "Dayan?" She whispered his name, suddenly very afraid.

At once he leaned close, his arm sliding around her slender shoulders. "Do not worry, honey. I will not allow anything to happen to you. Not now. Not ever."

"Something's wrong, Dayan, I can feel it. Let's get out of here. Maybe the police should go in with us."

"The police will never stop this group."

"I don't care if they can stop them or not. I think the point is not to get hurt right now. If we ask them, they'll go into the house with us," Corinne pleaded with Dayan. As she looked at him, she found herself touching his mind. She read his resolve. Dayan was determined, casual about the danger, completely confident in himself. Corinne sighed. "You're going in there, aren't you?"

"Of course I am. You and Lisa need clothes."

She caught his arm. "Dayan, forget it. We can shop for clothes. Nothing is worth your getting even a scratch. I don't like the feel of the house. I think someone is either in there or watching it."

He leaned close to kiss her irresistible mouth. "I think you are absolutely right. The house is being watched. But you are perfectly safe right here."

"I'm not waiting here while you go alone. If you insist on being pigheaded about this, I insist on going along. I can do extraordinary things, Dayan. I know I'll be of some help." She was not about to let him go off alone again.

Dayan smiled, his teeth very white in the darkness, making him look like a predator. Why the image flashed into her mind she had no idea, but she shivered all the same. Occasionally she caught glimpses in his mind of predatory wildlife. Weird things, like leopards and night raptors. Swirling images of mist and fog, of lightning bolts and fierce storms. It was all there in his mind mixed up with what and who he was.

There were images of Dayan as a child with other children, running free in a wild jungle, but alongside him were leopards, savage-looking guardians that seemed to be watching over him. She was uncertain whether she was catching glimpses of actual memories or a jumble of memories and fantasy images. It was a dark world, unsuitable for the poet she thought him. In these visions he was a dark predator running with jungle cats in search of prey.

Corinne locked those images away to examine later. She was aware that Dayan was not exactly what he seemed. Dayan was a strong psychic with enormous talent. She had no idea what he was capable of.

"There you go again, honey"—he sounded amused—"scaring yourself for no reason at all. Such thoughts! You stay here while I check to see that the house is not occupied."

"Is it?" She was curious as to whether he could tell from a long distance away.

"Actually, there is no one in the house, but there is one man waiting in the yard just out of our sight. I can read his thoughts. There is another at the back door. He is whistling to himself. A third man is smoking a cigarette across the street, three houses down from yours. If you watch closely you can see the glow of the cigarette, just there, on the porch." He smiled again, this time without humor. "He is fantasizing quite a scene. I am afraid I cannot allow his twisted dreams to come to reality for him."

"You can read his thoughts from this distance?" She believed him. She knew he was telling her the truth. A part of her mind was struggling to put the puzzle together, but there were too many missing pieces. She trusted Dayan, yet she didn't really know him at all. It felt as if they had been together all of their lives, as if they *belonged* together, although she had just met him.

Dayan shrugged, a casual ripple of muscle and sinew. Of menace. Corinne bit anxiously at her lower lip. "You always seem so gentle, Dayan, yet you give the impression of being very dangerous. You can be quite intimidating—did you know that?" She was trying to laugh off her apprehension, but she perceived the violence in him, smoldering just below the surface.

His arm circled her slender shoulders, pulled her body close into the shelter of his. "All men are capable of violence, honey, if a loved one is threatened. Carpathian males are born protectors; it is a quality imprinted upon us at birth. We have been that way since the beginning of time. Your safety and health are my number one concerns."

Why did everything he say seem so rational when it wasn't at all? Was it the hypnotic cadence of his voice? Its remarkable beauty? The need and hunger radiating from him when he was so close to her? Corinne only knew that when she was with him she felt as if she had always known him, always belonged with him. She reached up and touched his jaw, her fingertips caressing. "I can move objects by concentrating on them. I know I can be of help to you."

He captured her hand, brought her fingers to the warmth of his mouth. "You have a tremendous talent, little love, and I thank you for the offer, but I will make sure there is no danger to you before you get out of this car. It is of paramount importance to me."

She had to look away from his mesmerizing eyes. She could fall into his eyes and be trapped there for all time if she wasn't very careful. Outside the car, the wind was rising, bringing tendrils of fog. It rose off the asphalt in long tails, swirling into a thick mist as it gathered over the street. It came in fast, as if from the ocean, smelling of saltwater and seaweed. Corinne forced her gaze away from Dayan's to stare out into the street. "Look at that, Dayan. Have you ever seen fog come in so fast or so thick?" In a way it was quite frightening. She knew they could never drive the car in such weather; no one could see in it. The fog itself seemed strange, as if bizarre shapes and forms were moving in it. She could hear a sound, a continuous whisper of voices buried in the fog.

"You are shivering, Corinne. Do not fear the cover. It is only that. I can safely move around in it without detection." Dayan spoke softly as he always did, but there was something disturbing about his casual observation. As if thick fog were an everyday occurrence. *As if he could command the fog.*

Corinne stared up at him, her eyes too large for her face. There were questions in her fascinated gaze, and answers in the steadiness of his return stare. The unblinking stare of a great jungle cat. Of a predator before it attacks its prey. Corinne moved, a subtle feminine retreat, but Dayan only tightened his hold on her. Her heart was pounding erratically again, loud in the silence of the fog-shrouded night.

"Corinne." He whispered her name. Or had he simply thought it so the sound brushed like the wings of a butterfly in her mind? His tone was sexy. Tantalizing. Intimate. He could make her insides melt with the way he said her name. He placed her palm over his heart, his hand covering hers. "Ssh, little love, listen to the sound of my heart talking to yours. You must learn to relax and breathe. Breathing is essential to your life, you know."

She inhaled; her heart was already following the strong pattern of his. She thought about that, the way he worded things. Essential to *your* life. Her long lashes lifted so she could study his face. Physically he was beautiful, sensual, very male. "Isn't it essential to your life?"

For a brief moment, humor flashed into his eyes, a fleeting glimpse only, and then his eyes were black and deep and fathomless. Hiding a thousand secrets. "Sometimes it is extremely essential. Like now. When I look at you, you take my breath away. It just happens. I find I cannot catch my breath."

Corinne found herself laughing in spite of her resolve not to. He was so outrageous, making her feel beautiful when she was pregnant. "I haven't noticed that peculiar phenomenon occurring. I'll have to pay closer attention."

"Then you must not realize you make my legs weak either." In the darkness, with the fog pressing close around the car and the strange insidious whispering, Corinne was grateful for Dayan's solid frame and the laughter he was generating.

"I think you're making things up just to get me to laugh and forget those men waiting in the darkness to hurt you." She was sliding her fingers up and down his arm absently. "I want to go with you."

His mind was a shadow in hers. She wasn't afraid for herself, she was afraid for him. She was determined to accompany him. "Meltdown." He whispered the word against her pulse, against her bare skin so that she felt him in her, deep inside. The word was a caress of black velvet, a sorcerer's tool.

Dayan felt his insides had gone into serious meltdown, turning his blood to molten lava. Thick and hot and moving through him with urgent demands. She was *everything*. Light and laughter, serenity and poetry and hot, steamy sex. She was classy and sweet, she was elegance and candlelit nights and lace and satin. She was the purity of frothy waterfalls and cool, dark forests. There was a wildness buried deep within her that surged to the forefront when she was with him. A wildness that matched his own. He sensed that it surprised

121

her because she hadn't known it existed. Yet she should have; it was there in her music, when she played so passionately, in the songs she wrote for others to sing.

Dayan drew her close to him, so that their hearts beat in the same rhythm, her heart matching his steadier beat. "You will stay in this car, my love, where the fog will protect and keep you safe. These humans cannot harm me. I will make sure they leave."

She recognized the "push" he used in his voice, the urge to obey that was nearly impossible to ignore. As irritated as it made her, Corinne was intrigued by the mesmerizing quality of his tone. Before she could really think about it, Dayan's mouth was capturing hers, whirling her away from anything as sane as thinking, removing every thought from her brain and replacing it with pure feeling. Then he was gone, slipping quickly from the car, leaving her sitting by herself, bereft.

Corinne drew her legs up onto the seat and nibbled at the tip of her fingernail. Dayan. He had crawled under her skin, wrapped himself around her heart, seeped into her soul so she couldn't stop thinking about him. Couldn't stop wanting to be with him. There was something different about him. Each time she thought she was close to the answer, he distracted her. He did it smoothly, casually, effortlessly.

She stared out the window and saw the thick fog. She could see nothing else, and the lack of visual cues gave her the illusion of floating in the sky, cushioned by billowy clouds. No one had the capability to command the sky, the weather. So why did she believe that Dayan had done something to bring in the mysterious fog? It wasn't natural. She had heard the whisper of voices, seen the shadowy shapes moving. It was frightening, yet he had gone out into it completely without fear, as if he *knew* he would come to no harm.

Why did he use such strange terms? She tapped her

chin with her index finger. *Mortals*. He had used that word as if it were natural and meant something. He had said the humans could not harm him. *As if he weren't human*. Corinne shook her head, attempting to dislodge the thought.

Of course Dayan was human. What else could he be? An animal? He certainly had an animal quality in the way he moved. He was like a large jungle cat. There was something in his eyes, in the way his body moved. What was she thinking? A mythical cat person? Corinne let her breath out slowly. It was too crazy to be sitting in the dark allowing her imagination to run wild while Dayan was out there in the midst of killers. He didn't think he needed protection, but she knew she could help him if it was warranted. Resolutely she reached for the door handle. As she did so, her hand trembled and she found she stopped midway. She actually broke out in a sweat. Everything in her demanded she stay in the car.

Very carefully, Corinne pressed her palms protectively over her baby. She was missing something important; she just couldn't fit all the pieces together. Dayan *was* different, he had tremendous power, but it was more than that. Little things didn't add up. Things no one else seemed to notice about him. Things she found in him when their minds were merged. At first she only heard his voice, but more and more small details were finding their way into her mind. Strange images. Facts. Vivid, detailed images of history, of time periods long gone by. The images were blurred, but they were there in his mind.

Dayan stood quietly by the car with the fog enshrouding him, wrapping him tightly in its coils. He touched Corinne's mind once more, smiled to himself at the way she was working her way toward the truth. Corinne. His heart and soul. His very breath. Corinne had touched things in his mind each time he merged fully with her. His past. Wars and the growth of nations. Vivid details etched in his memories. Feats of strength. Various time periods. It was all part of what had shaped his character. His family. Darius. The vampires attacking their family unit because of the two females. Concerts. Thousands of concerts. Some given as wandering minstrels, others in football stadiums. Horse-drawn carriages and old-fashioned automobiles. Every memory shadowed by the dark of night. *Creatures of the night.* Their world.

Dayan placed his hand on top of the car, right above her head, knowing he was completely invisible, knowing she was worried about him. She was attempting to resist his softly whispered command for her obedience. His heart was melting at the idea that she was determined to protect him when she was so small and delicate, her health so fragile. His love for her, growing with each moment he spent in her company, was becoming an all-encompassing thing.

He stared down at his hand, holding the picture of the change in his mind first. His hand distorted, curled, claws extending where his fingernails had been, fur rippling over his skin. He moved away from the car as the transformation came over him. He reached for it, embraced it, reveled in the complete freedom. The creature had been there in her mind, sharing her thoughts. Cat person. He liked that. She had caught glimpses of his world, of the hunts using the body of a big cat to provide himself with sustenance. Inside the leopard's compact, sinewy body, Dayan smiled. She was closer to the truth than she knew. He was inexplicably proud of her for that.

Silently, the magnificent jungle cat moved on its large, padded paws through the fog-shrouded street. It walked on cushioned feet, confident in its incredible hearing and night vision. It commanded the nocturnal haunting realm; the night was its undisputed kingdom. Dayan used the leopard's body to "see" objects around him. He knew exactly where his prey was. In the body of the leopard, Dayan moved ever closer to the object of the hunt. His muscles rippled like sinewy ropes beneath his fluid skin as he crept near.

The man crushed out his cigarette beneath his boot and repositioned his shotgun across his lap. The fog was making him restless. It was thick, impossible to see through, yet he could swear there were figures moving in it. He leaned out away from the porch, listening as hard as he could for any sound of someone approaching. All at once he was nervous; a faint tremor started deep inside and spread throughout his body.

Nothing was out there, nothing he could see, nothing he could hear, yet he felt threatened. Stalked. Nervously he stepped off the porch, thankful the owners were away for a few days. It had been easy enough to find out that the couple was taking a vacation. This property was the perfect vantage point to keep an eye on the Wentworth home. He paced back and forth. Never once did he see the cat approaching him, its body low to the ground, creeping forward inch by inch. Silent. Deadly. Dilated eyes boring into its prey. Never once did the man suspect that an enemy far more powerful than he was only a scant few feet from him. When the attack came, it was fast and explosive. The animal was on him, its strength enormous, its claws grabbing and piercing his vulnerable throat in total silence.

The leopard leapt onto the roof of the house, taking the carcass with it. It cached its prey between a dormer and the sharp slant of the A-frame. Dayan had to wrestle with the instincts of the big cat, hungry for its prize. It had been harder and harder to defeat the darkness growing and spreading within him, yet now with Corinne in his life, making him complete, he was strong again. He had someone to live for, someone to love. Someone to make it all worthwhile. Dayan breathed deeply and directed the leopard back toward the street.

The jungle cat leapt easily to the ground, moving swiftly through the thick fog up the street toward the Wentworth residence. A man waited in Corinne's backyard for her to come home. He had a gun and a knife, and orders to bring her back to a laboratory or kill her. The cat could smell the man even through the thick fog. A second man was huddled in her doorway, with the same orders and the same determination. They were very alert, afraid even. Two of their friends had disappeared without a trace. The society wanted answers fast. The Wentworth women were going to provide them.

The leopard moved with the same calm confidence, the same silence as when it had begun to stalk its prey. The wrought-iron gate was cleared with one easy leap, and the animal landed softly on cushioned paws. The fog was moving now, small eddies at first, becoming a thick, swirling pudding with a life of its own. It brushed against the legs of the man in the yard. The man glanced wildly around, looking for something alive that might have touched him.

With an oath he paced from one side of the lawn to the other, peering down toward his feet. The fog moved again like a giant snake, wrapping loose coils around him from his feet upward. He was moving toward the house when he noticed the unusual phenomenon. With a pounding heart, he pushed at the vapor, and his hand traveled right through it. His relief was tremendous. "Mike?" He called out to his partner, suddenly wanting to get out of the oppressive fog. It was so thick, he felt as if he couldn't adequately breathe.

Mike, inside the doorway, heard the muffled call and

turned, trying to see through the thick mist. "Drake?" He thought he saw a tall, pale figure moving in the fog, but it was vague and shadowy and not at all of the same build as his partner. Squinting, he leaned closer into the thick, soupy stuff, certain now there was more than one figure moving. He brought up his gun, trying to center on the amorphous, almost transparent shapes.

It was an animal, not a person, he decided, lowering the weapon. He was listening, but the strange fog cushioned the sounds so it seemed he was locked away from the rest of the world. Definitely not human, the shapes inside the white veil took on the forms of large cats. As he stared at them, nonplussed by the strange phenomenon, the cats seemed to turn to stare back, fixing glowing eyes on him. Red eyes. Eyes that flamed and seemed eerie and threatening in the midst of the fog. To reassure himself, Mike took a firmer grip on the handle of his gun even as he took a step backward to flatten his body against the wall, making himself as small as possible.

If it was an illusion, why was a cat moving forward, emerging out of the fog, staring intently, ferociously, at him? Its ropes of heavy muscle rippled like fluid beneath its mottled fur; its head was down, yet it never took its eyes off its prey. Mike tried to bring up the gun, his finger working at the trigger over and over in a desperate attempt to kill the thing, but his hand seemed paralyzed. The gun must have jammed. Nothing worked right.

He was still staring intently into the flame-red eyes when something hit him hard in the chest and he coughed once. It was the last sound he ever made. The leopard was so strong that when it attacked it crushed the man's chest even as its razor-sharp claws pierced his throat for the kill. The leopard dragged the body of the man out from the doorway and into the yard toward the other human.

Drake was fighting his way through the terrible bands of fog toward where he believed Mike was waiting. Coils of the stuff seemed to wrap around him as if he were a mummy. He thought he could feel the coils brushing here and there against his body, yet when he tried to shove them away, his hands went completely though the mist. It was a frightening feeling. He felt claustrophobic in the soupy stuff, and he hated the insidious whispers coming from inside the fog.

"Mike?" he found himself whispering, moving his feet carefully, cautiously, feeling his way through the grass. He was searching for the brickwork signaling he was close to the house. The toe of his boot hit something solid. It didn't feel like brick. Gingerly he felt around the object with his foot. A sick feeling began in the pit of his stomach. "Mike?" he whispered again as he bent down to feel with his hand.

Breath exploded from his lungs. It was Mike. Drake gasped aloud, swinging this way and that, his gun in his hand, his eyes wild as he searched for the enemy. With his free hand he explored the body, looking for a pulse. His palm landed in thick fur. He inhaled sharply, his hand moving of its own accord over the shape of a skull. The whiskers, the open mouth with sharp canines. Drake tried to scream, but the cat had already launched itself, burying its teeth deep in his unprotected throat before he could get off a warning. A sound gurgled deep, then died away.

Dayan shape-shifted immediately, catching the man in his arms, placing the gun in his waistband as he collected the second body. He took two running leaps with the men slung over his shoulders. Their weight was nothing to him as he soared through the sky under cover of the thick fog. He took a moment to snag the third body from the rooftop and once again headed for the forest miles out of the city.

It took minutes to dispose of the bodies the same way he had the other two. He incinerated them with a lightning bolt before burying them deep and strewing vegetation over the site so that it seemed undisturbed. The guns were buried deep in the earth with the ashes. Then Dayan returned to Corinne, dropping silently out of the fog beside the car.

Chapter Seven

'I am here with you, honey.' Dayan made the calm announcement before he touched the door handle of the car, afraid of startling her. He was a shadow in her mind, knew she was already afraid, and worried about his safety. The fog was oppressive to her. He could feel how uncomfortable she was, sensed that the baby was kicking strongly, but her heart and lungs were laboring. He sent the warmth of his love into her mind, strong and intense, his reassurance that he was in good health.

Corinne reached for the door even as he opened it. At once she flung herself into his arms, uncaring what he might think. "I was so worried about you."

He held her tight, savoring the feel of her fragile body against his. "Breathe, honey. You scare me to death when your heart tries to work so hard. I was never in any danger. Never. I told you that. You need to listen to me when I say important things." He buried his mouth against her soft neck, inhaling her fragrance, breathing evenly, willing her lungs to follow the steady pattern of his.

Corinne rubbed her face against his broad chest. "I never know what is actually important and what is sheer nonsense," she admitted teasingly, trying desperately to lighten the mood when she really wanted to cry in relief.

Dayan laughed softly, obliging her. "You are so good for my ego. Everyone else obeys me; I think you should too."

She pulled reluctantly out of his arms and looked around in astonishment at the rapidly disintegrating fog bank. It was melting away as if it had never been. "I'm the one everyone listens to, Dayan," she pointed out, her mind puzzling over the peculiar phenomenon.

Dayan intertwined his fingers with hers to bring her back to him. He kept her locked firmly beneath his shoulder as they walked toward the house. "And I am certain we all obey." She fit perfectly, her smaller frame moving against his, soft and feminine, reminding him continually of their wonderful differences.

Corinne glanced up at him, studying his features, then ducked her head to hide her expression. His eyes held warmth when they looked at her, but they took on a merciless stare when he looked away. He seemed more animal than human. Even his movements, fluid and powerful, seemed inhuman. She struggled to understand exactly what it was about him that she found intimidating.

Her heart, instead of matching the rhythm of his, was pounding very hard and fast. Her mouth was dry. "Dayan."

"Why are you frightened of me when I treat you so gently?" His voice was soothing and tranquil. He never sounded annoyed or irritated by her thoughts. Dayan took the keys to the front door out of her hand and unlocked it.

Corinne thought a long time before she answered.

Just how afraid was she of Dayan? She looked up at him, at the rugged angles and planes of his face. At his strong jaw. At his sculpted mouth. "I don't think I am, really," she mused aloud. "There's something different about you, Dayan—something dangerous. But not to me. I don't think the threat is directed at me." Her chin went up. "You know, I've always detested the way everyone wanted to tell me what to do with my life because of my health. I have a good brain and I can figure things out for myself. If you choose to spend your time with me and you want to care for me, knowing full well the repercussions of what can and probably will happen to me, then so be it. It's your choice, Dayan." She reached up and framed his face with her hands. "Just know that if you care too much, death can be very painful to the one left behind."

"Would it stop you, Corinne?" he asked quietly, his dark gaze drifting broodingly over her face. "If I were the one with the bad heart, would you walk away from me?"

A slow smile curved her mouth, lit her face and dispelled the worry hidden in her eyes. "I love life, Dayan. I believe in living it. I would never pass up love or laughter or knowing you because I was afraid of pain. It would be a small price to pay for your company. But then, I've known pain and experienced things others haven't. I've learned the value of love and laughter."

Dayan turned his head slightly even as his gaze remained fixed on her face, devouring her. He kissed her hand, drew her finger into the heat of his mouth.

At once her body clenched and a thousand butterflies brushed at the walls of her stomach. He made her feel beautiful, and sexy and very wanted. "What do you think you're doing?" She faced him with her heart in her eyes and her breasts rising and falling in anticipation.

His tongue did a slow, silky caress along her finger, then reluctantly released her. "Seducing you," Dayan admitted without remorse. He bent his head to find her mouth with his, kissing her leisurely, a long, slow kiss meant to tell her what he couldn't seem to convey with mere words. Poet or not, there were no words to say how much she meant to him. No words to say he would follow her anywhere. That she was life to him.

"You say it just fine." She whispered the words into his mouth, into his soul.

Dayan tensed, his arms imprisoning her, holding her tightly to him. There had been no blood exchange. Yet she was reading his mind. Slipping in like a shadow, with skill and ease, going where only those of Carpathian blood should go. Had she learned *too* much? Her heart wasn't laboring any more than normal. Carefully he touched her mind. Corinne hadn't even noticed what she had done.

She pulled away first, in a small, delicate retreat that made him smile even as he opened his arms to allow her escape. "What attracts you so much to music?" Dayan asked, surveying the neat stacks of music magazines on the coffee table.

"Music takes me to all the places my body will never let me go," Corinne told him, glancing up at him almost shyly. Her soft smile made his knees weak. "I'm able to feel the sensation of jumping out of an airplane or swimming beneath the ocean by just selecting the right piece. No matter where I am, or how difficult it is to breathe, if I can hear music, I know it will be all right." Her grin was self-conscious. "That probably sounds silly to you, but you're strong and free. I'm a prisoner trapped in this body. What my heart and soul and brain want are things I'll never experience, so I use music to soar."

Dayan said nothing. He couldn't speak; the lump in

his throat was blocking his ability to breathe. It was the way she lived her life. Corinne accepted what had been given to her and lived wholly despite her limitations. She embraced life. Tasted it. Experienced it. He could imagine her flying as a bird in the sky, swooping through the treetops. He would always have to stay close to her, watch over her, or Corinne would go for the stars.

"Don't feel sorry for me, Dayan," she said softly. "You see, I've been incredibly lucky. I treasure each day I have." She turned to look around her home. "I've had so much in my life, so many unexpected things. Come with me, look at this. Lisa is an absolute cretin when it comes to musical instruments so she didn't appreciate this at all, but you will." She caught his hand and tugged. "I know you will."

He went with her because he had no other choice. He would have followed her to the ends of the earth. She took him through the hall to the open room with the piano, quickly exposing the ivory keys. Her fingers were tight around his as she pulled him to the bench, nearly pushing him onto it.

"Listen to this. Listen to the sound." Her hands skimmed across the keys, fluttered and settled to play a sonata he immediately recognized.

The sound was beautiful, the notes true. Dayan watched her fingers glide over the keys. She played effortlessly, with a certain abandon, losing herself completely in the music. She played the way she lived life. The way she would love him. Passionately, with everything in her. Giving freely, generously. A complete merging of her body and soul and heart.

She was so beautiful to him. Her head bent over the keys, her eyes closed, her hair tousled and tumbling around her face, her expression one of concentration and rapt enthrallment. Dayan reached around her, planted both hands on the piano so his arms created an effective wall. He bent to taste the temptation of the nape of her neck. Her natural fragrance drew him, assailed his senses so that he could think only of Corinne. Of her soft skin and inviting body. Of the passion in her, the magic.

Corinne's fingers stilled on the piano and she turned into his embrace, half rising to meet the heat of his mouth. She found fire and flames. A burst of sunlight and a shattering need more compelling than life itself. They fed off each other, devoured each other, unable to get close enough. His mouth was hot and commanding. Hers was silken and insistent. She lost herself in his mouth, in his masculine taste. He couldn't get enough, feeding on her, taking the sweetness she offered like a starving man.

Her hands slid beneath his shirt, his hands were tugging at her blouse. The fire was explosive, the heat an inferno. There was no rational thought, only the feel of skin, hers satin soft, his firm and defined with hard muscle. He shifted her, his knee thrusting between her legs so she was riding on the hard column of his thigh.

Dayan made a soft sound, an edgy note of ravenous hunger welling up from his soul. The tone pierced her heart, invaded her mind so that she wrapped her arms around his head to cradle him to her, giving him everything, anything. Wanting to be whatever he needed. He pushed her shirt up out of his way, all the while his mouth and hers performed a tango of seduction.

His tongue stroked and teased, danced with hers. His teeth nibbled at her lower lip, the corner of her mouth, settled over her dimple. His lips drifted over her skin, down her neck and throat, leaving flames in their wake. He lifted his head then. Inhaled. Drank her scent in, deep within his lungs. His half-closed eyes slid over her.

Rested on her breasts. Soft. Creamy. Firm and tantalizing.

Her bra was a lacy dusky rose, lovingly cupping her full breasts. Corinne heard the hitch in his breath as he slowly bent his head to her. His long hair slid over her skin, brushed at her like silken caresses. His hands were incredibly gently as he cupped the soft weight of her, lifting one breast free of the bra. His tongue swirled over her nipple. Waves of sensation rocked her, shook her. His mouth, hot and moist, closed around her aching flesh. Corinne's legs almost went out from under her. She leaned back into the piano, the keys playing a jangling note. Streaks of lightning sizzled in her bloodstream, raced to the very core of her.

Her body clenched, dampened. She closed her eyes and gave herself up to the pure ecstasy of feeling he was evoking with his mouth. With his hands.

A small, discordant note invaded his consciousness. A whisper of trouble. Her breath was labored, her heart struggling. At once Dayan lifted his head, buried his face in the hollow of her shoulder. Her hands were exploring his back, driving him to the very brink of insanity, so he caught her wrists and held her still.

When he could breathe again, when it was safe again, he lifted his head to look at her. She was so beautiful with her thoroughly kissed mouth and her wide, dazed eyes, he was nearly undone. "Your heart and the baby," he reminded her. "Another couple of minutes and we were not going to be able to stop. I do not want you going unexpectedly into labor. Your safety and that of the baby come first. I was being selfish, and I ask your forgiveness. In truth, I was not thinking clearly."

His voice was a blend of haunting notes, so beautiful it brought tears to her eyes. It wrapped her in a cocoon of safety, a dark melody of love and sensual hunger. "There's nothing to forgive, Dayan. It was both of us. I wanted you as much as you wanted me. Thank you for being strong enough for both of us." Her hands crept protectively over her baby. She smiled up at him. "In truth, I wasn't thinking clearly either, and if you really knew me, you'd know how rare that is."

His eyes drifted over her face, intense, hungry, melting with warmth. "You are my heart and soul, Corinne. You do not know me, because you cannot merge your mind with mine, but I can read your thoughts, your memories. I know you as no other ever could. I do not need days, weeks, months to get to know you. I have only to touch your mind to know what you are like. I know how intelligent you are. I know how very much this baby means to you. We will be much more careful."

Very gently he drew her shirt down over her swollen, aching breasts. She circled his neck with her arms and leaned into his larger frame, allowing him to take her weight. "I'm sorry, Dayan, I didn't mean for things to get out of hand. I know better." Her hand slipped down his chest, rested on the front of his jeans. "I don't want to leave you this way." She could feel the bulge of his erection, so heavy with desire.

His body shuddered with excitement, anticipation, hardening more, his blood thickening. Dayan took a deep, steadying breath. "You mean the same way I have left you? Aching and unfulfilled? I think we will be partners, Corinne. When I am able to take care of your needs, you will take care of mine." He brushed a kiss along her temple. "We are in this together."

She pulled back to look into his eyes. "You really mean that, don't you?"

Dayan nodded. "I am no saint, Corinne. You are looking at me with stars in your eyes. I want to devour you right now. I think the safest thing for us to do is pack up your things and Lisa's and go back where we will no longer be alone."

Corinne leaned closer, pressed a kiss to the corner of his mouth. "I hate to tell you this, but my things are in the bedroom." She laughed softly, teasingly, and stepped away from him, knowing she was perfectly safe with him. Her legs weren't completely steady but she managed to walk without falling. He followed her into her bedroom, watching her with dark, intense eyes. She felt the weight of his gaze on her as she moved about the room, and it did nothing to calm her own storm of desire. Resolutely she gathered her things without looking at him. He robbed her of good sense, and for both their sakes, she needed to be responsible. Corinne continued into Lisa's room, pausing for a moment to place her hand over the baby. Dayan had protected both of them.

"Is she kicking?" Dayan asked softly, managing to make the question sinfully intimate.

Corinne nodded, afraid to look at him, afraid she would lose herself in his terrible hunger. In his poet's soul. Dayan moved up behind her, as silent as any jungle cat, and wrapped his arms around her, his palm over the small mound of her belly. He bent his head so his mouth was dangerously close to her frantically pounding pulse. "She is very strong. Such a miracle. All around the world people are finding out they are having babies, yet they do not appreciate what a miracle it is. Perhaps if they had no women, no babies, they would understand what is supposed to be treasured. As I treasure you, so do I treasure this child."

Corinne closed her eyes and allowed his words to seep through the pores of her skin. How could he say such beautiful things? How could his words always be so perfect? Why had she found him now, when she had so little time left? For a moment she leaned against his hard strength, inhaled his wild, untamed scent, was grateful for his enormous strength and poet's words and the way he made her feel that her child was a part of him too. Totally accepted. Without reservation.

"I want you to feel that way," he said softly, his breath warm, inviting, "because it is the simple truth."

"You are temptation personified," Corinne scolded, but her voice gave away her pleasure, and she covered his hand with her own. "You could have any woman, Dayan. Why in the world are you with me?" Her heart ached for him. She didn't want him to be hurt.

"There is only you. I can see no other, nor will I," he answered, completely certain. "You are everything."

Corinne pulled away from him gently, regretfully. "And what if I don't feel the same way? What would you do then?" There was a wealth of interest as well as humor in her voice.

He reached around her to pick up both suitcases. "You forget I read minds. If you truly did not want me, then of course I would have to accept such a thing, but you are my lifemate. There is no mistake. I see in color. I feel emotion. I look at you and there is meaning to my existence. You look back at me."

Corinne smiled then—she couldn't help herself. "I definitely look at you, I can't very well deny that. And I want to be with you. I knew John practically my entire life. I loved him, yet I couldn't give him passion, I couldn't give him my soul. I look at you and everything in me wants you, wants to be everything you've ever needed."

Dayan shook his head. Corinne was confused by the intensity of her emotions, the sheer chemistry between them. He didn't want her to feel guilt for not having shared her passion with her husband. "I am your life-mate, you were meant for me. We know each other, recognize one another because we're meant to be to-gether. You loved John as a dear friend, but you belong with me. Lifemates do not lie to one another. I am telling you the truth."

She reached out to touch his strong jaw, her fingers gently caressing. "Thank you, Dayan." She took another look around the house. "I think we have everything."

He took possession of the suitcases and made certain the house was securely locked before following her down the brick pathway and across the large expanse of immaculate lawn. Corinne stopped suddenly, looking up at the abundance of stars overhead. Stars that couldn't be seen earlier. "Aren't they beautiful?"

Dayan nodded and continued to walk to the car. Corinne was very pale, and he could hear her struggling to breathe. She acted as if she were normal, as if she were strong, but he was beginning to be alarmed again. He wanted to swoop her up and fly across the night sky with her, taking her to the nearest healer to demand she be put right. "You need to get in the car, honey," he advised softly.

She nodded, hating the weakness that prevented her from enjoying so simple a pleasure. Headlights caught her in a bright spotlight as a car whipped around the corner and raced straight toward her. Corinne stood frozen, her heart stammering, her baby kicking as a rush of adrenaline flooded her mother's body.

Dayan dropped the suitcases and moved with preternatural speed. He caught her up into the safety of his arms and leapt over the speeding car, taking to the air as he did so. Below him, the driver was spinning around, fishtailing, the occupants yelling with excitement. He could see them clearly, and for the first time, rage was beginning to smolder deep within his soul. He wanted no more humans threatening Corinne. A low growl rumbled deep in his throat, and he leaned over her silky hair, intending to whisper a command to her.

Corinne clutched Dayan's arm as they raced across

the sky. He wasn't running anymore. She was certain his feet weren't touching the ground. No one could move that fast. No one. She felt the warmth of his breath against her ear, felt him merging with her mind, the waves of reassurance, of love and commitment. "Don't tell me to forget this," she countered sharply. *'Don't order me to forget, Dayan. Not yet. Let me see you.'*

She was seeing him for the first time. Before, she'd had glimpses, tantalizing clues, but she couldn't fit the pieces together. Now he was sharing her mind, and she saw things, memories, images; she saw Dayan in different time periods. His memories didn't make sense to her, but she knew they were real and not from history books. They were too detailed, too vivid. And he had saved her from the speeding car, leaping into the air and virtually flying with her.

'Your heart must match the beat of mine. Listen, Corinne, for I will not lose you. Breathe with me and do not be frightened.'

"I'm not afraid of you," she whispered aloud. *'I'm not afraid of you.'* She didn't want him to use his telepathic ability to rob her of this memory. Was she seeing the reason Dayan was so lonely, so utterly alone in a world where everyone seemed to be drawn to him? He was completely different. He could do magical things.

Dayan took her to the safety of the rooftops, settling her gently in the shelter of a dormer. He glanced at the sky, and immediately clouds began swirling overhead, building fast and furious. The thick fog bank was returning with the unstable weather.

Corinne watched his every move carefully, noting that his expression was exactly the same, but deep within his eyes burned a red flame of retribution. "You're going to confront them, aren't you?"

"I want you to concentrate on your heart, Corinne." He made it an order, delivered in his black-velvet voice.

141

"It needs to be a nice steady beat. Hear it, feel mine." He brought her palm to his chest, right over his heart. "Feel that rhythm? You can control it to some extent."

"How could you move so fast?" she asked, her eyes wide with wonder. Corinne had been handicapped physically all of her life, so Dayan's abilities were wondrous to her.

"We will talk later, honey. I have a few minor details to attend to right now."

She reached out and caught his arm. "Be careful, Dayan. There's such a thing as being *too* confident."

He bent his head to brush her forehead with a kiss. And then he was gone. Corinne blinked and Dayan had disappeared. She drew up her knees, breathing slowly and deeply, concentrating on her heart as he had commanded. For the moment, she allowed herself the luxury of belonging to him, of knowing he wanted her. Only her. *What was he? Who was he?*

Dayan felt enormous power sweeping through his mind as he dissolved into droplets of mist. Streaking though the layers of fog, he moved swiftly toward the car that was roaring through the streets. A jagged lightning bolt slammed to earth directly into the path of the car. The vehicle lurched and fishtailed before it raced on. Hail poured out of the sky; ice the size of golf balls rained down on the roof of the car so hard it dented it. Visibility was destroyed by thick fog and sheets of ice. The driver slammed on his brakes, and the car slid to a halt. At once the deadly fog invaded the vehicle, pouring in through the windows and filling the empty spaces until it pushed out all the air.

Within the fog was a peculiar mist, a vapor trail of a shadowy color that left an impression of great menace. The driver reached for the door handle, but it was already too late. The fog was winding around his throat like the coils of a snake. The strangely colored mist wound tighter and tighter until the driver was choking, gasping, turning gray, then blue, his eyes rolling back in his head.

Both men in the back seat reached simultaneously for the doors. The fog seemed alive, fibrous, with tentacles that reached out to envelop them, slipping coil after coil around them like ever-tightening nooses. They struggled frantically, but their struggles caused the loops of fog to squeeze them more tightly until they were gasping and choking, reaching up to tear at the coils around their throats. Their hands simply went through the fog as if it were mist and nothing else. They died silently, without a chance to cry out for help.

Dayan guided the vehicle through the thick fog, using his peculiar radar so that he could keep the cloud cover around him as he removed the car from Corinne's neighborhood. These men would be found, but their deaths would baffle any coroner. Dayan had left no marks on any of them. All three appeared to have choked to death or strangled on something, but there were no drugs in their systems, no marks or evidence of foul play. Dayan was tired of being chased, and the members of the society had gone too far this time. They were determined to capture or kill Corinne and Lisa. Dayan could not allow the society to threaten his lifemate. By leaving the men dead in their car a few blocks from Corinne's home, he was sending his message loud and clear to the society members. They would continue the pursuit at their own peril. Corinne and Lisa were under his protection, and he would destroy anyone who threatened them.

The swirling black clouds overhead were dissipating along with the trails of fog. Corinne lay back on the roof, watching the patterns of the clouds, the lightning arcing from one black cauldron to another. It was a beautiful display, but it was frightening too, because it seemed so intense, so personal. *Like Dayan.* Everything about him was intense. He was always outwardly calm, tranquil even, yet she sensed so much more beneath the surface. Swirling like the dark clouds above her head.

Just as fast as he had gone, Dayan returned, standing over her, tall and powerful. She blinked up at him in total amazement. She closed her eyes when he reached for her. Tall. Elegant. Powerful. That same wildness was on him, clinging to him along with a lethal menace. It was something she couldn't quite define, but that was nonetheless real.

"I told you to keep your heart rate steady," he greeted her very softly, the menace strong in his voice. He lifted her in his arms, cradling her against his chest so that her heart immediately began to tune itself to his. "You said you were not afraid of me, honey, yet your pulse is racing."

"You appeared out of nowhere," she said defensively, thumping his shoulder with her clenched fist. "I am human, you know." She looked up at him with large, steady eyes. "Are you human, Dayan?"

He bent his dark head, his teeth very white in the night. "What do you think?" The words were whispered softly against her throat, against her pulse. "Do I feel human to you?" His voice was temptation itself.

Corinne knew better than to listen, she was so easily distracted by the sheer enticement of his voice. Her hands of their own volition found the thick abundance of his hair and tangled in the silky strands. "How do you do that so easily?" she asked, knowing her eyes would have given away her feelings even if he couldn't read her mind. She *loved* being with him, everything about him. She wanted to erase that look from the depths of his eyes for all time. The emptiness. The loneliness. "I'm beginning to think you're bad for my heart,

Dayan. You can melt a woman at twenty paces. You can. And you made the weather change."

Dayan's mouth continued to explore the soft column of her throat. "I did? I must be very talented. I hope such a feat earned your everlasting admiration." He sounded slightly distracted, as if it were more important to discover the softness of her skin than to hold a conversation. "You are very tired, Corinne. We ought to start out to meet the healers this night, but I think you need to rest. You have had enough excitement for one evening."

Her head rested on his shoulder, her long lashes fanning her cheeks. She was tired, more now than ever. As he carried her to the edge of the roof, he moved with such smoothness, she felt as if she were floating. "I loved dancing with you," she murmured without opening her eyes, enjoying the breeze blowing in her face. "I love the way you move."

"So I am making progress after all," he said. He floated with her to the ground easily, his mind fully merged with hers so that he could control her impressions of what was happening, fogging the memory a little at a time so it was slowly fading away. He had wanted to reveal what he was, who he was. He wanted Corinne's acceptance of him, yet he knew her body was weak, her heart failing. He couldn't take a chance yet. When she found out the truth, he wanted the healer's assurance that her heart would withstand the shock. As he drew a hazy veil over the evening's shocking events, he stressed different memories: his kisses; her response. Retrieving the suitcases, he made sure her seat belt was snug before he pulled the car away from the curb.

Corinne sat quietly on the seat beside him, astonished at how tired she was. The stress of the pregnancy on her body was beginning to tell on her. Dayan was driving carefully through the streets, his fingers en-

twined with hers. "Isn't it strange?" she mused. "If someone hadn't tipped Lisa off that you were playing in that
bar, we would never have met."

"I would have found you." It was a statement of fact,
quietly delivered.

Corinne was silent the rest of the way home. Her
mind was pleasantly blank. She was tired and strangely
happy just to be in his company. Minutes earlier, she
had scented the wildness in him, but now she felt his
tranquillity, an utter calmness that seeped deep into her
soul. Dayan seemed content to drive through the night,
humming softly under his breath. The tune was one she
had never heard before. It was hauntingly beautiful.

Lisa was waiting on the small balcony, trying not to
look like she was worrying. She watched anxiously
while Dayan courteously helped Corinne out of the car.
He would have carried her, but Corinne was all too
conscious of eyes on them.

'*You are being silly.*' The words brushed her mind
tenderly. '*Who cares what anyone thinks?*'

Corinne summoned up her courage to answer him
in her mind. The sheer intimacy of their communication appealed to her. '*I don't want her to think I'm not
feeling well.*'

'*You are not feeling well.*' He pointed it out very
nicely.

Corinne looked up at him from under her long
lashes, just one swift reprimand before she smiled at
Lisa. Above her head, Dayan found himself smiling.
That was his Corinne. Sweet and sassy at the same time.

"Are you feeling okay?" Lisa asked, her eyes anxious.

"Of course. I'm just a little tired," Corinne admitted.
"I thought I'd lie down for a while. What are you doing
still up?"

"Waiting for you." Lisa glanced at Dayan and looked
away. She wasn't certain why she trusted him when she

was with him but felt suspicious when he was out of her sight. He made Corinne act out of character. Corinne had never looked that closely at men, not even when she had been single. Corinne was practical, businesslike. She wasn't the type to cling to a rock star. Lisa tried not to glare at the man.

Dayan felt sympathetic to her. Lisa was disgusted with herself that she was jealous. She didn't want Corinne looking at Dayan with stars in her eyes. She didn't want Corinne looking at anyone like that. She wasn't willing to change her relationship with Corinne in any way, but she didn't like herself very much for her possessiveness.

"It's almost dawn," Corinne said gently. "You should be in bed, Lisa, not worrying about me. You knew we were going to get our things. It was bound to take a little bit of time."

"So there were no problems," Cullen said, wrapping his arm around Lisa's shoulders in a show of support.

"Well—" Corinne seemed confused, a slight frown crossing her small face. She glanced up at Dayan for help as she nervously shoved a stray strand of dark hair from her face.

Dayan immediately flooded her mind with warmth and reassurance. She was bewildered and disoriented for a moment, unable to recall exactly what had happened. She was searching her memories, and they were a jumble of confusion. "Nothing we could not handle," he answered easily, truthfully. His hands settled along her hips, anchoring her to him. "If we had known you were worried, Lisa, we would have called."

"Of course I was worried," Lisa said in challenge, her chin up.

Corinne leaned back heavily against Dayan, weariness sweeping through her. "Lisa," she said quietly, drawing on the strength of their relationship.

At once Lisa reached out and took Corinne's hand. "I'm picking a fight again. Just come and lie down, Corinne. I don't want you to become ill."

Dayan indicated Lisa's suitcase with his chin. "She was very careful to get everything on your list." He was moving Corinne toward the bedroom where she'd slept the night before.

Corinne knew Lisa was worried about her, but she didn't have the energy to reassure her further. All she wanted to do was lie down and close her eyes. Her body felt like lead, and each step was like wading through quicksand.

Lisa watched Dayan's every move—the way he held Corinne so gently, the way his eyes moved over Corinne's face tenderly, possessively. Lisa heaved a soft sigh and moved closer to Cullen. He responded by tightening his hold on her, and she looked up at him and smiled rather sadly. Her world was changing, and Lisa wasn't someone who managed change easily. Corinne looked very tired and fragile. It always frightened Lisa to see her looking like that. Her fragility highlighted the fact that Corinne's heart was fading.

"I couldn't bear it if anything happened to her," Lisa whispered to Cullen. "I really couldn't."

Dayan, with his superior hearing, heard her whispered confession. He knew exactly how she felt and could sympathize with her. He couldn't bear the thought of anything happening to Corinne either. He bent forward to brush the top of Corinne's silky head with a kiss, but he couldn't leave Lisa feeling so upset. He glanced back to capture her anxious gaze with his black one. It only took a few seconds, but it was enough. He sent her waves of reassurance, pushing a little further into her mind so he could implant a feeling of warmth toward him.

Corinne took her time getting ready for bed. Dayan

had pulled up his guitar, and she dawdled as he began to play. The music seemed alive, a part of the harmony of the earth and sky, a dreamy ballad. At first his voice was so soft she could barely make out the lyrics. She hurried out of the bathroom into the bedroom so she could listen to every word. His voice was mystical, beautiful, dreamlike. He looked up at her and the world seemed to stop spinning, standing still so the moment was locked in her memory for all time.

'*You take my breath away.*' She thought the words to him, not wanting to interrupt his singing, not wanting to miss one single word of the ballad. It was a song of haunting loneliness, of a man, a wanderer, a troubadour, searching through time, century after century, for the one woman who could love him.

His sensual mouth curved into a smile, and his gaze drifted over her before his lashes lowered and his hand moved over the guitar. His fingers worked so fast she could hardly follow them as they played the haunting melody. He sang of a dark shadow slowly spreading over his soul, a stain that would be impossible to eradicate once it took him over. A powerful beast that roared continually for release from within. As time went on and he did not find his lady, colors and emotions faded, along with all hope, leaving him only his guitar and the words of his song.

It was a dark melody that brought tears to her eyes. Corinne curled up on the bed, intently watching his face as he played. The light bothered her eyes, so she casually flicked her hand to turn it off. All that mattered in her world was Dayan and his perfect voice singing this hauntingly beautiful song. She had a sudden desire to hold him in her arms, to be the woman who was needed so desperately.

The music changed subtly, introducing a hopeful strain, one that rose to a joyful crescendo. She found herself smiling there in the dark, her eyes glued to his face. He was an artist, a poet without compare. She loved watching his expression as he played, as his soul poured out its music. Corinne's eyelashes lowered onto her cheeks. She was very tired. And Dayan was there with her, solid and real, impossibly strong and healthy.

For one moment the guitar was silent as Dayan stretched out beside her, laying the instrument across his chest.

She smiled. "Are you going to play for me until I fall asleep?"

"Absolutely." She heard his answering smile in his voice. "You have sweet dreams, honey. Dream about us together." His fingers once again glided over the strings, producing a soft ballad.

She was dreaming. Daydreaming. Nightdreaming. She only knew it was wonderful to be with him as she drifted away on his music. He made her feel alive and very feminine. She could even pretend to be healthy. In the midst of her dream, trails of fog began to slowly wind through the stars. She frowned, felt Dayan rub his index finger gently back and forth over her forehead.

"Go to sleep, honey. I want you to sleep all day until sunset." He brushed a kiss across her forehead, taking away her frown. "Do you understand me, honey? Sleep deeply until I call for you to wake."

She was more asleep than awake. "You're ordering me around again, aren't you?"

"Yes. I expect you to obey me." The sounds of his guitar filled the room, filled her heart and soul. "You know you are my life, you know it. Tell me you do."

"I wish I were your life." She was almost asleep, not certain what she was saying.

"You are definitely my life."

She was silent for so long, Dayan thought she had drifted off to sleep. He lay beside her, his fingers moving lovingly over his guitar, his body close to hers. He wanted this moment to last for all time. Corinne was beside him where she belonged. Light was beginning to streak through the darkness, turning the inky blackness to gray. He lay there savoring the feel of her beside him, missing the sound of her voice, her laughter, the way her eyes danced when she teased him. The way she looked at him as if he were the only man in her world. Corinne. He knew what poets wrote about. He knew why his soul had cried out for her. He knew why he had waited centuries for her.

"Dayan"—she murmured his name drowsily—"are you human?"

Startled, he stared down at her. Corinne's eyes were closed, and she was breathing as if she were asleep. He had covered her memories with a veil, not removing them completely because he wanted her to know the truth soon. He didn't want it to be a complete shock to her; he couldn't risk that kind of shock with her damaged heart. He wanted her to have the memories to draw on when she needed them, but his command should have prevented her from wondering.

He examined her thoughts as she lay there beside him. She was drifting in and out of consciousness, having a beautiful dream. She was unafraid. Dayan relaxed, a slow smile curving his mouth. She was moving closer to the truth. Closer to accepting him. *'Sleep, honey, while I visit you in your dreams.'* And he would. He couldn't bear to be away from her, not even while they both slept. He would be forced to seek refuge in the ground as the sun rose, yet he didn't dare protect her with normal safeguards. If she were to attempt to leave the dwelling despite the guards, the stress could cause problems with her weak heart. As it was, he was afraid if she did go too far away from him, she would begin to feel the effects of separation from her lifemate.

Although he had not said the ritual words to her, he and Corinne were already bound in heart and mind.

He bent once more to kiss her, needing to touch her, wanting to remain with her despite the danger to himself. He knew it was impossible to stay, but it didn't stop him from longing to be with her. *'Sleep until I rise, Corinne. Sleep safe.'* He murmured the command softly, needing to find a way to protect her while he slept.

When he was satisfied that she had obeyed him, he lay quietly, freeing his mind, seeking his brethren. *'Darius. Our need for a healer grows greater with each passing moment. She is much weaker this night. I do not know how much longer she can continue.'*

There was a wait and then Darius was there. Strong. Reassuring. Calm as always. *'Join with her. We will link—Julian, Desari, Tempest and I. You work, and we will supply you with as much help as possible to keep her going until we can come together.'*

Dayan let his breath out slowly. He should have realized Darius would think in terms of the family strength. His family was there for Dayan, as always, standing shoulder to shoulder with him to fight for his lifemate and the child. He reached for the merge, embraced his family and let go of his physical body to once more attempt a healing. This time with help.

Chapter Eight

Desari, lead singer for the Dark Troubadours, tapped out an edgy rhythm with her fingernail on the tabletop as she looked at her brother. "Dayan's lifemate is not going to last much longer, Darius. I don't like this situation at all. Dayan cannot claim his lifemate, nor help her while she is with child. What did Gregori say, Darius?"

Julian circled Desari's waist with his arm, bending to brush his lifemate's temple with a brief, reassuring kiss. "Gregori and Shea are really very good, Desari. They'll figure out how to help Dayan. Gregori is impressive when he works, and he is your brother, of your lineage. You know how powerful that makes him. It's too bad Gregori and Savannah didn't make Lucian's wedding. Running into the vampire delayed them, and now this news will cut their reunion with Lucian short."

"I'm not certain they will reach Dayan in time. Barack and Syndil are returning from the Carpathian Mountains. That's a long way, Julian." Desari, clearly worried, bit at her lower lip.

Julian leaned down to brush a reassuring kiss along Desari's temple. "They bring with them Shea and her lifemate, Jacques, brother to the Prince and a very powerful Carpathian. You are used to relying on your family in these matters, but in truth, there are many others— brethren, kin—who are moving to help us."

Darius shrugged his broad shoulders as he looked at his sister, his black gaze steady and calm. "We can do no other than to aid Dayan until they arrive. Gregori and his lifemate will be here soon enough, and we will travel together to reach Dayan and the one who would join our family. Dayan has no choice but to keep her alive, and he will do so."

Julian nodded. "Both Gregori and Shea feel it is too risky for Dayan to do a blood exchange with her while there's a baby in her womb. Dayan said the infant is female and a strong psychic. That will help, but until the healers arrive to aid the baby, we dare not risk interference."

Desari frowned. "If Dayan's lifemate's heart should give out, we will lose them both."

Julian's arm tightened around her. "Dayan will not allow such a thing. His lifemate's heart is very weak, but we should be able to keep her going with our linked energy until the healers are in position to aid her and the infant." He met Darius's eyes over the top of his lifemate's head. The situation was grave. Barack and Syndil were rushing back, bringing with them Shea Dubrinsky, lifemate to Jacques. Shea was an extraordinary Carpathian. A doctor, a researcher, a healer of great talent. With them traveled a human male. A friend to the Carpathian race, Gary Jansen was aiding Shea in her research to find a way to keep Carpathian children alive during the crucial first year of life. Gregori had sent information about him ahead, asking for the protection of the human from all Carpathians. The band members didn't know Gary, but Gregori's word would be obeyed unquestioningly within the Carpathian world.

"It is near dawn," Darius mused aloud, "but if necessary we could continue a couple more hours under cover of a storm."

"We said we would meet them here," Tempest protested. "And this campsite is secluded. It is a good place to go to ground."

Darius rubbed the bridge of his nose thoughtfully as he smiled down at his lifemate. Tempest stood with her hands on her hips, giving him that little frown that always made him want to take her somewhere secluded and kiss it right off her expressive face. "Barack and Syndil are on their way back, honey. They'll catch up with us at the house in the Cascades. We have to travel fast if we're going to get to Dayan quickly."

Tempest tilted her head, her flame-red hair glinting in the moonlight. "We didn't say we were meeting Barack and Syndil, Darius, and you darn well know it! We're meeting Gregori and Savannah here. You want to leave because your *other* big brother is coming and you're nervous about meeting him. Julian told you so many tales of the dark one, you probably have nightmares about him." Maybe Darius didn't, but Tempest did. And she couldn't help teasing her husband every chance she got. They had only been together a few short weeks, and he still could take her breath away with one sensual look from his beautiful eyes. She had the feeling he always would.

Tempest sounded far too smug for his liking. Darius glared at her in warning, one eyebrow shooting high. "Nervous? I have no experience with such a thing. I have heard the tales of the dark one, a bogeyman the elders made up to frighten small children. The stories are impressive, but the man is no doubt a mere man."

Julian's eyebrow shot up. "Mere man?" A definite smirk settled over his face. "I've heard Gregori described as many things, but a mere man is not one of them."

Desari reached out to her brother. "Darius, do you find it strange to think we have three elder brothers after all this time? First we met Lucian and Gabriel, the dark twins in the legends, tales you told us when we were children. And now Gregori, the dark healer. It is amazing to me that they live and breathe. Lucian and Gabriel were wonderful. I'm excited to meet Gregori."

"We never knew them," Darius pointed out. "Lucian and Gabriel were long gone, their existence no more than a myth. And Gregori was all-powerful with many responsibilities. You were a babe and I but six years old when we were lost. He was already a full-fledged male, grown in stature and strength. I doubt if he thought about us overmuch." Again he shrugged carelessly. He had certainly thought about his brother in those days, so long ago. He had hero-worshiped him, listening to each impressive story and filing it away to take out when he was alone.

Tempest slipped her hand into his larger one, a silent gesture of love. She touched the mind of her lifemate and found he was simply stating the facts as he saw them. He was making no judgment. Darius had long been without emotion until she had come into his life, and he possessed a will of iron and tremendous discipline. She leaned into him and reached up to find his mouth with hers. His apparent lack of emotion still intimidated her at times. She was feeling her way into Carpathian life, still struggling to be part of a family when she had always been so solitary.

Darius responded the way he always did, his kiss hot and possessive. Tempest melted into him, instantly pliant, her arms stealing around his neck. "I think of you too much," she pointed out.

"I fear for Dayan, Tempest. This problem is a difficult one. I honestly do not know if we can save his lifemate." With Tempest, this once, he would allow doubt to intrude. With her, he could be vulnerable and show his tremendous love for his family. "If it were you . . ." He trailed off, his gut lurching in protest.

"It isn't me," Tempest pointed out. "I'm healthy and strong. And you won't fail Dayan. You have been there for him over the centuries, and you will be the rock he leans on now."

Corinne turned over, snuggled closer to warmth. She knew who lay beside her and she didn't bother to open her eyes. "Dayan, you aren't sleeping. I can tell by the way you're breathing. Tell me what's wrong."

Dayan tensed. Her voice was drowsy, sexy, arousing his body when he had been utterly relaxed. "You are supposed to be asleep until the next rising." He meant it literally. He had given her a command.

Corinne rubbed her face along his chest and laughed softly. "You have to admit you phrased the order rather oddly. I was to sleep safely until you rose. What exactly does that mean?" She yawned sleepily, covering her mouth politely. "If you don't ever go to sleep and just lie there all night staring at the ceiling, does that mean I don't have to obey? Or does it mean I have to stay asleep until you actually rise from the bed?"

Dayan found himself grinning at the ceiling. He had been lying there beside her, simply enjoying being in the same room with her, wondering at the beauty of the night. Outside the room he could hear the night creatures stirring. The wind was rushing through the trees, and he felt vitally alive. "For your information, I was not staring at the ceiling. I was staring at you." He leaned over and kissed the corner of her mouth, laughing softly. "You little witch. How did you manage to wake up when you're supposed to be asleep?"

"It was a fairly wimpy command, Dayan," she pointed out, lifting her lashes so her green eyes could laugh at him there in the dark. "I mean, I heard you giving it to me, and felt the push, and I allowed myself to sort of go with it but all the time I was thinking that I wouldn't necessarily obey it."

"Wimpy? It was not wimpy. I was careful of your . . . er . . . *condition*. I was being sensitive. I object strenuously to your using the word wimpy. I was firm but gentle."

She rolled over to pillow her head on his shoulder. "You underestimated me. Admit it. You're so darned used to making people do what you want, it didn't occur to you I could resist."

His eyebrow shot up. "You did it on purpose."

"Well, of course. You can't just go around trying to force people to do what you want them to do." She turned so she was nearly nose to nose with him. Glaring. "Like Lisa. You have to stop influencing her, Dayan. And don't deny it, I know you do."

"I was not going to deny it. I told you, it is important that she accepts me in your life." Dayan linked his fingers behind his head. "Lisa has an unusually high resistance to my persuasion."

"Because Lisa is not like the rest of us. In her own way, she is different too," Corinne explained. "She is inherently good, and I think she is gifted with a protection of sorts. Lisa has to be allowed to work out her relationship with you on her own." She traced his lips with the pad of her finger. "You're rather ruthless at times, aren't you?"

His tongue flicked out, swept along her finger. "I stand on the stage night after night, performing, surrounded by people who do not know me. I have a need for space. Is it so wrong, after giving the best I have to give, to ask for that space? I do not harm them, merely ask for consideration."

Corinne smiled down at him. "I'm asking for consideration for Lisa. Give her time. She'll come to accept you. She wants me to be happy. If I'm happy, she'll be happy with my choice."

"Am I your choice, Corinne?" Dayan nibbled at her finger, his teeth teasing her, sending tiny flames dancing over her skin.

"And you're arrogant as well as ruthless," she pointed out.

"You may as well add that I am a thief to the long list of my sins, since you are taking an inventory of them." He slid his hand inside his shirt and pulled out a small notebook. "I could not possibly leave C. J. Wentworth songs behind. You left this treasure sitting in the middle of your bed."

Corinne had to look away from his mesmerizing gaze. He was a miracle, a genius with music, yet he was complimenting her work. She knew she was glowing. How could she not? Praising her music was one of the highest compliments Dayan could give her.

"Silly—" His voice was tender. He lifted his head to kiss her soft mouth gently. "You must know I am hoping you will join our band. What an asset you would be. You are capable of playing several instruments, and your songwriting is wonderful."

"I'm nowhere near being a legend as you are," she said, "but thank you for such high praise."

"I have been lying here beside you reading your beautiful lyrics. I watched you sleeping, Corinne, and wondered what I had ever done in my life to deserve you."

Warmth spread deep inside her at his softly spoken

words. "I write what's in my heart, about all the things that matter in life. All the things we encounter. There's such beauty all around us, Dayan. Everyone has to cope with everyday problems. Finances, sickness, even death, loving someone who doesn't love us back." She twisted the ring on her finger. "But we can still live life, see the beauty everywhere around us. It's there for the taking. That's what I try to write about in my music. Hope in the midst of heartache. Joy in the midst of pain. Experience life—don't watch it passing by."

Dayan reached out and gently took her hand, brought it to his mouth in a tribute. "I have never met anyone who lives life with the fullness you do, Corinne. And already, you have shown me such wonders. I look at something small, like the leaves on the trees, and find they are more beautiful than I had ever imagined."

"Leaves shine silver in the moonlight," she said. "I often sit in my backyard and watch the way the breeze makes them glitter at night when the moon is out." She lay back shivering, cuddling closer to him as if the talk of being outdoors chilled her. "It's cold in here." She beckoned with her hand toward the cupboard. The double doors flew open and a thick quilt tumbled out. It rippled like a magic carpet as it floated across the room and spread itself over them.

It wasn't cold, but her body was not regulating its temperature properly. Dayan suppressed the apprehension shimmering in his mind. He forced a smile. "You are showing off, Corinne. You are supposed to be sleeping and gaining strength, but instead, you are waving your hands about and making blankets dance in the air."

Her breath fanned his neck. Warm. Intriguing. Tempting. She laughed very softly, the sound joyful in the stillness of the room. Suddenly his smile was real. "At night when I was very young, I used to imagine myself flying on a magic carpet. I didn't dare set the blankets floating; I was afraid I would get caught."

"So what did you do instead?" he asked.

"I read, of course. Everything I could get my hands on. Books could take me to all the places I never could go on my own." She traced the indentation in his chin. "I've read so many books—fiction, nonfiction, encyclopedias, anything I could get my hands on. And I had the music."

"How did you manage to learn to play, especially when you were living on the streets a good part of your life?" He shifted her, wrapping his arms securely around her, curving his body protectively behind hers so they fit like spoons.

Corinne's laughter was soft, like the rain on the roof. "There was a small club, a bar, where live bands played all the time. Locks meant nothing to us, and we often slept in the back room there. Instruments were left behind all the time. I'd watch the band play, and then I'd practice until I could play the forgotten instrument with the same sound as the person on the stage. I'm lucky enough to have a good ear, and I can remember music easily. The piano was easiest for me because I could watch the performer's fingers and see how a particular piece was played."

"Do you realize how truly rare such a thing is, Corinne?"

She smiled. "I had many hours to practice."

Dayan slid his hand down her ribcage to her stomach. "She is moving. The two of you need sleep. I am keeping you up."

Corinne felt her insides turn to mush when he laid his hand over the baby in a protective gesture. Instinctively she knew that was what he was doing. She felt close to him, connected with him, content to lie beside him and listen to the sound of his voice and feel the heat of his body. It was one of the things she counted as beautiful in the world. One of the things she was thankful she had experienced.

"So—" Gregori's silver eyes burned over his brother. "You are Darius. I have heard much of your exploits. The miracle of keeping so many children alive, including two of our females." He clasped Darius's arms just above the elbows in the formal greeting of one warrior to another.

Gregori emanated power from every pore. He had long black hair like Darius, and a stockier, more muscular build than most Carpathian males. His eyes were a piercing silver, and as they rested on the brother he hadn't seen in centuries, an affectionate gleam glimmered in the depths.

Looking at him, Darius was at a loss for words. He had memories of this man locked away, placed carefully where they would never be tarnished. He had always been proud of being Gregori's sibling. In the earlier days, when life was hard and Darius struggled to safeguard the other children, he had drawn heavily on those memories of his legendary brother. He had honed his will of iron by comparing himself to his brother, by pretending Gregori was watching him, judging his actions. As a child, lost in the wilderness with infants to care for, Darius had tried hard to live up to the legendary image of his brothers. The twins were a myth, the greatest vampire hunters known to their people. Gregori had been so much more real to him.

Gregori stared into the steady gaze of his brother. "No one could be prouder of the things you accomplished than I. It was indeed miraculous that you saved both girls and saw Barack and Dayan through the long centuries of darkness. I thank you for giving me back my sister." He turned his head to look at her. Desari. She was tall and straight, with a voice like an angel. "A true gift to the world."

Desari went into his arms, tears swimming in her dark eyes. "I am honored to meet you at last."

"The honor is mine." Gregori hugged her long and hard before handing her back to the tall, golden warrior waiting to greet him. Gregori reached for his lifemate, bringing her in front of him, his arms securely around her. "May I present my lifemate, Savannah. My sister Desari and my brother Darius." There was pride in his voice.

"And you must know Julian." Desari clasped hands with her handsome lifemate. "He knows much of you."

Savannah laughed at Gregori's expression. "I can see I will have to insist we talk together, Julian." She kissed Desari's cheek and laughed again when Gregori firmly removed her from Julian's reach.

"You can stay away from him." Gregori pinned his brother with a steely eye. "How did you come to allow our sister to associate with this barbarian?"

Darius's eyebrow shot up. "Yes, I was meaning to take you to task over your lack of judgment. Whatever possessed you to send him to us? Your lack of foresight amazes me. He took advantage of the situation, as you can well see. I hold you responsible."

Julian smirked at the brothers. "It was fortunate I was around to guard the women of our race while the two of you were off chasing vampires, trying to hone your skills. In the end, I had no choice but to stay and guard what our race holds dear. I might point out that my relationship with Desari has officially made me your brother." He grinned complacently at them.

"I had hoped you might whip him into shape," Gregori confided with a deep sigh. "But I see it is impossible. He never obeyed a single law."

"You sent him to me to be rid of him." Darius feigned

a scowl. He had come to respect Julian for his independent ways and welcomed him into his family.

Gregori reached out to clasp Julian's arms in a warrior's greeting of respect. "I thank you for all you have done for my family. I am indeed grateful that it is you looking after my sister."

Julian grinned at him. "I am most grateful for the job."

"I trust your brother Aidan is well and knows why you have chosen to be apart from him." There was a subtle edge to Gregori's voice. "Had you spoken with Mikhail or me, we would have aided you in your battle with the vampire. You were a child, Julian, with a child's perception of guilt and responsibility. Mikhail and I are proud of the choices you have made to safeguard your people and your brother. You did talk with Aidan." It was more of a statement than a question.

Julian grinned sheepishly. "I took Desari to meet Aidan and his lifemate Alexandria. He had much to say about my protection of him. He obviously spent more time with you than I had first realized. He is well, as is his lifemate."

"This is Tempest," Darius said, drawing his red-headed lifemate to him. "She has not been long in our world."

Desari immediately shifted to stand close to the shorter woman. Julian glided closer as if protecting her, the family closing ranks to ease the newest member's fears. "Tempest has great courage. Without her, we would not have Darius. Our family owes much to her."

"Welcome to our family, little sister," Gregori said. "I thank you for my brother's life. It would not do to lose one so valuable."

Tempest smiled shyly, grateful for the support of Desari and Julian. She leaned into Darius as she tried not to be intimidated by the sheer power emanating from Gregori or his peculiar, soul-seeing eyes. "It's a pleasure to meet the rest of Darius's family. We've spoken of you often and looked forward to your visit with us."

Savannah leaned over to kiss her cheek. "I know all this must be new to you and perhaps a little frightening, but I can see you are well loved."

"Desari and Syndil have welcomed me as a sister, and Dayan, Barack and Julian are protective elder brothers." Tempest smiled lovingly at Darius. "And Darius makes it all worthwhile. I'm not afraid, just a little overwhelmed. And I do want children someday, so I'm putting my faith in you, Gregori, to solve the tremendous problems we all face."

"I promise to do my best." Gregori inclined his head. "With so many working, we hope to find answers much more quickly. Gary Jansen has been doing research into the different lineages, trying to ascertain how often a child was usually born to Carpathian couples. It appears, with the exception of a few lines, most children were born fifty to one hundred years apart. Savannah's line is an exception through her grandmother's side of the family. Sarantha, Mikhail's mother, had four children quite close, three males and one female. And my mother also had the two of you, Desari and Darius, close together. Yet Desari is the only female child who survives in our lineage." Gregori smiled at his brother. "Thanks to you, Darius. We owe you much."

"There are so few of us," Desari said sadly.

"But our ranks are growing as we discover that ancients are scattered throughout the world," Gregori replied gently. "Gabriel and Lucian still live. They live and have found their lifemates. Gabriel's lifemate, Francesca, has sent one of her healing quilts for Corinne. We would have liked to visit longer with them before returning to the Carpathian Mountains."

Desari reached out to link her hand with her lifemate.

"Julian told me the sad story of such heroes. It was a privilege to meet them at the wedding."

"They are true ancients. Mikhail is hoping they will be able to aid Shea and Gary in their research into the high mortality rate of our infants," Gregori said. "I have long sought the answer to this problem, but have not yet succeeded in defeating our worst enemy."

"The fact that we do not have female children," Savannah sighed. "And the difficulty of keeping our children alive the first year. You will solve the mystery. You are no longer alone, Gregori. You have Shea and Gary and now Francesca. You will find the answer, and we will have the children you wish for."

"Twins," Julian supplied. "Two little girls to run wild, with their father chasing after them." He looked well pleased with the idea.

Gregori bared white teeth at Julian across the table. "I see you are having much fun at my expense, Julian, but remember, I have known you many, many years. Desari, my young sister, there is much we have to speak of."

Julian laughed. "I wish you would speak to her, Gregori. She has surprising gifts, as Darius and I have found out." He kissed his wife. "I do not suppose you would want to sing your brother into a tree trunk for me."

Gregori's eyebrow shot up, a habit he shared with Darius despite the long separation between them. "Desari can use her voice in such a manner?"

Desari laughed, blushing a soft rose color. "Of course not. He is exaggerating. I use my voice to soothe and heal others, to bring them joy."

"Or reprimand elder brothers and lifemates when they do things she does not agree with," Darius offered helpfully.

When Gregori's silver gaze rested on her thoughtfully, Desari sighed. "All right, it is true I once used a net to entrap them." She smiled conspiratorially at the other women. "As you age, your gifts will come to you, and they will be useful in ways you did not imagine."

Gregori hauled Savannah closer. "I am taking you back to our country, where you will never hear this kind of feminine nonsense."

She rose on her toes to kiss him firmly on the hard edge of his mouth. "My mother lives there, and as I recall, you said my father allowed her to run amok, creating chaos and havoc in her wake."

"I would like to meet your mother," Desari said. She caught her brother's arm. "Let's plan a tour of Europe. We can go home to the mountains. It would be such fun. Barack and Syndil wanted so much to stay there and visit, and I'm certain Dayan would want to bring his Corinne to meet everyone."

"First we must see to it that Dayan will be coming with us," Darius reminded her.

"The situation sounds grave," Gregori commented.

Darius nodded. "Dayan is worried, with good reason. I had never thought to come up against such a problem. He cannot convert his lifemate with the baby unborn. But Corinne's heart is enlarged and overworked. I doubt if it will last until the baby is old enough to be born, and I am certain it will fail during labor."

"How long do you think her heart will hold out?" Gregori frowned, his dark brows settling into lines of worry. "You have examined her through your link with him. Do you feel we have enough time?"

"I do not honestly know," Darius admitted. Feeling emotion had some drawbacks, he was discovering. He loved Dayan as a brother. He could feel Dayan's pain, his perpetual heartache, and Darius was raw with the need to ease his brother's suffering.

Gregori allowed his breath to leave his lungs in a long sigh. He had thought Darius and Desari lost to him for all time. The joy of discovery, the affection swamping him, was overwhelming enough, but to feel as if he might fail them when they needed him most was truly daunting.

Reading his mind, Savannah reached up to soothe Gregori, rubbing the pad of her finger back and forth over his frown lines. "You will save her. I know you will, Gregori." She could feel the sheer magnitude of his emotions swamping him as he looked upon kin he thought lost to him forever.

Gregori's arm circled her waist at once, locking her beneath his broad shoulder. "I cannot imagine what this man is feeling with his lifemate so threatened." His silver gaze slid over Savannah. "There are few threats that would shake me, but such danger to you would leave me decidedly rattled."

A slow grin curved her soft mouth, and her eyes sparkled like gems. She was willing to provide the laughter for him, the teasing to ease the overpowering emotions. She was his lifemate, and *he* was in *her* care, however much he thought it was the other way around. "*Decidedly* rattled? I do love the way you put things. That is such an understatement. If I stub my toe, you lose your mind."

Darius's eyebrows shot up and Julian snorted, a blatant smirk on his face. "I would like to see that, Savannah. The dark one losing his mind is an image I will savor for some time." Julian exchanged a grin with Darius. "I seem to recall, Darius, he often lectured Mikhail on how a lifemate should obey her master."

Savannah swung around to pin Gregori with a glare worthy of her heritage. "Master? Obey her master?"

The silver eyes slid over Julian, deadly, gleaming with a promise of retaliation. "I am certain I never used the word 'master.'"

"I believe, Savannah, Gregori was rather severe with

168

your father at times for the amount of freedom he allowed Raven," Julian informed her. "And actually, I am certain the word 'master' was used more than once. I know 'obey' was." He tilted his head to one side. "You might speak with your sister—she has not yet grasped the concept of obedience."

Desari made a face. "Do not allow him to fool you, Savannah. Julian and I have a true partnership. He likes to grumble, but it works out quite well."

Savannah smiled up at Gregori. "That does give me hope, then. I just have to grow into my powers a bit."

"And what then?" Gregori caught her by the shoulders and gave her a little shake. "The very idea of you with any more power than you already have terrifies me. I cannot imagine what you are thinking of doing."

"Why, helping you, of course." Savannah patted his muscular shoulder.

"We have much to talk about," Darius said, "and little time to visit. I feel Dayan's anxiety even now, across the distance. I had thought we might continue our journey through the dawn to draw closer to them, although this is a safe area to spend the day deep in the ground."

"Link with Dayan, Darius, and I will link with you. I wish to examine her myself and see what we are up against," Gregori decided. "With all of us holding, we should be strong enough to permit an examination."

Darius nodded and reached at once across time and space. *'Dayan. The dark one has arrived. He is strong and capable and wishes to "see" what he is up against. I feel your anxiety. Has something more happened to cause your fear?'*

Dayan glanced down at Corinne. She was half awake, half asleep, floating somewhere in a dreamlike state in between. *'She is restless tonight, even after our healing session, Darius. And her body is unable to regulate her temperature properly. I feel that she is moving*

Christine Feehan

away from this world and approaching the next.'

'Link with her and allow him to see what is happening.' Darius kept his voice calm and sure. More than anything, Dayan had to believe they could keep Corinne alive.

There was a slight hesitation. *'You trust this man?'*

'He is my brother, lifemate to Savannah, daughter of the Prince.' Darius sent reassurance. *'I stand with you, Dayan. Gregori has traveled far to aid us.'* Deliberately Darius used the plural, reminding Dayan they were a family, together in all things. Dayan had all the instincts of a Carpathian male protecting his lifemate. Gregori was a stranger to him and therefore suspect.

'Then I can do no other than thank him.' Dayan's arm encompassed Corinne. There were tiny white lines near her mouth, marks he found alarming. Dayan conveyed the worrisome detail to Darius as he freed himself from his body. He became light and energy, a healing spirit wanting only to perform a selfless act, giving himself up completely in that moment to be anything Corinne should need.

Dayan felt Darius with him. Familiar. Strong. Enduring. Darius had a way of providing complete confidence. It had always been so, as long as Dayan could remember. Darius had been mother and father to him, elder brother, best friend, leader. Dayan was grateful he was there now. Darius didn't seem to question that they would save Corinne. Her salvation was necessary, so it was already a fact. Dayan took hope from Darius's pragmatism.

The strength pouring in from the combined Carpathians was vast. Dayan felt the power as they merged with him. He felt the dark one moving through him, seeing what he saw, the enormity of their task.

'The heart is deteriorating rapidly. It is necessary to slow it down until we can reach your side.' The calm

170

voice reminded Dayan of Darius. It exuded the same confidence. *'I am going to do what repairs I can. She must be brought fully into our world soon. The child is in surprisingly good health. Most of the oxygen and nutrients are going to her little body. She is, indeed, a strong psychic. We must not lose either of them.'*

Dayan felt the heat and power as the healer began working, moving carefully around the heart. Working to get blood to flow more strongly, carrying precious oxygen throughout the body.

'That is as much as I can do for her from this distance. Send her to sleep. Even while you travel, try to keep her asleep, but be careful not to overtax her heart with any compulsion she may fight. She has strong barriers. I will meet you soon, Dayan, and we will see to it that your lifemate survives, if there is any way to do so.'

'I thank you.' Dayan replied formally as he returned to his own body and felt the withdrawal of the others. Using such energy over a long distance was not easy. He knew his family and the healer would seek the rejuvenating soil, as he must too. Beside him, Corrine stirred, drawing his attention.

"Why am I feeling so different?" Corinne asked, looking up at Dayan. Her eyes were clear, and she was breathing much more easily. The tiny white lines of strain around her mouth had disappeared.

The relief Dayan felt was overwhelming. He lay beside her trembling with hope, with joy. "The healer is near. He linked with Darius and the others to provide you with more strength. He was the one who worked on your heart."

Corinne was silent a moment, surprised at how much she believed in him. In the strange ways of his family. She did feel better each time Dayan used his telepathic abilities to aid her. She couldn't deny that whatever he was doing worked.

"I want you to sleep now, Corinne," Dayan said. "The dawn is here and you need rest. I will sleep soon too. Rest will allow your body to heal even more."

"I am tired," she agreed, then smiled sleepily at him. "Although I suspect you are using your gift to give me a push in that direction."

"If I am doing so," Dayan said noncommittally, "it is a small one." He pulled her more tightly into the strength of his arms. "I love holding you, Corinne, and lying beside you. The baby is peaceful now—have you noticed? She was kicking before, but she has drifted off now, safe in her little world."

"I love your voice when you talk about her." Corinne's voice was soft, drowsy, as her consciousness faded into sleep.

"You love my voice all the time," Dayan replied smugly, brushing a kiss onto her temple. "Sleep now, my love. Wake when I call to you."

Chapter Nine

"Corinne—" The voice penetrated deep layers of sleep, dragging her back from a shadowy world of dreams. Someone was shaking her shoulder and demanding she wake immediately. It took a few moments before the desperation in the voice penetrated the shadows. Alarm spread, and she forced her eyelashes to lift. "Cullen, what is it? What's wrong?" Her heart was pounding and there was a hard pressure in her chest. "Is it Lisa?"

"She's gone. I woke up and she was gone. She left you a note." Cullen was shoving a piece of paper in her face.

Corinne took the letter, her fingers, slightly shaking, curling around the edges of the pale lavender paper. She didn't need the note to tell her where Lisa had gone. She knew Lisa, knew the way she thought. Lisa was programmed to wake up early, and she must have thought about the contract she had signed and talked herself into believing there was no danger. Lisa didn't want there to be danger, so it was simple enough for her to dismiss it. That was Lisa. The world was a place where she changed what she didn't like. People were supposed to be polite and kind, so Lisa simply imagined them that way. When other women didn't like her because of her looks, Lisa was very hurt and did everything in her power to change their opinion of her.

Angry with herself for not having foreseen such a possibility, Corinne threw back the covers and reached out toward her robe. It moved on its own, jumping from the hook on the back of the door to dance across the room to her hand. Corinne didn't seem to notice as she slipped into the terrycloth folds and paced restlessly across the room.

"What was that?" Cullen asked suspiciously.

Corinne glanced up to see him staring at her in shock. "What?" The word slipped out before she realized what she'd done. Of course Lisa wouldn't have explained about her; Lisa didn't want Corinne to different from others. She shrugged with feigned casualness. "Just this little thing I can do, no big deal. Get out of here so I can get dressed. I know where she's gone and I'll get her back."

"The photo shoot," Cullen guessed in disgust. "She didn't want to give that up. I thought she called and canceled it." He raked a hand through his hair. "She's such a defenseless little thing, why wouldn't she tell me? She knew I thought she was in danger. She should have listened to me."

"She listened to you, Cullen, she just didn't *hear* you. You'll find Lisa says things to appease you because she doesn't like arguments, but in the end she does exactly what she wants," Corinne said. She was pulling her clothes out of the suitcase and rushing for the bathroom.

"She knew how dangerous it was," Cullen said, trying to convince himself. "Maybe she didn't really go; maybe she started to and changed her mind."

Corinne yanked on her jeans, calling out to him through the bathroom door. "No, she didn't, Cullen. She pretended to believe us because it was what we all wanted to hear and Lisa doesn't believe in upsetting people. I'm telling you, Lisa doesn't argue. This is my fault. I should have known she would do this. Don't worry, I'll bring her back." She was buttoning the small pearl buttons of her blouse as fast as she was able, smoothing the material, her hand lingering for one small moment over her baby. She glanced at her watch. It was four-thirty in the afternoon. How had she slept the day away again? Using cold water, Corinne splashed her face in an attempt to clear the fog from her brain. It was strange how tired she was. Was her heart giving out so soon? Abruptly she pulled her thoughts away from her mortality and concentrated on the problem at hand. Lisa was in danger, and nothing else mattered at that moment.

Running barefoot back into the bedroom, Corinne swept up her hair haphazardly and fastened it into a semblance of a ponytail. "Where are my shoes?" Even as she asked the question aloud, she focused on the missing items and drew them to her. The shoes found their own way out from under the bed and presented themselves to her open palms. Cullen stared at her in amazement. Ignoring him, Corinne sat back on the bed and pulled on the sandals. "Stop staring at me, Cullen," she commanded. "I didn't know where the darn things were. Lisa must have taken a cab. We'll have to use your car; mine is still at the house. Where is it?"

"Right outside on the street. Don't bring it in here," he responded dryly.

Corinne's vivid green eyes flickered over him, then began to dance in spite of the gravity of the situation. "I wonder if I could. Where's Dayan?" He had been with her when she fell asleep. She remembered that quite distinctly.

Cullen cleared his throat. "It's a little early for him, but he'll know where we've gone when he wakes up. He always knows." He tried to sound reassuring.

Corinne's hands stilled around the strap of her purse. "Why don't you wake him up?" There was something in Cullen's demeanor that made her suspicious, but of what, she didn't know.

"He didn't stay here last night. After you went to sleep, he left. He likes his privacy," Cullen added a little lamely.

"Isn't that strange, when he's so quick to invade mine," Corinne murmured. She snatched up her purse and headed determinedly for the door. "Come on if you're coming. I want to make sure Lisa is safe."

"I'm coming, all right, and I'll have a few things to say to Lisa when I see her," Cullen added, holding open the door for Corinne.

"It doesn't do any good to get mad at Lisa," Corinne counseled as she slipped into the passenger seat. "She doesn't view things like other people. Yelling doesn't work with her, it only distresses her. I don't want her hurt, Cullen."

"Isn't that what we're trying to prevent?" he asked between his teeth.

"That isn't what I'm talking about. She's very vulnerable. I'm sure she told you about her brother's death."

"Which is exactly why she should be taking this seriously," he pointed out. "She's too trusting."

"There's nothing wrong with that, Cullen," Corinne said gently. "That's what makes Lisa Lisa. She is trusting and genuinely sweet and good." She glanced at his set features. "I've never seen her with a man the way she is with you. She talks a great deal, but she doesn't really fall for anyone. Don't do anything to hurt her."

Cullen laughed unexpectedly. "I believe she was planning to have this exact talk with Dayan about you."

Corinne tossed her head, her hair swinging against the window with an independent little swish. "I am perfectly capable of looking out for myself. Lisa, on the other hand, is not." Her eyes flashed at him in warning.

"I hear you, Corinne," Cullen admitted with a small grin. "I'm not the playboy type. I can't believe she even looked at me. And these same people who murdered your husband are after me. I know what they're like. I would never have acted on my feelings if she hadn't already been in danger. The minute I met her, I was attracted to her. I had no idea she would be at all interested in someone like me." He drove fast but expertly. After Lisa's wild driving, Corinne was appreciative of his skill. "I could easily fall in love with Lisa if I allowed myself to spend any time with her. In the last few years, I've never looked at a woman in that way." There was a heartbeat of silence. "I never thought I could—not again."

"What is Dayan like?" Corinne asked in spite of herself.

Cullen shrugged with studied casualness. "Dayan is a law unto himself. No one can predict what he might do. He's a genius with a musical instrument, and his voice is beautiful. He's loyal to a fault, but he isn't a man another man would ever want to cross. I don't know how to explain Dayan. But I've never seen him like this over a woman. Whatever he feels for you is genuine. He isn't a ladies' man."

"Why am I hearing a *but* in there somewhere?" Corinne asked astutely.

"I didn't say 'but,' " he denied.

"You have reservations about Dayan," Corinne guessed. "What are they?"

Cullen looked at her very soberly, concentrating on

putting his vague uneasiness into words. Finally he shrugged, shaking his head. "He's just different. Dangerous, maybe, I don't know how to explain it to you. The entire band is different. Darius is a very scary man. Seriously, Corinne, Dayan is just different. I don't know how else to explain it. The whole family . . ." He trailed off helplessly. There were no words to adequately describe Dayan's family.

"Dangerous to me? He isn't the type of man to hurt a woman." She believed that with her heart and soul. She *knew* it with every fiber of her being. "What aren't you telling me, Cullen? Does it have something to do with my heart? The pregnancy? Or something to do with Dayan disappearing each time I wake up?"

Cullen glanced at her set face. "Corinne, he doesn't want to be with anyone else. If you think he has someone else stashed somewhere, you're wrong. I'm not worried too much about your heart condition; I even tried reassuring Lisa, because she's very afraid. But Dayan's family can work miracles.

"I never imagined Dayan with a woman, so protective and . . ." He trailed off, shaking his head. "But I've seen it before in the band members. You should meet Darius. Now, there's a scary man, but with Tempest he acts entirely different, the way Dayan does with you."

Exasperated with him, Corinne stared out the window at the passing traffic. Clearly, Cullen was concerned about something, yet he wasn't going to tell her. Maybe it had nothing to do with Dayan and everything to do with her. Maybe Cullen didn't want his friend mixed up with someone like her. She was pregnant. She had a bad heart, and she moved objects around with her mind.

With each passing mile she felt more tired, more strained, her heart laboring so hard it was difficult to breathe. And she thought of Dayan. Worried about him when she should have been worrying about Lisa. What if Dayan had returned to their home again and someone had hurt him? Perhaps he was lying injured somewhere, needing her help, and she was unaware of it.

"Dayan didn't go back to my house last night, did he?" There was a little catch in her voice that she couldn't prevent.

Cullen shook his head. "Not a chance. He had no need. He took you with him to retrieve the things you and Lisa wanted. I was surprised he did that, by the way. I would have bet my last dollar that he would have tied you up at our house to keep you safe. How did you talk your way around him?"

"He's very reasonable." Even as she said it, the car was taking her further and further from him, and her heart was laboring harder and harder.

"You're certain he didn't go back to the house? We ran into trouble—did Dayan tell you?" She tried to sound matter-of-fact about it.

Cullen pinned her with speculative eyes. "No, he didn't say a single word. What kind of trouble?"

Corinne rubbed her pounding temple. She was feeling sick to her stomach. And the terrible dread was increasing with each passing mile. "Things. A peculiar fog bank. There was someone at the house. Dayan went out into the fog, and then we went into the house. There was a car . . ." She trailed off, trying to pull the memory out of her hazy brain. "I can't think—I feel sick."

"Do you have medicine you should be taking?" Cullen was concerned about her color. Corinne was deathly white.

They were approaching the large park where Lisa was to do the photo shoot. To their left, Cullen could see the vehicles crowded together. An area was cordoned off for the cameras and crew. Corinne put both hands protectively over her stomach. She was feeling very sick, struggling just to sound as if she were breathing normally.

"Corinne!" Cullen said sharply. "Do you have medicine with you?"

She nodded toward her purse. Her heart was pounding hard, erratically. The baby was moving in alarm. Cullen spilled out two tablets into his palm, very afraid for her. He never should have brought her with him to this place.

'Corinne.' The voice was soft and steady, a brushing like butterfly wings in her head. *'What is wrong with your heart? You must calm down.'*

Dayan's voice alone managed to calm her. Where was he? The fact that he could reach her reassured her that he was alive and well. Corinne took the tablets and made an effort to breathe rhythmically. *'I am okay now, Dayan.'*

'You are not where I left you.' It was a clear reprimand. *'Where are you?'*

"Corinne?" Cullen asked anxiously. "I shouldn't have brought you. If anything happens to you, Lisa and Dayan will kill me."

It was strange to carry on two conversations at the same time. "Nothing is going to happen to me, Cullen. See, I'm much better." *'We've come for Lisa. She went to a park where they're photographing her.'*

'No! It is not safe. I cannot come to you yet. Leave that place at once!' It was a clear order, delivered tersely with a hard "push" behind it.

She wanted to obey him. Needed to obey him more than anything else in the world. Everything in her demanded she do as he told her, but there was Lisa. As much as her entire heart and soul required that she comply with that order, she could not leave without Lisa. *'Don't be upset, Dayan. I will get home as soon as I have Lisa safe with us. Cullen is here too.'*

Dayan lay helpless beneath the earth, seething with rage. With fear that amounted to terror. He didn't dare make his command any stronger. Corinne was strong-willed and she was fighting him. Her loyalty to Lisa demanded that she get her sister-in-law to safety. Dayan knew her heart would not survive a struggle against him. He subsided, a shadow in her mind. The time until sundown seemed to tick away with agonizing slowness.

"Maybe you'd better stay in the car," Cullen said uneasily. Dayan was working on him, pushing at Cullen's mind so that he felt it was of paramount importance to protect Corinne. "It won't take me long to collect her."

"You'll never get through security," Corinne replied, resolutely pushing open the door. She slipped out before her reluctant body refused to do as she asked.

Cullen leapt out of the car and raced around it to take her arm. She walked determinedly along the walkway to the path that cut through to the interior of the park. At the area cordoned off for the shoot, she waved to the nearest security man and flashed a smile at him. "Frank! I didn't know you'd be working today or I would have come sooner. How's Lisa doing?"

The man in uniform grinned at her. "My favorite woman. I was desolate without you. You know how Lisa's doing. She couldn't make a mistake if she wanted to." He reached across the rope to loosen the latch and let her through.

Inside Corinne's mind, Dayan was suddenly very still. He wasn't prepared for the surge of adrenaline sweeping through his body, the flood of black jealousy at the stranger's words or Corinne's obvious affection for him. She was far too attractive and didn't seem to realize when men genuinely admired or wanted her. Dayan had come to resent the dead hours of the day when his body needed to rejuvenate. Even in his sleep, when he

181

lay as dead, he missed her. Needed her. Craved her like a drug in his blood.

"This is Cullen, Frank. I've hired him as a personal bodyguard for Lisa. We've been getting weird phone calls, and I've been so paranoid since John's death. I know I'm being silly, but I just don't want to take any chances with Lisa."

Corinne was looking up at Frank with her vivid green eyes, and the security guard was melting on the spot. Even Cullen could see that. Dayan could see it too. Inside him the beast was roaring with anger and a terrible rage. Hot lava was boiling up through his bloodstream even as his body lay paralyzed, locked beneath the earth. It took a tremendous amount of self-control to keep from using Corinne or Cullen to retaliate against the guard. The man wanted Corinne, but Dayan couldn't really fault him.

"Should I put my crew on alert, Corinne?" Frank asked, his blue eyes worried. "Are you expecting trouble?" John's murder had shocked them all. John had loved his sister and had come often to watch her photo shoots. Lisa was different from the majority of the other models, the ones who never spoke to the security crew. John and Corinne had almost always been at Lisa's shoots and had gone out of their way to speak to everyone. The three of them were unfailingly polite, warm and friendly. They remembered everyone's name and inquired about family members.

Corinne glanced up at Cullen, a question in her eyes. He nodded, his gaze slowly sweeping the area. There was a large crowd watching the proceedings, and a large crowd was a nightmare to him. Corinne smiled up at Frank. "Just ask them to watch for someone different—I don't know, anyone who looks like he might have a gun."

Frank nodded, all business. At once he spoke into

his radio and waved Corinne and Cullen toward the group where the filming was going on. Cullen leaned down to whisper close to Corinne's ear, "They're here somewhere. I know they are."

Corinne's breath caught in her throat. She looked around rather wildly, desperate to find Lisa. Dayan's soft voice, as calm as ever, brushed at her mind. *'What is it, honey?'*

'Cullen says Lisa's in danger; those men must be here.'

'That means you are in danger also, Corinne.' Dayan was holding his breath, counting the minutes, the seconds, until it was safe for him to rise. He was Carpathian, not vampire; he could rise before the setting of the sun, but not now, not when the sun had reduced his great strength and power to nothing. He waited, conserving what little energy he might have so he could aid Corinne should it become necessary.

Corinne walked across the uneven lawn toward the spot where the lights were set up in the middle of the wooded park. A small, frothy waterfall fell with a rush into a deep pool hollowed out of rock. Ferns grew in every nook and cranny surrounding the pool. Lisa was standing beside the pool in the midst of the greenery, looking slim and cool and beautiful. Corinne wanted to cry, she was so proud of her. Lisa was a professional and very thankful for the job and the money it provided her and her family. She was easy to work with, followed directions carefully, and the camera loved her. She had become very popular with photographers and clients for just those reasons.

Cullen simply stared at her, astonished that she had ever given him more than a casual glance. She looked nothing like the shy, vulnerable young woman he knew her to be. She looked like a goddess to him. She was a seductress in front of the camera, then turned to laugh easily with the photographer, joke with the makeup artist, tease the hairdresser. When she noticed Cullen, her face lit up and she waved. For one moment he forgot he had come on a rescue mission.

"Keep your mind on work," Corinne reminded him. "You're supposed to be her bodyguard. No ogling the client."

Cullen grinned sheepishly and edged his body in front of Corinne's as his gaze swept the crowd, looking for familiar faces. He was high on the society's hit list, branded a traitor by the organization. Somewhere in that crowd were men with guns—he was certain of it. "Maybe you should get back in the car," he told Corinne.

"You'll never get Lisa to come until this is over." Corinne was walking carefully through the maze of cable toward Lisa. She waved at a photographer she knew. "Are you on a break? I need to talk with Lisa." She held up one finger, indicating a quick chat.

The photographer nodded at her. "We can't decide if she looks better standing or sitting. Lisa can carry anything off."

"She's getting eaten alive by the mosquitoes," the hairdresser called as she patted Lisa's shimmering hair, then swatted at a bug landing on her own arm. "Honestly, Matt, these wilderness locations are dangerous."

"Not too much longer, Lisa," the photographer called back. "We'll lose the light pretty soon anyway."

Corinne had nearly reached Lisa's side when she glanced up and saw a man hidden above Lisa in the rocks. For one moment she thought he was part of the shoot, a male model, before it registered that he was short and plump and not at all handsome. As he half turned, the sun's rays glinted on something in his fist. Her heart in her throat, Corinne hurled herself at Lisa, catching her around the waist and driving both of them backward into the shrubbery. "Cullen!" she called out, terrified the unknown man would be able to get a clear shot at Cullen.

Both women fell heavily in a tangle of arms and legs. Corinne didn't care—she was concentrating on the object in the man's hand, fixing on it with her mind, determined to spoil his aim. She actually felt the intensity in the man as he fought for control. She saw people running toward her, saw two more men in the rocks out of the corner of her eye. Nothing mattered but covering Lisa protectively and keeping the man from shooting Cullen. She heard Dayan cry out in warning, felt his withdrawal from her mind. He had been providing emotional support, and it hurt that he left now when she was most afraid, when she didn't want to be alone.

Deep within the ground, Dayan shook with fear for her, raged at his inability to break free of the terrible paralysis that gripped his race during the daylight hours. He merged with Cullen, "seeing" through his eyes. Security guards were racing around in all directions, people were yelling, and Cullen was trying to make his way toward the two women. He was looking at his destination rather than at the wild crowd. Dayan drew a deep breath, let it out slowly to control his own panic. He forced Cullen to stop running and take a long look around himself to give Dayan a clear view of what was happening.

First he took care of the man struggling with Corinne for possession of the gun. Instead of attacking the weapon, Dayan went for the throat of the man, closing off his airway so that he had no time to think about shooting anyone. He let go of the gun, and it clattered downward through the rocks. He grasped at his throat in an attempt to fight off the unseen hands squeezing him like a vise. Only when the assailant fell from the rocks did Dayan, using Cullen's eyes, do a slow sweep of the crowd in search of other possible threats.

One man was dragging Corinne backward, away from the rocks toward the deeper thicket of trees, out of eyesight of the fast-moving security guards. The guards were converging on Lisa, who was still on the ground. Two women were screaming, and the scene was fast turning to chaos. Dayan forced Cullen to follow Corinne even though the human male wanted to go to Lisa, who was clearly sobbing, trying to fight her way past the security people to get to Corinne.

Dayan thought only of the man holding his lifemate. He allowed nothing else in his mind. He stared directly at the arm around her throat in an L choke hold. Almost at once the muscles in the man's arm began to swell. He yelled and released Corinne's neck, only to shove her in the back as she attempted to run from him. Right before Dayan's eyes, she went down hard, her hands going out to try to protect the baby from the rocky ground.

Swearing eloquently to himself in the ancient language, Dayan used his last remaining surge of power to buckle the earth so that Corinne's assailant fell hard, his head striking a jutting rock. At once more rocks tumbled down, dislodged by the minor quake, at first slowly, then raining down in a concentrated shower, striking the man's head and chest so that he was partially buried beneath the heavy stones.

That was all Dayan could do until the earth renewed his strength and the sun began to wane. With one last look at Corinne, lying small and fragile in the dirt, he reluctantly broke the mind merge with Cullen, his spirit retreating to its resting place, where his body already lay paralyzed.

Cullen turned to look at Lisa, who was struggling wildly with the security guards. "Corinne! Cullen, get to Corinne. Someone call an ambulance." Tears were streaming down Lisa's face.

Cullen was sprinting toward Corinne's fallen body when something hit him hard from behind, spinning him halfway around. His breath slammed out of him, leaving him gasping for air. He registered Lisa's high-pitched scream, saw people throwing themselves to the ground and running for cover. He never heard the gunshot. He wasn't even certain what actually happened, but when he tried to continue his forward momentum to reach Corinne, his legs turned to rubber and he found himself sitting abruptly on the edge of the grassy lawn.

"Cullen!" Lisa did manage to break free for a moment before a security guard threw her to the ground and covered her body with his.

It was Frank who aimed his gun very carefully, his hand steady when the gunman continued running toward Corinne. Frank called out a warning, loud and clear, hoping the man would stop. Instead, he turned and fired at the security guard, all in one smooth motion. The bullet thunked into a tree beside the security guard's head. Without flinching, Frank squeezed the trigger. He found he was whispering to himself, "No. No, don't." The gunman stood still, staring in dismay at Frank, his gun falling in a strange slow motion from his hand. He looked down at the crimson stain spreading across his chest and then up at Frank before he fell onto his knees and then face down, half on the rocks and half on the lawn.

For a moment there was only the sound of sobbing, and then people slowly began to look at one another, realizing the violence was over as quickly as it had started. Frank kept his gun aimed steadily on the stranger who had shot at him as he walked slowly toward him. Sirens could be heard in the distance, coming closer fast. Frank glanced anxiously at Corinne. She was very still, face down in the rocks.

Minutes later Lisa was climbing into an ambulance with Corinne, clutching Corinne's purse, tears running down her face. Cullen was being loaded into another ambulance. Lisa pressed a hand to her mouth to keep from crying out loud. "I did this," she whispered to Corinne.

Corinne was so pale she looked gray. Around her lips was a distinctive blue color that horrified Lisa. "She's pregnant," she said unnecessarily to the paramedics, "and she has a bad heart."

An oxygen mask covered Corinne's face. She looked small and helpless, very vulnerable and fragile. Already broken. As if she had already gone far away from Lisa. Lisa took a firm hold of her hand, wanting to cling to her, to prevent Corinne from slipping away. "Is she going to be all right?"

The ambulance was moving very fast, the paramedics talking on their radio, putting things into Corinne's IV. None of them looked directly at Lisa, and none answered her question. She touched Corinne's stomach, the baby. John and Corinne's baby. She didn't want to lose either of them. And if the worst happened and Corinne's heart gave out, Lisa wanted that tiny little part of her to live. "It's too early for you, baby," she crooned softly. "Way too early."

At the hospital Lisa was hustled out of the emergency room. She could only watch helplessly as they rushed Cullen into a cubicle beside Corinne. A policewoman came in after a long while to talk to her, but nobody said anything about Corinne or Cullen. Eventually the waiting room was filled with people: her photographer, her agent, Frank the security guard. The one person she looked for, waited for, knew she could lean on, the one person she dreaded most, didn't come.

Dayan. She would never be able to look him in the eye. Why hadn't she just listened to them all? Lisa hadn't wanted it all to be true. Murders didn't happen to regular people; she and Corinne were finished with that world. She had worked hard and found a new life. One that didn't include murder. She sat quietly, her fists clenched tightly, wanting to cry and cry forever.

Dayan lay locked in the earth, counting the minutes until he could rise without danger. He burst from the soil, dirt spewing like a geyser as he shot into the sky, shape-shifting as he did so. The sun was low but had not set, and the light hit his eyes so that they burned and wept. Or maybe it wasn't the sun. Dayan didn't know for certain as he winged his way swiftly across the sky toward the hospital where she lay.

His world. His life. The best part of him. She lay dying in a hospital. He knew it. He felt it. He kept his mind firmly merged with hers so that she couldn't possibly release her spirit from her dying body. *'You will hold on.'* He commanded it with every fiber of his being, bent his entire will to ensure her obedience.

'I am so tired.'

'Rest then, but you will not let go.'

'I hear them talking. They do not think they can save my baby.' There was sorrow in her mind, in her heart. A terrible weariness as if she had given up along with the doctors, as if she could no longer continue to struggle against the tremendous odds.

'Do not leave me alone!' he cried out. It was a plea. An order. *'No one needs you as I do. Do not leave me alone ever again.'*

'Dayan. You are strong. So very strong. There will be another for you.'

Even in her darkest hour she was thinking of him. Of Cullen and Lisa. She was piecing it together in her mind. Their future. Their happiness. She arranged it the way she thought would work best.

Dayan surrounded her waning spirit, locked her

firmly to him. *'There will never be another for me. Never. Should I survive your loss and continue for all eternity, I would no longer be me, but something hideous, an abomination. An evil monster. I will not become such a creature. I would choose to follow you into the next life. We are one, Corinne. One. There is no Dayan without Corinne. You have no choice but to live. For the daughter you carry inside you. For me. For our unborn children. For Lisa. I will not release you. Not now. Not ever.'*

He was much closer now, moving swiftly as the sun sank below the horizon. Colors splashed the sky blood red, and the wind was beginning to pick up, an ominous sign. Dayan was no longer the easygoing poet, the gentle man Corinne knew. He was a male Carpathian at full strength, and something was threatening his life-mate.

He strode unseen past the doctors and nurses, leaving a freezing cold in his wake. Past Lisa, huddled in the room where Cullen lay pale and bandaged and still unconscious. Dayan spared his friend a quick glance, attempting to assess the damage as he hurried to Corinne. Without her, he couldn't help Cullen or anyone else. His first thought, his first duty, was to Corinne.

She lay on the bed, hooked up to lines and bottles. She was very pale, almost transparent. Despite the oxygen, there was a blue tint around her mouth. Corinne looked small and thin beneath the single cover. She looked a mere child, a waxen doll. She was laboring hard for each breath. Leads ran from her heart to a machine and from her abdomen to another machine. Dayan stood looking down at her, his heart in his throat. She looked so fragile, he was afraid to touch her.

There was a familiar stirring in his mind. Warmth. Reassurance. Total confidence. *'Dayan? We are much closer. Bring her to the healers. We are gathering.'* It was

Darius. His friend. His family. Darius could always be counted on.

Dayan allowed himself to breathe. *'Cullen is in need. I cannot take the time to attend him. I will hold Corinne to me as long as I am able, but should I lose her, I will choose her path at once. I did not bind her and there has been no blood exchange, so I do not have the control needed for such a fight.'*

'You do have it, Dayan. You will not allow her to slip away from you.' As always, Darius was completely confident. *'I will send help to Cullen. Barack and Syndil will go to him. He knows them and he will not be distressed. Come to us now. Bring your lifemate that together we may save her life.'*

Dayan knelt beside the bed and took Corinne's hand. For a moment it lay there in his larger palm limply, but then slowly her fingers curled around his. He watched her long lashes flutter before she managed to open her eyes. "Dayan." There was a smile in her voice. "I think I was dreaming about you, or were we just talking?" Her voice was so low, such a faint thread of sound, he would never have heard her if he didn't have such acute hearing.

"I do not suppose you are aware that I love you." He said the words against her temple, his lips brushing her pulse tenderly. "Did they talk to you? The doctors?"

"They don't have to talk to me. I know I'm dying." Her eyes filled with tears. "I don't want to lose the baby. I want her to live."

"Do you trust me, Corinne? Really trust me?"

Her eyes closed again as if it was too difficult to keep them open. "Yes, of course."

"No, honey, you have to know what you are saying. Do you trust me with your life? With the life of your baby?" He willed her to open her eyes and look at him.

She blinked up at him. "I know what I'm saying."

"I am going to take you out of here."

"They won't let you." She closed her eyes again. It was a struggle just to breathe. Carrying on a conversation was far too difficult.

"They cannot stop me."

Dayan studied the lines running in all directions for a few minutes, then as he unhooked her carefully, he produced the same rhythms as the monitors, simply using his brain to work them. He lifted her carefully into his strong arms and strode boldly right out of the room into the hall with her. He moved easily among the humans, shielding Corinne and himself from human eyes as he made his way out of the hospital and into the night.

It was darker now and storm clouds were beginning to swirl above their heads. In his arms Corinne shivered, unable to maintain her body temperature. Dayan automatically did it for her, holding their mind-merge, breathing for her, aiding her failing heart. He took two running steps and leapt into the air with his slight burden held close to his heart.

Chapter Ten

Corinne heard the whisper of a voice. Faint. Far off. She loved that voice, the way it caressed her name, turned it into something sinfully intimate. Dayan was calling her. She was dreaming, though, and it was a beautiful dream. She struggled to open her eyes. Voices surrounded her, seeped into her heart and soul. Strains of music. The sound of water. She became aware she was lying comfortably on something other than a bed. It seemed a great stone slab, but it didn't feel hard. She lifted her lashes and stared up at the ceiling of a cave. She was in a crystal cave!

Corinne looked around herself in sheer amazement. Everything was beautiful, a world of crystal and steam with the flickering light of a thousand candles. The air was scented with an aroma she had never smelled before, but she inhaled in an attempt to take it deep into her lungs. It was soothing, tranquil in this place, surreal even. She knew she was dreaming again, but if such a place could never actually exist, Corinne was grateful she could visit it in her dreams.

She watched the dancing shadows flickering on the walls of the cave. The steam rose and swirled lazily, forming interesting shapes. It was difficult to focus on any one thing, and Corinne allowed her gaze to drift around the large chamber. She seemed to be in a subterranean city of some kind. There were many entrances and large open areas that she could see, almost as if the cave had a network of tunnels and chambers that ran deeper and also rose above where she was resting. The chamber she was in seemed very large, and a pool of steaming water was to her left. When she looked closer, she could see she was in a series of underground caves, with large cathedral ceilings and a stream that moved through a maze of tunnels. Stalactites formed huge sculptural works of arts, hanging from the ceiling. They were dazzling to look at. It seemed a sparkling world of gems and colors.

It took a few moments to realize she wasn't alone. There were several people in the large chamber with her. They were all around her and chanting in a foreign language. It was like a beautiful melody, dark and mysterious, a sacred ritual of some kind. The men were very handsome, their faces sober and intent, the women beautiful beyond description. The chanting filled the underground chamber with the haunting rhythm of the earth itself so that Corinne began to feel it in her veins. It was running through her like a river, ebbing and flowing with the cycle of life.

The ritual didn't alarm her; in fact, she felt very secure lying there watching them all. She studied each of them for some sign that they were familiar to her. The men were exotically handsome. They wore their hair long, their bodies were trim. All of them were intimidating to look at, yet, strangely, she wasn't frightened. They resembled Dayan, as if they could be closely related. All of them were chanting, and their voices were beautiful.

Corinne turned her attention to the women. Three of the women had long dark hair flowing nearly to their waists, while the fourth had rich red hair. All of them were graceful in their movements. Corinne found herself watching them singing, admiring the way they moved, their gestures and voices, their uncommon grace. The pattern of their hands and the swaying of their bodies were mesmerizing to watch.

After a time she became aware of the hand holding hers firmly. Carefully, because it was almost too much trouble, she turned her head toward that side of her body. To her astonishment, Dayan was standing beside her, his fingers woven tightly with hers. He was chanting the same foreign words as the others in the cave. As dreams went, it was strange and yet utterly beautiful. Had she died? She felt she was deep within the ground, maybe near the center of the earth. It was warm, with steam rising from several of the pools of water, yet the frothy falls cascading out of the walls were icy cold.

Corinne was certain she hadn't died, because her head was throbbing terribly from where it had struck the rocks. Her body felt bruised and battered, and she was terribly tired. It hurt just to breathe. She could feel her heart pounding in her chest. She was definitely alive, she decided.

Dayan leaned down to brush a kiss across her forehead, his warm breath a healing balm to the scrapes and bruises there. "This is my family, my people. I do not want you to be afraid, Corinne. Strange things may happen here, but one of our greatest healers will attempt to strengthen you and save your baby. I will be with you every step of the way."

Her eyes moved over his face. "You look so worried,

Dayan." Her voice was soft and very loving in this un-
guarded moment.

Tears burned in his eyes, in his throat. He was
breathing for her, regulating her heart, keeping her
alive as effectively as the human machines had done.
He bent closer so he could look directly into her eyes.
"I want you to live, Corinne. Do you understand me? I
need you to live for me."

She nodded, sudden tears swimming in her eyes. She
wanted to be his world, the air he breathed. She wanted
to listen to the sound of his beautiful voice for the rest
of her life, watch his eyes go from bleak emptiness to
sudden desire for her. Her body was slowly fading, and
she knew that his faith in his healers would come to
nothing. It was too late for her.

The chanting continued around her, and Corinne settled back into her dreamlike state. It didn't matter to
her if any of it was real, she concentrated on the beauty
of her surroundings and the symphony of voices to
keep the fear of dying at bay. Most of all, she didn't
want to think about her child. She had failed to give
her daughter the necessary time to grow.

"Honey." Dayan's voice intruded again, catching her
attention.

Corinne watched as a tall, slender woman with long
black hair approached her. The woman smiled reassuringly. "Corinne, sister kin." She touched Corinne's
hand with gentle fingers. "I am Desari, lifemate to Julian
and sister to Dayan, now to you." Her voice was musical, soothing, a healing in itself. "We have with us one
of our greatest healers." She turned to gesture toward a
man with slashing silver eyes.

Corinne watched as the man glided to her side. He
was more muscular than the other men, with long blue-
black hair. Power emanated from him. He smiled down
at her, softening the cruel edge of his mouth. He took

her hand. "We are awaiting Shea, one well versed in the care of our infants. Please allow my brother Darius and me to do our best to delay the child's arrival until Shea's journey is complete."

For a moment Corinne could only stare at him, dazzled by his raw power. She was reluctant for the healer to touch her, to learn the truth. Like Dayan, Gregori seemed to believe he could somehow do what all the doctors had failed to do.

Desari gestured again and a second man came forward. He looked very much like Gregori, only with black eyes that seemed to suit his dark good looks. "My brother Darius, now your brother. He will assist Gregori in this attempt."

Darius bowed, a courtly gesture, then raised Corinne's limp fingers to his mouth. "Welcome to our family, little sister. We wish your permission to attempt to heal you."

Dayan brought Corinne's small hand to his mouth. "Please, honey. I know this is strange to you, but for me, please try whatever they ask of you. Shea and Jacques have not yet arrived, and we must delay the birth until we have Shea here. Without her, the chances of saving the baby are much less."

Corinne looked up at Dayan and was instantly lost in the black abyss of his eyes. He looked so vulnerable; his feelings for her were stark and unprotected, written in every line of his face. Dayan leaned closer. "I need you to do this, Corinne. Please trust me, baby; this one time, do this for me." His words were whispered intimately to her, his need so great it brought tears to her eyes.

Corinne nodded and allowed Gregori to take her left hand. How could she ever refuse Dayan anything when he looked at her like that? Her right hand remained firmly in Dayan's. She didn't want to be alone with her failing body and strangers with slashing eyes and far too much power.

Gregori closed his eyes and sent himself seeking outside his own body and into the mortal lying so frail before him. Her human heart was nearly useless. It was Dayan who supplied the power to keep Corinne going. Gregori moved on to examine the baby. The child was female. Aware. Too small to be born yet. Gregori reassured Corinne and moved quickly out again.

'There is little time. Without Dayan aiding her she would have died, and the child with her. Darius, the child is female and a strong psychic. We cannot afford to lose either of them.' Gregori spoke to his brother, but he used the common mental path every Carpathian used so all those present would understand the dire need. *'I will work on the woman, as it is imperative she live for both of them. You take care of the child.'*

I have only done such a thing with Desari when she was an infant, never a babe in the womb.' Darius moved up beside Gregori and glanced once at Dayan. *'I will do what needs to be done.'*

'She will need your blood, Dayan, and she must not fight the transfer. She does not have any strength to waste so make sure she accepts it willingly. Darius will monitor the baby to determine whether her body can accept your blood. You cannot convert your lifemate while the child resides in her. The child would not live through such a difficult transformation. At this time, neither would Corinne.' Gregori was in complete command, his voice confident as he gave instructions.

Dayan half lifted Corinne so he could sit on the slab, cradling her on his lap. He bent his head toward hers, enclosing them in a private world. "What I offer you is life, Corinne. For both of us." His breath stirred the thick mass of hair tumbling over her shoulders. She felt his lips traveling over her bare skin, his teeth scraping gently back and forth over her irregular pulse. He murmured something soft in his strange language.

Corinne felt herself slipping further and further into her dream world. With Dayan's arms around her and his body so close to hers, she felt safe and protected. And then white lightning streaked through her, something between pleasure and pain. She lay passively in the crystal world of dreams and music. The flickering flames cast reflections on the wall from the pools of water, reflections that danced and mesmerized, tiny flames of orange and gold.

She felt the presence of the healer once again. Corinne felt a peculiar warmth as if another's spirit shared her body, just as when Dayan had attempted to heal her. It was strangely comforting. With the other presence, her heart seemed to labor less. She was tired, though—very tired. It was too difficult to keep her eyes open even though she wanted to observe the beauty of the chamber and the people in it.

Dayan closed the tiny pinpricks after taking enough blood for a ritual exchange. He shifted Corinne in his arms while he opened his shirt with one hand. "You will do this for us, my love," he commanded softly, gently, using a tone that banished her free will, that ensured she would do as he ordered. One fingernail lengthened into a sharp talon. Dayan opened his chest with a swift slash and pressed Corinne to him. "Drink, Corinne. I offer my life for your life. I offer my life for the life of our child."

Corinne was rather horrified that her beautiful dream had taken such a twisted turn. She couldn't quite force her eyelashes to lift, so she couldn't really look around, she could only lie in Dayan's arm, swallowing the warm liquid. In her dream she could be analytical about it. None of it was real anyway. She was cradled in Dayan's arms, belonging to him; he had taken her blood first, then given her his as if he could make her strong and physically fit. It all made some kind of weird sense, what with vampire stalkers thinking she was a vampire anyway. What was particularly strange to her was the fact that she didn't seem to mind taking his blood.

Gregori moved toward the struggling heart, seeking to find ways to control the damage. Without the baby, Dayan could give Corinne the necessary blood to survive, but that choice wasn't available to them until the baby was born. Gregori watched the healing blood pour into Corinne's frail body. At once her starving organs soaked it up like a healing balm. As Darius's spirit stayed close, monitoring the baby, Gregori went to work on the stuttering heart, meticulously repairing the damaged valve, utilizing the blood flowing freely into his patient. It wasn't the same as treating an injury. This damage was caused by a disease that had been slowly, insidiously wearing away at her heart. In her favor was Dayan's powerful blood flowing into her, along with his iron will, his heart and soul, his total, unconditional love.

Darius hovered close to the baby, soothing her, offering her reassurance and encouragement. As the blood of an ancient flowed into her little body, the transformation began. Her hearing would be superior, her looks enhanced, her body stronger. Corinne could only benefit from the blood, but the baby wasn't wholly formed yet. Reshaping her organs was going to be dangerous to the child. When the baby became frightened, bewildered by the strange sensations, Darius flooded her with warmth and reached out to make a telepathic bond with her. He told her stories of their world, of the Carpathians in need, of how precious she was to their people, how important it was that she hang on and stay with her mother who loved her so very much.

The small amount of blood Corinne had drunk was

now cycling through the child's body. Darius was merged with the baby and felt the rush like a fireball. '*Stop!*' he ordered sharply.

Dayan immediately inserted his hand to gently stop Corinne from feeding. He whispered the order to her, watching her face anxiously. Corinne was astonished when a tall, blond stranger with golden eyes leaned over and casually closed the deep wound on Dayan's chest with his tongue. He kept one hand on Dayan's shoulder, a gesture that spoke volumes to Corinne.

"Are you Julian, Desari's lifemate?" she startled them all by asking.

The man bowed slightly from the waist, his golden eyes on her face. "I am indeed Julian, lifemate to Desari and brother kin to Dayan. I am pleased to meet you, Corinne. We had hoped and prayed that Dayan would find you."

"Are you real? Is all of this real?" She was looking at him because he looked much more approachable than the other males.

He smiled at her, his teeth very white, very straight. "Do you want it to be?"

Corinne tightened her hold on Dayan. He was her reality. In her body, the baby was moving almost violently. She pressed one hand over her stomach protectively. "She doesn't like this, Dayan. I think I'd better be dreaming."

Gregori and Dayan both glanced apprehensively at Darius. He was still merged wholly with the baby. His concentration seemed total. Dayan leaned close to Corinne. "I know Darius. His strength of will. There is no way he will allow our baby to slip away from us." He bit gently, insistently at her knuckles to keep her attention focused on him. "Tell me how you are feeling, honey. Your color is slightly better." He was still merged with her, helping to regulate her heart and lungs, terrified of allowing her to try it on her own. "How do you feel?"

Mostly she was afraid for her baby. She took a moment to breathe evenly and stop her panic before it became full-blown. She did feel better; it wasn't such a terrible struggle just to breathe. She still felt weak and tired and wanted to sleep. "Dayan—" She said his name very softly, looking around once more. She was still in an underground chamber and there were still people around her. "Am I awake? I can't seem to tell the difference anymore, and it's alarming."

"Right at this moment you are very much awake, Corinne. Some of my family are here with us," Dayan said with gentle reassurance.

She examined his chest. His shirt was immaculate, unbuttoned, but his chest muscles were smooth, without a single blemish. There was no wound where she had fed. No sign of blood. For some reason, that provided the solace she needed for peace of mind. She was clearly mixing up her bizarre dreams with reality. "Tell me where Lisa is."

"At the hospital with Cullen. Do you remember what happened?"

"There was a man in the rocks above Lisa. He had a gun. I tackled her and fought with him . . ." She trailed off, looking around at the strangers. She lowered her voice. "You know, in my rather weird way. Everything is jumbled after that. I remember falling and trying to protect the baby." She rubbed carefully at the bump and scrapes on her forehead.

Dayan winced. Already dark bruises were beginning to show against her pale skin. Gregori had been far too busy to heal Corinne's superficial wounds, but it bothered Dayan that she was the least bit uncomfortable. He could feel her headache, pounding and throbbing, although she didn't complain. Questions were going around and around in her mind. Dayan provided answers. "Cullen was shot, honey. He's alive, and Barack and Syndil are on their way to the hospital to aid him. They will see to it that he does not die. Syndil is well versed in healing and has special gifts. Cullen knows Barack and Syndil, and Lisa will not be afraid, because she knows they are members of our band. She will allow them into his room." He didn't add that Lisa's permission was of little consequence as they could walk unseen past any guard at any time. Barack and Syndil were Carpathians at full strength, able to control the minds of the humans around them if necessary.

"Was it bad?" There was a tremor in Corinne's voice, and Dayan gathered her closer to him protectively.

"Honey, there is no need to worry about Cullen. If he was in trouble I would know. I am telepathic, remember? Barack and Syndil can easily communicate with me. They would report instantly if they could not handle the situation, and they would request that either Darius or Gregori come to the hospital at once." Dayan indicated the man with the slashing silver eyes and the small, dark-haired woman. "Gregori and Savannah have traveled from New Orleans to be with us. We owe them much."

Corinne rubbed her forehead again. She was grateful for everyone's concern, but she wished they'd all go home. She was tired, and there were too many of them. She wanted to sleep, not entertain, and her baby was still kicking violently. None of the others seemed to notice that the one they called Darius seemed to be in a trance of sorts.

She closed her eyes and rested her head against Dayan's shoulder. "Thank you all," she murmured, as politely as a child, her voice drowsy and weak.

Dayan glanced apprehensively at Gregori, who nodded at him in reassurance. *'It is good if she sleeps, Da-*

yan. I can take more time healing her, and Darius can work with the baby. She needs rest more than anything else. The repairs will not hold forever. This is temporary. I cannot give her a new heart. Help her to sleep.'

In the hospital Lisa sat with her head resting beside Cullen. She had cried until she was certain there were no more tears left. The doctors had told her Corinne was going to die. It was only a matter of time. They said they would leave the baby in her struggling body for as long as possible, but there was little hope the baby would survive once born. Then they told her they had no idea if Cullen would live or die. It was a waiting game. He was in bad shape, and the bullet had torn through lung and tissue, destroying everything in its path. They didn't know how he was still hanging on. As if that weren't enough, there had been a terrible commotion coming from Corinne's room as hospital staff, security guards and finally the police milled about. Fifteen long minutes later, when Lisa expected to hear that Corinne had died, they told her Corinne was gone. Vanished into thin air.

There was no way Corinne could have walked out of the hospital, everyone agreed on that, and no one had been seen near her room. When the monitors had signaled heart failure, the nurse had rushed in, only to discover the patient was gone. Lisa was terrified the men who had tried to murder them had somehow taken Corinne.

It was her fault. She had gone to the photo shoot even though they'd all told her she was in danger. Corinne had flown across the park, tackling her, protecting her without a thought for her own weak heart and the consequences to her and the baby. *They had tried to kill me!* Lisa tried to digest that information. Someone really wanted her dead. They had guns, and they would have shot her if Corinne and Cullen hadn't shown up to save her.

Lisa lifted her head to look at Cullen. He seemed so pale, and there were bandages everywhere. Lisa had lied and said she was his fiancée so she could stay with him. Once Corinne's disappearance had been confirmed, the hospital staff left Lisa strictly alone, posting guards at the door to Cullen's room. Obviously, no one knew what to say to her. Lisa didn't know what to do. John and Corinne had always handled the details of their lives.

She stuffed her hand into her mouth, biting hard to keep from screaming. She was responsible for this disaster. If she had listened, Corinne and the baby would still be safe. Cullen wouldn't be near death.

"But he will not die," a soft feminine voice said from behind her. "Do not be alarmed—I am Syndil and this is Barack."

Startled, Lisa spun around, nearly falling off the chair. She hadn't heard a thing, and the security guard hadn't escorted anyone into the room, yet two people were standing just inside the door. Her heart pounding in alarm, Lisa debated whether to scream for help. It took a moment before she recognized the names. Barack and Syndil from the Troubadour band. Dayan's friends.

"How did you get in here?" Lisa whispered. She didn't understand anything that was going on.

"Cullen has been our friend for a long time. He risked his life to warn us when we were in danger. We would never allow him to die," Barack told her. He smiled gently, looking directly into her eyes. "You must be Lisa, Corinne's sister. Dayan has told us much about you."

Lisa burst into a storm of fresh tears. "They've taken Corinne."

Syndil circled Lisa's shoulders comfortingly. "Corinne is fine, Lisa. She was dying here. Dayan could not allow such a thing. Gregori, one of our greatest healers, has come from New Orleans to help her. We are determined that Corinne and the baby will live." She squeezed Lisa's shoulders gently in reassurance and then glided the short distance to Cullen's side. At once her expression changed. "Barack, he is so pale. There is much damage." She touched Cullen's shoulder with gentle fingers. "It is difficult to see him this way."

"He will not be so for long," Barack answered confidently.

Lisa drew herself up to her full height. "Tell me about Corinne. Where is she? Dayan had no right to remove my sister from the hospital when she was so deathly ill. He had no right." For the first time in her life, Lisa was not going to hide from the truth, no matter how painful it might be.

Barack glanced back at her. "Lisa"—his voice was soft but compelling—"you know Dayan. You know that he loves Corinne and wants her to live. He needs her to live. He took her to the only people who have a chance of saving her. You wanted him to save her, remember?"

Lisa blinked rapidly. She found herself nodding, wondering why she was so upset. Of course Dayan would take care of Corinne. Anyone could tell he was crazy about her. She moved to stand beside the bed, reaching for Cullen's hand.

"Sit here near him and stay close while we work," Syndil invited softly. "No one will come in to disturb us."

"Corinne is really going to be all right? She's with Dayan?" Lisa sat in the chair because the relief was so tremendous that her rubbery legs threatened to give out.

"Gregori is reputed to be the best in the world." Syndil's voice was melodic, easy to listen to. "And yes,

Lisa," she continued, "Dayan is with Corinne and will not leave her side."

"Where? I need to see her."

Barack reached down and caught her chin, tilting her head so she was forced to look up at him. "You will see her soon, Lisa. Right now, your place is with Cullen. He needs you here. You know Corinne is in the best of hands, but Cullen is alone. He needs care. As soon as he is able to travel, he must be taken to a safe house which Syndil and I will secure. You will care for him there until he can go with you to where Corinne and Dayan are. It is what you want, and you will rest easy over Corinne's health, trusting in Dayan to inform you of her progress. Dayan must stay with Corinne; it is where he belongs." Barack's voice was mesmerizing, hypnotic. Lisa felt as if she were falling forward into his dark eyes.

Barack made perfect sense to her. She *had* to stay with Cullen. She was responsible for his terrible wound, and there was no one else to take care of him. Dayan's place was definitely with Corinne.

"I am going to teach you a healing chant, Lisa," Syndil said softly. "It will help us to aid Cullen. The words are in an ancient language, and they are very beautiful. Listen to the pattern of our words and repeat them with Barack. You will hear my voice rising with yours, but I will concentrate on healing Cullen. I have some small talent in this area—certainly not like Gregori's, but I believe I can do some good. Please lend your voice to us." Syndil sounded very gentle, her tone so pure and pleasing to the ear that Lisa could have listened to her forever.

Barack took several candles from his backpack and lit them, filling the room with a soothing scent. Lisa leaned close to Cullen. It was peculiar, but she could hear Syndil's voice chanting softly in her head. She was certain Syndil wasn't speaking aloud, yet she heard the words clearly and began to follow along with them, at first to herself, then joining Barack when he began to chant aloud. Lisa followed his example, repeating the beautiful-sounding words over and over. It was difficult to get the accent just right, but Lisa was determined to try. She had a strange feeling that Syndil really could help Cullen.

Syndil closed her eyes, focusing totally on the human male lying so still on the bed. At first images arose. Cullen smiling at her. Walking in the forest with him, talking and laughing. Cullen guarding her and Desari when someone had kidnapped Darius's lifemate. Cullen. He was held in high regard by the entire band. He was under their protection. Syndil took a deep breath, let it out slowly and sent herself outside her own body and into the one lying so still and wounded.

The wound was terrible. The bullet had ricocheted through Cullen's body, causing tremendous damage. Syndil began the delicate work of repairing from the inside out. The doctors had done a miraculous job, but Cullen was in trouble. She took her time, wanting to be meticulous. Barack would direct the hospital staff away from the room while she worked. If any of the society made an attempt to enter the hospital to kill Cullen, Barack would know. She kept her entire attention focused on repairing Cullen's organs. It was painstakingly slow work.

Exhausted and swaying with weariness, she made her way out of Cullen's body and back into her own. Barack immediately caught her around the waist to support her. "I'm so proud of you, Syndil. You really came through for him."

'He needs blood, Barack. Despite all the aid I have given him, he is still in danger. Our blood will ensure his recovery.' Syndil was drooping with weariness.

'*You need blood too.*' Barack's words were a whispered invitation.

Lisa jumped up and all but pushed Syndil into the chair. "Is he going to live?" she asked, almost ready to believe in a miracle. Barack and Syndil inspired confidence when she needed to hold on to hope desperately.

Syndil reached out and took her hand. "We will not give Cullen up to the other world just yet, Lisa. He deserves happiness, and it has been long since he has known such a thing. You care very much for him." She made it a statement.

Lisa nodded even as she hedged. "I just met him. But he's different. I really enjoy his company. And he was hurt trying to save me," she confessed in a little rush.

"He is not safe here, Lisa," Barack told her carefully. "You must realize that. The men who wanted to kill you and your sister want Cullen even more. The security guard placed at his door is very inexperienced. If Cullen remains here, the society will attempt to kill him. The security guard and Cullen and perhaps you will all die. Cullen has no other family. Our band is his family. We would like you to come with us to a place we know is safe. We must take Cullen there to safeguard him. We cannot be with him at all times, and he will need someone to help him while he heals."

Lisa's fingers curled into a fist. She didn't know what to do, whom to trust. Dayan had said much the same thing about Corinne, and he had been right. "This all started when we went into that bar," she accused recklessly.

Syndil looked directly at her. Her voice was gentle but very firm. "You know that is not true. Your brother was murdered by these same men. Just because you do not want something to be true, reality does not change. You must live in the real world, Lisa, not one of illusion. You are in danger, just as Cullen is. I will not force you to accompany us, but we are going to protect Cullen. I am asking you to trust us of your own free will."

'I will take her blood and insist on obedience.' Barack was annoyed with the woman. She was ridiculously stubborn.

'She is the one Cullen has chosen. Out of respect for him and for Dayan's lifemate, we cannot do such a thing.'

Barack snorted his opinion of that. "It was your refusal to accept reality that initiated this crisis. We could have lost both Cullen and Corinne. Did you want him shot? If so, you managed to accomplish it."

'Barack!' Syndil hissed a reprimand. *'What are you doing?'*

'I think we should take Cullen to safety and wipe his mind clean of this childish woman. She looks good, but what is that without substance?'

Cullen's hand moved, his fingers creeping toward Lisa's. "As I recall, Barack," he whispered, "not so long ago you wanted to shoot me yourself. I seem to inspire that reaction in people. What happened to me?"

Syndil leaned close to him, her hand gentle as she stroked back the hair from Cullen's forehead. Lisa was weeping quietly again. "You were shot protecting Corinne and Lisa. As always, you played the hero," Syndil answered him.

"Still trying to show me up in front of beautiful women," Barack said, grinning affectionately down at Cullen.

Cullen's gaze sought Lisa's, but she avoided his eyes by hanging her head even as she clung to his hand. "You never seem to appreciate a woman until I point out her good qualities, Barack."

"Do not seek to get me in trouble with this reminder

of my former behavior, Cullen," Barack said, keeping his tone light despite his worry. Cullen was almost gray. Barack looked anxiously at Syndil.

His lifemate smiled reassuringly at Barack. "It is true, Cullen," Syndil said. "I have a long memory, and you are the one who made me feel I could live again. You must rest and do as we say."

"I want Lisa taken care of." Cullen was looking at Lisa with love in his eyes.

Barack cleared his throat but subsided quickly when Syndil glared at him.

"Lisa, don't cry," Cullen said softly. "You're breaking my heart."

"He's right, though—it was my fault. I went to the photo shoot because I didn't want to believe there was a problem. And now you're hurt and so is Corinne."

"Corinne?" Cullen turned his head to look at Barack. "Where is Corinne?"

"She is with Dayan," Barack said soothingly, bending down to look into Cullen's pain-filled eyes. "You are to rest and heal, Cullen. Dayan will care for Corinne, and we will see to it that Lisa is safe. You have my word on that."

"Lisa is under your protection," Cullen insisted.

Barack sighed softly. "Of course, Cullen, she is under our protection. I give you my word. Now go back to sleep and stop ordering me around in front of Syndil. She likes it too much."

Cullen closed his eyes obediently in response to the hypnotic suggestion in Barack's voice. Immediately Syndil leaned close to Lisa, looking directly into her eyes. *'You must have the security guard escort you to the cafeteria while the nurse keeps an eye on the room. It is urgent that you get something to drink immediately.'* Syndil was feeling weak from the exhausting work of repairing the terrible injuries to Cullen. She needed sustenance, and Cullen needed Barack's ancient blood to complete the healing process. They could not give it to him and then allow the hospital to take a blood sample. Cullen needed to be moved where they could watch over his health properly and protect him.

Lisa leaned over Cullen to brush his forehead with a kiss before she turned in obedience to the hypnotic compulsion Syndil had used on her.

Chapter Eleven

Corinne heard the music first. Soft. Sweet. Perfect. It was so wonderful, it brought tears to her eyes. The voice singing the lyrics conveyed a husky blend of male sensuality and outpouring love. She knew who it was and found herself smiling. "Dayan." She whispered his name softly.

The music continued, but she felt the slight shifting of the bed where she was lying. "Corinne. I thought you might sleep forever. I want you to know you took several hundred years off my life. I cannot afford another scare like that. The next time I send you to sleep, I expect to find you where I left you."

Her soft mouth curved into a smile, but she didn't open her eyes. "Listen to you. You sound almost as if you're *attempting* to order me around." She sounded amused, drowsy, incredibly sexy.

Instantly his blood turned to molten lava, a slow burn that consumed his body and wrapped his heart in flames. She was so beautiful to him, lying quietly beneath the blankets, her hair spread out around her face, a dark silky mass he couldn't stop himself from touching. Dayan placed his guitar carefully beside the bed and leaned over to kiss her irresistibly lush mouth. "I command and you obey. That is the way it is supposed to be." His voice was a tool of seduction.

"Really?" Her smile widened to reveal her intriguing dimple. "I hadn't heard that. I've always thought it was the other way around."

"You have been talking to the wrong people."

Corinne's long lashes fluttered, and with a small effort she managed to open them. She lifted her hand to his mouth and touched the lines of strain with a gentle fingertip. "You really were afraid for me. I didn't mean to worry you."

His hand captured hers and he brought it to his mouth, kissing the center of her palm before he placed it over his heart. "You did more than worry me, honey. Do you remember what happened?"

"It's vague, like a dream. I'm not certain what I remember, what you told me, or what I dreamed. Are Lisa and Cullen all right?"

"I believe they're safe." He hoped it was true. Syndil and Barack had not touched his mind with news, good or bad.

She stared into his eyes, trying to read his thoughts. "I need to know Lisa is alive and well and that Cullen wasn't hurt too badly."

"As soon as I know the details of his condition, I will pass the report on to you. Lisa is being guarded, and nothing will happen to her. I can promise you that."

Corinne nodded her acceptance of his word. "My baby's alive." She said it softly, lovingly, her tone turning his heart over. "I can feel her moving."

Dayan smiled at her, but the expression in his eyes was grave. "She is going to stay right where she belongs until she is strong enough to survive on her own."

"Has anyone ever told you how good-looking you are?" she asked. "Because you are, you know. Incredibly good-looking. But more than that, you're very sweet."

Dayan groaned loudly. "Do not say that, Corinne. That is the worst thing you can say to a man. Sexy. Masculine. Brooding. Manly. I can think of a million adjectives I would like, but 'sweet' is not one of them."

"There's nothing wrong with being sweet, Dayan," Corinne told him. Her voice sounded far away to her, yet other sounds seemed too loud. Crickets. Night insects. The wind outside rattling the tree branches. "Tell me what happened."

"You deliberately ignored my order to sleep and went with my idiot friend Cullen to find Lisa." He bit out each word between his white teeth, reminding her of a wolf.

"You don't mean to call Cullen an idiot," she chastised gently, not in the least intimidated by his ferocious expression.

"Cullen knew he was at the top of the society's hit list and he went out unprotected, and took you with him. I do not consider that good judgment on his part. Hence the term 'idiot' might apply." His tone was severe.

Corinne went back to rubbing the lines of strain on his handsome face. "Of course it was good judgment. What else could he do? Lisa had taken off, and if he hadn't followed her, they would have killed her," she pointed out reasonably.

"He took you with him." It was a mistake that Dayan considered unforgivable. Under the circumstances, Dayan thought he was being extraordinarily understanding about it.

She opened her mouth to reply, but there was a nameless expression in his eyes, something wild and

215

untamed, something primitive. "I'll bet someone has told you that you're very intimidating," she teased him, trying to ease the tension. "Not that I'm intimidated by you, but I can see how other people might be."

"It would be best for you if you found me intimidating." He could not be severe with her no matter how hard he tried. She looked up at him, small and fragile, so incredibly beautiful, her sweet, compassionate nature shining out of her eyes, and he was instantly lost. It was enough to drive him to the edge of madness.

"Do you think?" She didn't look intimidated, she looked amused. There were dark circles under her eyes and bruises on her forehead, yet her eyes were dancing with laughter. "I'm not at all sure that would be good for you. Don't think I haven't noticed the undue adulation all those fans give you."

One black eyebrow shot up. "*Undue* adulation? I totally deserved adulation. Get used to it, woman. Night after night while I am up on the stage playing, you will have to sit there sharing me with my fans. There is no need to be jealous, Corinne. I will see only you while I am performing."

"Such a comedian." Corinne gave a passing thought to sitting up and dismissed the idea as too difficult. "I have no intention of sitting through your performances. Private ones will be enough for me. And I don't have a jealous bone in my body. We don't have to worry about childish things like that."

He rubbed the bridge of his nose. "Childish? That is a strong term. Harsh. Very harsh." She was smiling again, that smile that could light up the world. Dayan had no choice but to fasten his mouth to hers.

The earth moved and time stopped and he couldn't find the discipline to make it a gentle, tender moment. She had scared him, stopped his heart, and he needed her. Needed to feed on her mouth, drown in her sweetness for just a few moments. Dayan forced his body under rigid control and slowly, reluctantly lifted his head. "Please do not ever do that to me again." His voice was a velvet weapon, and he used it shamelessly. Briefly he rested his forehead against hers. "I found you. In the darkness, where there was no hope for me, where I struggled and battled the monster every second of every night, you came to me. You saved me, Corinne. You cannot abandon me now. I cannot go back to a life alone. No one can ask that of me, not even you. How can I make you understand? I cannot go back. You must make up your mind to live, if not for yourself and the baby, for me. Love me that much. Do it for me."

At once tears swam in her large green eyes. "Dayan." She whispered his name softly, hopelessly, lovingly. "Don't you think I would promise you if I could? I want that more than anything—I do, but I'm only human, I can't do the impossible." Her fingers tangled in his thick, dark hair. "I had a strange dream that your healers came to me and tried to help me. I know the doctors said I was dying—I heard them talking to Lisa. I heard her crying. Yet I'm still alive, and so is my daughter. Tell me."

"Gregori did his best to repair your heart, Corinne, but the improvement is temporary, to give the baby a chance to grow. Darius said the child is strong and wants to live. We have that in our favor. It is a delicate balance, waiting until she is big enough to survive without you. Gregori wants a few more weeks for her. He is working with your heart to give us that time."

"Then it wasn't all a dream." Corinne caught his head and lifted it so that he was forced to look at her. "What are you, Dayan? Was part of it a dream, or were you there too, helping them in some way?"

For the first time ever, his black gaze slid away from

hers. He sat up straight, fussing with her covers. "I love you, Corinne," he said softly. "I love you more than anything or anyone on this earth. You need to know that."

"Look at me." Corinne took his hand and brought it to her mouth, her breath warm against his skin. "Dayan, look at me, please."

He sighed, and she could hear his heart pounding strongly. His reaction was unusual, and she knew it was significant in some way. "What is it that you think I can't love in you? Because that's what I feel. You're giving me a part of you, but you don't want me to know all of you. I feel connected to you. Strongly connected. We're two halves of the same whole. I've been married, Dayan. I knew what I was supposed to feel. I loved John, but not in the same way. With you I feel everything and more. I could listen to you talk forever. Or simply sit beside you quietly without words. It would be enough for me. I want to be with you, but I don't know who you are. You say you can love me because you know me through my mind. I don't have that advantage. In order for me to know you, really know you, you have to talk to me. There's a part of you closed off to me. Don't you trust me to care for you no matter what it is?"

"You do not trust yourself. I can see into your mind, Corinne. I see you wrestling with doubts. You think it all happened too fast. That it is simply chemistry. Purely sexual. Or that it is just because you are pregnant and you need someone. You give yourself many reasons, many excuses for your feelings toward me. You do not say to yourself that you love me."

Her eyes searched his black gaze. There was pain there, in the dark depths. He was hurt, and it upset her. "Dayan, you have probably always had the ability to read minds, so it is second nature to you, but to some- one who isn't telepathic it is uncomfortable. I am used to censoring my thoughts, choosing how I want to present myself to the world. You can see into my mind, but for some strange reason, it doesn't bother me. If it were anyone else, including John or Lisa, I would be horrified that someone could read my thoughts. That should tell you something right there."

"You think it tells *you* something, Corinne. I already know why you feel that way. You are my lifemate, the one who holds the light and compassion, guards these treasures for me. You are my anchor in a world of darkness and violence, of bleak emptiness. You are the other half of my soul. The best half. I know I need you far more than you will ever need me. I know these things. You have not come to terms with what you feel because you do not trust it. You do not entirely trust me."

"How can you say that, Dayan? I'm here with you instead of in a hospital. I just met you, and some fairly bizarre things have happened, but I'm still with you."

He laughed softly. "As I recall, you had no real choice in the matter. I picked you up and carried you out of the hospital. You were not in any condition to argue with me."

"That's not the point." She was trying hard to find the energy to sit up. "I'm not the type of person to just go off with someone—that's the point. Obviously, I feel *strongly* for you." She plucked at the quilt with idle fingers. "The healer believes my heart will give out eventually, doesn't he?"

"You knew it would. I have looked closely at your memories. You have been to many doctors. There is little hope," he answered cautiously.

"Then you know I cannot possibly survive, Dayan," she said quietly. "I don't want you to think I'm *choosing* to leave you. I don't have a choice."

"You have a choice," he replied softly. But he knew

he wasn't telling her the truth and he looked away from her, unable to tell the lie and look into her eyes. She didn't have a choice because he wouldn't allow her to die.

"You aren't looking at me, Dayan," she said softly. "You can't have it both ways. If you're not going to tell me the truth, don't expect me to trust you implicitly. You don't have to hide anything from me. If the healers told you my heart was failing, that isn't exactly news to me."

Dayan touched her mind with warmth and reassurance. "Your heart *is* failing. But I intend for you to live at any cost." He said it starkly, without embellishment.

Her palm framed his face, studying his expression carefully. "I see what's in your mind. I don't know how, but I can read your thought right now. You think that somehow, miraculously, you'll save me, even if the baby isn't ready to be born when my heart fails. I don't know how you think you can perform such a miracle, but, Dayan, if there is a chance for the baby, that's what I have to concentrate on. She has to be saved."

"The healer is doing his best for her, Corinne, but do not ask me to choose the child's life over yours, because I will not." This time he did look her directly in the eye, wanting her to know he was serious.

"Dayan," she reprimanded softly, "the baby comes first. If there is a choice to be made between my daughter's life or mine, you will instruct the healers to save her. If you can't make that promise to me then you'll have to take me back to the hospital and Lisa, where they'll follow my instructions."

Dayan shook his head. "They cannot do anything for you at the hospital. Gregori believes there is a good chance to save both of you. We are awaiting Shea, as she is our expert with infants. I will not take you back to the hospital. It would be a death sentence."

"Then you will promise to put the baby's life before mine." She spoke sternly, her eyes wide and steady on his.

His fingers tightened around hers. "*You* are my life, Corinne, my world. I intend for both of you to live. You and the baby."

"So tell me what the healers did." She was struggling slightly, having every intention of sitting up.

"What are you doing?" Dayan touched her mind gently, learning that she wanted to see if she could sit up on her own before attempting to walk to the bathroom.

"I'm sitting up," she said, trying to sound casual when she was really breaking out in a sweat with the effort and feeling shaky with fear for the baby. "Don't change the subject. What did the healers do? It's important to me, Dayan, for a lot of reasons. I have to feel in control. I want to know what's happening in my life so I can plan things out. I'm a planner. Very organized."

His eyebrow shot up. "A planner? Organized? I did not realize that about you. That changes everything, of course." He reached out and casually lifted her into a sitting position, holding her close to him while she clung to his broad shoulders. He grinned down at her, his wild scent enveloping her. "I take your breath away, admit it."

Corinne tried to calm her beating heart. Strangely, when she consciously thought about it, it seemed as if her heart actually followed her directions. She became aware of everything then, the sound of their combined heartbeats, the ebb and flow of their blood in their bodies. The baby's heartbeat. *She was hearing the baby's heartbeat!* Wide-eyed, she stared up at him, accusation in her gaze. "You can't count this time as legitimate breath robbing. Something strange is going on. You wouldn't happen to know anything about it, would you?"

221

Dayan looked completely innocent. He bent his head to brush a kiss on the top of her silky head because he couldn't resist. "What are you accusing me of now, honey?"

She gave him her haughtiest expression. "I'm getting up." She made it an announcement.

He stared down at her, observing rather pointedly that she was securely trapped in his enormously strong arms. *'Enormously strong. Enormously. Are you getting that?'*

Corinne burst out laughing. "Of course I'm getting that. Lucky for you I don't perceive it as a threat. Enormously strong. You sound like a teenage boy." She tried to ignore the way he could turn her heart over with one melting look from his black eyes. "And why am I wanting to speak back to you in my mind? Am I becoming telepathic? Has that ability mysteriously rubbed off on me?"

"Everything about me is rubbing off on you. You are crazy about me."

"You're attempting to brainwash me," she accused, trying not to laugh. He got away with far too much because she found him far too attractive. "I really am getting up, Dayan. You have to let go of me."

"You do not have the strength to walk to the bathroom." Dayan could read the determination in her mind. He rose with a fluid motion, taking her with him, and crossed the room to the bathroom.

Corinne wrapped her arm around his neck. "Where exactly am I?" She was looking around herself carefully. It was no cave. The bedroom was very spacious with high ceilings and beautiful walls. The furniture was expensive and ornate. She stared at the room in awe. "Where am I, Dayan?" she asked again.

"In my lair. I am a big bad wolf and I have captured you." Very gently he set her feet on the tiles of the bathroom floor, his arms around her, holding her carefully. "You are shaking, honey. Is it because I am all male and you cannot help yourself, or because you are too weak to stand?"

"Good exit line," she observed. She pointed to the door. "Out!"

Dayan hesitated. He had been teasing her, but he knew her body was weak. "You had better call me *immediately* if you need help. You do not have to call aloud to me—thinking is enough."

"Get out!" Corinne said emphatically. "And stay out of my mind. I want *privacy*, Dayan. It's humiliating enough having to be carried to the bathroom like a baby. I'm an independent woman, totally self-reliant at all times."

Grumbling, Dayan gave in to her demands, leaving her alone in the room and going so far as to close the door behind him. Outside he began pacing back and forth with restless energy. *'The healer said you needed complete bed rest.'*

'Dayan!' She half wailed his name, half laughed. *'You're not getting it.'*

'I am keeping vigil. Standing guard.'

Corinne refused to laugh and she wasn't going to give him the satisfaction of replying. She stared at her pale face in the mirror, mildly shocked by her reflection. She looked different. She felt different.

'Doing my duty. Watching out for my lifemate.' Dayan managed to sound put upon and abused.

Corinne shook her head, laughter bubbling up despite her resolve to ignore him. There was every amenity in the immaculate bathroom, and she took full advantage. She took her time brushing her teeth, mainly because it was difficult to stand and she needed to lean against the sink. She was surprised at how weak she was. Her legs felt rubbery, but her breathing was much easier.

'Okay, Corinne, that is as patient as I can be under the circumstances. I feel your weakness, and you are still being stubborn. I am coming in.'

'I want to brush my hair.' As soon as Corinne sent the message back to him, she realized she had communicated with him telepathically. Easily. Naturally.

Dayan shoved open the door and picked her up, his black eyes moving over her anxiously as he inspected her. "Do not panic simply because you have done something totally natural. I am your lifemate—of course you can talk to me. It is not the first time."

Corinne was grateful for his hard strength, resting her head on his shoulder. "There was a difference, Dayan. You read my thoughts. I directed them to you in answer maybe, but you were reading what was in my mind. This time I *sent* you my thoughts, my words. That's a very big difference."

"Why should that alarm you?" he asked curiously, placing her carefully back in the bed. His hand rested on her small stomach as the baby moved inside her. He smiled. "See? She is happy and healthy. And she recognizes my voice now. She likes to hear me sing to her." His impossibly long lashes came down to conceal his expression. "I wrote a lullaby for her."

His words were a hesitant offering of love, rendering a seemingly invincible man vulnerable, and her heart melted again. She stretched both arms up to capture him, to bring his head down to hers so she could find his sculpted mouth with hers. Corinne couldn't help herself, she just relaxed and allowed the world with all its troubles to whirl away from her until there was only Dayan. Dayan with his broad shoulders and strong arms and perfect mouth. There was no thinking when Dayan kissed her, only feeling. Pure feeling. He swept her into another world where there were no limits, where time and space meant nothing at all.

Her body flared to life, melting and shaping itself perfectly into his. She paid no attention to her crazy heart, the way it raced just because he was close to her. Nothing frightened her when he was kissing her. She felt strong, his other half. She felt as if she belonged. Corinne never wanted to stop. It was the baby, kicking strongly, thumping Dayan right through Corinne's skin, that had them breaking apart, laughing softly in wonder.

"She is strong, isn't she?" Corinne said softly, not hiding the expression in her eyes from him. She was tired of attempting to be practical. Dayan was the most wonderful man she'd ever met, and she wanted to be with him. Now more than ever. He made her feel beautiful even in the middle of her pregnancy. He made her feel as if she were the only woman in the world when her hair was tumbling out of control and she was wearing a man's shirt to bed.

"You know how beautiful you are, Corinne," he said, bringing her hand to his mouth. "You can touch my mind; you see what I feel for you."

She tilted her head to look at him. "I know I can, but I'm not certain I want to actually do it. What am I going to find in there?"

His black eyes shimmered with hunger. Blatant. Stark. Raw. A terrible need. Corinne blushed and shook her head. "When I woke up, you weren't singing the baby a lullaby. You wrote a song for me too, didn't you?"

"Every song I write is for you." He leaned close to her. "I must call Gregori and Darius to us. They wanted to know the minute you opened your eyes." His grin was unrepentant. "We do not have to tell them everything."

"What time is it?" Corinne was looking around the beautiful room. "And where am I? I should at least know that in case someone asks."

He was a shadow in her mind, and he burst out laughing at her outrageous thoughts. "Of course you are still on planet Earth. I am not an alien."

She shrugged. "Just checking—you never know these days. And you are a bit bizarre. Is your entire band here?" She tried to sound casual.

He tucked her hair behind her ear. She sounded apprehensive. "You are a bit of a chicken, Corinne. I did not realize that."

"I am not," she denied indignantly and then glared at him. "You're doing it again. Every time I ask you a question, you deflect."

His eyebrow shot up. "Deflect? I have no idea what you are talking about."

"Dayan"—her fingers tightened around his—"where am I?"

"This home belongs to Gregori and Savannah. They do not reside here year-round; in fact, it is vacant most of the time. They have offered it generously for your recovery." He looked around the room. "I am on the road most of the time traveling. It is a unique experience for me to stay in a place like this."

"Do you mean a home?"

He shook his head, watching her carefully. "Home is wherever you and I are. On the road, traveling, as long as you and I and the baby are together, it will be home."

"So you have it all planned out."

Dayan nodded, still watching closely for her reaction, monitoring her thoughts. "You will come to love the others and the life we have. It is a good life, and we see many interesting places." It occurred to him he would see each place differently now. There would be color and laughter and beauty. *He* was different now. He would see the beauty as he traveled through each city, each country. She had given him that priceless gift. Never again would his world be one of shadows and darkness.

"It's nice that you have such optimism, Dayan," she replied cautiously. There was no point in arguing with him when he was so set on believing she could survive the birth of the baby. The last thing she wanted was to bring up the fact that she had no future. She wanted Dayan to promise her that his healers would save the baby if there was a choice to be made.

Dayan shook his head as he read her thoughts. She would live. He would move heaven and earth if he had to, but she would live. "I have summoned Darius and Gregori." He wanted to prepare her for visitors, knowing she found it difficult to be with strangers. Corinne had led a solitary life in the midst of people. She was very private and reserved with those outside her family. "Darius is my family, Corinne—a man I know and would give my life for. I trust him and his judgment."

Her small teeth bit down nervously at her lip. "I feel better than I have for some time, Dayan. I don't think it's really necessary to see them now, do you?"

"You know it is. They must monitor the baby and your heart carefully."

"What did they do different from what a doctor would do?"

Desari came through the door first. She was a tall, beautiful woman radiating light and comfort. She had a soothing, tranquil demeanor and seemed to flow rather than walk. Corinne recognized her at once from her bizarre dream. "Do you remember anything at all?" Desari asked gently in answer to her question. Her voice was soft, warm honey, compelling like Dayan's. There were no sharp edges to Desari; she was peace itself.

"I'm not certain what was real and what I dreamed," Corinne found herself answering honestly. "I don't understand why I feel so much better, when the doctors said I was dying and nothing could save me."

"There are those among our people born with the ability to separate themselves from the physical body and use pure energy to find the problems inside the body of a sick or wounded person. We heal from the inside out. There are no cuts made on the outer body, no sutures. The healing is done with light and energy," Desari answered matter-of-factly. "Darius has this gift, as does Gregori. We all do to a small extent, but they are very powerful."

Corinne turned the information over and over in her mind. It sounded insane, something from a science fiction story, but the fact remained that the doctors had given up on her and she was supposed to be dead. Her fingers remained tangled with Dayan's for support. "I feel much better."

Desari's smile was beautiful. Her raven-colored hair was in a thick braid hanging to her waist. She tossed it carelessly over her shoulder. She looked so poised, so beautiful and healthy, so alive that Corinne found herself close to tears. She herself would never look that good, not in a million years, and beside her was Dayan, the perfect male specimen.

'There can be no other for me, honey.' His voice whispered intimately in her mind, a soft reprimand. He flooded her with his feelings, everything at once. She sensed aching love, so strong that nothing could ever come between them, not even death. Physical desire, a raging fire in his blood, a hunger and need to unite them for eternity. *'You are the most beautiful woman I have ever seen. I do not see another.'*

There was something wildly erotic about talking to Dayan in her mind. It was so private and sinfully intimate. Corinne blushed for no reason at all. She was so pleased with his response to her thoughts, she barely noticed the two men who had entered the room.

Gregori cleared his throat politely, inclining his head toward her. "I hope you are feeling better, Corinne."

Her fingers tightened around Dayan's. "I am, thank you very much." She blushed, realizing she sounded like a child thanking an adult.

"What we did is temporary, Corinne." The healer's silver eyes glittered at her. "I do you the courtesy of telling the truth. The disease has progressed beyond our abilities to cure it. I will treat you as often as necessary to ensure that your daughter has time to grow strong. She needs a few more weeks. Every day, every hour counts for her. You must stay on bed rest and not tax your heart. Do not fear the birth; we have no intention of allowing you to slip away from us." Gregori smiled his encouragement. "Darius is with me, and I know he can appear quite intimidating. I do not want his manner to frighten you. He is my younger brother, and if he snarls at you, I will take him to task as befitting a younger sibling."

Corinne blinked. It took a heartbeat or two to realize the predatory man with the slashing eyes was teasing her. Teasing his brother. She glanced at Darius. Her mouth twitched, but she managed not to smile. "I'm certain you heard that, Darius. I'll take full advantage if you get all snarly on me."

For all her teasing manner, Corinne still gripped Dayan's hand hard when Darius loomed over her. Like his older brother Gregori, Darius wielded a power that seemed to fill the entire room. Dayan's enormous power was strong but subtle. Gregori and Darius were altogether different. A bit shorter than Dayan, they carried most of their weight in their wide shoulders and muscular arms. Each had pulled his long black hair back with a leather thong at the nape of his neck. While Gregori had peculiar silver eyes, Darius's eyes were as black as coal. Both looked very dangerous. Corinne couldn't believe she had dared to tease them.

"Good evening, little sister," Darius said courteously. "I am glad to see you have awakened. I was beginning to worry, something I prefer not to do. You will do well to remember that." He leaned close to her ear, speaking in a fake whisper. "Just so you know, Gregori does not travel with the band."

Corinne found herself smiling. "Thanks for cluing me in. I guess I won't be ratting you out after all. He probably just wanted an excuse to pound on you."

"Most likely. He has a certain reputation—a myth, you know—but he likes people to believe he is the bogeyman. Do not let his severe frown get to you. How is your daughter behaving?"

Corinne smiled at him. "She seems very strong, kicking quite a bit."

"That is the answer I wanted. You gave your lifemate quite a scare. Do not do that again." He made it a decree, as if everybody obeyed him. She suspected everyone probably did.

"Is your breathing any easier this evening?" Gregori asked.

Corinne studied Gregori's handsome face. There was a definite resemblance between Desari, Gregori and Darius. *'Gregori is the lifemate of Savannah Dubrinsky. Do you recognize the name?'* Dayan wanted to remind her that Gregori was taken. He owed the healer much, but he couldn't shake the notion she might find him attractive.

'Of course I do. Savannah Dubrinsky is a famous magician. In any case, you are the only man I find remotely attractive,' Corinne assured him, secretly amused. She thought he was the handsomest, the most charming

and romantic man in the world. How could he possibly be concerned she might look at anyone else? *'You're very silly.'* It didn't occur to her in that moment that she was easily reading his anxiety.

"I am going to check the baby," Gregori said, deliberately bringing her attention back to him. "She is strong and she wants to live. She has rare talents, much like you have. She is very precious to our people."

"You have to save her, no matter the cost." Corinne didn't look at Dayan. She sensed the strength of will in the healer, his complete determination to save her daughter.

Gregori's silver eyes shimmered for a moment like molten mercury, and then he shook his head. "There will be no trading of life, Corinne. You have a lifemate. We will not lose either of you. Each couple is needed. Both you and your baby will be saved. Dayan will not allow otherwise. You must believe that completely. Your daughter is very aware of you and already is bonded. She will not want to trade her life for yours. And we cannot lose her either. There will be no trade."

Corinne watched him closely. He was breathing deeply, regularly, then seemed to go into a self-induced trance. The same trance she had observed in her bizarre dream. She glanced up at Dayan. *'I was really in that cave, wasn't I?'*

He sighed audibly. *'Do you really want the answer, honey?'*

"Corinne," Darius said very calmly, "your heart is beginning to accelerate rapidly. Breathe and keep it under control. You must be aware of your heart rate, and when it begins to quicken, you need to relax and focus to bring the rhythm back to normal. You are capable of doing so. You must start believing."

Corinne immediately obeyed, suspecting there was a hidden compulsion in the softly spoken order. *'Don't put me off this time, Dayan. I was in that cave.'* She kept her eyes steadily on Dayan's.

His black eyes became aggressive, trapping her stare in their dark mystery so that she couldn't have looked away from him even if she'd wanted too. *'I do not wish to alarm you, honey, and each time we speak about what I am or what is happening, your heart gets jumpy. If you are certain you want the truth and are ready to accept it, then I will give it to you gladly.'*

She tilted her chin determinedly. *'I always want the truth from you, Dayan. Without that between us, we have nothing at all.'*

'I agree with you.' He took a breath, counted to ten and let it out slowly. He was careful to be a shadow in her mind, ready to erase any revelation that might be too difficult for her to accept. *'The cave you were in is deep below the surface of the earth, below the mountain formed of fire and ice. It is a place of power, and we needed such a place to perform the healing ritual. The candles were made of herbs and compounds known to promote healing through aroma. The healing ritual was conducted by the two healers, their lifemates and my family. It was a large gathering. While we were attending to you, two other members of my family, Syndil and Barack, were rushing to aid Cullen.'*

Chapter Twelve

"Come here to me, my love," Barack said softly, gliding to his lifemate even as he gave the command. He enfolded her in his arms. "You are drooping with weariness and you must feed."

"Cullen needs blood fast, Barack, or he may not make it. I am not a true healer like Darius or Gregori. I have never attempted such a healing before." Syndil rested her head on his chest, her fatigue catching up with her. "I do not know if I have done enough for him. My gift is in healing the earth, not humans or Carpathians. You must give him blood."

"You come before Cullen, Syndil," Barack said gently, his voice an invitation. Beneath her ear his heart was a steady beat; she could hear the beckoning of his blood, the ebb and flow of the essence of his life. Her arms circled his neck and she moved against him, restless and in need.

Syndil said his name softly as she slowly began to unbutton his shirt, her fingertips smoothing over the heavy muscles of his chest. She felt his body clench in answer, in anticipation. As always, she wondered anew at the beautiful mystery of their union. Barack. Her lifemate. She had known him throughout her long existence, and yet had not known the wonders of a true union until recently. The simple act of feeding was no longer just that. It was erotic and filled her with pleasure, with needs far beyond satiating hunger. She nuzzled his chest, smiled when his hands gripped her hair and his body moved aggressively against hers. Teasingly she nipped his chest, swirled her tongue over his jumping pulse, allowing the movement to trigger her incisors.

Barack groaned and pulled her tightly against him, wrapping her close while she fed. In the midst of the danger, with Cullen at the top of the society's hit list, Barack still felt the jolt of urgent need riding him hard. Syndil was careful—he could feel the hunger in her, sharp and fierce—but she took only enough to sustain her so Barack could give Cullen necessary blood as well. Afterward, Barack would always have a connection to Cullen, and Cullen to Barack, but they had no choice. If the mortal was to survive, he needed their healing blood to aid in repairing his damaged organs. Very carefully she closed the tiny pinpricks with the healing agent in her saliva and lifted her head, her eyes drowsy and slumberous. Barack bent his head at once to find her mouth, kissing her hard. "I am very proud of you, Syndil," he said softly.

"He is brave," Syndil replied, "and a good friend to us. He has risked his life many times. I wish Gregori or Darius had come to do this."

"You did fine." Barack reluctantly released her and sat on the edge of the bed. "I will give him blood, Syndil, and then we must take both of them out of here. Do not allow the woman to give you any trouble. Take control of her at once. No chances."

Syndil ruffled his hair as if he were a mere boy instead of the enormously strong man that he was. "Stop with the woman bit, Barack. Have you not touched her mind?"

"Who would want to except to command?"

"She was terribly traumatized. She does not see things she is afraid of because her mind does not allow it. She is merely protecting herself. It is the only way her mind could remain sane. Lisa is reliant on Corinne and clings to her as a safety net. Corinne is much stronger and must have realized it at an early age. She protects Lisa from the outside world, and Lisa knows she cannot get along without her. I have looked into her mind. She knows she needs a buffer."

Barack ducked his head, ashamed. "I do not deserve you. I never have."

"Very true," Syndil said complacently, "but I think I will keep you around anyway." She watched as he bent and lifted Cullen into his arms. Observing the expression on his face, her heart skipped a beat. Barack felt strong affection for the human, something few of their kind ever experienced. It was always necessary to keep a distance from humans so that no one ever found evidence their species existed. It was becoming more difficult as computers and travel made the world a much smaller place.

Barack murmured the ritual healing chant softly as he forced his blood into Cullen. A small amount only to aid in the healing of his broken and torn body. By their laws they should not have done so. They should have allowed him to die naturally, but Darius ruled their family, and to them he was a higher authority than the Prince of the Carpathians. It was Darius who had decreed Cullen was to be saved if possible. To Barack and Syndil, that meant they could use any means possible.

Syndil brushed back Cullen's hair with gentle fingers. "I am happy he is the one who found Lisa. He will always care for her and appreciate her goodness, where another man might see only her weakness."

Barack's black eyes fixed on her face. "I have apologized for my error."

She smiled at him. "It was an idle comment, not directed toward you, Barack, but I am glad you feel remorse for prejudging Cullen's choice so harshly before you touched her mind to find out if she was worthy of him. She will love him and be faithful. She will want only to please him and make him happy. Theirs is a good match. He needs to be needed, Barack."

Barack stopped the flow of blood from his wrist with a casual stroke of his tongue. "I am certain you are right, Syndil." He touched Cullen's mind to be sure that he was breathing easier, that his body had accepted the small amount of blood and was utilizing it to heal the terrible wounds. "We must take him out of here quickly, Syndil, to the safe house where we can better protect him. Call Lisa back to us."

Syndil took a step toward the closed door, then stopped abruptly, her alarmed gaze going to Barack's. "They are here. They have come for Cullen. We should have known they would move quickly to eliminate him. They consider him a threat and a traitor. Of course they would want to finish the job."

Barack could feel the vibrations of violence in the air, coming toward the room. "Four of them." He said it unnecessarily, tersely; Syndil could pick up the thoughts of violence as easily as he. "I will take Cullen, while you remove Lisa from danger. Call me if you have need of my aid to shield the two of you." He was already scooping Cullen easily into his arms, creating the illusion that Cullen remained lying helpless and still in the bed alone.

Syndil gave a very feminine cough of derision. She was an ancient, capable of walking unseen among humans and keeping Lisa from being seen as well. She dissolved instantly into mist and streamed from the room as the four human assassins shoved open the door. They stood a distance from the bed, pointing weapons at the motionless body they perceived to be there. The sound of the guns was muted, like a soft spitting that no one would hear beyond the door. Barack dulled it even further, directing the security guards and nurses away from the area to keep the humans as safe as possible.

Barack, waiting in the corner with Cullen in his arms, watched as the assassins repeatedly shot into the bed. None of them saw Barack—he had cloaked his presence—but they could feel the unusual coldness permeating the room. One of the society members moved forward to check the body, and as the others watched, Barack slipped past them. He heard their shouts of consternation and angry frustration that they had been so easily tricked, and once again Cullen had escaped their vengeance.

Hurrying down the long hall away from the assassins, Barack called out to warn Darius of the plot. *'They are here,'* he communicated simply. With Darius, there was no need for embellishing. Darius protected his own, and he considered Cullen part of their extended family. Darius would come in all haste and bring justice to the assassins.

There was no need for Barack to inform Syndil of what was happening since he was always a shadow in her mind. He was well aware of her taking control of Lisa and shielding both of them from prying eyes as they made their way out of the hospital. Syndil put Lisa in a hypnotic trance in order to transport her in the fastest way possible, through the air, just as Barack was doing with Cullen. The two humans would be taken to a safe house deep within the mountains where they could be more adequately guarded.

Corinne sat in her bed regarding Dayan steadily. The healers were chanting softly, she could hear them in her mind. The atmosphere was soothing, tranquil even, but she was on the verge of a discovery. What was it she was thinking? That Dayan wasn't human? Not of this world? What, then? An alien being? She shoved at the hair tumbling around her face as she studied Dayan's mesmerizing features. Did it matter so very much one way or the other? How had they taken her to a cave deep within the earth and performed an exotic healing ritual that had actually worked? Was all of it real, or only parts of it? She pushed the idea of a blood exchange out of her mind.

She laced her fingers through his. "Tell me, Dayan, the truth about all of you. I need to know. What are you?"

The healing chant stopped abruptly at her softly spoken words. Desari glanced at Darius. "Perhaps we can return at a more convenient time to check on you, Corinne," Desari offered gently. She smiled sweetly at the healer. "Gregori, would it be an inconvenience to return at a more suitable time?"

Gregori lifted an eyebrow at his sister. Aloud he sighed. "I think it would be best. We will return later."

Darius cautioned Dayan silently. *'Be very careful, Dayan. She must not be upset in any way. Gregori will monitor her heart from a distance, and I will watch over the infant. She has need of answers, and I believe she is more receptive than you give her credit for.'*

Corinne watched as the three Carpathians left the room and quietly closed the door behind them, leaving her alone with Dayan. He stood up abruptly, restlessly.

She looked up at him with her large, clear eyes. "I think it is time for you to talk to me about what and who you are. Start at the beginning. Where are your parents?"

"They are dead—murdered, as your mother was," he answered starkly. Dayan paced restlessly across the room, swept a hand through his long hair, leaving it disheveled in the wake of his marauding fingers. He suddenly reached down and caught up his beloved guitar, holding it close to his body like a talisman.

Corinne smiled to herself. His guitar. She was beginning to notice that he needed it in his arms when he was nervous, and he was nervous now. He was adept at asking her questions and invading her mind to get to know her, but he didn't like that same spotlight turned back on him. She had never seen him so nervous. "Dayan." She said his name softly, gently, and patted the bed beside her. "You look like a caged leopard in a zoo, pacing back and forth." She didn't add that he reminded her of a little boy clutching his favorite blanket. "Is it so bad to trust me with the truth?"

He looked down at her, his black eyes brooding and moody. "What happens if you cannot accept me as I am? What happens if I frighten you with the truth and your heart fails you?"

"Do you think I'm that weak, Dayan?" she asked gently. "My body is fragile—I've learned to accept that— but *I'm* not a weak person. I never have been." She held out her hand to him. "Stop pacing and sit by me."

Dayan stood for a long moment, his guitar across his chest, his eyes reflecting inner turmoil. Slowly, reluctantly, he crossed the room to sit carefully on the bed beside her. He enveloped her small hand with his larger one. "*My* heart could not take your rejection, honey. Not for one moment. Be very sure that you want to have this conversation now."

"I am certain, Dayan. You think your feelings for me

are very strong. Well, I have loved before. John." She said her husband's name and silently watched Dayan's involuntary wince. "Don't feel that way about him, Dayan. He was a remarkable man and deserved far better than a woman who didn't love him the way he should have been loved. I know how strong my feelings for you already are. I tried to tell myself the attraction was purely sexual, but I think about you—your expressions, the way you smile, the turn of your head. Everything. Even the silly things like how you can be childish sometimes. I find myself thinking it's an endearing trait. That's not due entirely to chemistry."

He sighed. "I am not going to ask what is childishly endearing."

She smiled at him. "No, you're not. You're going to tell me about your childhood. About yourself, so I get to know you."

He brought her fingers to his mouth, wanting—no *needing*—the reassurance of being close to her. "I grew up with Darius, Desari, Barack, Syndil and another called Savon. We were alone as children, with no adult to guide us. It was Darius who took responsibility for us. He was six years old and already showing signs of great power and strength of will. It was Darius who took most of the risks for us."

His teeth were nibbling anxiously at her fingertips, but he seemed unaware of it. Corinne regarded him steadily. "How did a group of children like that slip through social services? How did you all manage to eat and sleep?"

"We were separated from our people and were believed to have been murdered along with our parents. There was a shipwreck, and we ended up in Africa. That is where we grew up. Our band travels with leopards; we raised them. We actually learned quite a bit from animals. It was a difficult time but also very rewarding."

Corinne's small teeth scraped at her lower lip. She believed him, although it seemed impossible that six children could survive in Africa alone. The continent was wild and untamed. Something in her recognized the truth in his simple explanation, yet she knew there was much more he wasn't telling her.

"Dayan," she said softly, bringing his dark gaze to hers. "You either trust me or you don't. You have to make up your mind."

"What if I tell you I am not human?" He said it quietly, his teeth biting harder at her knuckles. "What if I told you my parents had died during the Turk wars? Would that frighten you away from me?"

Corinne's heart accelerated for a moment, and she was glad for the diversion, happy to be able to concentrate on slowing it down, giving herself time to think. She had suspected there was something not quite human about Dayan, but to hear him confirm it was something else altogether. *The Turk wars? What did that make him?*

"I would hope I'm not that big a coward. Are you something other than what you've shown me? Because the man I'm attracted to is gentle and caring and unbelievably wonderful." She was feeling her way, trying to encourage him and yet give herself the time she needed to assimilate the information he was giving her.

He looked away from her, unable to face her condemnation. "I want to be gentle and caring, Corinne, but in truth I am a predator," he said regretfully. "You are all that is good and right within me."

Corinne shook her head in denial. "You're so much more than a predator, whatever that means, Dayan. You're a poet without equal. The words that pour out of your soul, the incomparable music you make—that is who you are. The other is a part of your nature, per-haps, but only a small part. You couldn't say the things you say, the beautiful words you give to me, without feeling them deep within you."

He opened her hand, studied her lifeline for a mo-ment before pressing a kiss into the center of her palm. "I felt so many things in my youth, so much music, it seemed I *was* music. I heard it everywhere, in the earth and sky, the trees, the animals. I heard it and knew it was my world. Slowly it faded away. It was terrifying to realize I was going to lose it, so I wrote songs, hundreds of songs, thousands of songs, pouring out the notes and words and committing them to memory. Over the years those memories were what I relied on to get me through the darkness. I didn't feel the words or music anymore, but I had the memories to sustain me. I could touch others who felt the joy of love and laughter and draw upon their emotions to create what I needed."

He studied her face, his black gaze drifting over her possessively, lovingly, with so much hunger and need she could feel her body melting under his scrutiny. "You cannot possibly understand until you are able to merge your mind fully with mine. I knew utter bleak-ness, a black, empty void. Without my music, without my soul, I wandered the earth not understanding what I was, not willing to accept what I was. What I am."

She touched his face with gentle fingers. "What you are is a man with exceptional gifts, Dayan. The things you are talking about I see occasional glimpses of—I won't pretend I don't—but that is not who you are."

His perfectly chiseled lips curved into a beguiling smile, and he deliberately drew her finger into the moist cavern of his mouth. "You think I am an alien being from another planet." There was teasing laughter in his voice.

Corinne found herself grinning at him sheepishly. "It could happen."

"I am Carpathian. We are as old as time, doomed to wander the earth until we make the choice to give up our lives. Our males are dark, deadly predators; the beast lies strong within us, ever growing until such time as we find our lifemates to anchor us in the world of light."

Corinne knew he was telling her something of great importance, but she truly didn't understand him. "I have never heard the term *Carpathian*. If I still remember my geography, there is a range of mountains, the Carpathian Mountains in Romania and Transylvania . . ." She trailed off as the significance of that region hit her. She remembered vividly the strange twist her dream in the cave had taken. She was silent for a moment, gathering her courage. "Did you give me your blood?" she asked very quietly, unsure whether she wanted him to answer her.

"Are you certain you want the truth?"

She shrugged her shoulders, a delicately feminine motion. "I want the truth, Dayan, though I'm not certain I can take it. I wasn't dreaming in that cave, was I? It all happened just as I remember it. All those people were there to help you save my life. And you gave me your blood. Why? What did that do for me?" She tried to be very analytical about it, afraid that if she dwelled too long on the subject, she would be sick. She swallowed hard. "Why did you feel it was necessary?"

"To save your life and the life of the baby." Dayan watched her expressive face carefully, was a shadow in her mind monitoring her thoughts. He listened to her heart and breathing for signs of extreme stress.

Corinne sat very still, allowed her heart to follow the stronger, steadier beat of his. She nodded, not fully comprehending but knowing she was getting closer to

243

the truth. If his blood could save her daughter, then it was worth everything to her. She gathered her courage, watched his face intently. "Are you a vampire, Dayan?" She felt somewhat ridiculous asking such an absurd question, but she had never seen him in the daylight hours. Also, he was *too* mesmerizing. And if her strange dream had been a reality, he had given his blood to her in a rather unorthodox manner.

Dayan wanted to smile at her thoughts. Corinne was struggling to understand, heading in the right direction, while at the same time totally disbelieving her own wisdom. He liked the idea that she found him *too* anything. He was also aware that she had banished the actual picture of receiving his blood from her mind.

The pad of his thumb rubbed gently, soothingly, along her inner wrist. "Not a vampire, honey, but we share some of the same traits. A vampire is the undead, a Carpathian male who has chosen to give up his soul for the momentary pleasure of feeling the power of the kill. He is deceitful, treacherous and depraved. Wholly evil. Carpathians hunt down and destroy vampires. It is necessary for the preservation of mortals and immortals alike."

She stared at him with enormous moss-green eyes. Her mind went from racing to perfectly blank. She just stared at him. Carefully she cleared her throat, stalling for time. He believed every word he was saying. Either Dayan was telling the absolute truth or he was totally insane. She took a deep breath, let it out slowly. "Obviously, I don't know what to say." Her voice was neutral.

Dayan leaned down to brush the top of her silky head with his mouth. "You are not crazy, honey, and neither am I. Think about it. What can you hear that you should not be able to hear?"

Corinne continued to gaze at him, looking very

young and vulnerable. Her face was pale, almost ashen, and it was becoming difficult for her to breathe. Automatically Dayan did it for her, taking over the job, directing her lungs to push air in and out. "By giving me your blood, did you make me like you?" Her voice was low, a mere thread of sound.

Dayan circled her slender shoulders with his arm. "We do not need to have this talk right now, my love. If you are not feeling up to it, I will remove your memories and we will try again at a later date."

Her eyebrows shot up. "You can do that? Remove my memories?" Suddenly she glared at him. "Have you done that?"

He shrugged casually, without remorse. "Partially. I made them hazy so you would not be frightened, but left them accessible should you ever wish to put the pieces of the puzzle together."

For a moment she stared at him; then she burst out laughing. "This really is crazy, you know, because I'm believing you and it's too bizarre for words."

"I cannot lie to you, Corinne. You have the ability, through our blood exchange, to look into my memories, into my mind, and see that I am telling you the truth. You are my lifemate. I would not attempt to deceive you for any reason."

"And a lifemate means . . . ?" she prompted softly, struggling to comprehend.

"For a Carpathian male, there is only one chance at true life. We lose our feelings early. We have the memories of emotion to sustain us, and we have the ability to touch others so that we can share their feelings, but after centuries of loneliness and bleakness, it is difficult to maintain the illusion that life has meaning. The whisper of power calls us continually, a dark stain spreading over our souls. Some give up and seek eternal rest; others choose the darkness and become the things of legend—vampires."

"If all this is true, how can I be your other half when I am not Carpathian?" She wasn't certain she wanted the answer. She felt like his other half. She felt as if she belonged with him. Every moment spent in his company only made the feeling stronger. She knew nothing about him, yet she felt as if she knew everything. But if she believed what he was telling her, she would also have to believe in the legendary vampires.

"You have psychic ability. Human women who have paranormal abilities often seem to be able to link with us—at least that is what I have been told. Syndil and Barack are lifemates. Desari's lifemate, Julian, is Carpathian. But Darius found a human woman. Her name is Tempest, and she came to us through an ad Desari placed for a mechanic to travel with our band. Desari embedded a hidden compulsion in the ad in the hope that it would draw the right person to us, and Tempest answered."

"Is she human still?"

Dayan brought her fingertips to the warmth of his mouth, nipped gently, tenderly. "Tempest chose to save Darius's life and in doing so was fully brought over into our world. It was her choice, Corinne. Darius did not want any of us discussing the possibility with her, because he did not want to take any chances with her life."

"Chances?" she echoed. She was very tired all of a sudden and wished for the familiar comfort of Lisa.

Or John.

Dayan winced visibly. He knew it was natural for her, as natural as it would be for him to think of Desari or Syndil. He had spent several lifetimes with them and loved them deeply. Yet it bothered him that Corinne wanted the comfort of another man's company, of another man's arms. He knew he would love the baby; he already felt a strong bond with her. And if he was successful in saving Corinne's life, it would be his blood running in the child's veins.

Dayan's heart turned over at the thought of his child in her body. He framed her face with gentle hands. "There have been mistakes—human women who were not true lifemates, and they became deranged. Darius did not want to chance such a tragedy with his lady."

"What about you? You say you've given me your blood. Are you so willing to take a chance with my life?"

Dayan leaned forward to kiss her soft mouth because he had to. He couldn't see and feel her distress, her growing fear, without needing to reassure her in some way. The moment his mouth touched hers, featherlight, a brush only, his body clenched hotly and his blood turned to molten lava. She could do that to him with a look, a touch, with the taste of her perfect mouth. His fingers slipped around her face to clench in her hair, holding her still for his exploration.

Corinne responded immediately, kissing him back without hesitation, the electricity arcing between them as strong as ever. Her body seemed to melt into his with total acceptance. He made her feel instantly sheltered by him, protected. "I would never take a chance with your life, Corinne," he whispered fiercely against the corner of her mouth. "How could you think that? You are my life. My sanity. My music. Without you, there is nothing. I have known that existence, and I will not go back to it. I believe my blood can save your life. That is what allowed Gregori to heal you to the extent that he did."

"But the repairs won't hold up," she guessed softly, snuggling deeper into his arms. She was very tired and knew she needed to sleep again, but she wanted to be as close to him as possible.

"No, honey, not for long. We are hoping for enough time to give the baby a chance. That is the biggest complication." He chose his words very carefully.

"If my heart won't last, why are you so certain you can save my life?" She murmured the words softly, not really caring about the answer. If he could save the life of her child, she would be more than grateful to him. It would be worth everything, every bad moment in her life.

"My blood would transform your internal organs, convert you to what we are. That is my intention, Corinne. I know you are my true lifemate and I know it will work. There are no doubts in my mind."

She raised her head, pushed at his chest to put space between them so she could look into his black eyes. "Make me like you?"

Her heart had skipped a beat, but went on steadily. She was simply watching him, almost as if she were observing the scene from a great distance. Dayan captured her hand, needing to hang on to her, suddenly afraid the blankness in her mind was a refusal of his intentions. "It is the only way, Corinne, the only thing that will save your life. If you live, I live. We have no other choice. Gregori said your heart was too far gone and he could only hope to keep it going long enough for the baby to be born."

Corinne framed his face with her hands, her green gaze steady. "Perhaps you should have thought to ask me what I might want. I believe in talking things over, and I certainly think a decision this big should be made *by* me, not *for* me."

Dayan nodded. "I will not lie to you, Corinne. I thought about discussing it with you and dismissed the idea. As it is, you are very weak; your heart is strained to the maximum. I would have had to explain everything to you—"

"Like you're doing now," she pointed out solemnly.

"I am attempting to explain," he conceded, "but I am monitoring your heart closely to be sure the information is not too frightening. It is not every day that one hears of another species."

"And that is what you are?"

Dayan nodded slowly, his black gaze holding hers, his mind firmly in hers to catch every thought that passed through her brain. "Yes. We are as old as time and we live long lives. Our blood is different, and we have many gifts. We can run with the animals, soar with the birds, become the mist should there be need. But there is a price for these gifts. You would inherit these abilities, but you would also pay the same price."

"Which is . . . ?"

"The sun is harmful to us. Our bodies become like lead, paralyzed in the light of day. Those of us who have not chosen to lose our souls can move about in early morning and early evening while the undead are locked beneath the earth, but we are vulnerable during the afternoon. There are those who hunt us."

Corinne lay back among the pillows, pale and small. She took his breath away with her slight angelic smile. "Don't look so anxious, Dayan," she advised softly. "I am having more trouble believing this than accepting it for myself. I have never been able to run like other children. Now I am stuck on this bed, so weak I can't carry my own baby without help. You are the one keeping my heart beating." Her long eyelashes fanned down, two thick crescents against her white skin. "I am locked to this bed as surely as you say you are locked to the earth. The idea of running with animals and soaring with birds is very appealing to me. And I am already hunted. Remember, someone killed John and made another attempt on me. Although the threat is frightening, I can't pretend it didn't happen."

The relief sweeping through him left him feeling weak. Corinne laughed softly without opening her eyes. "Don't get too sure of yourself, Dayan. I haven't decided if you're a certified nutcase and I should be screaming down the house for help. I'm too tired to figure it out right now, so you're relatively safe at the moment."

"At least you are giving me a chance, Corinne, and I cannot ask for more than that. If it becomes necessary, I can remove your memories permanently."

"You can leave well enough alone, Dayan. I want to know you before I commit my life to your life. I met John when I was eleven years old. I thought I knew him well, but the truth is, I didn't."

He brushed his hand through the silk of her hair, a soothing caress meant to ease the tension in her. "You knew him. He did not know you."

She felt tears welling up out of nowhere. John. She never should have married him, never should have promised what she knew she couldn't give him. She had loved John, but not in the way she should have. Not in the way he deserved.

"Do not cry, baby, you are breaking my heart," he whispered softly, bending to kiss away her tears. He pulled his guitar into his lap, cradling the familiar instrument to him. His fingers began to move, flashing over the strings as if a spell had been cast over him. His offering. His comfort to her. A pouring out of his deepest soul.

Dayan played softly, his voice filling her mind with love and happiness, with dreams of a life together, with fantasies of running through the woods in the form of a wild cat, of flying through the air like an eagle, free and content. Of silk sheets and candlelight. Of children playing in the moonlight, singing along to his music. Of life. He was offering her life.

Chapter Thirteen

Lisa raised her head and looked carefully around the room. Her heart was pounding very loudly and her mouth was dry. She had no idea where she was or how she'd gotten there. Her last coherent thought was of getting something to drink from the hospital cafeteria. She was definitely not in a hospital now.

Cullen lay stretched out on a bed, a king-sized mahogany bed, his skin color much less gray. If anything, Lisa thought he looked even more handsome than before. She touched his face with gentle fingertips, an unnamed emotion rising sharp and fast out of nowhere. She barely knew him, yet he seemed to mean so much to her already. That frightened her, as everything frightened her. Life itself frightened her. Lisa knew there was no real stability; people you loved, people you thought you knew, could turn into monsters right before your eyes and plot to destroy you.

She had no right in getting involved in this man's life. He was too good, a steady rock, someone capable of attempting to protect her against killers with guns. She

251

was damaged, and she would never be all right. Where Corinne had grown strong and accepted life, had learned to be find beauty and goodness in the world, Lisa thought in terms of shadows. She was so afraid all the time. No matter how hard she tried to overcome her failings, she knew she could never face the world on her own. Where was Corinne? Where was her brother? She couldn't go on alone.

'But you're not alone.'

Lisa spun around, staring wildly. The room was empty. She was the only one there. And she hadn't spoken aloud. There was only . . . Lisa turned back to the bed. Cullen lay with his eyes closed, but his hand was moving slowly across the comforter to find her fingers. Immediately she laced her fingers through his. "Thank God, Cullen. I've been so worried."

A faint smile touched his mouth. "I should be sorry I worried you"—his voice was quiet but strong—"but the truth is, I'm glad you cared enough to worry."

"Thank God you're awake," she said staunchly. "I don't know where Corinne is, and we aren't at the hospital. Your friends came and took you out. They said those people would try to kill you if we stayed there. I thought they'd take us wherever Dayan and Corinne are, but . . ." She looked around rather helplessly. "I don't know, maybe they are here; I just woke up myself. I'm not even certain how we got here."

Cullen's lashes fluttered as he tried to pry open his eyes to see her face. She sounded forlorn and lost and he wanted to gather her close to him. "Barack and Syndil from the band came, remember? I was talking to them. I thought I heard Darius too."

She pulled his hand to her chin, held it close against her bare skin. "I don't know any Darius. I can't remember hearing that name before."

"Darius is our lead singer's brother. He handles security for the band. When Darius is around, you don't have to worry too much about anything. If he gave the order to move Corinne and me to a safer situation, they would do it."

"I only saw Barack and Syndil. They were pretty nice, especially Syndil," Lisa said. "I've been so scared, Cullen. The doctors said you might not survive the night and they told me Corinne and the baby both were going to die. And then Corinne just disappeared without a trace." Lisa was trying very hard to keep the wail out of her voice, but it was there all the same and she hated it.

Cullen managed to get his eyes open to look at her. He inhaled deeply, taking in the faint peach fragrance that always clung to her skin. She was so beautiful to him, it hurt to look at her. She tried hard to be strong, to be something she wasn't, and criticized herself because she didn't measure up in her own eyes. "It's going to be all right, Lisa. I promise I'm not going to die. Barack gave me his blood."

She blinked at him without expression, not comprehending what he was saying. "You needed a transfusion and he gave you one? I heard Syndil say you needed blood, but the memory's vague." Lisa found her memories of the band members were hazy. She couldn't form a distinct impression of any of them, though she had just been with them. She rubbed her forehead; her temples were pounding.

Cullen tugged at her hand to get her attention. "None of that matters, honey. Let the others take care of everything else." He smiled at her. "I'm glad you're here with me. I know you'd rather be with Corinne, but I need you here. Dayan's a good man—he would never allow anything to happen to her."

"Where was he? Why were *you* with Corinne, instead of Dayan?" Lisa tried to keep an accusatory tone out of her voice. A big part of her disliked Dayan tremendously—unless he was standing directly in front of her. Then, she didn't know why, but it was almost as if her entire opinion of him changed. None of it made sense to her. Lisa swept a hand through her hair and looked bemused. "I'm very confused about Dayan."

Cullen thought she looked more beautiful than ever. "Dayan is good for Corinne. I know him, Lisa. If you value my opinion, at least trust me on this one issue. I know him—I know what he's like. He would never betray a friendship, and he's the closest thing to family I have. The band took me in when I had no one. Everyone I loved was dead, and I had no future. They disregarded the fact that I had actively helped to hunt them and instead allowed me to travel with them for protection. They not only offered protection and friendship, but they took me into their family and made me feel a part of it. Very few people would have been that kind to a total stranger."

Lisa sat quietly, strangely happy in Cullen's company. She felt at peace when she was with him. There was a soft knock on the door, and Lisa turned quickly as Syndil pushed it open and smiled at them.

"Good, you are awake. Is he being good and staying down?"

Lisa found herself smiling, she couldn't help herself. Syndil was a tranquil, appealing woman, and Lisa couldn't imagine her being anything but honest and sweet. "He's being reasonably good," she answered, brushing at Cullen's hair to keep it out of his eyes. "I think his color is better and his voice is strong." She turned to Cullen. "Are you hurting anywhere?"

She sounded so anxious, Cullen smiled, tightening his grip on her hand. "Surprisingly I feel pretty good. But I wouldn't want to repeat the experience. It was fairly scary."

Lisa and Syndil exchanged a very feminine look. "You were out most of the time, Cullen," Lisa noted. "We were terrified for you."

"I'm going to show Lisa the house," Syndil told Cullen in her gentle voice, "while Barack takes a look at you. He wants to explain a few things to you." She took Lisa's arm firmly. "Come with me; I will show you around so you can find everything. If there is anything you need, please tell us immediately." As she led Lisa through the door, she bent closer with a conspirator's whisper. "It is obvious Cullen prefers your company to any other's."

Lisa found herself smiling up at Syndil, never feeling the cold air brushing her as Barack slipped past her unseen to go to Cullen's side. Barack waited until the door was closed and he could hear Syndil talking to Lisa about the food in the kitchen before he materialized beside Cullen.

Cullen watched him with patient eyes. "I knew you were there. You gave me your blood, didn't you?"

Barack shrugged his broad shoulders as if the tremendous gift of life had been a casual one. "You know how the women feel about you. I could do no other than to save your worthless hide or they would have been after me for centuries."

"Darius?" Cullen said the name softly.

Barack grinned at him. "I would not want to be in your shoes when he comes to see you. It is not so much what he says; it is the look he gives you when you nearly get yourself killed that makes you wish your enemy had not missed. He is not happy you placed yourself in such a position. And, of course, there is Dayan."

Cullen groaned aloud. "I don't want to think about Dayan right now. How is Corinne?"

Barack sighed. "She does not have long to live if Dayan does not give her his blood and bring her fully into our world. But there is the complication of the child. It is said she is like Corinne, and we do not want to lose her either. They are trying." He glanced at the door. "We have much to speak about and little time to do it. Lisa is anxious to be back in your company."

"You are too hard on her, Barack," Cullen said.

"So Syndil tells me," he responded. "You know you are different now. You are connected to me for all time. You can touch me when you wish; there is an open path between our minds. The blood bond between us will remain for all your life. You know what we are part of the time, but we shadow your memories most of the time so you are not in danger. It is different now. You will always be a threat to our species. Should your blood be examined, you would endanger us."

Cullen nodded his head, his eyes steady on Barack's face. He had already guessed as much. He had known the moment he had awakened. His hearing was far more acute. It was night, yet he could see clearly in the dark. He felt different, stronger, healthy despite the terrible wounds. He was also aware that his body was healing at a phenomenal rate of speed.

Cullen had been traveling with the band members for some time. He had learned to accept the fact that sometimes he knew what they were and other times his memory of them was hazy and he couldn't conjure up an image of what they looked like. On some level he knew it was necessary to protect the band from any other human seeking information about them. And it was necessary to protect himself from any vampires who might scan the information in his mind. As he traveled in the company of the band, it was likely he would someday encounter one. He knew that everything had changed for him when Barack had given him blood.

"You are under the protection of the family," Barack said softly, "and Darius wants you to know you always will be. But we cannot undo what has been done. There are decisions to be made. We made the choice to save your life, and the blood was freely given because of your place within our family, but only you can make the rest of the choices for yourself. We will respect whatever you decide."

Cullen nodded, understanding more than Barack knew. When his memories of them were clear, he remembered every detail and he had learned a great deal about their species. They were offering him a choice, and he was grateful that he was even being consulted.

"It is not a decision to be made lightly, Cullen," Barack counseled. "You must know I will always be able to read your mind, whether you choose full knowledge or to have your memories removed. I would know if you betrayed us to anyone, including your future wife. I see clearly into your mind. You want Lisa to be your partner, but she will never be able to accept our species as we are. She must always see us as human. She could not accept Corinne's differences, and she would be unable to live with the knowledge. If you choose us as your family, you can never reveal what we are to her. You are someone who values honor and integrity. You want a full partnership with your wife. She will always be in our lives, because she loves Corinne and Corinne loves her. To Corinne, Lisa is family, as you are to us. But you will have to keep this knowledge from Lisa for all time. We have lifemates. We understand the bond between male and female. If you choose to remove the memory of us, we will understand. Remember we will still have the same feelings for you, and you will remain under our protection. It is up to you."

Cullen smiled, his teeth very white. "You are my family."

"As Lisa will be."

"Exactly. As Corinne will be. Lisa loves her as a sister. My wife will be connected to you for the rest of her life.

257

Christine Feehan

If I choose to forget, then I can't give her my protection and help to shield her from the things she can't accept. I know what Lisa is like. She needs a protected environment, someone willing to shield her from the things she can't accept. I want to be that person. Not you or Darius. Me. I never thought I could feel alive again. You know strength, Barack, but you don't know what it's like for someone to struggle like she has to do to live in a world with people capable of doing monstrous things she can't understand. You have it in you to kill if need be. She is incapable of shouting at anyone. It hurts her when people raise their voices at one another. You think of that as a weakness. I look at her and see someone too good to live in a world like this one. I want to shield her. I want the chance to have her love me."

"We will love and accept the one you choose to share your life with. Forgive me, Cullen—I will work on my failings. Syndil has pointed out this same flaw, and I do not intend to continue with this behavior if I can help it. I will get to know Lisa and I will always protect her. You can count on that."

"Thank you," Cullen said quietly. "I'll retain my memories and work to guard our family, as you, Dayan, Julian and Darius always do. I don't want to forget any of it. Neither the good nor the bad. You are all I have."

"Then so be it." Barack gripped Cullen's hand hard for a moment, then backed off. "I have sent your answer to Darius and the others. If you have need, you have only to follow the path in your mind and you can speak with me." He grinned. "Of course, you can do the same with Darius."

Cullen stared up at him for a moment, thinking that over. He should have known that Darius had taken his blood to open a channel to his mind. Darius *always* protected his family. It was his nature. "Go away. I like looking at Lisa better. But tell Dayan we are praying for Corinne and baby."

Corinne slept fitfully, with strange images flitting in and out of her dreams. When she woke, sometimes the healers were in the room with her, but most of the time there was only Dayan. There were times he lay beside her. Often he sat quietly holding her hand and staring lovingly down at her face. Other times she woke to the sound of his music, a soothing harmony of voice and guitar. She tried a few times to overcome the terrible lethargy that seemed to have invaded her body, but it was too much trouble and she closed her eyes time and time again with the image of Dayan filling her mind and heart. Strangely, she wasn't afraid anymore, not for herself and not for her baby.

She had no idea how much time had passed before she managed to really wake up. She lay quietly taking inventory of her body. Corinne could hear her heart beating, as well as that of her child. She moved her hands protectively over the baby and murmured softly to the child, wondering if she could hear her. As she talked to her daughter, she looked around the beautiful room. It was full of treasures, from the artwork to the carvings on the high ceilings. The room was very large, the colors muted and elegant. The carvings looked like strange, beautiful hieroglyphics. Some of the symbols were soothing to her, while others made her heart pound if she stared at them too long.

Her hand moved over the thick quilt covering her. It was art too, a beautiful blend of colors with similar symbols woven into it. Each character was wide and clear, the surface smooth to the touch. She found her fingers continually seeking out the different symbols and tracing them carefully over and over.

She felt Dayan beside her, just lying quietly, his body

wrapped protectively around hers. Corinne turned her head to find him watching her, his black gaze loving. There was so much tenderness there, so much emotion, he robbed her of breath. She smiled, her soft mouth curving as she lifted a hand to touch his face with gentle fingertips. "Hello," she said softly. "Have you been waiting there long?"

"Several risings," he answered honestly, shifting so that he could prop himself up on his elbow to better study her face.

"What are you doing?" she asked, slightly embarrassed by his close scrutiny. He was watching her with unblinking eyes.

"Memorizing your face," he answered truthfully, his gaze drifting over every inch of her classic features. "I want to close my eyes and still be able to see you. I used to welcome daylight as a relief from the ever-present whisperings of darkness, yet now I resent those hours because I cannot be with you. I want to talk to you, just be silent beside you, look at you, reach out and touch you, know you are real and not some figment of my imagination." He traced her mouth, her eyebrows, his thumb lingering on the corner of her lips. "I do not want to sleep anymore because I cannot take you with me."

"Do you have to sleep away from me?" she asked, running her hand up and down his arm, needing to touch him almost as much as he needed to touch her.

He bent to brush a gentle kiss across the temptation of her mouth. "When I sleep, it is as if I am dead. I shut down my heart and lungs and do not breathe air. Our species does not have to seek the earth to sleep, and many of our people do not, but they sleep in chambers below ground where they are relatively safe from human hunters and accidents. Most of us do seek the rejuvenating sleep of the earth because it is safer and more natural to us. I would prefer to be beside you always, but it would be unsettling to you to wake and find me as if dead."

"Not if I was expecting such a thing. Why are you so distressed, Dayan?" She pushed her fingers through his hair. "I'm beginning to be able to read you, and you are having a difficult time. If something is wrong, just tell me."

"Everything is going the way the healers have predicted with your health," he answered vaguely, his black gaze slipping away from her.

She curled her fingers around his wrist. "What is it?"

He shrugged casually. Too casually. "There is a ritual between lifemates. It is necessary to bind us together. Until we are formally bound together, I am still a slight risk to others. There is nothing to be done about it, Corinne, until your health is better. It is just uncomfortable for me." The beast was struggling for supremacy from within. He felt it growing stronger with each rising. He needed her more than ever to anchor him. He needed her soul bound to his, her heart to complete him, her body for a safe haven.

"What ritual?" she asked curiously. "And don't shrug and put me off. If we're a partnership, then you have to give me the trust you insist on having from me."

He sighed. "You are getting tough on me, Corinne. Am I losing my charm?" He made an attempt to tease her, to make light of a dark situation.

"I don't think you could ever do that," she reassured him with an answering smile. "But I want us to be very certain we're together on this. It's important to me, Dayan. I don't want to do the wrong thing and take a chance of hurting you. This has happened very fast. I'm someone who has to think things through thoroughly before I make decisions. And you are asking me to take a lot of things on faith."

"We might come from two different worlds, Corinne, but you know we belong together."

"Maybe," she agreed noncommittally. "So tell me the ritual."

He circled her waist with his arm and leaned down to kiss her again. This time he lingered over the simple pleasure, savoring the moment. "When a Carpathian male recognizes his lifemate, he recites ritual words to bind her. The words are imprinted on him before birth. It is much like a human marriage but more permanent. Once said, the words bind the two, heart and soul and mind. She cannot escape him. They cannot be apart after that. They must touch one another often, using mind touch or they become . . ." He hesitated, searching for the right word. "I don't know—they need to be with one another or they can be very uncomfortable."

"He just says a few words and she belongs to him?" She pushed at his chest with her small hand, glaring. "That doesn't sound very fair to me."

"Now, Corinne"—his voice was as soft as velvet and just as sensuous—"I was not the one who created the ritual. It is thousands of years old. I can do no other than what my heart and soul demand."

"You said the words to me?"

He shook his head, his thick blue-black hair falling around his face. "I cannot while you are so ill. I do not know if your heart would be able to stand a separation from me during the hours I must sleep."

"And it's hard for you because you haven't bound us together?" Her small white teeth bit at her lower lip as she struggled to understand what he was telling her. Words like *risings* and *rituals* belonged in someone else's world, not hers. She was very practical. When he began to laugh, she frowned at him, trying to look severe. "You were reading my mind again, weren't you?"

He shrugged, that intriguing ripple of muscles beneath his immaculate shirt. "Naturally. I am your lifemate."

"How do you keep your clothes so perfect? And your hair. Why don't you have morning breath?" Self-consciously she put her hand over her own mouth. *How did he look so perfectly sexy and inviting, when she was disheveled and looking pretty much like a beached whale?*

Dayan really laughed then, he couldn't help it. Her image of herself was so far from the real thing that it was ludicrous. He couldn't imagine Corinne's soft, curvy body looking remotely like a whale. He lay back on the bed with her beside him, real, alive, her heart still beating, and he laughed out loud. It was a perfect moment in time.

She started laughing too, just because he was so silly, his joy so evident. Corinne thumped him hard on the chest. "Stop laughing at me."

"I cannot help it, honey. A beached whale? I can hardly tell you are pregnant. That is not a good analogy at all." He put his hand over the mound of her stomach. "And I like you disheveled." He caught her face in his hands and dragged her mouth to his.

The earth seemed to move beneath the bed, a curious rolling effect that brought dancing whips of lightning arcing through the room. The air vibrated with hunger and need. He lifted his head reluctantly and stared into her green eyes. "I love you as you are, Corinne. Right now, in this bed, while we cannot make love and there is a child growing within you. I love you with your hair all over the place and that slightly confused look on your beautiful face." He rolled over to place his hands on either side of her head, pinning her to the bed. "I love how you look at me as if you want to take care of me, though I am the one who is the male."

She touched her fingertips to his perfectly chiseled mouth. "We can take care of each other." Her voice was soft and inviting, a temptation he found impossible to resist.

Aching with love for her, he bent his dark head slowly so that she watched as he came closer, his black gaze hot and hungry and full of terrible need. Corinne circled his head with her slender arms and met his mouth with a hunger of her own. He was heat and light, a symphony of music that lit her very soul. He made her heart beat wildly and her spirit soar high above the clouds. There was no one else for her, whether human or of his species. There was only Dayan with his poet's soul and hungry eyes and dominating mouth. His hard masculine body and his perfect hands that moved over her body with the same talent as they moved over his instrument.

It was Dayan who pulled away first, putting inches between them, but he was breathing heavily. "Your heart is pounding."

Her mouth curved slowly, her eyes dancing. "That's yours, not mine." It wasn't strictly true; both hearts were beating out a syncopated rhythm together.

"The healers are going to come in here and give us a lecture," Dayan whispered, glancing at the door.

She ruffled his hair, enjoying the luxury of touching the silky wayward strands. "What will they do if they catch us?" she asked, smirking at him. "Be shocked?"

"Order me out is more like it," he said gravely. "I would be given a lecture about how irresponsible and selfish I am. Which I am. I should be very careful of you at all times, not giving in to temptation every time you smile at me." He frowned at her when she pushed at his chest. "What are you doing?"

"Getting up. I have to go to the bathroom. I take it that's not something your species has to do much." She was teasing, but the smile faded when he continued to look at her steadily. She held up her hand. "Don't even go there. I don't want to know. Just get out of my way and let a mere mortal do her thing."

"My love"—the words came out a whisper, velvet soft, and seemed to shimmer in the air between them— "I cannot allow you to run around. The healers said complete bed rest. I must insist you obey."

"They didn't mean not go to the bathroom. I seem to remember you carrying me the last time, but it isn't necessary." When he refused to move, she sighed heavily and changed tactics. "All right, carry me again. But this is embarrassing, and I'm afraid it's becoming a bad habit."

Dayan lifted her easily, cradling her in his arms. "I do not see why. You think of the strangest things."

"I'd like to be in your mind once in a while and see what goes on in there," she challenged him.

He set her carefully on the tile floor beside the wide marble sink. "You can read my mind anytime you like, honey. My mind is always merged with yours. I stay a shadow in there so I can find out all those fascinating things you try to hide from the world." He smirked at her. "You are just too much of a chicken to actually look into my mind and see what thoughts are lurking there."

She stood there, gripping the side of the marble sink, staring up at him for a few moments. "Well?" She waited. "Out! You can't think you're going to stay in here."

"I cannot leave you alone," he said mildly.

"I mean it, Dayan. Get out this instant. No arguing. Out!" She was very firm and tough about it.

Dayan looked helpless for a moment, then shrugged and glided out of the bathroom, deciding the old adage "Discretion is the better part of valor" held true.

The door closed with a hard thud behind him at a wave from Corinne's hand. "Make sure your mind goes with you," she called out, then found she was smiling because she could wave at doors and faucets and set her toothbrush in motion and it didn't seem to bother Dayan in the least.

'I do not know why you would think my mind would not go with me and stay with you at the same time.' His voice brushed at the walls of her mind like the flutter of butterfly wings, sending waves of warmth coursing through her.

For the first time in a long while, Corinne found she was truly happy. Standing in the bathroom, leaning against the sink, making an attempt to do something with her wild mass of hair, she was perfectly happy. Once she had pulled her hair free from the thick braid, it was too heavy to manage. She found she was too tired to lift her arms to tidy it. She sighed very softly.

'What is wrong?' There was anxiety in his voice.

Corinne didn't actually reply, she knew she didn't, she just sighed again, but it was enough to bring him rushing in, scooping her up as if she were precious porcelain. Her hair tumbled in all directions, fanning out over his shoulder and across the dark shadow on his jaw. "Just can't stay away, can you?" she asked, secretly grateful he had raced in to rescue her.

"I knew you needed rescuing," he said with great male satisfaction.

"Was I thinking *rescue?* That was the actual word in my mind?" She shook her head as she settled onto the bed. "I don't think *rescue* was the precise word. I can't imagine using a word like that."

"Oh, it was *rescue* all right." He wasn't going to let her off the hook that easily, not when her green eyes were sparkling with laughter and her intriguing dimple was very much in evidence. He especially loved that dimple. He knew he could spend hours looking at that dimple and never get tired of it.

He took the brush out of her hand. "It is amazing what the males of my race are called upon to do."

Corinne waved her hand toward the center of the room. "Go over there and do something." When he sat there, she pushed him, "Go on, do something."

"Something?" he echoed as he moved obediently into the middle of the bedroom. "What kind of something?" He sounded wary.

"I don't know exactly. Something cool. What do you like to do?" She was looking at him from under her fringe of long lashes.

Dayan suddenly grinned like a mischievous boy. "Anything at all?"

"Sure. Something really big."

His black eyebrows shot up. "If I show you, are you going to show me?"

"Sounds like a dare to me," Corinne said. "I can't resist a dare."

"Then you go first." He folded his arms across his chest, regarding her with his black gaze. "If I go first, you are quite likely to faint from shock."

"*Faint!* I am not the fainting type. *Nothing* you do could scare me that much now that I know you can do it," she replied haughtily.

'*You do not altogether believe I can do it.*' His voice whispered in her mind, sinfully intimate. It was temptation, it turned her body to molten liquid.

Corinne found herself staring at him, almost mesmerized by his black-magic spell. He had woven his dark melody so completely, so perfectly, she hadn't realized she was immersed in his music, in his soul. To cover up her reaction to the sheer intimacy of a mind merge, Corinne forced her wayward thoughts under control and concentrated. At once the brush in his

267

hand jumped free and moved through the air to resume the task of taming her flyaway hair. With intense concentration she divided the mass into three sections, using the power of her mind alone, and wove the long hair into a thick braid. A scrunchie came dancing out of the bathroom at her call and fastened itself to the end of her hair to complete the job.

Corinne looked up at him then, a trace of apprehension marring the perfection of her joy. "Well?" She looked like a little girl, unsure whether to feel pride or fear.

Deliberately he grinned at her, a taunting male grin of sheer competition. "Watch this." He held out his arm, his eyes fixed intently on her face, his mind wholly merged with hers in case she was frightened by the change as it came over him. Fur rippled along his arm, muscles contorted and popped.

Corinne watched in wonderment as the man slowly shape-shifted until a large male leopard was standing in the center of the room staring at her with that same unblinking stare. For a moment she stared, almost frozen in place, but then the cat moved, its powerful muscles rippling as it glided silently toward her. She recognized him! She knew it was Dayan. There was the same fluid grace and power, the same hungry eyes devouring her. Her heart rate accelerated, but it wasn't out of fear. Amazement. Fascination. Never fear. Not when it was Dayan.

The leopard nuzzled her so that she buried her hand in the glossy fur, astonished at the texture, at the joy of being so close to something belonging in the wild. She laughed aloud as she caressed the animal's head with her fingertips. For a moment she rubbed her face along the thick neck of the leopard, loving the feel of the fur against her skin. It was exotic, a rare privilege to be so close to a wild animal. The leopard nuzzled her back, its eyes staring at her, mesmerizing, trapping her in the untamed depths. Dayan. Her Dayan. She would know him anywhere, in any shape.

Without warning, a dark shadow seemed to creep slowly into the room, invading the air like a thick foul oil. Corinne froze in place, her entire body going perfectly still. She felt Dayan's reassuring presence in her mind. She watched in horror as the shadow seemed to take shape on the far wall, a grotesque bent figure, a skeleton stick figure with long, bony fingers that seemed to be tipped with daggerlike talons. Her heart thudded in alarm, and instantly Dayan's body was solidly in front of her. She felt the others joining with her too, merging minds—Desari a soothing, calming influence, and Gregori and Darius powerful and, she sensed, deadly.

All of them protected her, shielded her from the creeping shadow. It was wholly evil, a thick oily presence probing, seeking, *hunting* something. Corinne felt certain the evil thing was hunting her. She sat very still, kept her mind firmly anchored in the sanity and calm of the others. Shockingly, her heart remained steady, beating in the same rhythm as Dayan's while her lungs breathed along with his.

It was Dayan that surprised her the most. Her poet, so kind and gentle, so giving and loving, was suddenly something altogether different. She felt the contrast in his mind first. She was so attuned to him she recognized the change immediately. It came swiftly, naturally, and she realized these qualities were as much a part of him as his music and his beautiful words. He was dark, dangerous, a silent, deadly predator, a killing machine. Merciless. Without remorse. Ruthless. The total opposite of her poet. The cunning, relentless beast he had named himself. He would be unswerving on the hunt.

And he would never stop until he had destroyed his prey.

Corinne felt Desari stronger than ever, tranquil, soothing, comforting, whispering softly in her mind, the words almost indistinguishable, yet Corinne knew she was aiding her to understand what manner of creature Dayan really was. She felt the momentary surge as the intruder reached for her in an attempt to draw her out. She was safe and protected within the walls of the cocoon the others had wrapped her in. There was no chance of the dark horror finding her, yet it touched the three male Carpathians.

She felt that. Felt the shock, the recoil. The thing shrieked, a hideous sound that was in her head, heard through the listening Carpathians, a high-pitched sound of anger and hatred and fear. It took Corinne a few heartbeats to realize the creature could detect only the males. The women were merged so deeply with the men that the beast could detect only the powerful males. The creature instantly withdrew, retreating with furtive swiftness.

Corinne blinked up at Dayan, barely able to comprehend the transformation in him from poet to predator. His hand brushed her face, her hair, incredibly gentle, seemed to linger for a moment, yet his body was shimmering, almost transparent. She watched, her heart in her throat, as he dissolved right before her eyes. In his place were droplets of mist. The mist streamed through the room and right out the door.

Just like that, Dayan was gone. From the room, from her mind. Gregori and Darius had also disappeared from the mind merge, leaving only Desari, who pushed open the door to the room and glided to her side with an encouraging smile. "You are not afraid, are you?" Her voice was rich with beauty.

Chapter Fourteen

"It all happened too fast to really understand what is going on," Corinne answered honestly, not certain how to feel. She looked past Desari to the two other women behind her. They were smiling in reassurance but hesitated in the doorway, so Corinne waved to encourage their entry.

"I believe we are under siege." Desari took Corinne's hand to comfort her and at the same time to check her pulse. "There is no need to be afraid. My brother Darius and Gregori are two of the most accomplished hunters we have. They are seeking the evil one, along with Dayan, to destroy that which is a threat to humans and immortals alike." She spoke calmly, as if chasing evil monsters were an everyday occurrence. "Naturally, they will see to it that Dayan does not come to any harm. After all, we are fighting to save you and the child. We will not lose Dayan to an evil one."

Corinne studied the other woman's face carefully. She could see only goodness, compassion, a light shining outward from deep within Desari's soul. She appeared tranquil even in the face of such an evil being. "It felt horrible," Corinne admitted in a low voice, "and I could tell that Dayan was shielding me somehow from the experience."

"It was a vampire," the shorter, raven-haired woman answered calmly, reaching for a glass of clear water. "Here, drink this. I'm Savannah, Gregori's lifemate, by the way. I know it sounds absurd and something that cannot be real, but I assure you, vampires exist and they actively seek women who have psychic ability. Especially a woman unclaimed."

"You're Savannah Dubrinsky, the magician. I saw your performance in Seattle a few months ago. You were wonderful." Corinne sipped at the water to give her mind time to comprehend the situation. "That thing was looking for me, wasn't it?"

Desari shrugged casually. "In a way. You drew it here, although it does not know who you are. When it probed, it found only the male hunters. It will not be a problem, because they will destroy it."

"If this is all true," Corinne demanded, "why hasn't one ever tried to find me before?" As much as it seemed impossible for Desari to lie, Corinne didn't want her explanation to be true. Maybe it would have been better to live without knowing any of it.

The redhead smiled at her. "I'm Tempest, and believe me, Corinne, I know how confused you must be by all this. I was in your shoes only a few weeks ago. Just remember this," she continued, revealing that she could read Corinne's thoughts; "you would be missing a great adventure, which life is, and you would miss knowing Dayan. Most importantly, eventually you would have chosen to use your gift, and the surge of power would have revealed your presence to the undead. They would have found you."

"I have used my talent before," Corinne asserted.

"Perhaps, but in small things—little surges of power that would not call to the undead unless you were already in close proximity to them. More and more you are becoming at ease with your talents. Any surge of power leaves traces. We can find one another through those surges, and so can the undead." Desari spoke matter-of-factly, calmly, as if she were speaking of the weather.

"On the other hand, this all might be some weird nightmare I haven't managed to extract myself from," Corinne suggested with a slight smile. "Dayan is worth it, though. I love to listen to him. He says the most beautiful things to me. He has such a beautiful voice, and a beautiful soul. He always makes me feel as if I'm the only woman in his world."

"To him you are the only woman," Desari said. "And truly, Corinne, how could he not fall in love with you? Look at you—the way you've accepted your physical problems and still held your family together, the way you've accepted the information that Dayan has given you. It cannot be easy for you, but you work at listening and believing and comprehending what he tells you. Who else would give him that kind of acceptance? After centuries of being alone, without an other half, he finally has a home, and he appreciates it. You are his home. No other. You."

"I don't think he has accepted my physical problems," Corinne said, embarrassed by the woman's words.

"Because he fights for you?" Tempest laughed softly. "You'll find that that is one thing the males of this species are exceptionally good at."

Savannah nodded. "Dayan is fighting for your life and the life of your child. In truth he fights for his life also. Without you he has nothing. Dayan has existed in a bleak, barren world—he will not choose to continue

273

without you. Should you travel to the next world, he will accompany you, as is his right as a Carpathian male."

"I'm very tired," Corinne confessed, her hand going protectively over her gently rolling baby. "I try to hide it from him, but he always seems to know."

Desari smoothed back Corinne's hair with gentle fingers. "He is your lifemate. Of course he knows. I have known Dayan my entire life. I am so happy he has found you. He tells us you are C. J. Wentworth, the songwriter. I am so pleased to welcome you into our family."

Corinne sank back among the pillows. "I'm glad he has you all." She wanted Dayan. Wanted to spend every moment she had left with him. She could feel her strength ebbing away, slowly but surely. "What about my baby?" She looked at Savannah and then Tempest. "I know they must have told you the truth."

It was Savannah who answered. "Your heart will not hold up forever. In one more rising we will conduct another healing ritual. Our goal now is to give your daughter a few more hours, or days, whatever time we can. Gregori says her will is strong, and that is half the battle. She is like you, a true psychic, and therefore very important to our race."

"You use the term *rising* because it is night, not morning, when you wake," Corinne guessed. "Do they think they can save her?"

"We are waiting for Shea to arrive. Jacques, her lifemate, insisted they rest before completing the journey. Shea is with child, and he is protective of her," Savannah reported. "My mother sent word ahead. Shea has done much research into the problems of keeping our infants alive. She is a tremendous resource to us all."

"I cannot believe she traveled all this way when she is with child," Desari said, slightly shocked. "Corinne, we have trouble bearing children; our race is bordering on extinction. Julian is hoping we can provide a child for our people soon."

"The interesting thing is," Savannah said, "Gary Jansen, a human friend of ours, a researcher, has been tracing the lineages of families in which children are born closer than fifty to one hundred years apart. There are only a couple of them. Sarantha, Mikhail's mother, comes from such a line, as does Gregori. Gary and Shea think the infrequency of conception is a form of natural birth control. Desari, you are a descendant of one of the lines. As far as we know, I'm the only other."

Tempest exchanged a long look with Desari. "Have you tried to get pregnant?" Tempest asked. "Darius and I only just found each other. I haven't thought of children yet."

Savannah laughed. "In truth, Gregori and I have only been together a few weeks. I would love to give him twins. Total trouble for him to frantically chase around and guard instead of me. As soon as we are finished here, we intend to return to the Carpathian Mountains, where we will make our home. Once settled, I'm certain we'll try to have a child. Jacques and Shea will travel home with us. All of us intend to fly to Paris first to visit with Gregori's older brothers, Gabriel and Lucian. Lucian was just married, but unfortunately, Gregori and I missed the wedding due to unforeseen circumstances."

"Is it dangerous for Shea to travel?" Corinne didn't want to think another woman had put her child in jeopardy for her sake.

"Jacques would never allow Shea to do anything dangerous," Savannah pointed out. "He's Mister Protective where she's concerned."

Tempest and Desari burst out laughing. "And Gregori isn't with you?"

Corinne frowned. "Where are Lisa and Cullen? Are they okay? Lisa must be so frightened."

The smile faded from Desari's face. She was silent for a moment before answering, obviously conferring with someone else. "Lisa and Cullen are relatively safe where they are. Barack and Syndil are with them. Julian, my lifemate, has gone to their aid and has removed all immediate threats to them. They are under his protection. He has something of a reputation in matters of security." Desari phrased it as delicately as possible so as not to disturb Corinne's careful balance.

Corinne paled even more. "I thought those people were trying to kill me. Is Lisa still in danger?"

"The society targets anyone with paranormal abilities, but its members do not seem to be able to distinguish those traits very well. Because Lisa is a member of your family, she was also put on their list. Cullen was already on it and had been for some time. After Dayan brought you here, another attempt was made on Cullen's life at the hospital. Of course, Barack and Syndil were there, so Lisa and Cullen were unharmed. We removed them to a more easily guarded place."

"Why didn't you bring them here? Lisa is easily frightened. This must be terrible for her. I need to go to her," Corinne said immediately, catching hold of the quilt as if to throw it off.

Desari laid a gentle hand over Corinne's. "You're not thinking clearly. Your first duty is to your daughter and your own health. You may be feeling better, but the improvement is definitely temporary. You cannot be moving around and making your heart work any harder than necessary. It would not do Lisa, Cullen or anyone else any good if you were to die." She leaned close so that her dark eyes could look directly into Corinne's. "You do know that, don't you, Corinne?"

Corinne blinked away the illusion that she was free-falling into space. "I know I love Lisa and she must be very frightened. Is Cullen going to live?"

Desari nodded. Corinne had extremely strong mind protection for a human. Dayan had told them it took more than usual strength to shield her mind or to persuade her. Desari didn't want to put any pressure on her that might alarm her. "Cullen sustained tremendous injuries, and the truth is, Barack donated blood to him, which is something we do not do lightly. Cullen cannot be fully brought over. He and Barack will be connected to one another for the rest of Cullen's lifetime. We have great affection for Cullen, and Darius would not allow him to die when it was in our power to save him. Lisa is with him and is helping to care for him. I believe it will be good for her to take responsibility for Cullen's health."

Corinne was watching Desari's face. "Because you think I'm going to die."

Desari shook her head decisively. "Because Dayan has no choice but to bring you fully into our world, and Lisa cannot follow you here. You will remain good friends, but you can no longer be the one to manage her life for her." Desari spoke as gently as possible, but her seriousness showed in her dark, expressive eyes.

Corinne bunched the quilt in her hand, her fingers rubbing nervously over the strange symbol sewn into the edge of the comforter. "Fully into your world." She repeated the phrase softly, under her breath.

"Dayan's world," Desari reminded her gently. "Just keep that uppermost in your mind. You will be in his world."

"What about my baby?" Corinne finally voiced the question she had been unable even to consider. She was terrified for her baby.

Desari smiled encouragingly at her. "Are you strong enough for the truth, Corinne? Because you have to know you want the truth when you ask for it."

Corinne found that tracing the strange symbol over and over on the quilt was soothing. It helped to keep her mind from shutting down with fear. "Is my baby going to live and be healthy?"

"We are doing everything in our power to make that happen. Dayan's blood, which we believe will save your life and will convert you, will also convert the baby if you are given the blood while you are pregnant. That presents us with a few problems and new territory we have never dealt with before." Desari's voice was hauntingly beautiful and tranquil. "I am being completely honest with you. We do not have the answers you seek. This has never happened before, at least not that I know of. Certainly, it has not happened to Gregori, and he is the acknowledged healer of our people."

Corinne's fingers found the next symbol in the quilt and traced the character. "I'm trying to understand what you're telling me. If Dayan doesn't give me his blood, I will die for certain. You're saying that's a fact."

Desari nodded solemnly. "We are only delaying the inevitable. He would have completed the conversion already if you were not carrying this child."

Corinne heard her heart racing and took a moment to slow it. "How does he do it? How does he complete the conversion?"

Desari's gaze held hers captive, almost as if she were sharing her courage. "There must be three blood exchanges. Each blood exchange will bring you a step further into our world. And of course, because you are his lifemate, Dayan will complete the ritual and make you wholly his."

"And you think this will save my life?" Corinne asked doubtfully, watching Desari's face carefully. Dayan believed it because he had to believe it—he had no other choice or he would go crazy—but Desari had no ties to her. "Do you really believe it, Desari?"

Desari sighed softly. "I believe the odds are in your favor if everything goes right and we time it all perfectly. You know as well as I do that your heart is in bad shape. Even with Dayan's strong blood reshaping your internal organs, you will have to have the necessary strength to go through the actual conversion. Gregori thinks we can get you through it, and I have heard he is capable of great miracles."

"He is capable of miracles, Corinne," Savannah affirmed.

Corinne smiled sadly. "Still, for the baby's sake, I must be near Lisa. If something happens to me, she is the one who must raise her. She'll be the baby's only living relative."

Desari was shaking her head. "When Dayan gives you his blood, the blood will pass through the placenta to the baby. The child will have his blood, his genetic code, not your former husband's. The child will eventually be one of us."

Corinne was silent, listening to the sounds of the house, the wind outside the window, the branches swaying and dancing. She could hear her own breathing and the heartbeat of the child growing within her. "He gave me his blood already. What did it do to the baby?" She was struggling desperately to understand.

"Corinne—" Desari began gently.

Corinne shook her head. "No, I don't want you to treat me like a child. Just tell me straight. What happened to my baby?"

"Your daughter would never have survived the birth," Desari said. "Your heart was barely able to provide for you, let alone for both of you. Without Dayan's blood, both of you would have died, and that is the truth. She already carries his genetic code, but she is not fully in our world. Darius monitored her along with Gregori during the exchange. When it became too much for the baby, the transfusion was stopped to allow her body to adjust." Deliberately she used the human term *transfusion* to soothe Corinne.

"I thought a human couldn't be converted unless he or she has a lifemate." Corinne felt numb, trapped, suddenly panicked by the repercussions of her decision. It was one thing to make such a decision for herself, to choose Dayan's world, but something altogether different for her child. Where was Dayan? Her lifeline, her sanity. *'Where are you?'* She reached across time and space to him. Her fingers clutched the quilt, a strange thing to find so comforting.

'I am here, my love, always with you, a shadow in your mind. I hunt the evil one to make our world safe, but I am never far from you or our child. I will return unharmed to you as soon as we accomplish what is necessary. We will face what is frightening to you together, as it is meant to be. Uniting our two worlds is not so difficult when we feel as we do. Our love for our daughter will aid us in our choices.' His voice was a blend of heat and light, music and melody, so beautiful it took her breath away. He felt strong and real and a part of her.

"Your daughter has a strong psychic talent, perhaps even stronger than yours," Desari said. "She can be converted without danger to her sanity, but there are other complications. It is not something we do lightly, Corinne."

Corinne could feel unexpected tears welling up out of nowhere. "I feel like I'm being given little pieces of a jigsaw puzzle one or two at a time, and the picture is so overwhelming I can't comprehend it. What other complications?"

"Our species has problems having babies, particularly females. Few of us conceive females, and those that do rarely carry them to full term. Even after they are born, our babies often do not survive the first year of life. It is a terrible tragedy and has contributed to the decline of our race. Because you must be given blood to save your life, the baby will be given the same blood—"

"No!" Corinne was adamant. "Her life is more important than mine. She has to come first in every decision. I know Dayan doesn't want that, but it is *my* decision to make, not his. I don't want to give her life only to have her lose it because I selfishly wanted to live myself. It would be better to chance giving birth to her now and allowing the doctors to do their best. They are performing miracles with premature babies. You said yourself she was strong."

Desari shook her head. "She would not have survived had you given birth the night Dayan removed you from the hospital. It took all of Gregori's strength and power to keep her alive. It is too late to turn back now. She has Dayan's blood in her system. She needs us now to help her survive. A human doctor could never save her life."

Corinne twisted her fingers into the quilt in agitation. "I feel helpless," she confessed to the women. "I've always been the one to handle the problems in our lives, and now I can't help my own child when she needs it the most."

Desari shook her head. "You are so wrong, Corinne. Now more than ever it is you who will have to have the strength of will to carry her. You are already monitoring your own heart and attempting to regulate it."

"I feel Dayan with me when I have trouble. He's the one regulating my heartbeat and pushing the air through my lungs," Corinne corrected. "I know he's there."

"Of course—he is your lifemate," Desari said complacently. "But he cannot save you if you are not willing to be saved. You are using your will, and it is considerable." She patted the quilt. "I see you like this quilt. Francesca, lifemate to Gabriel, made it for you. She is a great healer who lives in Paris. When she received word that you were carrying a baby and you needed aid, she made this specifically for you. It is a healing quilt. Along with the healing symbols, she used other symbols to aid in your protection should there be enemies that find you."

"It's so beautiful," Corinne said honestly. "I didn't want to give it up. I hope I will have the opportunity to thank her for such a unique gift."

Desari patted her hand. "I would like to examine you and renew the healing process if it is possible. Do you remember what it felt like? Savannah and Tempest will lend me their strength, and we shall at least make you more comfortable. Lie back and we will begin."

Dayan, streaking through the air, appeared as a long trail of droplets, much like a comet moving rapidly through the night sky. Gregori and Darius were on either side of him, formidable hunters both, but it was Dayan's lifemate who was threatened, and he was the one who must save her. He felt the beast rising within him, struggling for supremacy. Gregori, renowned for his storms, generated a fierce squall, and dark clouds rolled in swiftly to cover their flight through the night sky in pursuit of the vampire.

Lightning zigzagged, arcing from cloud to cloud, intense and ominous. Hues of deep purple and black smeared the sky so that the stars were slowly obliterated. Thunder reverberated through the valley, echoed down the canyons, heralding a storm of great magnitude. Far below, as the three hunters streaked across the roiling sky, wild creatures sensing dangerous predators hastily found shelter and remained very still. Domesticated dogs yelped in fear and hid as the dark shadows passed overhead.

'Dayan.' Gregori's voice was compelling, a soft command. *'The beast is strong in you. Remember, you are in twofold danger. Your lifemate is not locked to you. There is no anchor to hold you to the path. The violence will trigger the rising of the beast. It is a time for care, not rage. Along with your life, your soul is in mortal danger.'*

Dayan could hear the purity of Gregori's voice and it washed through the red haze of anger clouding his mind. For a moment he could see and hear clearly again, but then the thought of the vampire seeking Corinne, threatening her consumed him again, and he continued his swift pursuit toward the enemy.

Darius and Gregori flying on either side of Dayan easily kept pace, senses flaring out to scan for any hidden traps. The vampire wasn't attempting to conceal his line of retreat. They knew from centuries of experience that if he was seriously attempting to evade them, he would be throwing up more of a blind.

Dayan was well aware of the vampire's intentions. He didn't care. He had tremendous confidence in his own strength and skill. Though he did not consider himself a hunter of the undead, he had often accompanied Darius on such hunts. It was his lifemate who was threatened now, and their code of honor dictated it was Dayan's responsibility as well as his right to remove that threat.

Suddenly an acid shower came from above the storm clouds, assaulting the flying hunters. Thin streaks of silvery light began to rain through the swirling black vapor. Almost impossible to see, the droplets burned with a caustic acid, searing the skin. The threads fell like poisonous darts straight at the hunters. They knew that the deadly shower was a delaying tactic of the fleeing vampire.

Immediately Gregori rose above Dayan, instinctively protecting him. As Gregori took the higher position, Darius sent up a flaming streak of orange-red light, pure energy, vaporizing the slivers of acid before they could reach their targets.

Dayan caught a glimpse of the vampire through the clouds, streaking across the sky. Dayan doubled his speed, moving straight as an arrow toward the fleeing vampire. He was a protégé of Darius, had learned from him. Dayan believed in directness, taking the fight to the enemy. He felt the presence of the evil one, a thick oily substance left behind so that the air reeked with the stench of the undead. Dayan shot out a wave of vibrations, a high-frequency sound that deafened the skies and knocked the fleeing demon from the clouds.

Just ahead they saw the figure struggling to shape-shift, to sprout wings. He was already dangerously close to the ground, and at the last possible moment, the vampire did an amazing athletic feat and spun, landing on his feet like a cat. At once he sought to cloak his presence from the hunters and the mortals occupying the area.

'Dayan!' Darius's imperious warning was sharp. *'It is a trap. Scan.'*

Dayan had automatically done so as he streaked in behind the vampire. There were four humans in a small cabin, all males. All fanatical. The stench of the society clung to them. Dayan knew they were not in league with the undead; The vampire was simply using them as another delaying tactic. Dayan was supremely confident in Darius and Gregori. Their reputations were legend. He didn't have to look to see that they were gliding in behind him. He knew they were there and trusted them to take care of the humans.

"I believe you wanted to introduce yourself," Dayan said softly to the vampire, his voice pure and melodious, the sound filling every atom of space around them though he hadn't raised his voice. "You will turn and face me, vampire. I am quite willing to accept your challenge."

The vampire shuddered with the effort to break free from the sound of that voice. It was made for golden tunes, truth and honesty. It was hideous to the creature, so that he pressed his hands hard against his ears in an attempt to block out the sound. He turned slowly, hands clamped to his head, his body swaying slightly. As he turned he opened his mouth as if to speak. A black swarm of insects erupted all around him, the air thick with them, so many they appeared as a solid wall, for one brief second obscuring Dayan's vision of the undead.

He was striding forward, easily blocking the stinging, poisonous bugs by deflecting them away from his body with a powerful current of moving air he produced with a casual wave of his hand. He continued moving rapidly, a blur as he whipped through the cloud of living shields. Dayan realized immediately that the vampire had used the insects to flee once again. He had disappeared as if he had never been, leaving behind an empty space in the air. Blankness.

Behind him, Dayan heard the shouts of the humans, the loud discharge of a weapon. The air vibrated with power, the storm raged, yet nothing mattered but that he pursue his quarry—the vampire who had sought his lifemate. He used the blankness to track the undead. The vampire was concealing his form, but Dayan wasn't fooled. The stench of his prey was overpowering, and he followed unerringly. He didn't glance behind him; he knew Darius and Gregori would be taking care of the enemy and would follow him as soon as possible.

The storm was fierce, a boiling, spinning mass of heavy black clouds. Lightning arced from cloud to cloud and there was a fast buildup of electrical charge along the ground. Bolts slammed from sky to earth, the sound deafening. The land shook. Nearby a large tree exploded in a fiery conflagration. Sparks rained onto vegetation. A wall of flames leapt at Dayan, solid, orange-red, a brilliant living, mindless antagonist roaring straight for him. At once he whirled quickly, a cloak of wet mist enveloping him as he raced through the fire with preternatural speed. He heard the sizzle of the mist as it heated and evaporated, but he was through and on the other side.

A dark shadow was just ahead, fleeing toward the darkened interior of a thicket of trees. Dayan took to the air, shape-shifting as he did so, a streamlined raptor racing through the canopy of branches to reach the undead before it managed to get to its lair. He came in from high above, dropping down out of the turbulent sky so fast the vampire had no warning. The large body of the bird knocked the night creature off balance, sharp talons raking viciously so that tainted blood splattered to the carpet of vegetation, withering it on contact.

Snarling, the vampire staggered, tearing blindly at the sky around him in an attempt to destroy his enemy, his head undulating back and forth like a reptile. He was a hideous, depraved being determined to live at all costs. Desperately he tried to regain his balance, his bearings, searching the sky and ground for his attacker.

Dayan was moving so fast he was a blur, a chameleon blending in with the trees, once more in human form. He struck straight at the abomination, the fury of the kill rising with the heat of battle. Flames leapt in the depths of his coal black eyes, and every vestige of the poet was gone, leaving behind the beast with the lust of battle on him. His fist plunged through the wall of the vampire's chest, a flimsy barrier, straight for the withered, blackened heart. The age-old lure of the beast was on him. Bloodlust was a red haze clouding judgment and honor, beckoning relentlessly. More, always more, it demanded, never sated, never satisfied.

Corinne heard the soft voice of the Dark Troubadours' acknowledged leader, Darius. A whisper of purity, soft and perfect, cleansing and healing like a fresh cool rain. *'Corinne. You are needed. You must summon him back to you. No other can save him now. I will feed your strength with my own. Call him to your side. You must do so now.'* The voice was calm, tranquil even, yet she knew immediately there was a terrible urgency. She didn't stop to question. She was so tuned to Dayan, the moment she reached out for his mind, she felt the killing frenzy, the implacable grip of the beast.

Corinne lay very still, instinctively taking a deep breath and letting it out to relax. She focused her thoughts on Dayan, blocking out everything else around her. The room fell away, the constraints of her physical condition fell away, even her awareness of Darius, until there was only Dayan in her mind. Her Dayan. Tall and sweet and loving. Generous. Giving. She closed her eyes until she could almost smell his clean woodsy scent. *'Dayan.'* Deliberately she used his name. Calling the man. Reaching for the intellect. *'Dayan, come back to me.'*

At once he was there with her, merged deeply so that she was in the heat of his battle with the smell of blood and the lust for the kill dominating his brain. She was quiet a moment, faintly shocked at actually witnessing the violent side of him she had always sensed. Corinne lay very quietly, stayed completely focused. Unknowingly she used her own talent, creating a surge of power. This was simply another side of Dayan. Her Dayan. *'Come back to me. Leave that place and return to where you are needed.'* She put all her energy into her call, but that didn't matter. Dayan was all that mattered.

She sensed the terrible struggle. Something else was fighting for him. Something shadowy, not tangible, but nevertheless, very powerful. She felt the dark stain spreading like a disease through him, the triumph of the beast as it threatened to consume him. At first Corinne believed he was locked in mortal combat with the vampire. Whatever it was, his adversary was evil and greedy and it wanted Dayan. Then she realized the vampire was dying. This other force struggling with her wanted Dayan's soul, wanted to turn him into the very thing he hunted and destroyed. She understood little of it, but instinctively she latched on to the mental strength flowing from Darius into her. She regulated her breathing, worked at regulating Dayan's. Adrenaline was pumping through his body, mixing with the frenzied savagery of the predator until he was more animal than man. Cunning, feral, a creature of the night.

'You are Dayan, a musician without equal, a poet with words that take my breath away. You are my lifemate, my heart and soul. Come back to me, Dayan. Leave that place. Leave that poor unfortunate aberration. Pray God will find him a better place. You can do nothing more for him. Come home to me.' She spoke from her deepest core, meaning every word, feeling every word. He was so deeply entrenched in her heart, buried so deeply in her soul, she didn't know where he left off and she began.

For a moment, reason and judgment shimmered in his brain, a whirling silver mist breaking through the red killing haze. *'Corinne?'* His voice was distant, a faraway thread of sound, drowned out quickly by a bellow of rage.

Corinne remained very calm, sending waves of love and tranquillity to Dayan. Darius was with her, guiding her from a great distance. On some level she was aware of his direction, but most of her actions were instinctive. This was Dayan, her other half, and he was out in the dark night somewhere with lightning and thunder crashing to earth around him, a fitting backdrop for the turbulence in his mind. They were merged so closely, she could feel the wild winds, the terrible vortex of violence, whirling like a tornado, strong and destructive, determined to sweep aside the man and leave the aroused beast. *'Dayan, come back to me. Leave that place and come to me. The baby is resting quietly and I'm very tired. I need you here where you belong.'*

She *was* tired. The mind link was difficult for her even with Darius's strength infusing her. Her body was worn and tired. A sound was beginning to impose itself into the violence of Dayan's mind. It was weak, irregular, a soft thumping like a distant drum. The code was strange and erratic. A beat. A miss.

Corinne felt Dayan move within her mind. A soft hiss, a groan of despair. *'Corinne!'* Her name was whispered in that velvet-soft voice. She closed her eyes, certain he would come. The beast could never hold him when she needed him. Nothing would stop him from coming to her. She felt the strength of his determination, knew he was wrestling for supremacy, to cage the beast within him. Corinne left him to it. Breathing was an effort now, her lungs laboring.

She felt Desari at her side, holding her hand, whispering a chant. She felt the healing energy of the three women. It was a warm tingling moving through her body. Desari was tranquil, she was always serene, yet Corinne sensed an alarm. It didn't matter, none of it did. Dayan was on his way, and she knew he would somehow make things right. She wanted to hear the sound of his voice.

Corinne drifted in a dream world. She heard his music, the beautiful poetic words that emerged from his soul as he expressed his need for love. His need for Corinne. Only Corinne. She believed him at last. He could do things others could not, and he would come back to her from the dark terrible struggle for his soul. She had faith. "Complete faith." She murmured the words aloud, but her voice was too soft even for the acute hearing she had acquired recently. *'Dayan.'* His name was her strength, her anchor so that she wouldn't drift too far from the real world.

'Corinne.' His voice whispered through her mind, filled her heart and lungs, so for a moment it was easier to breathe. Her long lashes fluttered as she tried to reassure the women she was still alive. Her lashes were far heavier than she remembered them being. In the end, it was too much of an effort to raise them, so she made herself smile instead.

'I knew you would come. Hurry, Dayan. I don't know why I'm so tired.' Corinne was certain she thought the words clearly in her mind, but they seemed to be slurred, running together like fine grains of sand. Her free hand moved slowly over the thick quilt, seeking something she needed.

Desari bunched up the comforter so that one particular symbol was under Corinne's moving fingers. At once Corinne's hand closed around it, tranquil once more.

Dayan streaked through the sky, faster than he had ever moved in his life. Corinne was fading away. He could feel her sliding away from him, moving in a direction he dared not allow her to go. Dark vapor parted as he burst through the clouds, a streak of blue-green against the roiling black of the heavens. Mist swirled in long tails along the ground and began to build up around the trees and houses.

Darius kept pace with him, concentrating on the child, whose hold on life was so fragile he was uncharacteristically worried. Gregori was attempting to hold Corinne to earth, focusing on her fading heart. The amount of energy she'd used to keep Dayan from succumbing to the lure of the kill had been more than her weak heart could stand. Corinne was fighting it, wasn't afraid—she simply trusted in Dayan, knew that he would be there for her as she had been for him.

Dayan could find no recrimination in her mind, no shock at the knowledge of his darker side. She was as accepting of him as ever, and her acceptance humbled him. As he moved across the night sky with the raging storm reflecting his inner turbulence, he gathered himself, preparing for the ceremony to come. He had no choice. He had to bind her to him for both of their sakes. He had to give her his healing blood. The baby was at risk, and Dayan, more than any other, knew the loss of her child was the one thing Corinne would never accept. She would trade her life for that of the baby.

Dayan shimmered into a solid frame, bending over Corinne as he did so, his large hand engulfing hers as he brought it to his mouth. Her lashes didn't lift, but her soft mouth curved. *'I knew you would come.'*

Chapter Fifteen

They were gathering. Dayan wrapped Corinne in the quilt she loved so much to transport her to the cave of healing. He held her easily, her weight no more than that of a child to him. He held her carefully, his most precious treasure in all the world, sheltering her body from the elements as he whisked her through the night sky.

Corinne rubbed her face on his shoulder, snuggling closer to him, once more feeling connected to him in a strange dream world. The wind was blowing hard, tugging at her body as they rushed through the air, but it was exhilarating rather than frightening. She felt perfectly safe, perfectly protected in Dayan's arms, even traveling at such a fast pace and in such a bizarre fashion. She turned her face up to the sky, observing the purplish hues streaking across the rolling black clouds. It was unbelievably beautiful, and she found tears burning in her eyes. This was Dayan's world, a place of magic. The night was his, and he could soar like an eagle or run through a forest as fast as a wolf. Corinne had never been able to run in her life. This was her moment, her last moment to fly.

Dayan, reading her thoughts, blinked back the tears threatening to burn his eyes and choke his throat. *'Not so, love; we have eternity.'*

As they sped through the waning storm, Darius and Gregori remained very close to Dayan and Corinne. Desari's lifemate, Julian, was also on his way to the cave, still a distance away. He had been designated the cleanup man, assigned to erase all evidence of the destroyed vampire and the human members of the society the vampire had used to try to throw the hunters off his trail.

Corinne was content to rest in Dayan's arms. She knew the others were arriving, some in pairs, some alone. She was fast gaining the attributes of Dayan's people. Her hearing was far more acute. She could see clearly in the night. Her talent was telekinesis, yet now she *felt* things much more deeply. She knew the Carpathian people were gathering to help Dayan save her life and the life of her unborn daughter. The healers were preparing for an early birth, perhaps even an attempt to take the child should Corinne not survive. She wasn't certain whether she was receiving the information from Dayan or she was so connected to the healers that she was reading their minds by herself.

Dayan glided across the floor of the healing cave, holding Corinne close to him. They seemed to be floating, feather-light, unconnected to the ground. Lights sprang up, hundreds of them, candle after candle so that the flames flickered and danced on the walls of the cave. It was beautiful. The multicolored crystals, some tall towers, others in rows of squat columns, shimmered with muted fire. Gems picked up the colors and flames, amplifying them and generating replicas all over the chamber, adding to the brilliance. The candles gave off that strange, soothing fragrance Corinne remembered from before. The combination of scents instilled a peaceful tranquillity in all who could take it into their lungs. She felt the power of the place moving through her body, as well as the combined strength of the healers.

Corinne made the effort to look around herself, wanting to see these people who had traveled long distances, some of them across oceans, to aid in the efforts to save her life and that of her daughter. She recognized some faces from her first trip to the cave, but there were more now. In her mind she could hear the soft chant of voices, not just of the people in the cave, but also those of unknown Carpathians far away. She knew from Dayan, that this was a well-coordinated effort on the part of the healers, who were determined not to lose her to death. Determined not to lose Dayan. Not to lose her baby.

Corinne was grateful to them all, but it seemed as if it were all happening to someone else. She was observing everything as if she were hovering above the scene, rather than in the center of it. There were males determined to save her for more reasons than simple sympathy. She was a female of great psychic talent, proven to be capable of conceiving a daughter of extraordinary psychic talent. Her daughter was already prized by these people, a treasure they would guard and protect should something happen to her. She felt it. She read it in their minds, merged as they all were together.

She turned her attention to Dayan. He was pale, lines etched deeply into his handsome face. His black eyes drifted over her face lovingly in a brooding, sensual study that melted her heart. He looked alone, raw, vulnerable. Corinne lifted her hand and touched his face, her fingertips gentle as they traced his mouth. "Don't look so sad, Dayan," she said softly. "You came back—that's all that matters."

"I should never have left you. There were other hunters who could have killed the vampire. I should have been strong enough to overcome my nature."

He was exposing more than his guilt to her; he was exposing his heart and soul. Laying them out in front of her, uncaring that she saw his naked vulnerability. His sorrow. His fear. "You are my life, Corinne, everything to me. I want you to fight. Not just for the baby, but for us. Know you are fighting for both of our lives. Keep that knowledge in your heart and mind and soul as you unite with me and with my people to preserve your life, all of our lives."

Corinne smiled up at him, a slow, loving smile. "I'm not afraid, Dayan, and I don't want you to be either."

He bent his dark head to close the inches between them, uncaring that there were so many witnesses. His mouth found hers, gently, tenderly in a dark melody of heart-wrenching love. He lifted his head slowly, reluctantly. Her heart was struggling now with every beat. They all could hear it despite the sound of the water pouring into the cave, despite the chanting of the ancients joining in from faraway countries.

Gregori positioned himself on Corinne's right side, took her small pale hand in his. Darius approached on the left, laid his hand gently over the small mound of her abdomen. Around the large cave, the Carpathians reached out to one another, linking physically as well as mentally. Julian and Desari stood tall behind Dayan and rested their hands in firm comfort on Dayan's shoulders.

'We cannot risk a repeat of tonight's events,' Darius counseled. *'You must bind her to you as you give her your blood. It is necessary, Dayan.'*

'I will not take a chance with her life. She would not survive a separation in her fragile state.' Dayan was adamant.

'*Then you must stay with her at all times, awake or asleep. I do not see that she fears very much. It is better to risk her knowledge of our weakness than another close encounter with the beast.*' There was a finality about the decree. Darius had led his group of Carpathians fearlessly down through the long centuries. They trusted his wisdom and skills. His word was rarely questioned.

Corinne knew that the man Dayan referred to as his brother was speaking telepathically to him. "I can feel his concern for you, Dayan. Whatever he wants you to do, please do it." She whispered the words against his throat.

"I do not want you to suffer any more on my behalf."

She smiled at him although her lashes were sweeping down. "I've never suffered on your behalf. What an idea! My heart has been failing since the day I was born. You have nothing to do with it."

"Are you certain? Be certain, Corinne. There is no going back. Each step forward you take is another step into my world."

"I have never been more certain. Whatever world you're in, Dayan, I belong there too." She could hardly speak now.

There was a moment of stillness in the cave. A waiting. Corinne knew the moment Darius and Gregori merged with her, Gregori traveling through her body to her daughter. '*I love you.*' She whispered the words to Dayan, wanting him to know, wanting him to realize that if this didn't go the way they all intended, he had been loved unconditionally, accepted unconditionally, even if they had never had the opportunity to consummate their love.

Dayan kissed her forehead, her eyelids; then his mouth drifted down to hers. He took possession with elemental hunger, with raw aching need, rocking the earth for both of them. "I claim you as my lifemate," he whispered softly to her, against her lips, amid the ancient healing chant. His mouth skimmed over her neck, feather-light, sensual, a whisper of satin and silk. "I belong to you. I offer my life for you. I give you my protection, my allegiance, my heart, my soul and my body."

White-hot pain lanced through her body, gave way instantly to a pure pleasure arcing through her, through both of them. Corinne felt drowsy, unexpectedly sensual. Her body clenched and burned with heat and need. She tried to stay awake, not drift, wanting to experience the beauty of what was happening, wanting to lend her feeble strength to that of all the others fighting for her life, but she found herself relaxing beneath the connection. She felt the sweep of his tongue as he closed the tiny pinpricks.

His mouth moved gently along her throat, up to the corner of her lips. "I take into my keeping the same that is yours. Your life, happiness and welfare will be cherished and placed above my own for all time." With her new awareness, Corinne sensed when Dayan further distanced her from what was happening. As though in a dream, she observed one fingernail lengthening into a single long talon, dagger-sharp. He slit his chest, opening the heavy muscle, pressing her mouth to him so that his blood ran into her.

She was astonished to find herself drinking almost ravenously, astonished to find she wasn't in the least repulsed. Strength seemed to pour into her body, a richness unlike anything she had ever experienced. This time she felt his power, felt the greedy way her cells and tissues absorbed the gift of life he was sharing with her.

Dayan was holding her with exquisite tenderness, looking down at her as if she were the most beautiful woman in the world, a treasure, a priceless gift he was guarding. Corinne felt tears burning in her throat, in her eyes. He was so handsome, so tortured, his face etched with lines of worry and sorrow she had put there.

"You are my lifemate, bound to me for all eternity and always in my care." He whispered the last of the ritual words, binding them together in the Carpathian ceremony as old as time. The words were imprinted upon him and all other males even before they were born. Each male had the extraordinary ability to bind his lifemate to him for eternity.

Corinne felt it immediately, her soul, her heart, even her mind, reaching for his. It was as if thousands of threads were weaving them together, forming an unbreakable bond. She became even more aware of what was happening inside her body. Gregori was working hard to repair the damage to her disintegrating heart, while Darius was monitoring the baby for potential problems caused by the rich blood pouring into her body. Inside Corinne, organs and tissues were actually reshaping, and the same thing was happening to her daughter.

Corinne knew the moment the richness and power became too much for the baby. She heard her own protest, made the effort of movement away from Dayan even as Darius gave him the command to stop. It was Julian who closed the wound on Dayan's chest with his own healing saliva. For a moment Corinne lay there, afraid to think or breathe, wrapped in the soothing quilt and the shelter of Dayan's strong arms. Her baby was struggling to survive. The blood was changing her tiny body too fast—it was uncomfortable and frightening for the infant. Corinne heard Darius whispering to the child, conveying images more than words. Beautiful, tranquil, soothing images.

The child was aware of her environment deteriorating, of the changes taking place rapidly in her body. Corinne added her own voice to comfort her daughter. Dayan joined with her, merging them together, offering his love and comfort and commitment to the baby. And then Gregori joined them. Corinne was astonished at the power and strength emanating from Gregori, the skill he used to keep the baby from leaving the uncomfortable home she was dwelling in. The baby's body was hot, her insides on fire. Gregori soothed her and provided a cooling balm for the twisting pain.

Corinne blinked rapidly as tears ran down her face. *'She's suffering because of me, what you're doing for me!'* The cry was torn from her heart. *'It hurts her. I can feel that it hurts her!'*

At once her heartbeat was irregular, sounding loud and uneven in the cave. Desari reached around Dayan to squeeze Corinne's hand. "Corinne." Desari spoke aloud so the sound of her voice would be an anchor of calm. "Dayan's blood is the only thing keeping both you and the baby alive. Conversion is difficult on the body, and it is painful. Darius is doing what he can to minimize the baby's pain, and we are adding our strength to his, but we cannot take all of it away. Her body is tiny, and a small amount of blood will cause major changes in her. You have need of conversion. The repairs to your heart are not going to hold more than a day or two, perhaps only hours. The child will be born, and we must be ready for that. We are giving her time you can ill afford. With this blood, with her body changing, we hope her heart and lungs will be mature enough to withstand the outside world. It is a trade-off none of us are happy making, but it is deemed necessary."

Dayan leaned down, his dark eyes moving lovingly over Corinne's face. "You cannot panic now, my love.

We have chosen a path and have already embarked upon it. We are on the journey together. She will grow strong—trust Darius. He is family. Our family, her family. And put your faith in Gregori. He is a great healer and will do everything possible to protect our unborn child. Neither Darius nor his brother lose the battles in which they choose to engage."

Corinne reminded herself to breathe oxygen for the baby, or perhaps it was one of the others reminding her. She was aware of the minds sharing together, a path slightly different from the one she used exclusively with Dayan. Theirs was private, seemed intimate, sensual. This was different, yet still felt comfortable and caring. Cradled as she was in Dayan's arms, she felt sheltered and cherished by his family and friends.

She was exhausted, and she didn't want to feel that way. They were all trying so hard, and Gregori and Darius were expending tremendous energy on her behalf. She wanted to be better for them all, but her heart was stuttering, and throughout her body a strange lethargy was spreading. It left her weak and unable to do more than lie in Dayan's arms, breathing in and out as slowly and steadily as she was able.

Desari glanced apprehensively at Darius's face. He was drawn and pale from the fight for the child's life. Gregori shook his head. "One rising, perhaps two at the most. The child will benefit from every hour we can win for her." He put his hand over Corinne's. "She is a fighter like you. She accepts what is happening to her, taking her example from you. I know this has been difficult—it is all new and completely foreign to you—but you are doing very well. We will not lose your daughter. She is willing to fight with us, and that is more than half the battle."

"Thank you." Corinne forced her voice to speak aloud, a thin, reedy whisper of sound, but Gregori heard her clearly. She gave up after that, closing her eyes and snuggling closer into the warmth and strength of Dayan's body.

"She can no longer regulate her body heat," Dayan said anxiously to Gregori. "Why is she not responding to the blood and your healing?"

"She did respond, Dayan," Gregori replied quietly. "Her heart is still beating despite the fact that it is disintegrating at a rapid rate. She is using all her energy just to live. When she can no longer continue with her strength of will, with the strength we are lending her, then you must convert her immediately. We must be prepared. It will happen fast. Pray it happens during our strongest hour, not when the sun is at its peak."

Dayan paled visibly. "That cannot happen."

"The child is aware of the danger," Darius said softly, his voice a perfect blend of power and velvet. "She will endeavor to hold on during our weakest hours. She understands and will fight to hold on."

"I am not completely powerless at that time and will help should the birth start early, but I can do nothing if Corinne's heart should fail her," Gregori said.

"Then I will convert her now," Dayan said, his black eyes flickering with the flames reflecting off the crystals. A cold wind seemed to sweep through the huge chamber so that the flickering lights of the candles grew and danced in a mad frenzy.

Corinne's small hand fluttered, found Dayan's mouth, her fingertips moving gently over his perfectly chiseled features in a gesture of tender recrimination. *You promised me, Dayan. I hold you to your word.*

At once he pressed a kiss into the center of her palm, held her hand to him tightly as if he could chain her to earth with him. *I can do no other than honor it.*

"Corinne." Savannah's voice was very soft. "Shea is a great healer. Before she became one of us, she was a surgeon, human, much like yourself. Remember? We spoke of her. I have called her; she is making her way swiftly to us. She will be of great help to us with your baby. Do you understand me?"

Corinne nodded. "I understand what you're trying to tell me. I'll hang on until she arrives. If it gives my baby a better chance, I'll do anything."

"Shea is an exceptional woman," Gregori added. "She has long researched this particular problem and is hopeful she has found ways to aid our children as they grow."

"Corinne is very tired," Dayan said softly. "Thank you all for your help."

Corinne was aware of movement in the chamber, another flurry of activity as a bed was prepared for her. There was no thought of returning her to the surface, to the house they had originally taken her to. She would remain with Dayan deep within the crystal world until her heart ceased to provide her with life.

Dayan held her close to him as he murmured his thanks to the vague, shadowy figures moving out of the chamber. Corinne was content to lie in his arms, feeling his solid frame, grateful for the strength in him. The chamber was filled with a fragrance that seemed to envelop her in tranquillity, serenity. She felt at peace, free to enjoy what she could of this strange underground world.

Darius leaned down to rest his hand on the top of her silky hair. "Welcome to our family, little sister. We are grateful you have been found." His hand slipped away and he moved silently, taking the sense of his enormous power with him.

Tempest bent to kiss her cheek. "Be strong, Corinne, and welcome." She took Darius's outstretched hand and followed him out.

Desari and Julian brushed a welcoming kiss of encouragement on her forehead, exchanged a soft word with Dayan and glided out.

Gregori and his lifemate Savannah were the last to slip away. They reassured Dayan they would be close by should there be need.

"At last," Dayan whispered softly, "we are alone." He settled Corinne comfortably in the bed. The sound of the waterfall should have been loud, but already Corinne had learned to mute her hearing so it was one less thing Dayan needed to do for her. He tucked the quilt around her. "After the baby is born, you will be fully healed, and I am going to spend endless nights making love to you. Has my hair turned color yet? I expect to rise with white hair after all these scares."

She smiled, her hand tangling in his long black hair. "I love your hair just the way it is. Don't get white hair on my account. Which one of us was the nutcase going out to fight the unholy dragon?" *'What was that, anyway?'* It was too much trouble to use her voice, so she slipped into the intimacy of mind merge. *'You thought you needed an adventure? White knight charging the burning fires with a bucketful of water?'*

He laughed softly as he stretched out beside her and once more gathered her close to him. "You're mixing up your stories." His fingertips slid over her beloved face, tracing each delicate bone, every classical curve.

"It's so beautiful here." Corinne's eyes were closed and her voice was drowsily contented. "I knew it would be like this. I used to dream about exploring new worlds. I wanted to swim in the ocean and see the coral reefs." Her fingers rubbed at his hair. *'You've given me so much in so short a time, Dayan. Thank you. I've flown through the sky like a bird. I was able to go beneath the ground and see crystals and gems.'* A smile tugged intriguingly at the corners of her mouth. "I met some very famous musicians—my life's dream, you know."

Dayan closed his eyes tightly, felt a hand squeezing his heart like a vise. His chest burned with terror. She was slipping out of their mind merge and using her voice, entirely unaware of it. "I love you, Corinne," he whispered aloud.

'I love you too.' She was drifting in his arms. *'Show me what it's like to be you, Dayan, to run and fly and have such wonderful freedom.'* She felt his terrible sorrow and instinctively wanted to ease his burden. Her fingers tugged gently at his hair, willing him to take her with him on an incredible journey through time and space.

"I can't take you traveling," he said softly, aching to give her anything she wanted, wishing he could cradle her in his arms and fly across the night sky with her. "The weather is turning cold and a storm is approaching. It wouldn't be safe."

"Where is your imagination tonight, Dayan? *Where is my poet? Sing for me and let me see your memories. I want the wild ones, of running and jumping, things I could never dare to imagine for myself.* Share that with me." She didn't open her eyes to look at him, yet he felt her inside him, deep where it mattered.

Dayan leaned closer, put his hand over her daughter, their daughter, John's daughter, to include her, to show her his world of the night. He felt the baby move in answer and he found himself smiling. Corinne slipped her hand over Dayan's, threading her fingers through his larger ones. He blocked out his fear, his terror of losing both of them to death, and he merged his mind fully with Corinne's.

She allowed his memories to sweep through her, to carry her off so she could feel the power coursing through her body as he shifted shape. Fur rippled across his skin, and his muscles became sinewy ropes stretching over his body. They merged together deep within the leopard's body. The cat padded slowly, confidently through the jungle, moving through dense vegetation almost lazily. It was amazing—she could feel the wind ruffling the leopard's fur, smell the scents in the air; she knew what was happening all around her from the tips of its whiskers.

'It's like radar!'

Dayan was happy he was delighting her. The leopard leapt casually from the forest floor to a tree branch six feet above its head. It was effortless, an easy movement of sleek muscles, similar to a casual shrug. All around was the dense jungle, the huge leaves and swordlike fronds reaching toward the sky. The overhead canopy was swaying with the breeze allowing banded rays of light to cast dancing shadows over the ground below. Corinne was amazed at the leopard's piercing intelligence. At first she thought it was because Dayan was occupying the large cat's body, but then she realized his mind remained hidden deep while the animal moved and hunted.

'You and the leopard coexist in its body.'

'This is a memory from my childhood. I needed to learn skills. Leopards are truly amazing creatures. They are quick and cunning, wary and always difficult to detect. They adapt well to various environments, from the jungle to the desert. We explored the various habitats in order to gain more knowledge. Animals provide tremendous knowledge of our world.'

Corinne found the subject fascinating, and was greatly impressed by his deep appreciation and respect for animals. *'Show me more.'*

This time the terrain was completely different. The leopard even appeared different. It had a longer coat and larger spots. Corinne examined it carefully. *'It looks like a snow leopard, but not exactly.'*

"This species is called the Amur leopard, named for the river border between Russia and China. We found them in a narrow mountain chain along the borders of Russia, North Korea and China. They are very beautiful, but game is scarce and they are hard pressed by the threat of extinction, much like our species."

At once he felt a rush of sadness, that seemed linked to his own. They were merged so deeply, he couldn't tell where she left off and he started. It was an intimacy he was unfamiliar with, yet it felt right. He had a home now, and her name was Corinne. She was his world, the very air he breathed into his lungs. He couldn't bear for her to be sad, even over such an important issue as a dying species.

Dayan called on his memories, conveying the stalk of the leopard as it moved relentlessly, with single-minded purpose toward its prey. The eyes were focused, intent, merciless. She could feel the wildness sweep over her, through Dayan.

Dayan felt Corinne draw a deep, excited breath. The baby jumped beneath his palm. At once Corinne reached out to the infant soothingly. Immediately Dayan added his own comfort. Her mother's happiness coupled with Dayan's reassurance allowed the baby to accept the new impressions more easily.

He changed the memory again, drawing on something less frightening, the simple mechanics of a cat's everyday life. The leopard stretched out on the limb of a tree and stood for a long moment, testing the wind for the wealth of information it would impart. It stretched lazily and leapt to the ground. Padding on silent paws, it moved through the jungle back toward the small stream where it could drink. All around were traces of smaller creatures, scurrying out of harm's way as the cat traveled quickly through the dense cover. It began to run, a sprint of speed and power, moving quickly for the sheer pleasure of it. It was Dayan's memory, his boyhood enjoyment of occupying the body of the leopard, and Corinne was grateful for the sharing.

He took her from that long-ago jungle to a modern-day concert, a large room crowded with people talking and laughing. The lights went low and there was a sudden hush of anticipation. The moment stretched out. Corinne waited with every bit as much excitement as the crowd for the appearance of the band. The Dark Troubadours, renowned for their music, for the beauty of their lyrics and phenomenal talent with instruments. Suddenly the band came running onto the stage and the crowd roared, rising, stomping and clapping wildly.

'You're incredibly handsome.' There was pride in her thoughts, a pleased, rather possessive pleasure that made him incredibly happy.

Dayan's fingertip traced the curve of her mouth. "My little groupie," he teased and bent his head to claim her lips. He couldn't help himself. He craved the taste and feel of her silken mouth. He was exquisitely tender, yet fiercely possessive, raw with aching need. Corinne responded with the same heated tenderness, her only way to express her growing love for this wild, lonely man. She slipped her arms around his neck to cradle his head to her, a tremendous effort when her body was so tired and worn.

At once Dayan felt her weariness and slowly, reluctantly broke the contact to kiss the corner of her mouth, her chin, the line of her soft, vulnerable throat. He ached with love for her, felt that same ache in her. It humbled him like nothing else ever could have. He could read her every thought, easily see into her memories. He had been alone for centuries, surrounded by people he only had memories of loving. She had changed his world, brought so much to him.

Corinne accepted him for what he was. She was gaining access to his memories and his thoughts through their continual mind merge, and now the binding ritual and his blood tie, but her acceptance ran deeper than all of that. He felt it, saw acceptance not because they were lifemates, but based on a deep love and commitment to him. Corinne had faith in herself and her judgment. She sensed good in him and embraced it. She loved the poet in him, the way he expressed himself in his music and lyrics. She accepted the darker side of him, knew it was his nature, part of who he was. She believed in him and who he was. What he was.

"I want you to sleep, my love," he whispered softly, his mouth traveling along her delicate collarbone. "I can feel that you are tired. Just let go and sleep. It will give your body a chance to rest. I will remain here beside you."

Her slender arms slipped reluctantly from around his neck to fall limply onto the quilt. His wandering mouth was robbing her of the ability to think properly. If she closed her eyes, burning tears sprang to life, tangled in her lashes. She ached for him, for his terrible sorrow. He didn't want to go to sleep. He was terrified that when he rose she would be lost to him. His normal calm was totally destroyed. Corinne recognized, with her new awareness, that she was becoming more and more like Dayan, gifted with enhanced abilities.

'Are you safe here with me?' She was soothing him, trying to reassure him.

Dayan captured her hand, brought it to his mouth. His strong teeth nibbled with extraordinary gentleness at her fingertips. She was turning him inside out. "We are deep beneath the earth. I do not always have to sleep beneath a blanket of nurturing soil. I would rather remain beside you. If you should wake before sunset, do not be frightened. My body will give the appearance of mortal death. But it is merely rejuvenating. It is a natural state for Carpathians, Corinne. I would not want you to become alarmed in any way."

She smiled at his assurances. Everything about Dayan was extraordinary. Magical. She could believe anything of him, even rising from what might seem a dead state. She had discovered images in his mind. Carpathians rested in a state much like suspended animation. She felt the welcoming of the healing soil as he felt it, as a natural state, in which he could be truly one with the earth and the sky.

"I won't be afraid, Dayan, if I wake. I'll be expecting you to appear like Sleeping Beauty." Her voice was so faint it was barely discernible to the human ear, but Dayan could hear her without trouble. There was a smile in her voice. "If I kiss you, will that wake you?"

"If you have need of me, Corinne"—he knew she was teasing him, but he answered solemnly—"I will hear you." Deliberately he laced his fingers through hers, holding her body close to his. "I will always hear your call to me."

'I know you will. I'm not afraid anymore, Dayan. I'm not. Whatever will happen, will happen. We've done the best that we can to prepare for this. Either I live through it and we get the happily-ever-after ending, or I don't. I want to enjoy my time with you, every minute, every second. Please don't feel so afraid for me.'

He could feel his heart pounding out a rhythm of fear in his chest. He took a breath, deep, dragging her scent into his lungs. Dragging in serenity, a tranquil state of mind. He allowed it to flow over him, through him, knowing that what she said was true. "I do not fear traveling to another world. If you are there, that is where both of us will be. I hope to stay in this time and place to share the beauty of this world with you. I want to be able to once again feel love for my family and raise our children here with them before traveling onward. But if it is not meant to be, then so be it."

Corinne lay beside him, drifting in a semi-dreamlike state. The baby moved inside her beneath Dayan's warm hand. It connected the three of them. Dayan felt that connection very strongly, and Corinne found herself smiling, relaxed and totally happy. He had given her a treasure beyond any price. He had loved her the way she was. With her heart disintegrating and another man's child in her body. He loved her with her strange talent and matter-of-fact ways. She had been accepted for who and what she was. No more and no less. No one could ask for more.

She wanted to hear his music, to drift off into her dreams of him with the sound of his songs in her ears. Dayan felt her wish in his mind, looked around the cave, suddenly aware that he was without his precious instrument, and that he hadn't once thought of it. He always had it in his hands, yet now when it was needed, it was nowhere in sight.

'Your security blanket.' There was a trace of laughter, as if she felt his panic welling up. *'Baby.'*

Dayan found himself laughing, relaxing in the warmth of her company. *'I cannot play for you without my guitar.'*

'I'm not letting you off the hook that easily. Sing for us—the baby and me. You don't need your instrument to sing to us.' She sounded incredibly smug, teasing and happy.

Dayan pulled her firmly against him so that her head fit snugly into his shoulder. He could do no other than oblige. His beautiful voice was filled with his love, the lyrics pouring out of him like molten gold. She fell asleep in his arms with a small smile curving her mouth. Beneath his hand, the infant snuggled closer and drifted off with her mother.

Chapter Sixteen

Corinne woke, her body rippling with pain. She heard the soft echoing cry of the baby, and was frightened that her time to give birth had come too soon. It was that small, forlorn cry in her mind that kept Corinne calm. She took a deep slow breath to provide her daughter with precious oxygen. "We're all right, baby," she crooned softly. "We expected this to happen."

It was very dark in the cave. Only the water shining like black silver gave off a faint light, a reflection from a vent far overhead, yet Corinne could see as clearly as if it were daytime. She took a cautious inventory of her body, excited, afraid, yet determined. She tried not to notice that her heart was pounding far too hard and laboring sluggishly.

She didn't want to think of dying, or to be frightened by it. She had loved. Completely. Totally. Without reservation. And she had been loved in return the same way. How many others could say that? And she knew she would accomplish this most important, most monumental task of her lifetime. She would leave a legacy of beauty and wonder. A treasure for the world. Her daughter. She closed her eyes and breathed deeply, centering herself. She could do this. She could always do what was required of her. More than anything else in her life, this was her important moment. Giving life to her daughter.

"We can do this, baby," she whispered softly. "Together. The two of us. We can do this." So many other women had gone before her and there would be millions after her, but this was her moment in time and she wouldn't fail her daughter.

Corinne turned her head slowly to look at Dayan. He lay beside her absolutely motionless. He was very pale, there was no discernible rise and fall to his chest. His skin, usually hot to the touch, was stone cold. He lay as if dead. She found his long, dark, silky hair and tangled her fingers in it to connect with him. She needed him, needed him solid and real beside her. Asleep or awake, he reassured her with his presence. The sun hadn't yet set, but instinctively she knew the time was close. It was strange not to have Dayan a shadow in her mind. He had been there so much, she took it for granted now, although she hadn't realized until just then that she felt so connected to him at all times. How much it mattered.

'So, my love, it is happening.' Her fingers tightened in his hair. She held the silken strands against her face. *'I think we're ready for it, as ready as anyone can be. I love you very much. Hear me, Dayan. I love you.'*

The wave started again, a long, angry ripple that seemed to rise higher and higher so that she breathed over the top of it, concentrating on the air moving through her lungs, winding its way to her baby. The child was uncomfortable, frightened. Something was squeezing down on her, pressing her to move, but she didn't want it to happen yet.

312

Instinct took over and mother and child began to work in a kind of union. Corinne commanded her body to stay relaxed and tranquil, breathing through the uncomfortable contractions, all the while soothing the baby with her mind. She found herself astonished that she could touch the infant's mind, that the baby was so intelligent and aware at such a young age. The baby would warn her before Corinne actually felt the onset of a contraction, enabling her to take a deep, calming breath and breathe her way through each one. She wished she could get up and walk around, knowing it would speed up the process, but didn't dare take the chance. Despite her determination not to panic, Corinne found fear flooding her as the contractions increased and a heavy stone seemed to settle in the vicinity of her chest.

She knew the instant Dayan awoke. He was there in her mind even as he drew his first breath, even as the sound of his heart filled the chamber with its reassuring, steady beat. Her rock. Her anchor. *'Dayan.'* She breathed his name, inhaled his scent. Of course he would come to her in her time of need.

His hand moved over her face, a loving, tender gesture. She could feel his love for her pouring out of his heart and soul and into hers. "You will never be alone, my love, not ever again. Whatever happens here this night, I will be with you."

"I'm glad you're with me. I wanted Lisa, but I know she would have had a difficult time coping. I couldn't lean on her too hard. That makes her feel so guilty. She doesn't realize she has given me so many other gifts. I don't need to lean on her to love her." Her breath caught in her throat as the next contraction began to swell like a great tide.

"It is time." He made it a soft statement. His voice was velvet soft. His black eyes met her moss-green ones, and instantly she was falling through time and space into a deep, fathomless well. Dayan shifted position even as he held her mesmerized within his hypnotic gaze. *'Her time has come. The baby is coming, and her heart is failing. We have need of healers now.'* He sent the call out into the night, knowing the others were somewhere close by, sleeping beneath the soil in the network of underground tunnels and chambers. His call would awaken them instantly.

He held her in the thrall of his gaze, removing the pain from the experience of labor to rest her heart. He could hear it, the terrible skipping, the heralding of disaster. Her body was already worn out, and she was just beginning.

"I can't feel the contractions anymore," she whispered. "I'm supposed to help the baby through this, Dayan. If I can't feel what's happening, how can I help her?"

"I am simply blocking the pain as mortals often do with medications when they give birth; you will feel the contractions without the discomfort of labor." He was outwardly calm, tranquil within his mind where she was safely merged with him. Deep inside where she couldn't see, a hand was squeezing his heart like a vise. "There is no need to put unnecessary strain on your heart if I can prevent it." He tried to sound matter-of-fact. The moment the contraction was over, Dayan pulled her into his arms, sensing her need to change position.

Corinne was devoting every ounce of will to keep her heart going, but the labor was depleting her energy quickly. Dayan buried his face in the silky strands of her hair, hiding there for a moment while he forced away his own fears. "I wish I could do this for you, Corinne," he murmured softly.

She tilted her head to kiss him. "Lisa is fragile, Dayan.

She's my family and I love her very much." Corinne found it difficult to catch enough breath to speak.

Dayan held her in his strong arms as if that would keep her from traveling beyond his world. "Ssh, honey, I will see to it that Lisa is protected and loved all her life. You do not need to worry about her."

'But what if I don't make it, Dayan? Who will tell her, how will she get here to be with the baby and you? Cullen—'

"Cullen is doing very well at the moment, resting comfortably with Lisa holding his hand," he assured her quickly. "Syndil and Barack are guarding them, making sure no harm comes to either of them. I can touch them at any time, as you are able to do. You have only to send your fears to our brethren and they will reassure you as I am doing. Syndil knows you are in labor; she is monitoring us as I am monitoring them."

'Don't let her tell Lisa anything is wrong. If something happens to me, you go to Lisa yourself. You go, Dayan. You must be the one to tell her.'

"I want you to remain quiet, honey. Conserve your energy. Your job is to stay alive through this, to give life to our child. Do not worry about something that may never happen, and certainly not about Lisa, who is perfectly safe."

The next contraction swept through her body, much more intense than the last. Her heart erupted into a violent, frenzied pounding. It was impossible to breathe. A stone was crushing her chest, and inside her, the baby went very, very quiet. Panic welled up as she fought just to breathe. She knew Dayan was aiding her, yet she couldn't draw air into her lungs.

Gregori shimmered into the room. One moment there was no one beside the bed, and in the next instant, he stood tall and straight, invincible. His smile looked reassuring, but Corinne was beginning to know him through their continual mind merges. There was worry in his mind. Darius loomed over her too, a larger-than-life figure so powerful he seemed unshakable. A woman emerged from what seemed thin air, transparent at first, then very real. She was small, with wine-red hair, and she gave the impression of total competency. She was the one who leaned close and put her hand on Corinne's abdomen, a slight frown of concentration on her face.

"This is Shea, Corinne," Gregori said softly. "Trust in her judgment as we do." Gregori took her hand. "Our people are gathering wherever they are and they will lend their aid also. We will do this."

Corinne glued her eyes to Dayan. *'Save my baby.'* It was a desperate plea. *'Something's wrong, I can feel it.'*

"Corinne—" Shea's voice was gentle but very firm. "I'm going to take the baby immediately. She's in trouble, and we need to get her out now." She looked up at Dayan. *'You must complete the ritual as I do so, Dayan. Bring her across fully into our world and we will hope her body will go through the conversion fast enough to sustain her life. Gregori and Darius will aid you in this. Julian stands by to give his blood, as does Jacques.'* As she spoke to Dayan, she was already prepping Corinne, deftly cutting through clothing, without any need of light. Her mind was directing Darius and Gregori without having to use words as they worked together like a well-oiled machine.

Dayan shifted position again, his arms encircling Corinne, her head resting on his chest. Shea was fast and efficient, a highly skilled surgeon as well as a Carpathian healer. It was obvious to Corinne that Shea knew what she was doing. She felt no pain; they were working in concert to prevent pain. She felt strange sensations as Shea did the emergency procedure, opening her womb to allow access to the baby.

Corinne felt disconnected from the entire procedure. She was drifting again in a dream world, uncertain what was reality and what was dream. She saw the red-haired woman cutting into her. She saw Dayan nuzzling her neck, his mouth drifting over her pulse, his teeth sinking into her skin. None of it alarmed her. Gregori had centered himself, moved from his own body to become pure light and energy, streaming into Corinne in order to slow down the death process and speed up the conversion.

Corinne heard voices chanting in an ancient tongue, saw the flurry of activity as others brought a small enclosure like an incubator into the chamber. Dayan lifted his head, his face a mask of torment. That moved her even when nothing else seemed to. She ached for him, for his sorrow. He looked older; there were lines etched deeply into his dark, sensual features. She saw him make a thin cut along the heavy muscles of his chest, over his heart. She saw him press her to him, holding her close, murmuring to her, commanding her to take what he offered so they both would live.

She saw herself attempting to obey his command, her movements weak and feeble so that Dayan had to hold her head to him, stroke her throat so she would convulsively swallow. At the same time, she saw Shea lift out the baby, a tiny form. Her helpers were moving even faster now, cutting the cord, working on the baby, Darius very much in the forefront. He bent over the baby, his manner protective, tender even.

Corinne felt the tears on her face. Happiness. It was done. Her daughter was alive and in a circle of people who would love and care for her. Drifting above it all, Corinne was so tired she just wanted to close her eyes and let go. Sleep a long, long time. An eternity maybe. It seemed she had been tired all her life.

'*No!*' The command was sharp. '*You are not finished*

here, Corinne. I forbid you to do this.' The voice was imperious, authoritative. It followed her into her dreams and shook her out of her dreamlike state. She found herself in Dayan's arms, her mouth pressed to her chest, warm salty liquid pouring down her throat.

'It is enough!' Gregori warned Dayan before Corinne could fully comprehend what was happening and panic, or be repulsed and fight. *'There can be no resistance on her part. She simply isn't strong enough to survive if she resists.'*

Dayan immediately allowed Julian to close the wound in his chest and he held Corinne to him, locking her mind to his. She was fading away—he could feel her spirit drifting further from him, yet her departure wasn't a conscious choice. She seemed unable to rally enough strength to keep fighting, even with his ancient blood, even with the Carpathians pouring their strength of will into her frail body.

Dayan rested his head on hers. They had waited too long. Her poor mortal body had fought as long as it was able, remaining just long enough to give life to another. Now the life force was slipping away from her. She was no longer feeling the blood coursing through her body. Her fragile heart was still pumping because Gregori was forcing the damaged organ to do its job, but Corinne seemed too far away to call back.

Dayan felt them all around him—his people, his family. The chant swelled in volume. He heard the baby's soft distressed cry as Shea worked with her. He inhaled the scent of healing herbs. For a moment he allowed himself the last luxury of taking it all in, the beauty of the chamber, the flood of memories of his life: shapeshifting, soaring, challenging the earth itself as he gained knowledge; his beloved music, so much a part of him. He loved it all, but the woman in his arms was everything. Nothing else would ever matter to him.

Without her, there would be no color, no light, no music in his heart or soul.

Dayan bent his head to brush her eyelids, the corner of her mouth, with his. *'I love you, Corinne. You do not go alone into a strange world. I am with you.'*

At once there was a loud protest. Sharp. Demanding. All of them. His family. From a distance he heard Barack's and Syndil's cries of alarm. He heard the echo of Cullen, who must have caught the objection from Barack's mind. He heard Julian's sharp denial and Desari's soft little murmur of dissent. Tempest called to him. Gregori and Savannah added their demands. But it was Darius whom Dayan had followed all his life, only Darius he answered to. And it was Darius who commanded him now.

'You will not follow her. You will save her.' The voice was incredibly soft, but Darius had no need ever to raise his voice to be obeyed.

'She does not wish to continue, Darius. I can do no other than allow her to rest.'

Darius's hand came down hard on Dayan's shoulder, connecting them physically. *'You can be her lifemate later, giving in to her every desire, but not now. You are Carpathian, Dayan. We embrace life. We hold on. We endure. You will not release her or yourself from this world.'*

'She has the right to make her decision.' He had the right to make his choice; Corinne deserved the same respect. It was the last thing he could give her.

'This was not her choice, Dayan!' Darius persisted. *'She was never given a choice. Death was inevitable, and she knew and accepted that. She is tired and worn, but this is not her choice. She embraced you, accepted you, knowing what you are. She did not resist each time you offered to bring her into our world. You were not keeping the knowledge from her; she always knew it on*

some level. Her choice would be life, you, her child. She cannot make that decision, so you must make it for her. You do not realize how tired and worn you yourself are, how much energy you have used in keeping her alive to give the child a chance. You are not thinking straight. You will not go with her. You will stay with us, and you will turn your will on her and prevent this tragedy.' It was no less than a decree. A command meant to be obeyed.

Darius suddenly crouched low and looked Dayan in the eye. "If you ever trusted me, trusted my judgment, if you ever believed in me, follow me now."

Dayan felt the strength of his leader, the man he named brother, flowing into him, and he nodded, a slow, grim smile softening the edges of his mouth. It had been long since he had known emotion around his family, and now his pride and love for them were overwhelming. He turned inward, swiftly pursued and caught up with that weak, flickering light that was moving so far away from him. He surrounded Corinne's spirit; his will a strong wall, an anchor to hold her in his world. *'Corinne. Know me.'*

He felt her response. Weak. Fluttery. But she knew him. Of course she knew him. She would know him anywhere. What had he been thinking? Corinne loved life. She embraced life. She might be accepting of the hardships life had handed her, but she found joy in all things, beauty in the world around her. She wanted to raise her daughter, she wanted to see Lisa's and Cullen's happiness. Corinne wanted a life with Dayan.

Dayan held her locked to him. Her spirit was being pulled away from him, away from her damaged body. He saw Gregori and Darius working, two points of pure light, massaging and stimulating her heart. He knew Gregori commanded that more blood be given, and it was Jacques, brother to the Prince, who supplied it to Corinne. Dayan saw the two healers work furiously at spreading the blood to the organs of Corinne's body in hopes of speeding the conversion. Both were exhausted from maintaining the out-of-body experience, but neither wavered in his task.

'I'm tired. Let me sleep for a while.'

It was those last six little words that convinced him. She wanted sleep, not death. Not eternal sleep. *'Not yet, my love. It is not over yet. One more thing. Just one, and I will allow you to sleep as long as you like. Join with me, merge into my mind so that I can keep you safe while you cross over fully into my world.'*

The first ripple of pain was shocking. It felt like fire racing through her bloodstream. Corinne's body contorted, jerked in Dayan's arms. He couldn't believe the force of the rush, a fireball consuming her. She cried out, the sound torn from her throat, loud in the hushed stillness of the chamber, so that it echoed up the vent into the night sky.

'Oh, God, she cannot survive this. I do not want her last moments to be such pain.' The words broke from him as tiny beads of blood oozed across his forehead. He could not take the pain away. He had dulled it, but it was something none of them could fully prevent.

'She must survive.' Darius was implacable in his resolve.

Dayan breathed deeply, allowed the pain to wash over and through him before he turned his complete attention inward to that fragile spirit huddling so weakly within the walls he'd constructed. Corinne astonished him. She was unafraid. She was as accepting of the conversion as she had been of her labor. She was weak, though, and unable to aid him in gathering strength for the coming battle.

The next wave of fire burned through her internal organs with a jolt so severe, she was nearly wrenched out of Dayan's arms. There was no gradual buildup. The healers were forcing the conversion to accommodate her disintegrating heart. It would have failed long before if the two healers had ceased their work.

Dayan held Corinne's head as she was violently sick, again and again. She was too weak to move or help herself. He took great care that she did not inhale, seeing that she expelled every damaging toxin from her body. He found himself clenching his teeth against the waves of terrible pain racing through her body. Deep within his mind he felt her spirit falter, the light flickering. *No!* He clung to her, turned every ounce of his will to prevent that light from being extinguished. They had come so far. Death must not take her now.

The chant was a continual murmur in his mind, and he knew it was aiding the process, but he needed something else, something to draw her to him. The baby was quiet, fighting her own battle for life with Shea's help. It came to him then. The one thing he could give her that he knew she loved. His music. He began to sing. Softly at first, a melody of dark, dangerous love. A ballad of need. Of a man's desperate fight for the one woman he loved above all else.

Desari joined in on the chorus, her beautiful, magical voice a gift from the heavens. She sang with him, helping him use his voice to draw Corinne from the jaws of death. The notes leapt into the air, silver and gold, dancing like glinting sunlight in the darkened chamber.

He felt Corinne's response then. Weak, but there. She clung to the sound of their voices, allowed the melody to take her away from the terrible burning in her body, the humiliation of her system ridding itself of human toxins. The loss of control, the helpless feeling of lying unable to move, while her body contorted and writhed with pain. She chained herself to those notes, his gift to her, and floated above the fire, holding to life, clinging to Dayan, her solid anchor.

He was humbled by her complete trust and faith in him. He had no idea if he would have given his life so completely into another's hands. He was awed and humble and grateful. Blood-red tears dripped onto the back of his hand, but his voice never wavered as he sang to her.

The ordeal seemed an eternity to him, and his new-found emotions were raw. But he sang with his heart and soul. His voice surrounded her, lifted her above the terrible pain and kept her anchored firmly to him.

'Now, Dayan.' There was relief in Darius's voice. *'Send her to sleep and we can complete the healing.'*

It took a few moments for Dayan to realize what Darius meant. The healers had managed to utilize his blood and the precious blood of the Prince's lineage to convert Corinne's failing human heart into a strong Carpathian heart. The danger was over. He could barely comprehend that it could be so. He felt as if he had fought ten thousand battles, as if he had been fighting for all time.

He issued the command to sleep, strong, compelling, instant. Corinne had no choice but to obey, and in her weakened state, it was easy for him to send her into the Carpathian method of sleeping. Dayan breathed a sigh of relief. At last she was beyond pain. He looked up, his broad shoulders sagging. He was completely drained of energy. He had given Corinne a large amount of blood, he had not fed, nor had he slept in the rejuvenating soil. His every ounce of energy had been utilized to keep Corinne's heart and lungs going, to bind her to him. The emotions he had withstood would have been enough to drain his great strength. He was dangerously weak and pale.

He looked around the chamber to the others who had offered so much for him, for Corinne. Shea was working on the baby. He found himself smiling, a slow grin that replaced his fatigue with warmth. His child. Corinne might think of their daughter as John's, and he understood, but in truth, she carried Dayan's blood in her body. While Darius and Gregori continued to work at healing Corinne, he studied the baby.

"Will she live?" he asked Shea quietly.

The red-haired woman glanced at him. "She's very strong and she wants life. Corinne, Gregori, Darius and you did a good job of instilling a strong will in her. She will have loving, nurturing parents. I think it will be best if she stays here for a few weeks to give her body time to adjust to the outside world, but she is doing quite well."

"Few babies survive the first year." Pain sliced through him at the thought of losing the infant. He felt fiercely protective of her.

"That is so," Shea admitted, "but I have done a tremendous amount of research and I think I can keep her alive. Diet is important. A Carpathian infant's body is different from an adult's. We can no longer nurse them the way humans can, and they need a mixture of nutrients. Our blood is too rich for them. That is why it was important the baby didn't convert before she was born. She is just too small to live through it."

"It does not make sense that a mother cannot feed her own baby. Has this always been so? Nature provides for the young."

Shea nodded. "Hundreds of years ago, according to Gabriel and Lucian, our people didn't have this problem. Something has happened in the intervening years to cause this dilemma. The change took place sometime around the late thirteen hundreds or early fourteen hundreds. I'm almost certain of it. I'm very close to finding out." She spoke confidently. "In the meantime, this baby has special needs. She is not fully human, nor is she fully Carpathian. Rather than try to bring her over,

I believe we should allow her to grow as she is, at least until she is older. I was not fully Carpathian and I managed to survive. Gregori and I have worked on a diet we think will aid this little one in growing strong. And should there be any problems, we can monitor from a distance and immediately aid you. She has a good chance, Dayan."

"Thank you for what you have done for us."

Shea smiled at him. "I am glad I could get here in time. The journey was long, and we could travel only at night, covering many miles quickly. I feel your worry for Corinne. Darius and Gregori will heal her body completely. When she rises, it will be with a strong heart and a perfectly healed body. She won't have any after-effects of childbirth. They will see to it that she feels no discomfort. Allow her to rest for several risings beneath the healing soil. The baby will be fine with us. She knows us, and although she wants the comfort of her mother, we will do for her."

"Who will care for her during the hours of daylight? She cannot go to ground as we must, and she is too weak to be unattended, commanded to sleep during our hours of sleep. We must bring Lisa here." Suddenly Dayan was thinking like a father, not a Carpathian.

Shea smiled her reassurance. "We have dragged poor Gary Jansen with us. He has been a tremendous help in my research and is fully under the protection of all Carpathians. He will tend the baby while we are deep within the soil."

Dayan looked skeptical.

Shea laughed at him. "Gary is perfectly capable of taking care of this baby. Trust me. I work with him all the time. And he was entrusted with the care of Falcon and Sara's adopted children during daylight hours."

Dayan nodded reluctantly and indicated the small enclosure. "What is that?"

"It is much like a human incubator. She is still too small to live entirely on her own, but with your blood and care, she will grow very fast." Shea cleared her throat carefully, her eyes suddenly shifting back to the baby. "When Corinne rises, she will want to see the infant, Dayan. It is natural for a mother to feel this way."

Dayan suddenly smiled, the flash of his white teeth dispelling the worn look from his sensual features. "Are you trying to tell me in your delicate way that my lifemate will not rise with the same appetite as I will have?"

Shea laughed softly. "I think she will have the same hunger, Dayan, but her instincts will demand she see her daughter."

"Corinne wanted to name her Jennifer after John and Lisa's mother. I read in her mind that she was afraid to give her daughter a name, afraid it would somehow jinx the baby." Dayan leaned over to look into the transparent enclosure. He stared at the child, a horrified expression on his face. "She would fit into my hand."

Shea laughed at him. "She weighs about four pounds. Don't worry, she will gain weight fast enough."

"Dayan—" Julian clapped him on the shoulder. "Congratulations are in order. You have a lifemate and you are a father. It is cause for great celebration. However, we must postpone any festivities until after you have fed and have gone to ground. This has been a long ordeal, and you need to rejuvenate properly. Your lifemate will heal beneath the welcoming soil. Darius and I will guard your resting place and your child with our lives." Even as he spoke, he was casually bringing his wrist to his mouth. Without so much as a wince, he tore a wound in his skin and pressed his hand to Dayan's mouth. "Take what I offer freely so you might grow strong to protect your lifemate and child."

Dayan gratefully accepted the ancient blood. It soaked into his cells and tissues, bringing a rush of power to his depleted body. Julian had offered freely, knowing Dayan wouldn't leave Corinne. He had gone through far too many traumas with Corinne to entrust her to any other. Dayan would guard Corinne himself, and Darius would guard the entire family as he had done for centuries. Julian, Desari's lifemate, had taken his position guarding Darius's back.

Barack and Syndil sent their joy winging to Dayan through the night air, a shower of sparkling gems like fireworks in the sky above the vent in the chamber's chimney. Dayan was grateful to his family for sharing in his happiness.

The band's beloved Desari leaned close to brush a kiss on his cheek, happiness radiating from her. Her lifemate, Julian, grinned with his familiar teasing look. They watched the other Carpathians leave the chamber, their mission of mercy accomplished. They were now free to return to their homes.

Besides Dayan's family members, only Gregori and Shea remained behind with their lifemates. The healers would be exhausted when they finished their work, desperately in need of blood. Their lifemates would supply them blood before they would hunt on their own this night.

Gregori emerged first, his body pale, exhaustion obvious on his face. Then Darius, stumbling so that Tempest and Julian both reached for him at the same time. His skin was almost gray. He circled his lifemate's waist lovingly. "It is done, Dayan. She will live, whole and strong."

Gregori nodded. "Allow her to rest beneath the earth for two or three risings. Shea and Darius and I will make sure the baby lives. Corinne's body desperately needs time to heal fully. It was the most difficult work I have ever done. I advise caution before rising; check her before you awaken her. If in doubt, call to me or Darius.

We will examine her for you and give you advice."

Behind Dayan, Julian laughed softly. "So, Gregori, perhaps you will accept my dark embrace to replenish you, after all. Savannah is rather pint-sized."

Savannah tossed her wealth of raven hair and thumped Julian on the chest as she pushed past his much larger frame to take Gregori's hand. "I don't know why the lot of you insist I'm short. I happen to think of myself as being *very* tall."

Dayan found himself smiling at the tender expression on Gregori's face as the healer looked down at his rather petite lifemate. He tried to recall all he had heard of the healer. Gregori. The dark one. He had a reputation as a renowned vampire hunter, an individual others walked carefully around. But Dayan doubted that Savannah was in the least intimidated by her chosen one; she seemed to be a woman very much in love and secure within her relationship.

Dayan knew Julian fairly well. As Desari's lifemate, Julian traveled with the band. He was definitely a law unto himself, confident and certain of his own abilities after traveling the earth alone for centuries. He could needle both Darius and Gregori easily with his taunting sense of humor, almost as if he were secretly laughing at the two men over their downfall with their women. Dayan liked Julian's sardonic, independent nature, although it had been difficult at first to allow him entrance into their family.

Gregori smiled down at Savannah, his features full of love, then he turned ice-cold silvery eyes on Julian. "I should accept your offer, Julian, and drain you dry. It would put you in the earth for a few days and out of your lifemate's hair."

Julian laughed softly, nuzzling Desari's thick mass of long, silky hair. "She loves me in her hair, right, Desari?"

Dayan could feel the relief in the room, the release

of tension into humor. Gregori was nearly gray with fatigue, but no one mentioned it. Savannah glanced up at the healer, and they both simply dissolved into mist and streamed from the chamber before Dayan had a chance to thank them. He knew he owed a huge debt to Gregori.

"We will leave you now," Desari said in her soft, musical voice, "that you may sleep undisturbed. I cannot wait to greet Corinne as a sister. I will check on Cullen this night as well. Do not worry, we are all bound by Darius's word. He has taken Cullen into the family, and with Corinne comes Lisa. They are human, but they are well loved. I will see to it that Lisa has all the news and knows that Corinne is out of danger. I will tell her you will bring Corinne and the baby to her the moment Corinne can safely travel. Syndil says Lisa will be much relieved when she hears news of Corinne."

Dayan shoved a hand through his black hair, leaving it more disheveled than ever. "Thank you, Desari. Corinne has been anxious about Lisa. And I know Cullen has very strong feelings for her."

"So Syndil tells me. Do not worry any longer, Dayan. It took some time for everyone to accept Julian into the family. Corinne and Lisa will also work out their places with time. I know you are concerned that Corinne may not want to travel with us because she has a baby, but she loves you. She knows that in your heart and soul you are a musician. As she is home to you, so are you to her." Desari leaned over and hugged Dayan. "I love you very much, and I am so happy for you."

Dayan kissed her and watched as Julian and Desari left the chamber, walking side by side. Julian had his arm around Desari's slender shoulders and was whispering softly, suggestively in her ear. Dayan heard her musical voice laugh softly, happily. The sound filled him with so many memories, flooded him with warmth.

Corinne was alive and out of danger. The baby was alive and safe within the enclosure. Darius opened the earth and gestured for Dayan to gather Corinne's body into his arms. Dayan hesitated. "You are certain this Jansen will watch over my daughter?"

Shea laughed softly. "You are already becoming a worried father. Gary is very reliable. I will be here with Jacques, of course. Darius and Tempest will sleep above you and Corinne. Gregori and Savannah are in the next chamber. Our people are everywhere within this network of tunnels. No harm will come to the baby while you rest."

Dayan took a last look at the baby, touched the top of the transparent enclosure with his fingertips, right over the tiny infant's head. Then he floated down into the rich, welcoming soil with Corinne, holding her close, his body protective as he allowed his heart to slow and eventually cease beating.

Darius closed the earth over their heads and turned then, into the arms of his beloved lifemate, Tempest, needing to replenish his strength.

Chapter Seventeen

Dayan woke deep beneath the surface of the earth with his heart pounding and his body on fire. Corinne. He turned his head to look at her, afraid, exhilarated, so hungry for her he thought he might go up in flames. She lay beside him where he had placed her, unmoving, completely still; she lay as if dead. She looked unbelievably small, fragile beside him. Her body was a woman's, soft and curvy, and he knew she had the heart of a lion, yet she looked like a child in her sleep.

It had been three risings since he had gone to earth with her. He had awakened each night to check that the baby lived and was doing well in her little cocoon. He knew Corinne would expect it, but he did it because he found he was filled with worry for the infant. Each time breath came into his body, fear for the baby, his daughter, would cycle through him. *Daughter.* He tasted the word. He was a father.

Dayan scanned automatically, searching the immediate area first for danger, then to assure himself that no others of his kind lingered near their resting place.

Darius and Tempest had risen and were some distance away. Shea was already awake and bending over the child, feeding her with some formula she had concocted.

'The baby is well?' He made the inquiry before he had even parted the soil of his resting place, anxious for news, anxious to gently touch the baby's mind with his own.

'She grows stronger with each rising, Dayan.' Shea's reply was gentle and patient.

Dayan concentrated on the other two healers, focusing his attention completely. *'I wish to bring Corinne to the surface.'*

There was a brief pause, as if the healers were conferring. It was Gregori who answered him. *'I will come at once.'*

Dayan waited impatiently as Gregori hurried to the chamber. Dayan waved his hand to open the soil above their heads. He waited anxiously while Gregori took his time, centering himself, focusing, moving outside his own body and into Corinne's to examine the repairs. He paid attention to the smallest detail, making sure Corinne was completely healed before she was awakened. Dayan watched Gregori come back to himself, raising an elegant eyebrow at Dayan's obvious anxiety.

"She is healed, Dayan, and completely ready to take up her life with you. I will examine the baby and get out of your hair," Gregori drawled, knowing full well what was on Dayan's mind.

As Dayan floated out of the earth with Corinne cradled in his arms, he cleaned both her and himself, examining Corinne's lush body for marks or signs of her ordeal. Not a single mark marred her skin, not even the long, wicked cut where she had been opened to take the child from her body. He clothed both her and himself, knowing Corinne's natural modesty.

Issuing the command to wake, he brought her safely to ground, bending his dark head to find her mouth, to capture her first breath. Corinne. His lifemate. *'I want you, love, more than my body can stand.'*

Merged so deeply with him that she felt the urgent demands of his body, she couldn't help catching fire, her body perfectly attuned to his. She was aware that his body was full and hard, his mind dancing with erotic thoughts and images. He allowed the nightly reassurances from Shea to replay in his head, so she immediately knew the baby was thriving.

Dayan carried her swiftly across the chamber to the small area where Shea had enclosed the baby protectively. Corinne cried out at the sight of her daughter. She circled Dayan's neck with her slender arms and burst into tears. She couldn't believe she was alive. Her body was strong and supple, her heart beating in perfect rhythm with Dayan's. Every cell felt alive, on fire. She wanted Dayan as much or more than he wanted her.

'That is not possible.' His voice was sinfully wicked.

She laughed in the midst of her tears, so unbelievably happy she couldn't take it all in. "I have to hold her. I have to have her in my arms." She looked up at Dayan with her heart shining in her large eyes. "Have you held her?"

He shook his head. "Only Shea and Gary have held her. Gregori and Darius have examined her daily, and all of us have been reassuring her, but it is you she wants."

Shea smiled at her. "She is very strong, Corinne. She definitely wants her mother. It is not good to have her out of her protected environment for any length of time. Together, Dayan and I can provide a shield for her while she spends time with you. But only for a few minutes. It is better to be safe."

"What is wrong with her?" Corinne asked anxiously.

"I want her immune system to be stronger. She has had a hard go of it and needs a little more time. Do you have a name picked out for her? Dayan thought you might want to call her Jennifer after John and Lisa's mother."

Corinne nodded, unable to take her eyes off her daughter. "She's so beautiful. Little Jennifer, at last we meet."

Shea lifted the baby carefully from the enclosure, placed the tiny body into Corinne's waiting arms. Merged as he was with Corinne, Dayan shared the instant bonding between mother and child, the unbreakable tie, the exchange of love and tribute. It flooded all three of them. The acceptance. The love. Dayan felt tears burning in his eyes. This was his family for all time. Eternity.

'We have it all, my love, I cannot believe our good fortune.'

Corinne crooned softly to the baby, rocking her gently back and forth while Dayan surrounded them both with his arms. "Look how tiny her fingers and toes are," he marveled. "She has everything, like a real person." He was almost afraid to touch the tiny infant; his finger looked very big as the infant clutched her fist around it.

Corinne laughed softly. "You've never been around a baby before, have you?"

He grinned at her, nuzzled her neck so that unexpected sparks seem to jump back and forth between them. "Does it show?"

"Absolutely. Do you want to hold her?"

Dayan looked like he might faint on the spot, and both women laughed openly at him. It was Corinne who sobered first. "I'm so sorry, Shea. Savannah told me you are expecting a child, and you had to make such a long journey to be here. I don't know how we can ever repay your kindness. Is your baby okay?"

Shea placed both hands on her stomach, holding her baby protectively, feeling her lifemate's breath on the nape of her neck even although he wasn't in the chamber with them. "It is difficult sometimes for our people to carry to full term. The baby is fine, but we had to travel cautiously to prevent complications."

"Dayan told me there's concern that Carpathian babies often don't survive the first year of life." Corinne looked anxiously at Shea.

Shea sighed and pushed her hand through her long wine-red hair. "That is true, Corinne. There have been problems for many centuries. Gregori has done much research on this, and I joined him a few years ago. We discovered that the problems have been occurring longer than we originally thought. It was assumed that during the fourteenth century when most of our adults and children were destroyed, many, many lifemates were lost to us. It was believed fairly universally that Carpathian women had some chemical makeup that made it possible for only the male fetus to implant successfully."

Shea leaned over and smiled at the sleeping baby. "I think it is much more than that. I believe it has something to do with the plague."

Corinne's head snapped up, and she clasped the baby protectively to her. "What do you mean?"

Shea laughed softly. "Jennifer doesn't have the plague, don't panic. The plague has been around for much longer than most people realize. We know of instances in China in 224 B.C. There was an outbreak in Rome around 262 A.D. that killed five thousand people a day. The crusaders carried the plague to Europe. It swept through the continent in the 1300s and early 1400s."

"How could our people have been affected? Human illnesses do not have any effect on us. Their drugs and alcohol do not either," Dayan pointed out.

Shea shook her head. "That's what is believed, but it is not necessarily true. Drugs and alcohol are pushed through our systems, so we do not feel the effects. The same happens with human diseases. It doesn't necessarily mean there are no traces left in our systems."

"Has there ever been a case of a Carpathian falling ill from such a thing?" Dayan could scarcely believe what Shea was saying. "I have lived hundreds of years— how is it possible that I would not have contracted an illness?"

Shea laughed again. "You Carpathian males. You have egos the size of the continent. I read your thoughts as easily as you read mine. Yes, my mother was human and my father was Carpathian. I am a researcher, Dayan. I am merely looking at a hypothesis. I don't much care whether you think I'm capable of understanding the makeup of a Carpathian or not. What matters to me is finding an answer to this puzzle. If it is found, we can save our children. In doing so, there is a chance we can save our race from extinction."

Dayan bowed courteously, elegantly, a courtly gesture. "I ask forgiveness for my thoughts, Shea. I have never seen a Carpathian with a human disease."

"Traces still might be left behind," Shea pointed out patiently. "The human descendants of the survivors of the plague carry a mutated gene. That gene seems to be responsible for giving them protection from the HIV virus. Our people must have at times been forced to use those who were ill for sustenance during that time. With as many as five thousand people coming down with the plaque daily, they might have had no choice. It was during that time that we began to lose our babies on a regular basis. It might mean nothing at all, might be merely a coincidence, but it is an interesting fact."

"How does all that affect Jennifer?" Corinne asked fearfully.

"I don't honestly know," Shea said. "I'll work closely with you to see that she thrives on the mixture of nutrients we give her. So far she is doing well on it. Another week or so and she will be able to be with you all the time. For now, she needs to be in her little incubator." She grinned at Corinne. "I suggest you and Dayan take some time to be alone together. Enjoy yourself—you've earned it. Gregori, Darius, Gary and I will be watching over Jennifer. Look at it as if she had to stay in the hospital. She will sleep for long hours. You will know when she awakens; her mind will reach for yours."

Reluctantly Corinne allowed Shea to take the tiny infant from her arms. "She seems so small and helpless."

"She is growing," Shea assured her. "Both of you are extremely pale. Go away for a while, doctor's orders," she added firmly.

Corinne watched Shea place the sleeping baby carefully into the transparent enclosure. Dayan wrapped his arms around Corinne's waist. "Do not be sad, honey," he whispered against her satin skin. "We will know when she awakens and we can be here immediately. Let us go and explore your new world." There was a raw ache in his body, in his mind.

She heard it in his voice. Dayan never tried to hide his needs, his vulnerability, from her. Something deep within her responded to him, heating and melting, so that she was pliant and soft with wanting him. Her hand crept around his neck, her fingertips gently massaging the tense muscles. She leaned close to him, wanting to feel the warmth of his mouth against her skin. *'I can't wait much longer to be with you.'* There was a breathless

Christine Feehan

catch in her voice that he found incredibly sexy. He
caught her up in his arms and moved through the
chamber to stream through the tunnels up toward the
stormy night sky.

Corinne lay in his arms, cradled against his chest. She
looked up at his face, worn from worry, seeing lines
etched there that she had never seen before. For her.
The wind rushed at them, cold and biting, but Dayan
immediately showed her how to regulate her body temperature so she felt perfectly warm. A cool mist sprayed
her skin as they moved through the air toward some
destination unknown to her. Below them were acres of
treetops, swaying and dancing in the wind. It was
strange how the leaves looked silvery in the blackness
of the night. It was then that Corinne realized she could
see the ground clearly, even as fast as they were traveling. She could see everything, down to the smallest
mouse scurrying in the pine needles to get out of the
rain.

The drops of rain glittered like gems in the night.
Dayan's body was hot and hard, and flying through the
sky was totally exhilarating. She turned her face into his
throat, nuzzled him, her blood thick, a molten lava
moving through her body. She just let it happen,
wanted it to happen. He had become her whole world.
The way he talked, the way he turned his head. His
slow, sexy grin. The way his eyes burned over her.

*'I am reading your thoughts. Do you want us to fall
out of the sky?'* He took a firmer grip on her soft body,
aware of every lush curve.

She kissed his throat, inhaled his scent. Deep within
her something was struggling for freedom. A wildness
she knew was there, wanting—no, needing—to come
out. Corinne smiled. She had always wanted the freedom to be that woman in her soul. Now she had it. Her
tongue found his pulse, swirled in a small caress. She

felt his reaction, the instant slam of his heart, the tightening of his body. Her mouth drifted up to his ear, explored and briefly teased before moving along his jaw. *'If you don't kiss me, I might die and we'll never make it to wherever you're taking me.'*

The raindrops were bigger now, droplets of glittering water that ran along her skin and sizzled on the heat of her body. The thin silk of her white blouse was immediately transparent, drawing his gaze to the beckoning enticement of her breasts and wreaking havoc with his ability to move swiftly through the sky. He was grateful the stone house he was seeking was looming up, nestled in the cliffs at the edge of a forest clearing.

They plummeted, nearly falling out of the air as he fastened his hot, seeking mouth to hers, possessive, exploring, craving more and more of her until he thought nothing he did would ever be enough. The wait had been endless. They landed somewhat haphazardly, not on the porch, but against it, a tangle of arms and clothes. Dayan dealt with that problem immediately, not waiting for the shelter of a roof, but ripping aside cloth and dispensing with footwear in every direction. He had to touch her, every bare inch of her satin-soft skin. Feel her. Memorize her.

His mouth was hot and moist and ravenous, giving Corinne no chance to realize they were still outside. All around them the raindrops splattered to earth, and sizzled and steamed against their skin. Her hands had a life of their own, touching his body, making her own exploration, tracing his defined muscles, his narrow waist and hips, then moving lower still to where he was thick and hard with urgent need. She felt his body jerk, felt the way the breath slammed out of him as her fingers moved over him.

Lightning arced across the sky and split open the heavens. The earth rolled beneath their feet as their mouths met again, welded together in heat and fire. They couldn't get close enough, skin to skin, desperate to be one. Dayan thought he would go up in flames, his body hot and hard and demanding. *'I have to have you, Corinne. I might go insane if I do not have you immediately.'*

Corinne's carefree laughter was muffled in the side of his neck. Her breath found his pulse; her teeth scraped and teased. There was such joy in her, spilling over into him. Her tongue swirled again, her lips following the path of his collarbone. All the while, her hands were testing the weight of him, thick and hard and so needy. Her fingertips skimmed and danced; her body moved restlessly with heated demands of her own. "You don't want to wait?" Her voice was husky, sexy, a promise of paradise. Her mouth was wandering over the heavy muscles of his chest toward his flat abdomen. His stomach muscles clenched while fire exploded in the pit of his belly.

Dayan's hand slid over her body, trying to memorize every inch of her satin skin. He lost his ability to think rationally, and it didn't matter. Corinne's hands and mouth were inflaming him further, her body willing, accepting, hot and as needy as his own. His fingers found her welcoming moist heat, probed, pushed, felt the rush of hot liquid, eagerly awaiting him. Dayan lifted her, whispered instructions in his mind, or maybe it was just an image.

Corinne's arms circled his neck and her legs circled his waist. She could feel him, hard and thick, pressing into her. She was open and completely vulnerable to him. She closed her eyes, savoring the moment, the exquisite pleasure, the heat and fire, as she enveloped him, took him into her body, uniting them as they were meant to be. The pleasure was more than she had ever dared to dream of. She heard her own small cry of happiness, and her hips began to move, almost of their own volition. She was riding him hard, taking him as deep into her as she could. Her breasts brushed his chest, and the raindrops ran down their bodies like lapping tongues stroking tiny caresses over their sensitized skin.

Dayan bent his head to her breast as she leaned back, her face lifted to the heavens in a kind of ecstasy. This was how it was supposed to be. Right. Perfect. Two halves of the same whole. His hot, seeking mouth found temptation, pulled strongly while her body tightened around his, a fiery velvet sheath he was lost in for all time. His teeth scraped, nipped, sank deep.

Corinne cried out, her fists clenching in his hair as white-hot fire raced through her body, a pleasure so acute it bordered on pain. She forced her eyes open to watch him feed, as his body took hers, surging strongly upward to fill her, the friction keeping her on the edge so that she was clenching her teeth as her muscles convulsively gripped him.

It was erotic to watch him, his mouth on her skin, his throat working, his black hair rain-wet and slick. It was then, in that perfect moment, in the wild wind and rain, that she noticed his hair was no longer jet black but a soft charcoal. She made a sound, a soft cry of love, of devotion, her eyes filling with tears. He lifted his head, his black eyes glittering like obsidian. From the two pinpricks on her breast, two thin trails of crimson merged with the raindrops. Watching her, he bent his head and followed them, returning to close the tiny pricks with his tongue. His dark sensuality triggered a like hunger in her. Deep. Elemental. Sensuous.

She felt her body tighten, clench around his until she was holding him in a slick, tight, fiery grip. Dayan deliberately pushed aside the wet strands of his hair. *'Come on, my love, for me. Do this for me. I need this.'*

She slowed her hips, using long, slow strokes, letting

the hunger wash over her. Slowly she leaned forward, watching him watch her. Very slowly she lapped at the water over his pulse. His body jumped and heated a thousand degrees. Her teeth nipped experimentally. She felt his answering response, his hips surging forward hard, a little faster. Corinne looked up at him, her eyes slumberous, sexy. *'I do this for me because I need this. I want all of you, Dayan. I want you to belong to me. I want you in every part of me, with every breath I take.'*

Without hesitation she let it happen. Reached for it. Embraced it. This was her life, and she trusted his leadership as she had every step of the way. She hadn't been repulsed by his need, his dark hunger; instead she craved him in ways she had never imagined possible. More than anything, she trusted him. She knew that if she couldn't follow through, he would help her; he had a mesmerizing quality, that would make it easy to follow him anywhere he led. Dayan loved her. He would never do anything to bring her or her daughter harm.

His body seemed to swell in hers, grow thicker and harder, while her body gripped at his. Brand-new instincts took over, her teeth sinking deep, and he flowed into her like nectar. She felt him gasp as the white-hot fireball raced through his bloodstream, as his hands gripped her hips and he thrust forward, surging with powerful strokes. Then they were exploding together, minds fragmenting while their bodies seemed to ripple and burn. The earth moved, a strong rocking under them. Corinne couldn't tell if it was real or imagined. She could only cling to Dayan breathlessly, every cell screaming with joy. She was alive! She had found her paradise, and it was very real.

Corinne closed the pinpricks and rested her head on Dayan's shoulder. They clung together, their hearts beating wildly, fighting to get their breathing under control.

"I love you, Corinne," Dayan whispered softly against her bare skin, his eyes closed, his black lashes emphasizing the paleness of his face. "I love you so much." He lifted his head slowly, reluctantly, looking down at her through half-closed eyes.

She was looking up at him, her heart in her eyes. Their bodies were still joined together, and her body was still rippling with little aftershocks. She reached up to touch his wet hair, to trace the perfection of his mouth. "Thank you very much for finding me."

He smiled then, a slow, tender smile that would always be capable of stealing her heart. "You are very welcome." Small droplets of water dripped from his hair to splash on her face. They both burst out laughing. "We did not make it into the house."

"I see that," Corinne acknowledged, looking around her as if she were waking up from a dream.

Dayan reluctantly parted their bodies, reaching to lift her into his arms. "Crazy woman. Next time you decide to seduce me, make it out of the rain."

She bent her head to lap the water from his shoulder. "I don't know. I rather like it myself."

The touch of her tongue sent flames dancing over his skin. Dayan pushed the door open with his foot and waved a casual hand to light the candles and the wood in the fireplace. There was a thick fur rug on the hardwood floor and he put her down, the fur immediately rubbing along her bare skin so that her body tightened again in anticipation. Dayan stretched out beside her on his back, his long body very male. "You are going to rest for a while." He made it an order. "I am not taking you back to the healers half dead."

Corinne laughed at him. "Do you think it's possible to die from making love?"

"The way we make love, anything is possible." He stared up at the ceiling, watching the flickering lights dance while the rain fell against the windows. He reached for her hand, laced their fingers together. "I never again want to feel like I did when I thought you were dying, Corinne. You were taking my soul with you."

She rubbed her face against his shoulder, against his thick hair, which was now threaded with gray. His badge of love for her. "You are such a miracle, Dayan, and you persist in thinking it's me." She looked at him with a critical eye. "Why are you so pale? You're never like this." She touched his face.

"I need to feed," he said simply. "In a little while I will hunt, but not right now. I want to spend every minute, every second, in your company."

She lay quietly for a moment, absorbing what he was telling her. "Will I have to do that, Dayan?" She rolled onto her side to look at him. "Because I'm not certain I can. With you it's different, but I don't know about anyone else."

Dayan's black eyes moved over her face in a kind of dark, brooding study. "I did not think of such a possibility. I do not like the idea much." He was quiet for a brief time while the rain and wind blew at the walls and windows. "Now that you have brought it up, I do not recall Tempest ever feeding in front of us."

"Tempest was human," Corinne said with hope. "She's Darius's lifemate."

"Yes, she was human when she came to us. I do not ever recall seeing her feed." A slow smile touched his mouth. "Darius would never tolerate her feeding from another male, human or otherwise. I think it is best for us to adopt the same policy. It is entirely possible I have a jealous streak."

Corinne laughed at him. "You cannot be in my mind

344

and ever be jealous." She tugged at his hand. "Come on, lazy, let's go outside again. I want to run."

His eyebrows shot up. "If you have an overload of energy, I can think of other far more pleasurable things to do besides running. I am being good because you need to rest."

Corinne laughed softly. "You think I need to rest?" She stretched, lifting her arms to the sky. "You're the one who stopped, not me. I want to get the hang of being a Carpathian. I want to run, Dayan. For the first time in my life, I can do it. I really want to run. Please, let's go running."

"Right now?" He lay back in lazy contentment, linking his fingers behind his neck, watching her closely, drinking in the perfection of her body. He loved the way she moved, loved the joy in her, the naturalness. "There is a storm out there."

Her laughter filled the room with warmth, filled his heart and soul. "I think there's a storm in here too. A little storm never hurt anyone." She bent over to kiss him, her hair sliding over his chest, the silky strands causing him to shiver with anticipation. "Don't say no. I'm not overdoing it, really, Dayan. I need to run."

"You are a crazy woman." He sighed heavily because he knew he was going to run in the storm with her. How could he resist her happiness? It was impossible for him. He wanted to snuggle up with her somewhere safe, but Corinne wanted life. She faced her new world with the same lack of fear she had faced her former life.

Corinne caught his arm and tugged. "Come on, lazybones, or I'm going without you." She was looking around the room. "What in the world did we do with our clothes?" She was blushing, crimson creeping up her neck to her cheeks so that she looked like she was glowing.

He shifted position, turning onto his side, propping

up his head on his hand as he regarded her naked body with glittering, hungry eyes. "I do not think you need clothes, honey," he observed matter-of-factly, his black gaze dwelling intently on her full breasts.

At once her body began to tingle with heat. "You stop it, Dayan." She backed away from his reach, but she didn't attempt to cover herself. She liked him looking at her with that intensely hungry gaze. "You were the one who said we had to stop. Come on." She turned her back on him and walked slowly, provocatively, to the door, her hips swaying in invitation and her firm bottom beckoning to him. She had beautiful legs and a long, elegant back. She took his breath away.

Dayan moved quickly, leaping to his feet, scanning the area outside the house to be certain there was no danger. She glanced back at him over her shoulder, her look frankly sexy. "I don't think running naked, when I'm built like this"—she turned to give him her profile, her hands coming up to cup her generous, firm breasts—"is a very good idea."

His body tightened at the sight of a nipple peeking out at him through her fingers. "Then *walking* naked will have to do, because I like looking at you." He caught her hand, his fingertips sliding in a caress over her silken skin.

Her eyes moved over his body, a smile tugging at the corners of her mouth. "I see that," she pointed out, completely happy. She could touch the baby's mind at will, know the infant was sleeping soundly in the care of the healers while she discovered the exceptional gifts Dayan had given her. She could have it all, experience it all, and she was determined to.

They moved together out the door onto the porch. Dayan tugged her closer, moving her beneath his broad shoulder for protection. "Remember to regulate your body temperature," he said. Her body was brushing his as they walked together, and their skin become so sensitized, electricity began arcing between them.

Corinne threw back her head, looking up at the night sky, watching the glittering silvery drops rain down from the shadowy clouds above them. A small sliver of moon slipped out briefly from behind a heavy black cloud to shine on the thick stand of trees swaying all around them. Shadows danced, the air was clean and crisp, and the sound of the rain on the vegetation was a musical melody.

She looked down at her bare feet, shocked that she could walk without shoes on sticks and rocks and pine needles. She seemed to glide over the surface, as an animal might, her body instinctively finding the quietest, easiest way to go through the woods. She marveled that she had such a talent. Not only was her body moving efficiently, but her sense of smell had also become acute, and she could see despite the darkness. Information flew in on the wind, almost through her very pores. It wasn't from Dayan this time; she was receiving it on her own.

She laughed softly, happily, unable to believe she was so alive. That the world around her was so beautiful and new. She was walking faster, listening to her heartbeat, reveling in its strong rhythm.

Dayan allowed her to slip out from under his shoulder, watching her body move, sensuous, enthralling. She lifted her arms again to the moon and dark clouds, her hair wild and rain-slick, her breasts rising as she inhaled sharply to take in the scents of the night. She looked like a goddess, a wild, untamed siren lifting her arms in pagan sacrifice as she turned in a slow circle. "I want to run, Dayan," she repeated.

"Then we will shape-shift, honey." Who could ever deny her anything? Dayan knew it would be impossible for him. "Remember what I told you before? It always starts in your mind. You must build a complete picture in your head and hold that image. It is an odd sensation, although not unpleasant. If it frightens you, Corinne, reach for me. I will be with you in your mind at all times."

Corinne stopped moving, abruptly, swung around quickly to look at him, her eyes wide with excitement. "I'm not afraid. Really, Dayan, I'm not."

"Picture a leopard." He did it for both of them, creating the image so she could capture it down to the smallest detail.

She made a little sound, a throaty purring as fur rippled along her arms, as her muscles contorted, her body stretched, and then she was running on all fours, a sleek jungle cat. Her body felt like a well-oiled machine. She ran quickly, reveling in her ability to do so. She had ropes of muscles and sinew. Cushioned paws. Running in this form was unlike anything she had ever experienced, complete and utter freedom. She bounded across the ground, her paws barely skimming the earth. Her pelt kept the rain from penetrating to her skin. Whiskers acted like radar so that she was aware of everything around her. *'Dayan! This is wonderful!'*

The male leopard closed the distance between them in a single leap, its larger, heavier body protectively close. He didn't want her to get carried away with her exuberance. She had undergone a terrible ordeal, and even if she thought she was strong enough, he couldn't take the chance of her being injured. Not even a stubbed toe. Not a chipped fingernail.

'I'm reading your thoughts, and you're being silly. I'm whole! Isn't it so great to be alive?' He could hear her excited laughter as she leapt up on a thick tree branch and lifted her muzzle to the wind and rain.

He was catching her joy. How could he not? She was bathing him in her warmth, her light, her total pleasure in the moment. He would have soared to the moon and pulled it out of the sky if she asked him. He prowled below her, his ears and eyes alert for danger, yet he was merged deeply with her, immersed in her childlike happiness.

Corinne leapt from the branch because she could. There was untold power in the cat's body. She wanted to use it, try it out, see what it felt like to be a leopard. Dayan was unbelievably sensuous in the body of the male leopard. She realized, with a slight shock, that she was taking on the attributes of the animal. It was amazing to her. She rubbed against the tall fronds of grass, enjoying the sensation.

'Baby, be careful here. We both are very heightened sexually. In this form, sex is possible between us, and you might trigger both of our instincts, but I am not certain it would be entirely enjoyable to you. Leopards are very dangerous at any time. When they mate, the male must hold the female in a submissive position for his own protection. You need much more experience to control animal passions. On the hunt this form is extremely difficult to control.'

Corinne was tempted to discover what he was talking about. The female leopard certainly wanted to mate, but, merged as she was with Dayan, she could easily read that he was worried, even though the male shared the same desire. She immediately controlled her impulses and took off running again, stretching out her sleek, muscled body. She was silent, her leaps taking her over fallen tree trunks and even wider streams. She loved the sensation and wanted it to go on forever.

'We can do this at any time?'

'Of course. You should practice with me often. There is much to learn, honey, and I can see you will take to it easily.'

'Can I fly?'

His laughter was a soft joyful sound in her head. *'It is raining. Birds don't like to get wet.'*

'This bird likes it. We can fly to see Lisa and Cullen.'

In the body of the leopard, Dayan shouldered her around, turning her back toward the shelter of the house. *'It is too soon. Lisa knows you were very ill and you have had the baby. She would expect you to take a few days to recuperate.'*

'It has been a few days.'

'I want you, Corinne. All to myself. I want to taste every square inch of your body. I want this rising and the next and ten more to make love to you.'

Her answering laughter was tender. *'Really? So why didn't you just say so?'*

Chapter Eighteen

Corinne looked around the crystal chamber with its steaming pools and flickering candles. Water lapped at the large rock formations and reflected colors from the various crystals along the curving walls and ceiling. This underground cave with its network of tunnels and large rooms was beginning to feel like home to her. The baby was growing stronger, gaining enough weight that Shea was certain they would be able to remove her from her protected environment soon. Corinne held her daughter for small blocks of time, very aware of the dangers outside the incubator. Both Dayan and Corinne often merged with the infant to comfort and soothe her. They wanted her to know she was loved and wanted and they couldn't wait for her to be out with them.

Desari and Julian were frequent visitors, and Corinne really liked them both. She found Julian's sense of humor a good conterbalance to his intimidating demeanor. She knew Desari didn't find him in the least intimidating. Desari had a sweet personality, and she welcomed Corinne as a sister. It was taking a bit of time, but Corinne was beginning to feel as if she might fit into Dayan's family. All of them seemed excited about the baby, even Darius, who was by the far the scariest man Corinne had ever met.

"Darius is not in the least scary," Dayan denied, moving up behind her to rest his head on her shoulder so he could look at the infant. "Jennifer's color looks better today."

"You're reading my mind again." Corinne leaned back, pressing her body into his much harder frame. At once his body stirred to life, tight against her bottom.

Dayan was always in her mind. He would always be in her body, too, if he could manage it. He didn't want to leave her side. Corinne caught the echo of his thoughts and laughed softly. "That will look good when you're playing with the band on stage. A little kinky, though. I'm not certain the censors would let us get away with it."

Dayan allowed relief to wash over him. Several times in the course of the last few days, Desari had gently made references to traveling on the road with the band, but Corinne had never answered one way or the other. When Dayan touched her mind in an attempt to gauge her mood on the subject, he always found she simply avoided thinking of it. "You are not opposed to traveling with musicians from town to town? Leaving everyone you love behind?"

Corinne moved her body provocatively against his. "Everything I love is right here with me. And Lisa. I can't stay home for her. Lisa has the money to travel, if she wants to visit us. If she really is in love with Cullen, as I keep hearing from everyone, then my guess is she will want her own home."

Dayan lifted the hair from the back of her neck to

press a series of little kisses against the warmth of her skin. "Cullen will decide what to do."

Corinne savored the feel of his mouth for a moment, then bent to put little Jennifer in the incubator. The action pressed her bottom tightly against Dayan, who took advantage, catching her hips to drag her even closer. She took her time, her happiness spilling out as she gently kissed her daughter and enclosed the sleeping baby in the incubator. She stood up, still looking down at the baby. "Isn't she beautiful, Dayan?"

His hands moved slowly up her body from behind, sliding from her hips to her tucked-in waist, traversing her narrow rib cage to cup her breasts in his palms. "She is truly beautiful, Corinne, just like her mother." He whispered the words against her ear, his tongue touching her skin, tasting her because sometimes he had to.

She leaned her weight into him, her hands covering his as his thumbs teased her nipples into hard peaks and her breasts swelled, aching with need for him. "Sometimes, when I first awake, my heart is pounding in terror because I'm so afraid this isn't real." She turned her face to look up at him over her shoulder. "I'm afraid you can't possibly be real, that I'll wake up and it will all be a dream."

His mouth wandered up the side of her neck. His teeth found her earlobe and nipped sharply. She yelped and glared at him. Dayan grinned without repentance. "Just wanted you to see I am very real." He swirled his tongue on her ear to ease the ache.

"I want to visit Lisa and Cullen today. I know Barack and Syndil are being very reassuring about his condition, but I want to see for myself. And even though Lisa is told I'm fine, I know she's anxious."

"All right, then, honey, we will go when Shea comes in to check on Jennifer." He buried his face in her neck, inhaling her fragrance. He was sending chills down her spine, while molten lava spread through her blood. He had only to look at her and she found she wanted him. More than wanted him. Corinne craved the scent of him. The feel of him. The sight of his naked body. The sound of his beautiful voice. She wanted to watch him making love to her, see his face etched with sensual beauty. She turned in his arms and blindly found his mouth with hers, arms circling his neck, her body at once soft and pliant and instantly inviting. "You are amazing," she whispered into the heat of his mouth.

His hand bunched her hair, tipping her head back to give him better access for exploration. He took his time, kissing her thoroughly, savoring the taste of her. "You are the amazing one," he corrected, finding her pulse with his tongue. "The way you trust me. The way you have thrown yourself into our world and embraced it with your arms wide open. You have required little aid even when you feed."

She raised her head. "I thought I was doing that all by myself. I admit I was shocked at myself. If I think about it, the idea repulses me, but when we're together . . ." She trailed off, leaning her body into his.

"I enhance your need and desire to feed," he admitted. "I do not want you to be uncomfortable. Over the centuries I have been in a few situations where the illusion of eating was not enough and I was forced to consume human food. Vegetables were not so bad, although my body immediately rejected them, but the flesh of animals that had been killed was wholly repugnant to me. I know you feel this way about taking blood. To our people, it is sacred and very natural."

Dayan groaned suddenly, caught her face in his hands and brought his mouth down once more on hers. He could hear Corinne's silent laughter echoing warmly in his mind. Her hearing was acute now, and she had picked up Shea's deliberate noise as she approached the chamber.

'It was nice of her to warn us.'

'It was necessary, but not nice. We have wasted our time alone here.' There was another groan, his breath hot on her neck. *'Stop laughing, I might have to walk all bent over.'* He allowed her to feel the painful fullness, the little jackhammers tripping in his head. Deliberately he groaned again, just for good measure.

Corinne laughed out loud, the sound carefree and happy. "Poor baby. Welcome to real life."

He wrapped his arms around her tightly. "I do not want real life. I want sex." He leaned close to her. "Hot sex, scorching sex." His voice was wicked in her ear, his breath stirring tendrils of hair and sending shivers along her spine.

"Now I really don't feel sorry for you at all." She pushed at the wall of his chest to put distance between them. She was laughing, her eyes dancing as she teased him. "You're a wicked man and you deserve to be hurting." He knew very well what he was doing to her body—the rush of heat, the spread of fire. He was totally unrepentant.

Shea moved into the chamber, still making noise to warn them of her coming. She could hear them laughing together, could smell the age-old call to mate with her heightened senses. She grinned at them as they broke guiltily apart. "I'll watch over Jennifer while she sleeps. Are you visiting Cullen and Lisa today? I checked on Cullen while they were sleeping just to make sure he was healing nicely. He's already wanting to get up. Gregori went twice too, just to make certain."

Dayan's hand slipped down Corinne's arm, his fingers shackling her wrist to his side. "That sounds like Cullen."

"Lisa has been very anxious to see Corinne," Shea

admitted. "Cullen doesn't want her to be worried, so he's decided to get up and find you both."

"That is where we are going now," Dayan assured the healer.

Corinne nodded. "I've been worried about Lisa, but Dayan thought it would be too soon for Lisa to think I could travel after all that's happened."

Shea shrugged as she bent over the incubator. "I think at this point, Lisa will be so glad to see you she won't question anything. She prefers not to confront anything that doesn't fit her view of the world."

Corinne tugged at Dayan. "Come on. I really want to see her. Jennifer's asleep—now is our chance." She suddenly grinned at him, her teeth very white and her eyes dancing with excitement. "We can fly. You can teach me to fly. Hurry, Dayan, I can't wait." She was dragging him toward the entrance to the chamber.

Dayan couldn't help catching her exuberance. She was bringing back memories of his childhood when he had first experienced his abilities as a boy. He stopped her. "See that chimney going up the vent? It is far faster to go up that way."

She studied it for a moment, uncertain whether he was teasing her. "It looks very narrow. How can we fit, even if we were birds?"

"Bats live in caves. They are small and can get into very tight places."

"No way. You can actually make yourself that small?"

"I can be the mist on the wind, molecules in the air. Of course I can do small. So can you. It is exactly like the leopard. Study the image in my head so you have the exact replica in detail, then focus and hold that image. You can do it." He would help her to hold the image, just as he had done with the leopard.

Corinne followed his lead without hesitation, willing to experience everything life had to offer. The sensations were completely different: the information pouring into the bat's body came differently than the leopard's senses. When she burst into the night sky, Dayan was already providing the next image, that of an owl. In midair, she made the transformation, this time aware of his aid, and accepting of it.

To soar across the sky was so incredible, she lost the image more than once and had to rely on Dayan to hold it for her. It didn't matter—she was entranced. High above the trees she circled, dipping her silent wings and scanning the earth for all she could see and hear. *'I could stay here forever!'*

He was experiencing flying and shape-shifting through her eyes. It was such a part of him, he had forgotten the joy of it. Or maybe he had never been able to feel it as strongly as Corinne did until now, not even as a child when his emotions were still intact. Or maybe the intensity of his feelings was because Corinne was with him, by his side, in his heart and soul, and he had someone to share every pleasure, every sorrow. Maybe that was the difference. He only knew she had made him whole, had changed the world into something new and shiny, and her joy was constantly spilling over to him.

Dayan turned her in the direction of the house where Syndil and Barack had taken Cullen and Lisa to protect them from the members of the society. Dayan knew Darius had tracked down the hunters and had succeeded in diminishing their numbers. He had done so once before. Hopefully, it would be some time before they could fill their ranks of soldiers and send new assassins after his family. He refrained from passing on the information to Corinne, not wanting her to have to face the harsher aspects of their life until it was necessary.

Below them the house appeared, a long, sprawling

structure surrounded by forest. The clearing contained a garden of wildflowers and ferns. To one side was a large oak tree. Hanging off a branch by a thick rope was a tire swing. The house looked well kept. Dayan glided to earth, guiding Corinne as she landed, scrambling for a purchase in the midst of pine needles and vegetation. The female owl nearly crashed into the tire swing. She shifted back into her normal shape, laughing aloud. It was Dayan who provided clothes.

"Dayan, this is so much fun. Did you see me? I thought I was going to smash into the oak tree. I was trying for a branch, but at the last second I was afraid I wouldn't make it."

Her hair was a wild mass of silk, her cheeks flushed with excitement, and her moss-green eyes were dancing again. She took his breath away and melted his heart. "You did fine, though your landing could use work."

His voice was teasing, a black-velvet melody that somehow played through her body and soul. Corinne touched his face. "Thank you, Dayan. I love every minute of this, I really do." She glanced at the house. "Is this where Lisa is staying? It's wonderful—who owns it?"

Dayan shrugged. "Carpathians own property all over and we lend it when there is need. Listen to me, honey, before we go in. Lisa must not know about us. That we are different. It will be better for her if she never finds out." Dayan spoke with extraordinary gentleness.

Corinne smiled lovingly up at him and framed his face with her hands. "I know Lisa better than anyone else, Dayan, and I love her. I would never want her burdened with more than she can handle."

He nodded his acceptance and bent his head to kiss her inviting mouth. "I fear you are looking far too beautiful to have gone through such an ordeal as you have.

I do not know how Lisa will take your recovery." His hand traced the slender column of her throat, moved lower to cup the weight of her soft, firm breast in his palm. He thought that touch would be enough, but need slammed into his body. Before he could stop himself, he bent his head lower to find her nipple right through the thin silk of her blouse, his teeth scraping gently, his mouth suddenly hot and urgent, pulling strongly.

Corinne closed her eyes and leaned into him, wanting him all over again, her body flooding with liquid heat. She circled his head and held him tightly to her. "What are you doing, Dayan? We're right outside the house; anyone could see us through the windows if they were looking." But she wasn't pushing him away as she should have; she was pressing him to her, arching her body to give him better access. Her breath was coming in ragged little gasps. How could she need his touch so much? She wanted him right there, that minute, again and again, his body hard and thick, thrusting into hers.

'We can be unseen if we so desire.' Even in his mind, his voice was husky, sensual, wickedly erotic. She could taste him in her mouth, feel him deep inside her, and yet he was only at her breast, his mouth demanding. The feel of his mouth, hot and wet over the silk of her blouse, was making her wild and hungry.

'You mean invisible?' The thought excited her. Having him right there, right at that moment. When she wanted. She was already moving against him, making her own demands. *'Tell me how.'*

'First you do whatever you see in my head.' His hand was sliding over her flat stomach, pushing aside her shirt so that he could feel bare skin.

He had pictures in his head, but Corinne was certain they had nothing to do with becoming invisible. She heard his soft laughter. *'You're so incredibly bad some-times.'* She meant to chastise him, but it came out soft and sexy. She was already responding to those pictures, trusting him to cloak them from prying eyes. She was pushing aside his clothing, her hands finding the hard length of him, fingertips dancing and teasing, making intimate promises to him.

Dayan removed their clothing in the way of his people, easily, simply, so that her body was open to his, so he could look at her curvy feminine form and marvel at its lush perfection. His hand slipped down her flat belly to the nest of curls and settled there, his fingers finding her hot and slick with damp need. "I could take you over and over and never have enough," he whispered, leaning back to watch her face while he pushed with his palm against her entrance. He loved to see her face, the way she moved into him, her hips begging for more, wanting him with the same eagerness he had for her.

"Dayan." She whispered his name. Softly. Her voice said it all. He bent his head again to find her mouth with his, at the same time inserting two fingers into her hot channel, stroking, teasing, matching the rhythm of her hips. She was fiery hot, and her scent called to him. Corinne moved restlessly against him, loving the way the breeze slid over her body like his fingers, teasing her nipples into hard, beckoning peaks so that Dayan couldn't resist her invitation. She loved him watching her pleasure, *feeling* her pleasure when he merged with her.

'I want to taste you, Corinne. I want every part of you.'

'I would deny you nothing, Dayan. You know that.' She loved the intimacy of their mind merge. The way everything between them was so out in the open. She didn't have to tell him she wanted him to push into her harder—he already knew it. He didn't have to tell her

that the way she was moving and showing her need of him excited him unbearably.

His hands spanned her waist and he lifted her, setting her bottom unexpectedly on the tire swing. He tipped her back so he had access to her sheath "You'd better be right about that invisible thing," she warned him, but her fists were clutched in his hair and she was already going up in flames.

Dayan delved deep into the sweet, hot core of her. She was shaking with need now, her muscles clenching tighter and tighter. She wrapped her legs around his back, moaning her pleasure, unable to believe she could feel so alive and ready to shatter at any moment. His hands were hard on her hips, pulling her to him as he deliberately took her over the edge into a mind-shattering release that seemed to go on forever. Satisfied, he stood, dragging the swing forward, pinning her hips so that he could bury himself in her to share her explosive pleasure. He moved in hard, deep strokes while her body exploded around his and her hands' grip on the rope was the only thing keeping her in touch with reality.

Dayan tightened his hold on the curve of her hips and allowed the wildness of his nature to claim him. Corinne was urging him on with little breathless cries, with her tight, hot body surrounding his, pulling him deeper and deeper into her. Lightning arced across the sky and split open the heavens, raining a shower of sparks around them. Or maybe it was just in their minds—Corinne wasn't certain. Electricity seemed to be crackling between them so that flames sizzled and danced along their skin.

He threw back his head, surging forward again and again, the wind in his face, his body buried in her hot velvet sheath, tight and fiery, dragging him closer and closer to the edge of the world. Corinne was so much a part of him, he couldn't tell where his pleasure started and hers left off. He felt the first ripple, the contraction, the strong gripping of her muscles around him and he willingly went with her, right over the edge of the world. They were free-falling through time and space, while all around them the earth rocked and rolled and fireworks seemed to scatter across the night sky in a fiery display.

Corinne found herself back in her own body, struggling to control her wild breathing, both hands clutching the thick rope. Dayan was watching her, his heart like thunder in their ears. His black gaze was so hungry and intense, Corinne's heart went into instant meltdown. They both smiled, the same slow grin of sated contentment. Of intimate conspiracy.

Dayan gently disentangled himself, helping her to her feet, holding her close to him. He loved holding her almost as much as he loved making wild love to her. Music was playing in his head, notes and lyrics running through his heart and soul. *Corinne.* He breathed her into his lungs, letting them both recover naturally.

"Was I yelling like a banshee? I can't honestly remember," Corinne asked.

"If you were, I must have been yelling right along with you," Dayan assured her. He allowed the wind to cool the heat of their bodies before he clothed their bare skin. Tilting his head to one side, he regarded her gravely. "You are so beautiful, Corinne. When I am up on the stage performing and you are either by my side, performing right along with me, or simply sitting in the audience with all those single men staring at you, I am going to have a few bad moments."

She laughed at him, flung her arm around his neck to kiss him soundly. "Crazy man, we just made the earth move. I know you aren't going to pretend you're not feeling arrogant and like the greatest lover of all time. What is all this sudden insecurity?"

His white teeth flashed, black eyes boyishly mischievous. "I knew if I planned it right, you would eventually get around to admitting it." He caught his mane of hair in one hand and secured it at the nape of his neck with a leather tie.

Corinne's fingertips tenderly brushed at the wayward charcoal strands falling across his forehead. "You deserve it this one time. I love you very much."

"At last. I never thought you would come right out and tell me! I was going to pry it out of you if you waited much longer. We are no longer invisible. I think we'd better go up to the house and get inside in case Lisa comes out here and notices we did not bring a car. I saw the curtains flutter upstairs."

Corinne turned eagerly to the house, hurrying up the porch steps to the front door. Before she could tap, the door was yanked open. "Corinne!" Lisa flung herself into Corinne's arms so hard, she nearly knocked them both over. Dayan saved them with a steadying hand on Corinne's back. Tears were swimming in Lisa's blue eyes, streaming unchecked down her face. The two women clung together, laughing and crying at the same time while Dayan looked on in helpless male horror.

"I was so afraid for you," Lisa said, clinging to her. "Let me look at you. They told me in the hospital that you were going to die. You just disappeared out of your hospital bed. Syndil told me your heart is strong and the baby is alive. Where is she?"

Corinne hugged Lisa to her as the words began to tumble out. "I didn't die. My heart is very strong, stronger than it has ever been. Dayan's family knows healers—incredible doctors, they saved the baby and me. Jennifer is still in an incubator, but I promise, as soon as they let me have her, I'll bring her to you. Tell me about Cullen. How is he?"

Lisa was leading Corinne through the beautiful

house, toward Cullen's bedroom. Dayan followed, keeping his distance, allowing Lisa to have Corinne's complete attention. "Cullen is really doing well, but he won't stay in bed no matter what I say. Yesterday morning he wanted to get up and fix me breakfast! He's like that—he's always wanting to do the sweetest things. I like doing things for him, but he doesn't want me to; he thinks he's imposing."

"Has he tasted your vegetarian lasagna yet? That should convince him you can be very domestic," Corinne advised.

Lisa stopped before pushing open the door. "I want to be with him, Corinne. I mean it—I've never met anyone like him, anyone I could just talk to for hours. I love being with him." She smiled. "He's sort of been a captive audience."

"That's good, isn't it?"

Lisa shrugged. "I'd give up modeling to be with him. You know how much it means to me to know I have a huge retirement fund, and plenty of money to fall back on. But I'd give it up for him, I really would."

"But . . ." Corinne encouraged gently.

Lisa glanced at Dayan, who was some distance down the hall, studying a painting. She lowered her voice. "Cullen hasn't said anything to me. I think he likes being with me, I know he's attracted, but I don't know how he really *feels* about me. Or how much. He's different from other men, Corinne, he really is."

"I'm happy for you, Lisa. I like Cullen. I think I could grow to love him, and I can't imagine that he wouldn't adore you as I do." She took Lisa's arm. "Before we go into Cullen's room, I should tell you that Dayan and I are married."

"What?" Lisa glared at her, clearly hurt.

"It was necessary to protect the baby. I love him, really love him, and I want you to love him as a brother.

He's been so good to me. He saved my life; he saved Jennifer's life." Corinne looked up at Lisa with a steady, almost mesmerizing gaze. "I intend to spend the rest of my life with him. I need you to accept him as family."

Lisa nodded, flinging her arms around Corinne again. "I owe him everything for saving little Jennifer and you."

"Lisa!" Cullen's voice was still slightly hoarse but he sounded strong enough. "What are you doing out there?"

Dayan knew perfectly well that Cullen could hear every word with his enhanced hearing. Dayan walked down the hall, reached past the two women to push open the door. "Hey, lazy boy, these two cannot make up their minds whether to cry or laugh or just stand there hugging each other. I need another male around for balance."

"We aren't that bad," Corinne denied, slipping her arm around Dayan's narrow waist as Lisa rushed forward to Cullen's side.

Cullen was sitting in a chair, a little pale, but looking stronger than Corinne had expected. There was something different about him. It took only moments, but when she glanced at Dayan he nodded imperceptibly. *'Power recognizes power. He cannot do what we can do, but he walks partially in our world. He shares a mind merge with Barack.'*

Corinne had known about it, Dayan had discussed it with her, but it was strange to her that she could see the difference in Cullen the moment she walked into the room. She touched his hand with gentle fingers. "I'm so sorry you were injured, Cullen, and that my heart was acting up at the same time. Poor Lisa and Dayan had to take the brunt of worrying about us. How are you feeling?"

"Like I could go dancing if anybody would give me the opportunity."

"You shouldn't rush yourself, Cullen," Lisa said anxiously. "What's the big hurry?" She laced her fingers through Cullen's with one hand while pushing at his hair with the other.

"A man can't very well ask a woman to marry him when he's dressed in a bathrobe and hasn't a proper ring. It isn't done," Cullen said.

Lisa looked at Corinne anxiously, as if she didn't dare understand him. "I don't think a woman would care one way or the other," Lisa said carefully. "Were you planning to ask someone to marry you?"

"I wanted to ask someone," Cullen admitted, "but she's beautiful and famous and far too good for me. I could pull it off dressed up in formal attire with a candlelight dinner and a ring, but bathrobes do something to take away a man's courage."

Lisa stood there looking so helpless, Corinne wanted to gather her into her arms. Evidently, Cullen felt the same way. He pulled Lisa down onto his lap, his arms circling her body. "Lisa Wentworth, would you consider marrying me? Before you answer me, I want you to be aware I have enemies. We will spend time on the road, traveling with the band, and when we're not, we will be hidden away in places like this. I can promise you I'll work my best to get out of danger so we can live somewhere comfortably, but in the meantime, we will have to travel around in safety with the band."

Lisa swept back her hair. "I want to be with you, Cullen. I'll have to find a way to get out of my contract, but I'll do it. I'll find a way."

"Barack and Syndil will help you with that," Dayan said. "Let them go with you to take care of it. Barack is a superb businessman, and since Cullen cannot go with you, one of us should protect you and your interests."

"That's a wonderful idea," Corinne said.

Lisa found herself nodding, blinking rapidly. Sometimes she felt as if she were falling forward into Dayan's eyes when he stared directly at her. It was the craziest thing. And she always seemed to agree to things she wouldn't ordinarily agree with. She looked at Cullen a little helplessly. "What do you think?"

"I think if I can't go, Barack should go with you. He knows a lot about contracts, and if anyone can find a loophole, he'll be able to. If you go, Lisa, you have to stay right with Barack and Syndil and do everything they tell you."

'Why does Barack have to go with Lisa? We should go, Dayan. She's uncomfortable with this.' Corinne objected.

'She cannot rely solely on you, honey. Barack and Syndil will protect her from any members of the society who should be lurking around, and of course, either of them can easily persuade those holding her contract to let her out of it. Let her depend on Cullen and the others.'

"Syndil thinks I'll have to hole up here for a few more days, but Lisa and I will join you before the first concert date," Cullen promised. "I'd like to get married as soon as possible." He looked up at Corinne. "Will you be terribly upset if we get married quickly? It would be dangerous to plan a large wedding with Lisa having such a famous name. It would draw the society members out for certain. I think we should do it in secret and then we can have a celebration with the band members. What do you think, Lisa?"

"I always thought I'd want a huge wedding with the long train and roses everywhere, but I really just want you. It would be nice if Dayan and Corinne could be there as witnesses."

"You name the time and place, Cullen," Dayan promised at once. "We'll be there." He was glad he'd said that when he felt Corinne's happiness blossoming inside him. She loved Lisa and wanted to see her married.

He slipped his arm around Lisa's shoulders, pulled her close to him. "Is Barack taking good care of you?" There was a slow draw to his soft voice.

Cullen laughed. "He's getting used to Syndil adoring me. She has from the moment she laid eyes on me. He just can't seem to admit it yet."

To Corinne's surprise, Lisa laughed with him. "Cullen is so mean to Barack. He's always winking at Syndil and blowing her kisses. He says outrageous things to her. Barack gets this look on his face—it's priceless, Corinne."

"I haven't met Syndil and Barack yet," Corinne admitted. "But Desari and her husband, Julian, are very nice."

Lisa nodded. "They've visited every evening. I can't believe I've met the entire band. Even the bodyguard Darius and his wife, Tempest. She's really nice, but Darius is intimidating."

Corinne was shocked that she caught the echo of Lisa's thoughts. *Like Dayan.* Lisa found both Dayan and Darius intimidating. She thought Barack was funny, and Syndil was a sweetheart. Corinne stretched out her hand to Lisa. "I want to tell you all about baby Jennifer. Come on, let's go talk while Dayan makes certain Cullen really is as well as he keeps saying he is."

"How much did she weigh?" Lisa asked.

"She's very small, only four pounds, but she is gaining weight. She should be out of the incubator soon. She has lots of hair, and little dimples by the corners of her mouth."

"Like you do," Lisa said.

Corinne laughed and hugged her. "I'm so happy, Lisa. Truly, truly happy."

Chapter Nineteen

Corinne woke tangled in sheets, her heart pounding erratically and a cry of alarm in her throat. There were tears on her face, and both hands reached protectively for the small mound that was gone from her stomach.

'What is it?' Dayan dragged her close to him, his arms closing around her, a safe shelter in the storm of her nightmares. *'Tell me, honey.'* He was scanning their surroundings, merging more deeply so he could see into Corinne's haunted dreams.

"I couldn't breathe, Dayan—for a moment I couldn't breathe!" Her heart was settling into the calmer, more steady rhythm of his. She lay in his arms, grateful for the strength of his body. She listened to the reassuring sound of her heart and the softer, almost imperceptible sound of her daughter's breathing. "For a moment, none of it was real—not you or the baby or my new heart. You were gone and I was left alone."

Dayan pressed his mouth to her temple. "You were resting in the way of humans, Corinne. You wanted to lie down on the bed here in our new home."

369

Corinne found herself smiling in spite of the echoes of her terrible dream. "Do people consider tour buses home?"

Dayan turned so he could look down on her face, his fingertips tracing the delicate bone structure. "We live mainly on the road, so these buses become home very quickly. I noticed you were very nervous around the cats."

His thumb was stroking tiny caresses at the corner of her bottom lip, sending little shivers running down her back to the base of her spine. He always made her so aware of the differences in their bodies. How hard his muscles were, his bones thick and strong; her body seemed soft and very feminine in contrast although her muscles were quite firm. She reveled in her new strength. Still, he made her always remember he was a man and she was a woman.

'My woman.' He reminded her he was always a shadow in her mind.

"Cats? Is that what you call those things? They aren't cats, Dayan, they're wild animals. Real wild animals. Leopards eat babies. Little Jennifer would be a tasty treat for them," she pointed out.

"Tasty treat? I like that." His hand spanned her throat as he bent to take possession of her mouth. A slow swirl of fire. When he lifted his head, his glittering eyes black with hunger, his hand drifted lower to find her abundant breasts. "Everyone needs tasty treats now and them." He bent his dark head so that his long hair slid over her skin like strands of silk, teasing every nerve ending into raw need. His breath was warm, and her body tightened in anticipation.

Corinne found herself smiling, relaxing inside where she was still hearing the echoes of her nightmare. Jennifer was out of the incubator and sleeping peacefully in the small built-in crib Dayan had designed for their new motor home. The tour was beginning in another week and they needed to get moving. Jennifer was so tiny, both Dayan and Corinne were almost afraid to hold her, so it was reassuring to have the other band members nearby to help out. Gary Jansen had elected to travel with them until Jennifer no longer needed his protection or Cullen and Lisa returned to travel with them.

"What time is it?" Corinne asked, suddenly worried.

Dayan moved closer to a beckoning peak, his mouth skimming creamy flesh so that her thoughts immediately scattered in all directions. Her hands bunched fistfuls of his charcoal hair into her palms, and she pulled his head down to her eager body. "Stop teasing me. We don't have all night."

His tongue stroked a caress. "I like taking my time. Every inch of you deserves attention."

"Absolutely," she agreed, "and we're in a bit of a hurry here, so if you're planning on giving me the attention I need, get on with it and stop making me crazy!" He was driving her crazy and he knew it. Her body in such close proximity to his was hot and aching with need.

His soft taunting laughter was in her mind when he finally gave in to her demands and took her breast into the hot, moist cavern of his mouth. Her body answered with a rush of damp heat calling to him. Dayan took his time, a long, lazy, very leisurely exploration of her body, caressing every hollow and curve, every secret shadowed place. His hands and tongue brought a thick molten heat to her bloodstream and a building urgency Corinne couldn't ignore. She was on fire, inside and out. Deep within her raged a conflagration, a firestorm burning so hot she thought she might explode. His touch was turning her inside out so that she could barely catch her breath.

Wickedly she found his body with her hands. Feeling her way through his mind, she discovered every secret thing that drove him crazy. Her mouth found his throat, nibbled and scraped at his pulse. She heard the echo of his heart slamming. Her hands caressed his firm buttocks, delved into the muscles, traced the etched lines there while she spread tiny kisses across the heavy muscles of his chest. He was thick and hard now, his skin hot as she moved along the line of his flat belly. His breath was ragged and his mind was a red haze of hunger.

Her tongue swirled a path along his hipbone, while her hands found the columns of his thighs. His muscles were hard and rigid with anticipation. Corinne let her breath wash over the velvet head of his heavy erection, while she cupped him in her hands, while her fingers danced and teased. She kept it up until he groaned and caught her head in his hands, dragged her to him. Her mouth was tight and hot, her tongue a dancing fire. His hips moved urgently, a hard rhythm he seemed helpless to stop.

Dayan muttered something, a thick, husky sound of sheer pleasure, and he suddenly used his enormous strength to take back the lead. He pushed her down on the tangled sheets, his hands catching her curvy hips while he knelt above her. He simply yanked her to him, his shaft thick and hard, demanding entrance. She was slick with welcoming liquid, her tight sheath enfolding him in a fiery welcome. He surged into her, hard and fast, his body a little wild, a little out of control. He watched them coming together, a tango meant only for the two of them, while in his head the musical notes swelled into a crescendo of heat and light and pure erotic pleasure.

Corinne watched his face as she moved with him. Loving him. Loving what he did to her. What she did to him. All the time the fire built and now she could hear his music, the wild, unrestrained notes dancing with flames inside him. His soul. Or hers.

Ours! The word slipped into her mind and they fragmented together, crashing into the stormy seas and shooting upward to the glittering stars. They clung to one another while the earth rocked and the wildness in them subsided.

Dayan's dark gaze never left her face. He bent to kiss her, to taste her again, wanting more but knowing they were out of time. "Our soul, Corinne. The music comes from both of us. Without you, I would never find it in me." He kissed her again. "Why are you just lying there? Aren't you the matron of honor in this wedding? I know I'm the best man. We were supposed to be there five minutes ago. Lisa will be panicking."

"I forgot! Darn you, Dayan, you always do that. Wipe that satisfied smirk off your face." She loved that look on his face. She sat up and caught his face in her hands because she had to kiss him, she was so happy.

"I was just showing you this is reality, not a dream. You should be grateful," he teased.

A loud thump on the door of the trailer had them breaking guiltily apart. Corinne burst out laughing, she couldn't help it. She found herself fully dressed while Dayan was sitting completely naked on the edge of the bed.

"Get over it, you two," Darius ordered from outside their motor home. "Everyone is waiting. You are holding up the show here."

"Thanks for the clothes," Corinne whispered to Dayan with a straight face. "That was very thoughtful of you."

He glared at her. "Darius has excellent hearing," he pointed out.

She shrugged, still secretly laughing at him. "Then

let's hope he's very discreet." She glanced at her clingy gown in the mirror. She looked sexy, feminine, elegant. Different. She was different. She was whole. Corinne smiled at her reflection as Dayan, fully clothed and looking extraordinarily handsome in a suit, came up behind her to encircle her waist with his arms. He bent his head to kiss her temple, and she could see his love for her shining in his eyes.

"I'll get Jennifer," she said softly, basking in his warmth. Her world was more perfect than she had ever imagined. "We can talk about those leopards the lot of you keep for pets on the way to the chapel. Lisa thinks you're all crazy too, although the little traitor petted one this morning with Syndil."

Dayan watched her pick up Jennifer. He stared at them for a long moment—his beautiful wife so filled with laughter and warmth—his tiny daughter, such a miracle to all of his people. The melody of his life had been dark for so long, such an endless eternity, yet it was gone in an instant, to be replaced for all time by the melody of love.

A SELECTION OF NOVELS AVAILABLE FROM PIATKUS BOOKS

978 0 7499 3747 8	Dark Prince	Christine Feehan	£6.99
978 0 7499 3748 5	Dark Desire	Christine Feehan	£6.99
978 0 7499 3749 2	Dark Gold	Christine Feehan	£6.99
978 0 7499 3761 0	Dark Magic	Christine Feehan	£6.99
978 0 7499 3785 0	Dark Challenge	Christine Feehan	£6.99
978 0 7499 3668 6	Dark Demon	Christine Feehan	£6.99